THE NIGHT PRINCE

LAUREN PALPHREYMAN

Copyright © 2025 Lauren Palphreyman
All rights reserved

The characters and events portrayed in this book are fictitious. Any similarity to real persons, living or dead, is coincidental and not intended by the author.

No part of this book may be reproduced, or stored in a retrieval system, or transmitted in any form or by any means, electronic, mechanical, photocopying, recording, or otherwise, without express written permission of the publisher.

ISBN: 9798315931126

Cover Design by: Damonza
Copy Edit by: Rachel Rowlands

Contact the author:
www.LaurenPalphreyman.com

Prologue
Blake

His footsteps echo as he walks down the endless prison corridor.

Shadows coil around his arms and legs, almost as if they are alive. They slink around his ankles like cats.

His nostrils flare as a sweet, familiar scent hits them.

She's peering through the barred window of one of the cells ahead, her back to him.

He tilts his head to one side. Is this his dream, or hers? Has he merely imagined her? Or is this a consequence of the bond between them?

Her red hair cascades down her back, almost the color of blood in the gloom. It's as if she's been plucked from her bed and dropped here. She's wearing his shirt, the one he gave Callum for her to put on after James bit her. It's too big for her. It caresses the soft curve of her behind, and strokes her thighs. Her calves and feet are bare. He swallows.

She stiffens like prey, and he wonders if she senses him watching. Then he follows her gaze. A writhing mass of shadow surges toward her. The jailer of this prison is coming.

Blake prowls toward her as she edges back. She bumps into his chest, and he hooks an arm around her waist—clamping a hand over her mouth before she can scream.

He brings his lips to her ear. "You shouldn't be here, little rabbit."

She stiffens in his arms.

And how he loathes her. He loathes the way her scent washes over him—even here. She smells like the slither of moonlight that would drift through the grate of the cell beneath the palace. Freedom, taunting him. The broken promise of something he cannot have.

He loathes how soft and warm she feels, how his cock stirs at her proximity. He loathes how the wolf he keeps on such a tight leash longs to sink his teeth into her.

Footsteps approach.

He drags her though an open cell door. It clicks shut behind them. Her attention shifts to the emblem carved in the obsidian beneath the barred window; a key with two crescent moons in the bow. He wonders if she knows what it means. Most Wolves would—it's a remnant of when the acolytes rose a century ago, but this symbol is not common in the Southlands. They don't worship the darker gods there.

Her elevated pulse drums in his ears. His arm tenses against her torso. "Shh."

The temperature drops, and Blake's breath mists in front of his face. Aurora inches back, as if desperate for warmth, even from him. He holds her tighter.

The footsteps fade, and Blake exhales. He removes his hand from her mouth. She twists in his grasp to look up at him, and the soft swell of her breasts presses against his chest. A crease forms between her eyes. "What—"

Her attention jerks back to the door.

The figure stalks back. Thick, unnatural darkness bleeds through the barred windows.

"Wake up. Wake up. Wake up." She's muttering under her breath. "It's just a dream. Wake up."

It's not just a dream.

He shuts his eyes. He wrenches her back. He doesn't hit the wall—instead, it dissolves. The cell door bursts open in front of them, but they're already falling through endless darkness.

He lands on his feet in the cell beneath the palace, and he knows they're inhabiting his dream now. A memory. He doesn't like it here, but it's not as dangerous as the place before.

There's a cot against one wall, the mattress stained brown with old blood. A bucket of waste sits in the corner. There are books piled against one wall, a candle flickering beside them. The scent of lemons mixes with iron and the cloying odor of bodily fluids.

Aurora stands in the center of the space. She's perfectly poised, her back straight, her chin slightly raised so she can look down her nose at her surroundings. Only her slightly elevated pulse and the fact that he can *feel* that whisper of her inside him through their bond—like a small thread of light—tells him she is not as unfazed as she seems.

He loathes that about her, too. She's always so well put together, but he's been able to sense the violence that simmers beneath her skin since he first set eyes on her. It makes him want to provoke her.

When he was a child, some of the older boys from the village used to throw stones at the ducks in the river. He didn't understand why they did it—even at six years old it had seemed juvenile to him—until he met her.

He'd do anything to ruffle her feathers. He wants to see what happens when she unleashes herself.

Perhaps he loathes her so much because he knows, deep down, he's the same. He wears many masks, too. He hasn't been given the luxury of losing control. He knows what dark secrets lurk within his soul, but he doesn't know what lies behind the mask she wears. He thinks it might be magnificent.

She faces him and he steps closer to her. He studies her face, her cheekbones, her blue eyes that peer up at him through thick eyelashes. Fuck, she's beautiful.

"Are you really here?" he asks.

She frowns. "Of course I'm here." Her forehead only reaches his chin, yet she manages to speak to him as if he's smaller. A dazed look flickers over her features. "Are you?"

Footsteps approach the cell door behind her, and he sighs. "You should go. I'd rather you didn't see this next bit."

She glances over her shoulder. When she turns her attention to him once more, his damned subconscious has dressed him in a blood-drenched shirt. His feet are bare and dirty, and his breeches are torn.

"Are you hurt?" There's a hint of concern in her voice, and he adds another thing to the list of things he loathes about her: she sounds like she might actually give a shit.

"Time to wake up, little rabbit."

"Where are we?" Her eyebrows knit together. "Where *were* we?"

"If you remember this in the morning, I'll tell you."

He grabs her arms, and shuts his eyes. He needs to wake up.

He pushes her into the wall.

They fall into endless darkness once more.

***

BLAKE'S EYES jolt open.

He's in his bed at Lowfell, and the crescent moon shines through his window. His heart is pounding. He's not sure what is more disturbing: the location of his dreams, or Aurora's presence.

He slides out of the sheets, grabs the breeches and shirt that are folded on his armchair, and pulls them on. He puts on his boots, not bothering to fasten them, and slips out of his chambers.

He pads through his castle. The darkness is almost as thick as it was in the prison. He passes the room he put Aurora and Callum in. Callum is talking in hushed tones, and he feels a twinge of her panic. She has woken as unsettled as him.

When he's outside, he crosses the small courtyard to the land outside the castle walls. The loch that surrounds Lowfell is as black as the sky, and the mountains on either side of it are shrouded with shadow.

Cold wind ruffling his hair, he delves into woodland, and wanders through the ash trees until a chapel comes into view.

He enters. The gloom is thick within. Fragments of glass crunch beneath his boots as he passes the rotting pews and makes his way down the aisle. The stained windows once showed the story of Night's triumph over the Moon Goddess, and how he trapped her within his prison.

He tenses when a flapping sound echoes around the space, but it's just a bird nesting in the rafters. He pulls himself onto the altar. He lies back on the hard stone, his knees raised, and clasps his hands behind his head.

He stares up at the emblem carved into the stone arch that supports the ceiling.

The door creaks open.

"I thought I heard you walking around." Jack's low voice rumbles around the small chapel as he strolls toward him. Blake's second in command drops onto one of the pews at the front, stretching his legs out and crossing them at the ankles. "Trouble sleeping?"

Blake makes a noncommittal sound before turning his head. Jack's dreadlocks are tied back from his face, revealing fading bruising around one of his eyes. Callum's handiwork, no doubt. Jack was responsible for keeping Callum out of the way while Blake persuaded James—the Wolf King—to ask for Aurora's hand in marriage. His sleeves are rolled up so Blake can see the tattoos curling around his corded forearms. Blake knows what that ink hides.

"She was in my dream."

Jack releases a soft chuckle. "You shouldn't have done it, you know."

Blake sighs. "Probably not."

Jack runs a hand over his mouth. "There are reports that Night's acolytes are gathering. Whispers that the Night Prince is creating an army in the Northlands for him to command."

Blake pulls a face. "The Night Prince? Fenrir, perhaps?"

"Still in the Snowlands. Last I heard, he killed an alpha and married his wife. Ingrid, I think her name was."

"Alex, then."

"Probably. I'll send someone to monitor the Grey Keep. He could make things difficult for us."

The thread of light that Aurora gave Blake wraps around his soul and pulses inside him. He shifts on the stone, stretching one of his legs and arching his back slightly.

Jack frowns. "What's wrong with you?"

"I can feel her."

Jack's nostrils flare, then he chuckles. "Luckily for you, she's not a half-wolf who's just about to go through the transition . . . oh, wait. . ."

"Piss off, Jack."

"I remember when I was first bitten. I didn't leave my bed for a week."

"Spend some quality time with your right hand, did you?"

Jack laughs as he stands. "And the left." He walks over to Blake and clasps his shoulder. Concern flickers across his expression. "Learn to block it out or it'll drive you insane."

Blake grunts, and Jack strolls to the door of the chapel.

"Get some rest," says Jack.

He steps outside and the door swings shut, sealing Blake and the darkness within. Blake rubs his face with both hands. He imagines a cage around his soul, so that Aurora's thread of light cannot touch the rawest parts of him. The worst of the feeling eases, though his blood still runs hotter than usual.

Exhaling, he stares at the carving in the stone above his head—the key with two crescent moons within. The symbol for Night's prison.

The Northlands wind slips through the caved-in roof, stirring the scent of old blood. He wonders how many people were sacrificed on this altar. It was known that the former alpha of Lowfell secretly worshipped the God of Night. The fool thought he could offer up innocent blood in exchange for power.

Night doesn't want blood, though. He wants souls.

More than anything, he wants the key to his prison so he can escape it and unleash his violence upon the world.

Night wants the Heart of the Moon.

He would offer unimaginable power to whoever brought it to him.

Chapter One

I jerk upright, gasping for air.

I'm tangled in the bedsheets. The shirt I'm wearing—oversized—is slick with sweat. I'm cold. So cold. Ice pumps through my veins, and I wonder if I'll ever be warm again. The world is dark. Grey. As if I'm seeing it through a veil of shadow.

A floorboard creaks. The mattress dips by my bare feet. A wave of heat washes over me, along with the scent of male and the mountains.

"Look at me." The words are gentle but authoritative. A hand cups my cheek—callused and strong, yet careful. "Look at me." More demanding. This is the voice of someone who is used to people doing as they say.

Helpless, I bring my gaze up.

"That's it. Eyes on me. Now breathe."

I suck in air, letting it fill my lungs, letting it clear away the darkness.

"Good lass. Come on. Breathe with me. In... and out..."

My heartbeat stops its cacophony in my ears. We've done this before, I think—in the kennels beneath Sebastian's castle.

Sebastian. Goddess. I killed Sebastian.

A fresh wave of panic cascades over me.

"Princess." The word is sharp and commanding. "Breathe. In... and out..."

A half-burned candle flickers on the bedside table next to a cup and a pile of books. A decanter of whisky sits on the mantlepiece where Blake left it. There's a throbbing pain in my side. James bit me—only hours ago.

Rain patters against the window.

"That's it. Come back to me, Princess."

Warmth radiates from the figure before me. The tight grip around my lungs eases, and my breaths come easier. "Callum?"

"Aye. I'm here."

Callum's expression is gentle, at odds with the tension in his body and the hard biceps straining against his shirt. His hair, the color of dark sand, is brushed back from his forehead, and his green eyes flicker with concern.

"Are you in pain?" His forehead creases. "Do I need to get Blake?"

"No... I... it was just a nightmare, I think." I release a breath.

"What did you dream about?"

I shake my head as I try to remember. "I was in a prison, and Blake was there, and something was pursuing me. And..." I tense as our conversation earlier this evening comes back to me. I bring my knees to my chest. "Goddess, I need to tell you something about Blake. He's plotting against you."

Callum frowns. "What?"

"Everything he did... that bond he created that links my life to his... It was all part of a plan to steal the Wolf Throne. He's going to help you become the Wolf King, then he's going to challenge you. He knows he'll win, because our lives are linked. You won't kill him, because if you do, I'll die too."

Callum tenses. "He told you this?"

"Yes."

Callum stares at me for a moment, his biceps like steel. A soft laugh escapes him and warms the cool air.

"This doesn't concern you?" I ask.

"Oh, it concerns me. It's just... I couldn't understand it, before. Why he'd done it. He threw everything away that he'd spent years working for. He set me free, he fought James, and when he saw you dying... His face..." He swallows. "He saved your life. I've been searching for the reason for it since we got here, and I could find none. I started to think..." He shakes his head. "I don't know what I thought. But this... *this*... makes sense. I find comfort in that, I suppose. Even if it complicates things somewhat."

"We need to break the connection between Blake and me."

"We do. But he won't try to kill me until I've won the throne."

My pulse quickens. "You think he'll try and kill you."

"I'm certain of it. I forfeited to James, and for years, people have speculated about what would have happened if we'd fought. It weakens his claim. Blake won't allow himself to be seen as weak." I grip Callum's wrist like I'm scared he's going to be ripped away, and Callum smiles. "He will not defeat me. We have time. Until then, he could be useful. Get some rest, and we can worry about it later." He runs his thumb along my cheek. "I'm sorry I left you alone. With all the chaos of the battle, it was the best time to get one of Blake's messengers into the castle to send word to Fiona and Ryan."

"I know. I understand."

My blood warms at the proximity of him. This time it's not fear that pumps through my veins. It's something raw and feral that wants release.

Callum's expression darkens. "Princess. . ." His voice is rough and low, almost a warning.

I reach for his face, desperate to pull him closer. Pain bursts in my side where James bit me, and I wince, my hand hovering above the sheets.

Callum's jaw clenches as his gaze drops to my waist. "Can I see?"

I inch back on the bed, then lie down on the pillows.

Callum peels back the bedsheets. He shifts, bringing one of my bare legs over his lap as he leans over me. Weeks ago, the thought of being exposed like this—in a man's shirt and my underwear—before the alpha of Highfell would have scared me. Now, it makes my breathing quicken.

He undoes the button, just beneath my breasts, then gently makes his way down. His thumbs and fingers lightly brush my skin. He draws the shirt apart to expose my midriff, and though the cool air touches me, I'm burning.

I want him, I realize. I want him urgently. Desperately. I want his hands on my body, and to dig my fingers into his muscles. I want the warmth of his mouth. I want to climb on top of him and claim him as mine. I want him in a way I've never wanted anything before in my life.

I don't know what has come over me. Perhaps I feel like this because I almost died tonight. Perhaps I want to cast away the cold shadow of whatever nightmare awoke me. But I want to feel warm. I want to feel *alive*. I want to expel this energy that's coursing through me.

Callum stills. I prop myself on my elbows. There's a long jagged scar across my waist and torso where James sank his teeth into me. The skin around it is red, but it must look a lot better than it did only hours ago when I was bleeding on the grass.

I should be worried about it, yet I watch Callum, fascinated. He looks so intense, so impenetrable. His expression is like stone, and he's every bit the warrior I first saw at the dog fight in Sebastian's castle.

The wolf flickers behind his eyes. For a moment, I wonder if he has sensed the change in me—this *need*.

While my anger is mostly directed at Blake for using me as a pawn in his games, Callum's seems wholly reserved for his brother. "He will die for this."

It sounds like a promise and it heats my blood more. It's not just that he cares that I'm hurt—there's something more primal to it. Possessive. As if he can't bear that his brother has marked my body.

I'm on fire. A furnace.

Goddess, I don't know what's wrong with me, but I need it to stop. I ache for him. My skin is sensitive, and I shift on the mattress. The strange urge to bite something comes over me. I feel almost feverish. A soft shaky breath escapes me.

Every muscle in Callum's body becomes rigid.

His gaze snaps to the place between my legs, which now throbs with need, as if he can sense what I'm feeling. I'm only thinly covered by my underwear, and I feel myself getting hotter and damper. He sucks his bottom lip. A soft growl comes from his throat.

When he meets my eyes, his wolf is there, dark and beautiful and powerful. He blinks a couple of times as if he's trying to pull it back.

"I thought I'd lost you, tonight." His words are strained.

"You did, for a while. But you found me." I smile. "Come here."

He takes a deep breath as he seemingly tries to settle himself.

I'm injured. No doubt, he thinks me a fragile thing that he doesn't want to break. Goddess, I want to be broken. I want to be consumed. I want to release this caged beast that's pacing, agitated, inside me. I want all the horrors of tonight to disappear.

"*Don't*," I whisper. "Don't be a gentleman."

"Rory. . . You're hurt."

"Don't you want to take care of me?"

He lets out a shaky laugh, and drags his gaze away to stare at the floorboards. "Aye, I want to take care of you. But I fear it wouldn't be right."

"It would."

One of his thumbs rubs frustrating circles on my leg, still resting across his lap. "I don't want to hurt you."

"You won't."

He shifts so he is kneeling on the mattress between my legs, and triumph bursts within me. His expression darkens.

"You need to get some sleep," he says.

"Then why don't you help me relax so I can?"

He groans. "You're a demanding wee thing, aren't you? Brave, too, to be tormenting the alpha of Highfell in this way."

"He doesn't scare me. I'm courting the future Wolf King, don't you know?"

He chuckles, a soft husky sound that fills the small bedchamber with warmth and dark promise. "Oh aye? You're courting him, are you?"

"Do you not think so?"

"What is he like? Handsome, I presume?"

"He's very handsome. And strong. And he likes to think he's a gentleman. He's not. He's a wolf."

"Is that so?"

He moves, lowering himself and forcing my thighs to part further to accommodate his broad shoulders.

"Yes," I whimper.

"I think we're way beyond courting, Princess." He plants a soft kiss on the damp fabric of my underwear. "Don't you?"

My back arches. "*Yes.*"

Sweat beads on my brow and I want to beg for more, something I've never done in my life. Yet as he hooks my underwear to one side with his finger, I stiffen. My body cools, as if I've been plunged into ice. Darkness creeps in at the edges of my vision and a panicked sound escapes my lips. Callum stills between my thighs.

A growl builds, crescendos, vibrates inside me. It's like there's something caught in my chest, thrashing against a cage, trying to break free. It wants to run toward something, but I don't know what. My skin is clammy. My hair sticks to my face.

"*Callum*," I whimper.

"Princess?" He's up, instantly, caging me within his arms. "*Ghealach*, you're burning up."

Dots flash before my eyes, and cold sweat beads on my skin. I try to cling onto consciousness, but a wave of darkness crashes toward me. The small bed, the fireplace laden with books, the embers in the hearth, Callum's face—they all turn grey.

"*BLAKE!*" Callum sounds faraway as he leaps from the bed.

I'm sinking.

Then blackness.

Chapter Two

I'm racing down a dark endless prison corridor. I'm a crumbling statue, and vines of shadow coil around my arms and legs. Damp cells, metal scalpels, and hearts dripping black blood flash before my eyes.

I'm sprinting through a forest at night. My dress snags on branches, and thorns dig into the soles of my feet. I don't know if I'm running toward something, or running away, but if I stop, I'll die.

Callum's blurry face appears before mine. *"What's wrong with her? Is it the bite?"*

"It's her wolf." Blake sounds like dark silk and it cools my burning bones. *"Aurora, darling."* A palm presses against my clammy forehead, and the beast that rages in my chest settles. *"Look at me."*

I peel open my eyelids and jerk back.

Blake's pupils dilate until they are empty black holes, and his mouth curves into a cruel smile that is too big for his face. He laughs. Harsh and cold and endless.

I know what you are, I scream inside my head.

What?

Monster.

The darkness takes me once more.

I'm trapped in a cold dark space, and there's water as black as pitch up to my waist. A great beast carries a rabbit in his maw as he runs through a dilapidated chapel. A whip tears through my flesh as male laughter shatters my eardrums. A woman cries amid a snowstorm.

Feral amber eyes peer at me.

"*Her body is assimilating.*" A voice dripping honey and poison. "*It wants to reject the wolf.*"

"*She was fine earlier.*" A voice rough with worry, thick with the Northlands. "*A wee bit restless, perhaps, but not like this.*"

"*She'll go through phases like this until she shifts for the first time. It will pass.*"

"*Did this happen to you?*"

"*Yes.*" A hand tilts back my head and pushes a chalice to my lips, filled with poison. "*Drink up, little rabbit.*"

No. No. No.

I swing my head against my pillow, helpless. Cold darkness trickles down my throat and spills from my lips. He bleeds into the shadows, and his voice echoes in my mind.

My pawn. My puppet. Mine.

I blink, and I'm padding through a castle. Cold air tickles my bare legs, and my naked feet slap against the flagstones. I savor the cold on my burning flesh. I savor the shadows that brush against my cheeks. My legs are weak. It's too dark to see, but I'm attached to a leash and I follow it. My fingers squeeze around the hilt of a silver blade. Something growls in my chest.

I'm not a pawn. I'm not a puppet. I belong to no one.

I enter the room. He sleeps in a bed that's pushed against the wall. I don't know if I'm awake, or dreaming. Everything is hazy, yet he seems more corporeal than before. He has his arm slung above his head, and his dark hair is mussed. He looks so soft. So peaceful. *So easy to kill.*

I blink, and I'm straddling his torso, a blade to his throat. My thighs clench his hips. He feels solid. Hot. His fingers curl around my wrist like a shackle. He opens his eyes, and something feral looks back at me. He blinks, long eyelashes fanning his cheeks, and the beast disappears, but something just as dangerous meets my gaze. He smells like blood and dark fairytales and the depths of the forest.

"*I don't recall inviting you into my bed, Aurora, darling.*"

He is carrying me. My cheek is pressed against his hard bare chest. I'm a doll, draped in his arms. A toy to be played with. A puppet to be controlled. I snarl and struggle, but he holds me tighter, and I cannot shake myself free. He passes me to someone else as if I'm nothing. Callum makes soothing sounds against my ear. I'm hot. So hot. So restless. When will it end?

"*Where did you find her?*" Callum's voice is thick with sleep and worry.

"*In my chambers.*" I hear his amusement. "*I think her wolf wants to kill me.*"

"*I think most Wolves want to kill you.*" A pause that lasts an eternity or a heartbeat. "*You speak of her wolf as if it's separate to who she is.*"

23

"It is."

"The wolf is part of who we are, Blake. Perhaps if you accepted that part of yourself—"

"Callum, if I ever want your counsel, I shall ask for it. And if I ever ask for it, I truly fear for the state of the world." Footsteps rumble like thunder through my ears. *"Keep a tighter leash on your pet."*

Shadows take me once more.

I'm in a carriage with Sebastian, and he has a slit across his throat. I have strings hooked into my arms, and a faceless being is making me dance in an empty ballroom. Blake prowls toward me, eyes alight with violence.

I'm running. I'm lost. Dark corridors twist into oblivion. There's a symbol. A key, with crescent moons in the bow.

Someone screams.

Someone sings.

Bright, blinding light.

I jolt upright.

I'm breathing hard. My hair sticks to my skin, and I'm tangled in bedsheets. I'm alone.

Grey light dances across the room, and rain patters against the window. A fire burns ferociously in the hearth, so someone must have been here recently.

My head throbs, and my mouth is as dry as a bone. I feel weak, as if my limbs have turned to twigs and could snap at any moment. A soft groan scrapes from my throat, and it feels like sand. There's a beaker on the table beside me, and I grab it. I sniff the clear liquid inside, smell nothing, then gulp it down greedily and set the beaker down again. It soothes my aching throat, and it's so cold I feel it travel to my stomach.

I think I had a fever. I've no idea how long it lasted for. I try to sift through the dreams and hallucinations. It all blurs together, a tangled mess that hurts my mind. I remember Blake's voice cutting through the veil of darkness, saying my body was trying to assimilate the wolf.

I fight the wave of fear that crashes over me. He could be wrong. He could have been lying.

Worse, he could have been telling the truth. I could be turning into one of the beings my kingdom has taught me to suppress, and to fear, for twenty years of my life. The part of me that the priest tried to whip out of me, that my father tried to poison, that condemned my mother to her fate. It could be real.

I remember something else—straddling Blake while he was in bed, while holding a knife to his throat. I shake my head. I would never do such a thing. A fevered dream, not a memory.

The air is stale in here, and smells like sickness. It reminds me of the mornings I spent on the edge of my mother's bed, and the weeks I spent ill, locked in my chambers, after her death. Only she didn't die of illness, like I'd thought. Anger simmers beneath my skin. My mother was murdered by my father.

I clench and unclench my fists, take a couple of deep breaths, and cage the feeling. I'm far away from him, now. Although perhaps, one day, Callum might help me gain justice for what he did.

I rub my face with both hands, then slide my feet out of bed. I was so thirsty when I woke up, I didn't notice the piece of parchment next to the beaker of water, or the hunk of bread on a small plate, with a butter knife beside it. I pick up the note.

Princess, I'm in a meeting with some of Blake's clan. I'll be back shortly. Eat your breakfast. Stay where you are.

I'm ravenous, so I follow one of his commands. My stomach groans as I force down the dry bread. It doesn't sit well, and I quickly swallow more water before setting the beaker down.

My entire soul protests at his second instruction. I don't want to stay where I am. The walls feel as if they're closing in on me. In the back of my mind, I hear myself as a young adolescent, pleading with one of the maids to let me go for a walk in the palace gardens, or join my father and brother for dinner in the Great Hall, or to ride my horse in the grounds like mother used to let me.

I can't be that girl anymore. I swore I'd be more than that.

I push myself to my feet. My legs are a little shaky, and it feels like there are blades scraping the inside of my skull. I groan and clasp the windowsill to gain my balance. I take a few deep breaths. The room I'm in looks out onto a gloomy courtyard. The sun is blocked by roiling grey clouds, and rain splats against the cobblestones below.

There's an armoire in the corner of the room, and I make my way toward it, hoping for fresh clothes. Only male clothes hang here, breeches and shirts and a kilt that is the same red tartan as Callum's. I wonder if Fiona, or someone else from his clan, arrived while I was sleeping to bring him this. I hope so. I hope Fiona is alright in the aftermath of Callum and Blake's betrayal.

The shirt I've been wearing is stiff with sweat. I pull it off, and select another. I'm not sure whose it is until I've slipped it on and the scent of dark pine curls around me. My pulse kicks up in protest, even as I fasten the shirt up. I don't want to wear Blake's clothes, or smell like him, but it will do for now. I pull on some breeches too, and cinch them in with a belt because they fall low on my hips.

Someone taps against the door. I freeze.

Callum would have just walked in. I look over my shoulder, at the butter knife sitting beside the plate of bread. I hurry over to pick it up, drop it in my pocket, then warily open the door.

A girl around my age and build, with long wavy dark hair, stands in the corridor. She is striking, with a sharp jaw and plump lips. Her dress is lovely, black with long sleeves made of lace. She looks somewhat familiar, though I don't think we've met.

"Hello?" My voice is hoarse from lack of use and I clear my throat.

"Blake requests your presence in his council chambers."

I incline my head. I may not appreciate being summoned by the alpha of Lowfell, but at least it saves me from searching an unfamiliar castle for Callum.

"Are you part of his clan?" I ask.

"Aye."

I smile, hoping to make a friend. "I'm Aurora."

She brushes a strand of hair over her ear, and I catch a glimpse of a scar or a tattoo on her wrist, which she hurriedly covers with her sleeve. "I know."

I wait for her to tell me her name. When she merely exhales as if I'm wasting her time, I frown and step back. I should have guessed the people in Blake's clan would be as obnoxious as their alpha. "One moment, please."

The only shoes I have are the bloodstained muddy slippers I wore when James gave me back to Sebastian. Wincing, I put them on.

The girl doesn't speak to me as she leads me through a labyrinth of narrow corridors. The style is not dissimilar to Castle Madadh-allaidh—the castle I was first brought to when Callum took me to the Northlands—but it seems more claustrophobic. Perhaps it's the lack of tapestries and clan colors that make the dark walls feel closer together. Iron sconces hold torches that flicker as we pass.

"—I won't risk her." Callum's thick accent sounds almost like a growl as we approach a door.

"Don't be ridiculous." Blake's tone is smooth like satin. "She'll be fine. We can handle-"

The girl knocks and the room falls silent.

There's a strange sense of anticipation building in my chest. I hate to admit that I'm somewhat curious about the place Blake calls home. Callum once told me that some people wondered if Blake—the half-wolf from the Southlands—was even an alpha. Anyone who questioned it usually wound up dead.

Yet, here we are, in his territory—in a very real castle in the Northlands.

How did he get it? Is this truly his home? Do his people like him?

"Come in," drawls Blake.

Chapter Three

There are three tall arched windows in the wall on one side of the council chambers, and mountains that are shades of orange and brown are visible through them. Torches in black iron sconces flicker between the windows, and a fire burns low in the curved stone hearth. The space is dominated by a large, oval table, and four men are standing around it. They all look at me as I walk inside.

Blake is at the head of the table with his hands flat on the surface. He leans forward. His white sleeves are rolled up, exposing corded forearms and the beginning of the scar on his elbow, which he must have got when he was bitten. Not for the first time, I find myself curious as to how he was turned into a wolf.

Callum's expression softens when his gaze locks onto mine. "Rory, what are you doing here?"

"I invited her." Blake's gaze brushes over the large shirt I wear, which belongs to him. "You're looking dashing today, little rabbit."

I offer him a clipped smile, because I'm sure he's trying to provoke me. "Thank you."

A male with dreadlocks and tattoos winding up the dark skin of his arms smirks. Jack, I think his name is. I saw him in the dungeons when Blake kidnapped me and tried to get me to marry James. My displeasure grows.

The fourth male in the room, I've not been acquainted with. He is as large in build as Callum, with short black hair and a neatly trimmed beard. His arms are folded across his chest, emphasizing biceps that strain against a black shirt. He wears an eye patch over his left eye, and faint scars crisscross his throat. Recognition jolts through me, though I cannot imagine where I would have met such a man.

"Please, come in," says Blake. "We were just talking about you."

I walk toward the table. "I heard," I say. "What were you discussing?" I don't like the idea that four men were talking about me, without me being present.

"You should be resting," Callum whispers, with a note of reprimand. "Did you not read my note? You've had a high fever for three days."

Three days? Callum is about to go to war with his brother, and I've been bedridden for three whole days. Questions pound through my already thumping head as I wonder what I must have missed.

"I couldn't bear to be trapped in that room any longer," I reply quietly. "I feel much better now."

"Hm."

Up close, Callum looks like he's barely slept. Stubble peppers his jaw, and there are smudges beneath his eyes. His usual scent of the mountains is overlaid by male sweat, as if he's not been washing. I put my arm around his waist and squeeze. On top of everything that has happened with his brother, he's had to worry about me.

The woman who brought me here huffs in the doorway.

"Will you be joining us, Elsie?" asks Blake.

"No." Elsie offers no deference to the male who I'm guessing is her alpha. She heads into the corridor, and her skirts make a rustling sound as they drag across the flagstones. The door swings shut behind her.

I breathe in quickly when I feel a sharp squeeze of emotion in my chest. It's coming from Blake, and it disappears so quickly I might have imagined it. I've not gotten used to the strange link between us yet, forced onto me by Blake. It feels like there's a thread of shadow in my chest that is wrapped around my soul. When he feels something, it seems to spread and tighten. I try to figure out what he's feeling. Yearning, I think. I wonder who this woman is, to him.

The burly male I haven't met before suppresses a chuckle.

"Has something amused you, Arran?" asks Blake, a slight edge to his silky tone.

"No." Arran's voice sounds a little hoarse, as if he doesn't use it much. He doesn't sound sincere. He leans closer to his alpha, whispers something in his ear, and Blake nods.

Arran strides away from the table, past Callum and me, and heads out after Elsie. He glances at me once over his shoulder, and again, I get that jolt of familiarity. The door swings shut behind him.

"As I was saying," says Blake, "I want Lochlan and some of his clan to come to Lowfell for Oidhche Fhada."

Callum's hold on me tightens almost imperceptibly. "And as *I* was saying, that's not a good idea."

"What is Oidhche Fhada?" My mouth stumbles on the unfamiliar words.

"It's a wolf ritual that will take place next week," says Callum. "We believe Oidhche—or the Night God, as you call him in the Southlands—has a prison in the sky in which he keeps *Ghealach*—the Moon Goddess—prisoner."

"I remember," I say.

"Oidhche moves her into a different cell each night, so she can never be found by those who seek her. On the night of the full moon, that is when she's closest to us. Once, though, every two and a half years, he moves her so deep inside his prison that her light cannot touch the earth. For a few moments, the world is cast into darkness. That is when we perform Oidhche Fhada."

I think he's talking about the lunar eclipse. We have a festival to mark it in the Southlands, where we light bonfires to honor the Sun Goddess, and cast away the darkness.

"And you don't wish to perform it this time?" I ask.

"It's not the ritual I object to, but the alpha Blake wishes to invite. Lochlan Christensen is the alpha of Glas-Cladach, and we cannot trust him."

There's a map of the Northlands on the table, and Blake taps part of the coastline. "Lochlan has the second biggest army in the Northlands, and we have a mutual enemy."

"James?" I ask.

Blake inclines his head. "I wish to persuade him to join our cause. If we want to move effectively against James, we're best doing it while he's licking his wounds after the battle with Sebastian. We have three weeks until the full moon. I want us to make our move just after. We'll need an army to get into the castle, and the support of at least four alphas to join us if we are to hold it. Lochlan can provide us with an army."

Callum grits his teeth.

"You don't like Lochlan?" I ask.

"I've nothing personal against the man," says Callum, "but while it's true that he and James don't get along, he has as much reason to dislike me."

"He thinks inviting Lochlan could put you in danger," says Jack. "Particularly after—"

Callum makes a low sound, a little like a growl, and Jack shuts his mouth.

"Why would it put me in danger?" I ask.

"Do you remember when I rode out to aid my brother while we were at Madadh-allaidh?" says Callum. "We lost the battle against Sebastian and I was shot with wolfsbane."

Fear had clenched my heart when Callum fell to his knees in his chambers, covered in sweat and gore. Blood ran down his arm from the bullet wound in his shoulder. A lick of shame flickers through me. I'd told Callum that morning that Blake was not as bad he seemed. How wrong I was.

I nod.

"The fort Sebastian took used to be a part of Lochlan's territory," says Blake. "The alpha who took over in his stead was someone Lochlan was fond of. He's likely dead, now, or worse."

"Sebastian was only there because he was looking for me," I say. "Lochlan may blame me for what happened." My voice is dull as I realize why I may have an enemy in Lochlan, despite never meeting him.

"Aye," says Callum. "We cannot trust his loyalties."

Blake sighs. "Lochlan will find Aurora delightful. Trust me." I don't bother pointing out that we can't trust Blake. "I've already invited him, anyway. This conversation is fruitless."

Callum's jaw hardens. "*What?*"

"Come on, Callum. You and I can handle him, and you know it. Why don't you tell your little pet the real reason why you're being so overprotective?" A dimple punctures Blake's cheek and my head snaps toward Callum.

"Blake." Callum's voice is laced with warning. Jack smirks.

"What is it?" My tone is sharp.

He pinches the bridge of his nose, then pulls a piece of parchment from the pocket of his kilt. I take it.

"Ryan and his lass, Becky, arrived yesterday," says Callum. Relief courses through me. The sixteen-year-old boy I spared in the Borderlands fighting ring is alright. "James let them go, but he sent them with this letter."

Callum McKennan is scrawled in ink across one side. The wax seal is broken, and I flick it open. I turn the parchment over, and read.

You have something of mine. I have something of yours. Want to swap?

My brow furrows. "What does he have of yours?"

"Fiona." Callum's tone lacks intonation, and he stares blankly at the parchment in my hand.

Panic and anger twist in my gut. Callum's bloodshot eyes are not just the consequence of worrying about my fever and the bite that throbs in my side. James has taken Callum's oldest friend prisoner. She's my friend, too, though I don't know her well. Fiona was one of the only people at Madadh-allaidh who treated me with kindness, and she did so knowing I was from her enemy kingdom.

My fear hardens to resolve. I touch Callum's arm. His bicep is clenched beneath his sleeve. "We'll get her back. He thinks you have something of his?"

Callum swallows. "Technically, I do."

"Then we should negotiate a trade."

"That's where it gets complicated."

"Why? What does he want?" I frown. "What do you have that belongs to him?"

He runs a hand over his mouth. His gaze darkens when he looks at my waist, where James's bite marks my skin. His eyes swim with regret when they meet mine. "You."

Chapter Four

I pull back from Callum. Hurt and confusion battle for dominance in my chest. "What do you mean? I don't belong to anyone, least of all James."

The rain has become more ferocious outside, and it drums against the arched windows as Callum drags his teeth over his bottom lip. "Technically, you do, Princess."

"What are you talking about?"

"It's wolf law." Callum's broad shoulders are hunched, as if he's carrying a great weight. I wonder how many times he's had this conversation with Blake and the others while I've been bedridden. "Usually, when a half-wolf is bitten, if they survive they become part of the clan of whoever bit them. The alpha of that clan must take responsibility for them. They essentially become the alpha's property. James is from Highfell. If he'd not been king when he'd bitten you, you would have been mine. James outranks me. He has a claim to you. Wolf law dictates that if he asks for you, you must go to him."

My legs feel shaky—from the fever or shock, I don't know. I place a hand on the edge of the oval table to balance myself. The thought that the male who attacked me, who has forever changed my life, thinks of me as his property makes my blood run cold. Anger twists in my chest, and my heartbeat thunders against my ribs.

Blake is backlit by the roaring fire in the hearth. Jack leans against the table. I hate that they are witness to this. I hate that they have all discussed this without me. I swallow my emotion, and bury it deep.

"That's ridiculous," I say. "Just because James says something doesn't make it so. I don't belong to him."

Blake drums his fingers on the map. "Be that as it may," he says, "if he asks for you back and we refuse, it puts us in breach of wolf law. The optics are bad—to have a future king refuse to adhere to the rules that bind all Wolves."

Unlike Callum, there is no emotion in his voice. He speaks as if me being another man's property is of no consequence to him. I note his wording, too. *A future king.* He doesn't want to be in breach of wolf law because it may ruin *his* prospects for the throne, not Callum's.

My gaze snaps to his. "So you plan to hand me to him?"

Callum puts his hand over mine. His palm is hot and calloused, and his touch offers me some comfort. "No. Never."

"There's a simple solution," says Blake. "Another alpha must claim you before James officially asks for your return."

I note that Blake doesn't name Callum as the alpha who must claim me, as if he himself is an option. Jack watches

Blake carefully, his lips pinched in the corners. He seems to have noticed this too, and doesn't look like he approves.

"What are you talking about?" I say. "I don't want to be 'claimed'. What does that even mean?"

Blake shrugs. "An alpha would mark you with their bite, and announce you as part of their clan in front of witnesses. The claim is stronger if it happens at a celestial event, or in the presence of a priestess, but it's not always necessary."

When I shake my head, it throbs. "Absolutely not."

"Not even if it would keep you safe?" asks Callum.

I flinch. He agrees with Blake. They have had this conversation before without me too, then. "No."

Callum brushes his thumb over my knuckles. "If you're worried about the pain—"

"No."

Hurt flickers across Callum's face, and I realize he thinks I'm rejecting him. Perhaps this is the way of Wolves—to dominate, and claim ownership over one another. Perhaps this is the way of all men. I belonged to my father. I was given to Sebastian. I was taken by Callum. I was used as a pawn by Blake.

For the first time in my life, I have tasted freedom here in the Northlands winds. I have smelt it in the pine-rich forests, and seen it in the wild mountains and rain-drenched valleys. I have felt it too in the warmth of Callum's arms. I have a chance here to be an equal instead of a prize. I won't give that up so easily.

I sigh. "I cannot belong to anyone again. Not even you, Callum."

Callum's expression softens. "It's not about belonging to *someone*. It's about being part of a clan. It would make it easier for me to protect you."

"I don't belong to you or your clan," I say. "I have a title already. I'm the princess of the Southlands. Perhaps, after everything that has happened, that does not count for much. I'm sure my father would execute me for treason if he knew I was not being held against my will. Still, I cannot denounce my position and title, nor defer to an alpha. I will not."

Callum's forehead creases. "It's not like that, Princess. It would keep you safe—"

"I'm not safe! From the moment you and Blake attacked James, you declared war on him. James has obviously realized that I'm of some importance to you. This will not stop him. He will come for me all the same. Are you going to let him take me?"

Callum's expression darkens. "*Never.*"

I take a deep breath to compose myself. "It doesn't matter whether he says I belong to him or not. He is trying to rattle us. We must get the clans on side so we can win this throne quickly, and we must get Fiona back. Before James has time to act."

There's a knock at the door. "Yes?" Blake asks.

A crop of messy copper hair comes into view as Ryan pokes his head into the room.

Callum exhales. "What is it, Ryan?"

Despite Callum's clear exasperation at the interruption, my lips curve into a smile. Ryan's freckled face breaks into a grin when he sees me. "Princess! You're awake!"

"Ryan!" Callum snaps his fingers, drawing the sixteen-year-old boy's attention back to him. "What is it?"

"Can I have a word in private?"

"Now?"

"Aye."

Callum's gaze sweeps across the room, and the men in it. "It can't wait?"

"No."

Callum squeezes my shoulder. "I'll just be a moment. Let me know if you need me, okay?" I nod, and he follows Ryan into the corridor, shaking his head. "I swear to *Ghealach*, lad, if this isn't important—" His words are cut off as the door swings shut behind him, and I'm sealed shut in a room with two Wolves who are plotting against Callum and me.

Tension tightens my throat, and my teeth tingle—like I want to bite something. The urge to either cross the room and sink my teeth into Blake, or gnaw my fingertips until they're bloody, is so strong that I ball my hands into fists.

When the feeling doesn't desist, I trace the jagged outline of the northern coast on the map, Blake's sleeve brushing against my hand. I catch a few names—*High Peaks, Oidhche Craig*. Highfell must be up here somewhere. I spot it by a patch of land named *Glen Ghealach*.

Blake whispers something. There's a shuffle, heavy footsteps, and Jack walks past me. He winks then disappears into the corridor and shuts the door.

My gaze moves slowly up to Blake.

I can't help but think of the fever dreams I had—of his eyes, as black as night, of his laughter skittering across my bones, of him bleeding into shadow and coiling around me like a viper. In the daylight, he is just a male—a wolf—and yet my pulse kicks up as if I'm prey.

"Alone at last, little rabbit."

Chapter Five

The Northlands kingdom stretches across the oval table between Blake and me. The wind hammers the rain into the arched windows, and the noise pounds through the gloom like the drums of war.

Alone at last, little rabbit.

When he first linked our lives together, I felt his emotions as strongly as my own. I think he has found some way to conceal them, because though I can still feel that dark part of him inside me, I can't identify his intentions.

How I loathe this male. I think I may loathe him even more than James. I can taste my hatred, bitter on the back of my tongue. My teeth tingle, ache, like I want to sink them into his flesh. He used me. The worst part is how much that hurts.

I've never had friends. As the princess, I always stood apart from others. I wasn't allowed to run around and play silly games with the other children. As an adult, no one talked freely around me. My brother, Philip, was cruel. Every male who ever spoke to me did so because they had something to gain from my father.

I thought this had hardened me, and made me a good judge of character. Now, I wonder if it made me even more susceptible to deception—so desperate to make a connection with someone, anyone, that I let myself be fooled by a snake.

It's not that I ever fully trusted Blake, but Goddess, a part of me had wanted to. I enjoyed conversations with him, even when he was trying to provoke me. He spoke to me as if I was equal to him—more so, perhaps, than even Callum did. A horrible, weak, cringing part of me wanted to be his friend.

I loathe him, and myself, for it.

"How are you feeling, little rabbit?" His voice is carefully smooth, casual, as if he's merely making small talk.

I may not have seen Blake's poison until it was too late, but I know he gains enjoyment from other people's pain. I won't give him mine. I force my lips into a polite smile—the same smile I've given many obnoxious lords while I secretly recoiled at their presence. "I am well. Thank you."

He tilts his head slightly to the side. I feel him, then. A cool prickle beneath my skin. The strangest feeling of shadowy vines that spread around my soul. When I felt his yearning, earlier, it seemed involuntary. This is different. It's like he's reaching for me, and trying to gauge my emotion. I tense, blocking the sensation, caging my emotions and keeping them close.

"Are you well rested?" he asks.

"I'm fine."

"Callum said you had nightmares. What did you dream of?" There is something pointed in his tone, as if the answer is important to him, though I can't fathom why.

"It was just the fever." I keep my voice sweet as honey. "Thank you for your concern."

I catch it. His slight flicker of displeasure. My smile aches a little less. My sweetness irritates him. Good.

He strolls toward me, his footsteps loud and steady on the flagstones. He stops close enough that his dark forest scent wraps around me, and he leans back against the table. It creaks beneath his weight. His face is close to mine, and his thigh almost brushes my hip.

I want to move back, to put distance between us, but I force myself to stay where I am.

This close, I see that he looks like he has not had much sleep, either. There are faint shadows beneath his eyes, and his dark hair is messy—as if he's been dragging frantic fingers through it. A soft curl brushes his forehead.

In my fever dreams, he had seemed ethereal and untouchable—a monster made of death and shadow. The realness, the solidity, of him—corded forearms, broad shoulders, a hard chest straining beneath his white shirt—makes him seem even more dangerous, somehow.

"You defied James, dragged a blade across Sebastian's throat, and all I get is a pretty smile and a 'thank you for your concern'?" His voice is low and seductive. "How disappointing."

"If I ever led you to believe I was trying to impress you, Blake, I apologize for the misdirection."

A dimple creases his cheek. "Are you angry with me?"

"Can't you feel it?" I ask.

"Right now, you're guarding your emotions. As am I."

Despite my unwillingness to ask for Blake's help, the question slips out. "How? How does this... thing between us work?"

He looks like he's considering whether or not to answer. "When I saved your life, I shared my lifeforce with you. It was like I gave you the end of a rope to pull you back, and I grabbed onto your lifeforce at the same time. I don't know how it feels to you, but for me it's like a thread of light from your lifeforce is still inside me. When you feel something particularly strongly, it wraps around my emotions and pulses, and I feel it too."

"How do I stop you from feeling me?"

"I can stop it myself by imagining a cage around my emotions, to stop myself from touching your light. You could try that." He cocks his head to one side. "Is that how it feels for you? Like a thread of light?"

I search inside me for that piece of him, that end of the thread, and shiver. "No. It feels like darkness."

"Well? Are you angry with me?"

"Why would I be angry?" I try to keep my tone smooth, but I can't quite conceal the bite behind it. "You saved my life." *And linked our lives together without my consent, all as part of your plan to take the throne and kill Callum.*

"We're friends, then?"

My soul protests, and from the glint in his eye, he knows it. We're not friends. I'm not sure Blake even knows how to make friends. Jack and Arran seem amiable enough with him, but Blake must have manipulated them in some way.

Perhaps they fear him, like the Wolves at castle Madadh-allaidh did.

I force myself to smile. "I made friends with a man in the Southlands, once. My father thought he was plotting against him and I was told to dance with him, sit with him, fill up his cup. He was a devious, cruel man. He hurt one of my ladies-in-waiting, I think, but I made friends with him anyway. I found out he planned to take over a territory, and turn the army against my father. It could have cost my father his throne."

"What happened to him?"

I recall that night when my father sent me away. I'd heard the shouting in the throne room, even from my bedchambers, as he tried to escape. "He died."

"It seems that being your friend is dangerous, indeed." Blake's eyes reflect the flickering torchlight. "Tell me, do you seek your father's approval, even now—knowing what he did to your mother?"

Rage billows in my chest like a tempest. Self-loathing crashes through me as well. I'm not sure why I told him that story. Did I wish to scare him? Impress him? I try to compose myself. I don't want him to know that one of his blows has landed. Yet even if he could not feel my emotions, I know he'd be able to sense this change within me as a wolf.

I step back, and nod curtly. "Callum will be waiting for me outside."

I walk toward the door.

"I'm sorry I couldn't give you what you wanted the other night." There's something suggestive in his tone, although I have no idea what the suggestion is. I know he's trying to rile me. I know I should keep walking.

Don't bite. Don't bite. Don't—

I turn back around. "What do you mean?"

"When you visited me in my bedchambers."

I frown. Every muscle in my body tightens. Red hot images flash beneath my eyelids—Blake's face soft with sleep, his hair mussed, his arm thrown back on the pillow, my blade pressed against his throat. His sheets were crumpled beneath my thighs, and the wolf shone in his eyes when he grabbed my wrist.

I'd thought it was a dream. A nightmare. A conjuring of the fever. It was. . . it was real?

Embarrassment, it seems, is a harder emotion to swallow than rage. It swells inside me until my cheeks are aflame and my pulse is pounding. I wish for the ground to open, to swallow me up, to take me away from the obnoxious snake before me.

Blake's mouth curves into a slow, satisfied smile.

I raise my chin, even though I know my face must be redder than my hair. "I have no idea what you're talking about." I stride toward the door again. I'm trembling. I'm on fire. I'm *mortified*. "Good day, Blake."

"Good day, little rabbit." I feel the cool whisper of his amusement. He goes back to studying the map.

I open the door, step out of the council chambers, and close it a little too forcefully behind me.

Callum and Ryan look up abruptly from the other side of the corridor. Both seem annoyed. Ryan's face is flushed, and Callum has his arms folded across his chest and his jaw is tense. Callum's brow creases in concern, a question in his eyes. I nod. *I'm okay.* He offers me a strained smile before turning to Ryan.

"No," says Callum. "And that's the end of the matter."

"But—"

"Everything okay, Red?" A deep voice comes from the shadows, drowning out Ryan's protest, and I jump. Jack leans against the wall with his arms folded across his chest.

I frown as I recall him plotting with Blake in those dungeons I was brought to before I was presented to James. *She smells like the Highfell alpha*, he'd said, and suggested that Blake bathe me.

"How original you are," I say. "Calling me Red on account of my hair."

"On account of your hair?" says Jack. "No, I was referring to your blush, *Red*. Are you feeling flustered?" His grin widens, flashing white teeth, and my cheeks heat even more.

"What are you lingering out here for?" I try to appear more composed. "Didn't anyone tell you it's rude to eavesdrop?"

"My mother may have mentioned it." He shrugs, then nods at the door to the council chambers. "Blake's had more suitable accommodation prepared for you. I'll take you there, now you've woken up."

There's a grunt of displeasure as Callum dismisses Ryan. The young wolf huffs and stomps away. Callum mutters something under his breath about insolent pups as he crosses the space between us and threads my fingers in his. The tension softens in his shoulders.

"Ready?" says Jack.

"Aye."

We follow Jack through a labyrinth of corridors.

"What was that all about?" I ask under my breath as our footsteps thump against the stone.

"Ryan wants to go back to Madadh-allaidh." Callum sighs, and again, he looks as if he's carrying a great weight on his shoulders. "The lad's come up with some grand scheme to rescue Fiona. He thinks he can trick James."

"Oh," I say softly. "That doesn't sound like a sensible idea."

"No. It doesn't. He's going to get himself killed if he doesn't listen to me. And he has a history of not listening to me."

"Is he close with Fiona?"

"Being part of a clan . . . we're family. She taught him how to ride a horse, and Fi, James, and I, we used to let him tag along when we went hunting." He shakes his head. "I think he used to have a wee crush on her, before Becky."

I squeeze his hand. "We'll get her back."

"Aye. And I shall make James pay for all of this—hurting you, claiming you, taking Fi. I could do without worrying about Ryan on top of everything else."

Jack points things out as we pass them—the doors to Blake's Great Hall, a drawing room, a corridor leading to the infirmary. Just like earlier, I notice the absence of any clan banners or tapestries within the castle. It's quiet, too. We pass a few people in the corridors—two women in brown dresses having a hushed conversation, and an old man in a black and grey kilt carrying a box of fish toward the kitchens. A young child—around four years old—with a mop of black curls tears down a stairway past us, causing Jack to tell him to run faster if he means to outrun his mother. Either Blake's clan is not very big, or they're residing elsewhere.

When Jack gestures to a spiral staircase leading to a library in the tower, I make a note of it so I can visit later. I want to find out how Blake connected our lives, so I can disentangle myself from him. The library seems to be a good place to start.

Finally, we stop outside a door on the second floor of the castle. Jack opens it.

The room is much larger than I expected. A huge four-poster bed dominates the space, covered in furs, and two armchairs sit on a sheepskin rug in front of the roaring fire. In the corner, a wooden partition partially hides a dressing area and a sturdy oak armoire. Despite the lack of decoration, there's a rectangle of lighter stone above the wooden mantelpiece, as if a picture once hung there.

"Blake thought it might be more suitable than the room you were in before," says Jack. "The former alpha of Lowfell used to reside in here."

"This was Bruce's room?" Callum's tone is dark as he looks around.

"You knew him?" asks Jack.

"Aye. Did you?"

Jack strides to the window, which looks out onto a vast expanse of water, and leans against the ledge. "Our meeting was short-lived." His eyes glint in the grey light. "Blake took a particular dislike to him. It's why he opted not to take this room for himself. He didn't want to sleep in Bruce's bed."

Callum leans by the door, mirroring Jack's easy posture. "Did he kill him in here?" He sounds as if he's merely enquiring about the weather.

"No. He did it in the infirmary."

A flicker of disgust surges through me at the reminder that Blake is a killer, who likes to inflict physical, as well as emotional, torment.

Callum's mouth pinches at the corners, as if he doesn't approve, either. "I see."

A smile plays on Jack's lips, as if our revulsion to his alpha is amusing to him. He straightens and gestures at the armoire. "There are some clothes that should be your size in there, Aurora, and the bath has been drawn if you want to freshen up." He points at a doorway in the corner that must lead to a private bathing room.

"Thank you." I keep my tone polite, despite my distrust of this male. It will probably work in our favor to keep Blake's clan on side, if we are to defeat him.

Jack's smile widens before he nods. "My offer stands, if you want to spar later, Callum."

"Perhaps you could train with Ryan," says Callum. "Keep the lad out of trouble."

Something seems to pass between them both—a challenge of sorts that I don't understand. Jack leaves and closes the door behind him. As soon as we're alone, Callum visibly slumps against the wall. He meets my eyes though, a flicker of heat in them even as his expression softens. He crooks his finger.

"Come here," he says.

Chapter Six

I cross the chambers, and stop inches away from Callum.

He leans against the wall, and I touch his chest and savor the reassuring solidity of him beneath his shirt. He sighs. It's as if my touch is as reassuring to him as his is to me. Without warning, he slides his hands beneath my thighs and lifts me up. I wrap my legs around his torso.

He carries me to the bed, climbs onto it, and lays me down on the quilt. My head sinks into the feather-soft pillow. He settles over me, and rests his weight on his forearms on either side of my face. He presses his forehead against mine. His skin is hot, almost fevered.

"I was so worried." His voice is as rough as sand.

I take his face in my hands. "Are you alright?"

"No."

My eyebrows lift at his admission. It's obvious he's struggling with everything that has happened over the past few days, yet I didn't expect him to admit it. Whenever I saw my father straining beneath the weight of ruling the kingdom, he would lash out at whoever was closest. Whenever my brother was in a foul mood, he would turn to the bottle.

Again, it strikes me how powerful this man—this wolf—is, to be able to show his emotions with no fear of them being held against him.

I brush my thumb against his jaw, and his stubble scrapes against my skin. "Talk to me."

"You were in pain, and I was powerless to stop it. James is trying to claim you as his. Fiona is a hostage. And Blake..." He shakes his head, then huffs a soft laugh. "I'm stuck here with Blake of all people, trying to pretend I don't want to tear him, and the men who work for him, apart. The only good news I've had these past days is that James doesn't have the Heart of the Moon. Blake has a spy in Madadh-Allaidh, who sent word yesterday."

Even though the Wolves shifted the night that James handed me over to Sebastian, this doesn't surprise me. The Heart of the Moon is an ancient wolf relic that is said to have been ripped from the Moon Goddess's chest. It would give the Wolves the power to shift at will, which would be a big advantage in the war between the humans and Wolves.

"I didn't think that Sebastian would have traded something so important for me," I say.

"Foolish man," says Callum.

"It's strange that you shifted though. At the time, I thought..."

Callum's brow furrows. "What?"

"I prayed to the Moon Goddess," I say, feeling silly. "I thought, perhaps, she answered."

Callum smiles softly. "Perhaps she did. She is said to involve herself in the fates of Wolves, at times." He strokes my cheek, then sighs.

"What is it?" I ask.

"I thought I would feel better when you awoke, yet I find myself feeling. . . restless."

I note the tension in his body, and the hardness that presses against my thigh through his kilt. My blood heats, and I stroke his cheek. Being with a man like this is so new to me, yet I cannot deny that I'm restless, too. "Can I help you with that?"

He captures my mouth with his. He makes a low sound in his throat as he deepens his kiss. He slides his tongue against mine—hot and dominant—and heat pools between my thighs. I shift against him. I curl my legs around his waist, pressing myself against his torso. I whimper as a jolt of pleasure surges through me.

He pulls back, trembling slightly, and shuts his eyes. "No. I fear that I'll push you back into a fever. I've felt guilty about it for three days."

"What do you mean?"

He opens his eyes, and blinks back the wolf. "As Wolves, when we're. . . excited. . . our more feral side tends to come out. When my mouth was between your thighs," my cheeks flame, but Callum doesn't seem remotely embarrassed, "I provoked your wolf. You spent the next three days trying to suppress it. If I were to do to you what I want to do. . ." He shakes his head. "I dread to think how long you will be unconscious. I won't do that to you again."

"You think you will give me so much pleasure that you will push me into a fever for days?"

His expression is so remorseful that I have to suppress my smile. "Aye."

"You certainly think highly of yourself, don't you?"

A soft laugh escapes from his lips. His eyes crease at the corners, and they brighten—the color of treetops being hit by sunlight. For a moment, he looks younger. Not an alpha with the weight of a clan on his shoulders, about to challenge his brother, but a young male full of mischief and light.

"I don't recall your complaints the previous times I have tasted you, nor every time I slid my fingers inside of you until you cried out my name."

I fight my blush and his grin widens.

"Do you not think I've earned my high opinion of myself?"

I bite my bottom lip. "I cannot remember. Perhaps you should remind me."

He growls, before nipping my ear with his teeth. "Demanding wee creature. Take a bath, then we shall go for a walk outside. I've been cooped up inside for days, as have you. The fresh air will do you good." He kisses my nose, then my forehead, before his expression becomes strained once more. "And for the love of *Ghealach*, change out of Blake's clothes, will you? It's taking all of my restraint not to rip them off you."

"I won't stop you."

He groans and rolls off me. "Bath. Now."

***

"I'LL BE glad to be out of this place." Callum's hand is clamped around mine as he leads me through the Lowfell entrance hall, toward the oak door. The area is small, with no decoration, and a stairway leading to another floor. "We're surrounded by enemies here. I've sent word to Highfell, but I can't imagine my men will arrive until after the full moon. It's why we'll wait until after before we make our move."

"Do you have a big army?"

The door creaks as Callum pushes it open, and the wind sprays rain into my face.

"Big enough to protect Highfell, but not to keep everyone under control when we get to Madadh-allaidh," says Callum. We walk outside, into a small courtyard. The walls on either side are so close together, it feels oppressive.

"That's why we need Lochlan," I say.

Callum nods and pulls me into a tunnel in the castle walls, which offers us a brief respite from the weather. There are tall iron gates at the end, and my lips part as we walk through them and turn.

We are surrounded by water. Mountains slope upward on either side of the dark loch, burnt orange, brown, and golden yellow. Behind us, the castle reaches up to the grey sky. It's smaller than Madadh-allaidh, but it's similarly austere in design—with angular stone walls, dark windows, and a rectangular tower.

The rain patters as it hits the loch, and the air smells like mud and wet leaves. Our boots squelch in the grass, and Callum tips back his head and sighs as we stop beneath a couple of trees at the water's edge. Rain rolls down his face and lips. He seems as in awe of the surrounding beauty as I am.

"Have you been to Lowfell before?" I ask. Blake was part of his father's wolf alliance, so it's feasible that Callum may have visited.

"No. I knew it was something of a fortress. Until I saw it the other night, I'd not realized how impenetrable it truly was." He tugs my hand, and we walk along the side of the loch. The water is the color of rust, and its waves lap over stones by our feet. "There's a strip of land that connects it to the rest of the Northlands around the back but it's only revealed at low tide. The only other way to approach is via the water."

"We're close to the Borderlands here, aren't we?" I say, thinking about the map in Blake's council chambers.

"Aye. Lowfell used to raid a lot of the Borderlands villages—plus some of the wolf territories as well—but no one could ever seize it. It's why my father was keen to get the former alpha on side for a while."

"Bruce?"

"He was a very unpleasant male. James would make a point of taking me out hunting when..." Callum shuts his mouth, his eyes darkening at the mention of his brother. "One day, my father completely cut ties with him. They almost went to war."

"What happened?"

"I think Bruce made a pass at my mother." Callum's gaze is focused on the woodland ahead. "My father was a jealous man, and that kind of insult would not have gone down well. Everyone thought Bruce would challenge my father for the throne—but then we got word he'd been killed and there was a new alpha of Lowfell."

"Blake."

"Aye." Callum chuckles darkly. "I don't know how that devious shite did it. This castle is near impenetrable, and Bruce had a particularly bloodthirsty clan. From what I've seen over the past day, it seems like Blake disposed of them as well."

I nod. "It's quiet here. There don't seem to be many people living in the castle."

"No."

"That troubles you." Ash trees sway around us as we enter the woods, and I almost slip on the wet fallen leaves on the ground. Callum grabs my arm, supporting me, and I wince as the bite mark in my side aches. Callum's jaw tightens, but I pull away and start walking before he can comment. "Are you worried his clan won't be useful in the fight against your brother?"

Callum's breath mists in front of his face as he falls into step beside me. "There were always questions about whether Blake was truly an alpha, but he managed to make people believe he had forces that supported him back home." Callum gestures around him. "Does he, though? Are the people at Lowfell right now the extent of his clan, or are there more hidden away somewhere?"

"Either way, he's good at hiding things," I say.

"Aye." Callum's face darkens. The trees get closer together and cast their shadow over us. "That's what troubles me."

As we delve further in, the scent of wet leaves and moss gets deeper, and a building comes into view among the trees. It's a small chapel, with a singular spire. As we get closer, it's evident that it's in need of some repair—the walls are crumbling, and the stained-glass window above the door has been smashed.

Callum's forehead creases. "That's interesting."

"Is it for worshipping the Moon Goddess?" I ask, knowing that Wolves don't pray to the Sun Goddess like we do in the Southlands.

"No." Callum approaches the door, and pushes it open. "We worship *Ghealach* outdoors, where the moonlight can touch us. You will see at the ritual next week. This is something different. Come."

He heads inside while I pause at the threshold. It's sparsely furnished, with only a few pews, and a stone altar beneath another smashed window at the other end of the room. Glass crunches beneath Callum's boots as he heads toward it.

My muscles tense. I've never liked religious buildings. Even though this chapel is a far cry from the extravagant houses of worship in the south, memories of the High Priest's crop flash through my mind.

"Aye, it's what I thought." Callum looks at the circular window above the altar. "This is one of Night's chapels."

"The god who keeps the Moon Goddess prisoner?" I ask.

"Aye."

Curiosity getting the better of me, I suck in a deep breath and walk inside.

"Why would any Wolves worship him? Isn't he one of the villains in your story about the Elderwolf?" My footsteps echo as I walk down the aisle between the pews, and stop beside Callum at the altar.

I recall the story Callum told me, about the origin of Wolves. The first wolf, the Elderwolf, had fallen in love with the Moon. She gave him the power to shift so he could fight the dark creatures who belonged to the God of Night. Until the Sun Goddess became jealous, and sentenced the Moon Goddess to the prison in Night's sky. Her imprisonment was what stopped the Wolves from being able to shift at will.

"Before the first men and the Elderwolf, Night's monsters roamed the earth—soul-suckers, winged beasts, water serpents." He turns to lean against the altar, hands clasping the edges of the stone. Grey light flits across his jaw as branches sway outside the broken windows. "When *Ghealach* was locked away in his prison, she tricked him into imprisoning all his dark creatures. Night was imprisoned, too, in the process. Before then, many Wolves prayed to Night, asking him to spare them from torment."

"They prayed to him because they feared him, not because they loved him," I say.

"Aye. Some Wolves continued to worship him, even after he had taken *Ghealach* prisoner. We call them Night's Acolytes. In my grandfather's day, they rose up against us—not just here, but in other wolf territories like the Snowlands too."

My eyes widen at the mention of my mother's homeland. "Why?" I ask. "What did they want?"

"They were determined to free their dark god from his prison."

"Is that possible?"

"They believe the Heart of the Moon is the key. It's why finding the relic would be a blessing and a curse. It would mean freedom for my people, and would help us in the war against the south. But—"

"It could start an entirely different war, with those who worship Night."

"Exactly." He shakes his head. "Why any wolf would choose to turn their back on their goddess is beyond me. Their means of worship are much darker than ours."

His gestures at the floor by my feet with his chin. The stone is stained dark brown.

My stomach curdles. "Is that blood?"

"Night's Acolytes would sacrifice people in the hopes he would bless them with his dark powers."

My breath mists in front of my face as I cast my gaze around the chapel—there are small symbols carved into the stone walls that I can't quite make out from here. Part of the roof has caved in at the far end and there are a few branches protruding into the building. It seems like a ruin of whatever it once was, yet there is a strange feeling in this place—cold and dark and eerie.

"Should we be worried that Blake has this chapel on his grounds?" I ask.

"Blake is a lot of things, but he's never struck me as a religious man. It's an old building, and it doesn't look like it's in use any longer. In fact, it looks like the windows were intentionally smashed. Like I said, Bruce was an unpleasant male, as was his father. This will have been their chapel."

My attention snags on the symbol carved in the stone arch above the altar. It's the image of a key, the bow comprising of two crescent moons facing one another. It seems familiar, though I can't place it.

"Come, let's leave this dark place," says Callum. "It smells like blood and despair."

I don't need telling twice. He takes my hand, and we head back into the woodland. Something loosens inside me as the air freshens, and the scent of rain and pine fills my lungs. Both our footsteps are a little less relaxed than earlier as we walk quickly away from the chapel.

Chapter Seven

Callum seems restless in the days leading up to Oidhche Fhada. I think he wants to ride out to visit some nearby clans, but he seems reluctant to leave my side after my illness. I think the over-protectiveness must be a wolf thing.

We spend our time exploring the dark corridors of Lowfell, and the grounds outside. The castle is quiet. People seem to come and go as they please, some of them delivering meat and grains from a nearby village, then heading back home before nightfall. We see little of Blake, and I dread to think what he's plotting.

Arran and Elsie frequently spend time together in the kitchens, while Arran cooks, and Elsie fusses over the small boy—Alfie—who raced past us on the stairwell on the first day. She must be his mother. We eat with them, one evening. They don't converse with us much, but they talk among themselves about innocuous things—the weather, the upcoming ritual, the fact that the alpha, Lochlan, will be arriving soon. When they leave, Callum frowns when Alfie scampers past. Later, he tells me the boy seemed familiar.

On the day of Oidhche Fhada, when we're taking a walk in the woods, Callum smiles when he sees Jack sparring with Ryan outside the stone walls of the castle. I recall that Callum suggested they train together.

"You want Ryan to spar with Jack?" I ask.

"At some point soon, we will be at war with Lowfell," Callum tells me under his breath. "Arran is built like me, and he's a Northlander. I know how he will fight. Jack is different. I want to get the measure of him, see how he has been trained, without him getting the measure of me."

"By having him fight Ryan?" I arch an eyebrow, skeptical. Ryan is smaller and younger than Jack; he's hardly going to push him to his limits.

Callum folds his arms and nods at the two. Ryan is more than holding his own against the stronger man. As if feeling our attention on him, and wanting to impress us, he pulls a maneuver that has Jack's wooden sword flying out of his hands. Jack chuckles as Ryan presses his blade to his throat.

"Ryan may not be physically strong, but he's excellent with a blade." Callum gives me a big boyish grin, and his green eyes glint in the weak sun. "I taught him."

My lips twitch. "I suppose you want me to be impressed?"

"Are you?"

I squeeze his bicep and roll my eyes. "You're very impressive, Callum."

His loud laugh causes a few birds to take flight from the woodland, and Jack to look in our direction and grin.

Later, the sky darkens through the window of our bedchambers, and my anticipation about the ceremony grows.

I sit in one of the armchairs by the fire, my legs curled beneath me, and flick through one of Blake's books. I took it from the library—a dusty room in the tower that Callum has been walking me to each morning, before complaining that he's bored.

Experiments: Book Two is handwritten across the front. I found a book like this in my old chambers at Madadh-allaidh. Similarly, it's an account of torture conducted on Wolves, that I presume was written by Blake. I don't want to read about the awful torment that Blake must have inflicted, yet there are sections within it about the full moon.

I read about the way in which a wolf's bones break and shift, the ways different stimulus can provoke the subject's inner beast, the way that reason and logic is replaced by primal instincts when the wolf surfaces. The lunar eclipse is tonight, and it's two weeks until the moon will be full. If Blake and Callum are right about me, then these things will happen to me, too. Tension coils in my chest and squeezes. I chew my fingers, and some of the knots unwind as I rip off the edge of my fingernail.

The leather armchair on the other side of the hearth creaks as Callum stands. Slowly, he unbuttons his shirt. I put my book down, transfixed, as he exposes his hard chest and the ridges of his torso. He shrugs the material off his powerful shoulders, and drops it onto the floor.

"What are you doing?" I whisper.

He sits back down in the chair, legs slightly parted. "Come here."

"No," I say, because I'm feeling restless, and I want to see what he'll do next.

"Aye. Now."

The corner of my lip quirks, as my pulse accelerates. The dark hunger in his expression compels me to obey. I slide my feet out from under me, and pad across the floorboards toward him.

He pats his lap. "Sit."

I arch an eyebrow, and try to appear unaffected by the powerful shoulders and the mass of muscle before me. "You're very bossy this evening."

"I'm an alpha. Now do as you're told." His eyes glint playfully, so I know he's only teasing.

I climb into his lap, and my thighs press against either side of his. He breathes in deeply as his hands find my waist. Warmth spreads through the woolen material of my dress as he squeezes.

"Can I help you?" I ask.

The corner of his mouth lifts. Slowly, he dips his face to my throat and drags his nose over the sensitive skin there. He inhales deeply, and I breathe in sharply. "Are you... smelling me?"

"Mmhm," he mumbles.

I curl my arms around his neck. "For any particular reason?" He opens his mouth, and his breath brushes my ear. "And don't say it's a wolf thing."

He brings his face back to mine and grins. His green eyes gleam in the firelight. "It *is* a wolf thing." He slides his big hands up my back, then nips my earlobe with his teeth. Heat coils low in my stomach. "It's been too long since I've been inside you. I want to check that you still smell like me."

I huff out a laugh. "Oh. It really is a wolf thing." He drags his tongue up the column of my throat, and I arch my back as a gasp escapes my lips. These Wolves are strange creatures.

"I want Lochlan to know exactly who he'll be dealing with, if he tries anything." His voice is low and rough, and something stirs within me.

"And? What do I smell like?"

"Mm. You smell like fresh snow, and moonlight, and honey. You smell delicious." He nips my skin with his teeth and a soft whimper escapes me. "But not enough like me for my liking."

He curls his arms around me and pulls. My face falls to his shoulder, and my chest is flush with his. His scent, and the heat of him, it overpowers me—mountains and dawn and Callum. My peaked nipples rub against his skin through the fabric of my dress as he rubs his arms up and down my back. I kiss his collarbone, and his muscles tighten.

"What are you going to do about that?" I ask.

He nuzzles my neck. "I'm doing it now."

"You can do better than that, can't you?"

He looks up slowly, and the wolf is in his eyes. I lower my lips to his. He leans forward and claims them. His kiss is hot and deep, and he slides his tongue against mine. A rough sound escapes him. It trembles through me, and I'm suddenly on fire.

I want him. I need him. From his erection that presses against my core through his kilt, I know he feels the same. I move, tentatively, against him.

He groans, and his hands find my hips. "I forgot how good your body felt against mine," he mumbles.

He moves me against him, his rhythm tortuously slow. Delicious friction builds as my arousal pools between my legs. It's like there's something coiling inside me, something that needs release. I capture his lip with my teeth and the sound he makes is feral.

"Now you smell even better," he groans.

"Because I smell like you?"

"Because you smell like you want me."

I do. I want his fingers. I want his mouth. I want everything. I want him to bury himself so deeply that all I know is him. I move faster against him, and he dips his lips to my throat and sucks on the skin. His teeth press into me, his canines sharp. I whimper. He groans against me, then suddenly jerks back. Ice floods me as his head hits the back of the chair. The wolf blazes behind his eyes for a split second before he shuts them, and they crease in the corners. "Fuck."

"Callum?" I breathe. "What's the matter?"

His cheeks are flushed, lips swollen, and his chest moves deeply. His hands hold me firmly in place. He looks like he's in pain. "My wolf." He grits his teeth. "I almost bit you. I don't. . . I don't have control."

I'm breathless, my pulse pounding. "Open your eyes." He obeys, and my breath catches at the beauty in those wolf irises. I brush my fingertips down the side of his face. "You don't scare me."

"I scare myself when I'm with you. The leash I keep myself on always feels frayed. I don't want to hurt you. I don't want to push you into a fever for days, again."

"I trust you."

"You wouldn't—not if you knew how loudly my blood howled every time you were near."

"So, you're never going to touch me again?"

The corner of his mouth lifts, and there's a wicked glint in his eyes. "I didn't say that." He sucks in a deep breath, tempering his emotions. Then he nods, resolute, as if he has made a decision. "I want to wait until after the full moon. I'm going to wait until you've shifted the first time, and I know you can handle me." He slides a hand onto my cheek, and his expression darkens. "I'm going to wait until your senses are heightened—touch, scent, taste. . ." He runs his thumb over my bottom lip, and my breath hitches. "Then I'm going to take my time exploring every inch of you." He dips his mouth to my ear. "And I'm going to let the wolf side of me off the leash."

I breathe in sharply. Desire coils inside me and throbs between my thighs. I turn my head and lean toward him, wanting to kiss him. His hands keep me in place, halt me. He holds me for a moment, as if showing me who is in charge, then he presses a soft, chaste kiss on my lips.

The sound of chatter and footsteps outside our chambers breaks the tension. Callum blinks, and the wolf disappears. "Sounds like people are gathering," he says. "Come on. Lochlan and his clan will be here soon. We should go."

Frustration pulses through me. I still feel him, hard, between my legs, so I know he feels the same. Stubborn wolf.

"Don't look at me like that." He smiles, somewhat sheepishly, and kisses me again. "I'm sorry. I just wanted to hold you, to kiss you. I didn't mean for it to get this far."

"You're a frustrating wolf, Callum McKennan. Has anyone ever told you that?"

He shrugs. "Some people may have mentioned it. If it makes you feel any better, I'm suffering, too."

I roll my eyes and climb off him. "It's suffering of your own devising." I turn away from him and brush down my dress. "I would have let you take your pleasure from me in any way of your choosing, if you weren't so stubborn." I smirk when he stiffens and curses under his breath. I grab my cloak from the foot of the bed and walk toward the door. I look over my shoulder. "Are you coming?"

He gets up, slips on his shirt, and grabs a black coat from the armoire. There's a dark look in his eyes as he stalks toward me, but it becomes playful as he hooks an arm around my waist, and nips my ear with his teeth. "Bold words, Princess. We'll see if you feel that way after the full moon."

Even though the mention of the full moon makes something harden within me, I keep the smile on my face. "What do I smell like now?"

"Mine," he growls in my ear.

***

THERE ARE about thirty Wolves gathered in the small courtyard when we arrive, and the night is filled with excited chatter. Everyone wears a dark cloak or coat—which Callum told me is tradition for this night. Callum threads his fingers with mine and pulls me through the crowd toward Blake.

The Lowfell alpha leans against the castle wall, in conversation with Jack. When the cold wind whips my hair and stirs my cloak, Blake's nostrils flare. A look of distaste flickers across his expression which he quickly hides. I'm glad the cold disguises my flush. Blake clearly knows exactly what we were just doing. From Jack's smirk, he does, too.

"Excellent, you're both here." Blake's breath mists in front of his face, and he rubs his hands together. "Are you ready?"

"Aye," says Callum. "When can we expect Lochlan and his clan?"

A short distance away, Alfie punches an unfazed Arran with his tiny fists, much to the exasperation of Elsie, who tugs him away by his collar.

"He'll meet us up at Dawn's Craig," says Blake.

My gaze snaps to Callum. "The ceremony isn't taking place at Lowfell?"

"No," says Callum. "We'll hike up a nearby mountain so we're closer to *Ghealach*."

A small thrill ignites beneath my skin. I've felt claustrophobic since we got here, and I long to explore more of the Northlands. I still ask the question. "Is it safe to leave?" Callum doesn't seem to trust the alpha who will be arriving tonight.

Callum squeezes my hand, as if sensing my worry. "Bloodshed is forbidden during the night of Oidhche Fhada. It's wolf law. Unbreakable. You're safe, Princess." He brings his mouth to my ear. "Plus, you smell like me, remember?"

Blake pushes off from the wall. "Time to go." He throws his arm up in the air to gesture to the other Wolves as he walks toward the tunnel that leads to the grounds.

More chatter fills the air as we follow him through the courtyard and outside of the castle walls. Wild grass tickles my hands, and mud squelches beneath my boots as the group of us cross the unspoiled land toward the nearby mountains. Only the soft glow of the half-moon lights our way.

I can't help but smile as we all make our way to Dawn's Craig to perform the Oidhche Fhada ritual.

Chapter Eight

I'm unused to hiking, particularly at night.

My thigh muscles ache, and I stumble on jagged protruding rocks. I'm quickly breathless. Despite the chill in the air, sweat beads my skin. I lag at the tail of the group while Callum, just ahead of me, jokes around with Ryan and Becky. With his muscles and wolf strength, I'm sure it doesn't occur to him that the climb may be a struggle for a human princess who spent most of her time sitting indoors sewing, or preening, or playing the piano.

Despite my discomfort, a smile plays on my lips. The air is so fresh I can taste it. The scents of rain-drenched grass, muddy earth, and the occasional whiff of animal feces travel in the wind. Childlike excitement bubbles in my chest when I spot a sheep grazing on the mountainside.

When I look over my shoulder, Lowfell Castle is a mere dot in the darkness, surrounded by rippling water that reflects the moonlight. My breath catches, and freedom fills my lungs. Despite everything that has happened—being attacked by James, Blake linking our lives, his plot against Callum—I'm glad to be here, rather than in the Southlands.

Blake's contrived laugh slices through the darkness and sets my teeth on edge. He's at the head of the group, speaking to Arran, Jack, and an older gentleman in a black-and-grey kilt. The small boy, Alfie, runs circles around them. My mouth pinches at the corners.

"You don't like Blake, I take it?" A smooth male voice, thick with the Northlands accent, makes me jump. A tall member of Blake's clan falls into step beside me. The hood of his cloak hides his face. "He tends to have that effect on people."

"Does he have that effect on you?" I ask, curious about what members of Blake's clan actually think of him.

"I find him... intriguing."

"How so?"

"He collects broken birds. Have you noticed? The bastard with one eye, the abused woman, the half-wolf from the King's City docks." I feel his attention on me, and my muscles tighten. "The Southlands princess. I've long wondered what he intends to do with them. Heal them, or pluck their feathers. Cage them, or let them take flight. Perhaps they just amuse him."

I frown as I make sense of his "birds". Arran, with his scarred throat and eye patch, must have been the first, and from Jack's Southlands accent, he could have originated from the King's City docks. I don't know who the abused woman is, though. Nor do I appreciate being referred to as broken myself. Even if it might be true.

"Are you a broken bird?" I ask.

The wind carries the sound of bagpipes as the summit of the mountain gets closer. Lochlan's clan must already be here.

"We're all a wee bit broken, aren't we?" There's a smile in his tone.

"How are you broken?"

He waves an arm beneath his cloak. "Nothing interesting, I assure you. Father issues, a lost love." He gestures at Callum. "I hear he kidnapped you."

"I chose to come with him."

I stumble over a jagged rock, and the man grabs my arm and steadies me. There is strength in his grip. I mumble my thanks and brush myself down.

"Why would a Southlands princess choose to come to her enemy kingdom?" asks the male.

"I was supposed to marry a terrible man. I wanted to be free."

"Ah, I see. Callum would have been powerless to resist."

"What do you mean?"

"I hear he enjoys a damsel in distress."

I have the strangest feeling this male is trying to antagonize me. I shouldn't be surprised that Blake's clan are as provocative as their alpha. "I'm not a damsel."

"No? Yet you let him save you from your perilous situation in the Borderlands, rather than saving yourself."

I'm stung by the slight shred of truth in that. "That is part of the story, I suppose. I'd also planned to gain information on the Wolves." I shrug. "I thought if I gave it to my father, I could barter for my freedom. My loyalties changed when I got to know Callum. More so when I learned more about my father, and the man I was supposed to marry."

"What truth did you learn?"

"That people in power mold their stories to serve their interests. That the Wolves are not the villains my people are taught to believe they are. Not all of them, anyway."

Blake calls over to Elsie and asks her to keep the little beast under control.

The track steepens. At one point, I need to use my hands to clamber over some rocks. I've never had to do such a thing before, and a smile spreads across my face when my palms get wet and dirty. Callum looks over his shoulder when we're on less treacherous ground and grins before playfully shoving Ryan toward the mountain edge. Ryan swears at him, face turning red, and Callum roars with laughter. I take a moment to catch my breath, shaking my head at the childishness of the alpha I find myself involved with.

The cloaked male steps beside me once more and chuckles. He must be as tall as Callum. He's not as muscular, but his dark cloak hangs off broad shoulders. "What's your name?" I ask, panting.

He inclines his head at the steep slope ahead, a blanket of stars above us. "Come on." He starts walking once more. "We're almost at the top."

We reach the grassy summit and find ourselves at the edge of a stone circle. There must be about twenty people waiting for us—drinking from flasks and gathered around whisky barrels. A woman plays the bagpipes, and the shrill yet joyful sound fills the air. They all wear yellow tartan beneath their cloaks. This must be Lochlan's clan.

The cold air is filled with chatter and the scent of wet earth. A soft laugh escapes me and mists in front of my face. For the first time in my twenty years of life, I have climbed a mountain.

"You have stunning hair, by the way," says the male. "Many Wolves in the Snowlands have hair that color."

My head snaps toward him at the mention of my mother's homeland, but he's watching the crowd.

Ahead, Ryan tugs Becky toward one of the whisky barrels, while Callum shouts after them to pace themselves. Jack strides toward a blonde woman in the middle of the revelry who wears a white dress. She's the only person who isn't wearing black.

"Is that the Moon Priestess?" I ask the cloaked wolf.

He nods. "Aye. She'll be conducting the ceremony, later."

Arran musses up Alfie's hair and leads him in the opposite direction, while Elsie seemingly exchanges a sharp word with Blake before following them.

"Is Lochlan here yet?" Callum's rough voice is carried by the cold wind. "I can't see him."

"I suspect we'd know if he was," says Blake. "He always likes to make an entrance."

"Gentlemen," says the male beside me. He lowers his hood.

Callum and Blake both turn. Callum's fist clenches by his side, while Blake's mouth curves into slow smile. "Ah, Lochlan, there you are," says Blake.

My stomach jolts. Lochlan has hair as red as mine. It's shorn close to his scalp at the sides, a bit like Callum's, but the hair at the top is much longer—braided then tied—and it reaches his lower back. His eyes glint with intelligence, and they're underlined with black kohl. Amusement dances on his lips.

Lochlan winks at me before he strides toward Blake and clasps him on the shoulder. "You're looking flawless as always, Blake." There's something like heat in his eyes.

A dimple creases Blake's cheek. "As are you, Lochlan."

Callum crosses the space between us, and puts an arm around my shoulders. There's something territorial about his stance, and Lochlan chuckles. "Rest easy, Callum. I have no quarrel with you. I've just become acquainted with your princess." He grins at me. "I like her."

Some of Callum's tension dissipates, though he still seems wary when he shakes Lochlan's hand. "Thank you for coming. I was hoping we could speak."

Lochlan makes a dismissive gesture as he steps back. "I know what you want to talk about but we'll have time for politics later. Blake has invited me to stay for a few nights. Let us enjoy the festivities tonight, and we can talk about your brother—and what I want from you in exchange for my support—tomorrow. I don't know about the rest of you, but I'm parched after the climb. My men brought a barrel of Glas-Cladach's finest whisky. Can I tempt you?"

"Always," says Blake, his voice smooth as silk.

Lochlan's grin is almost wolfish. "Excellent. Callum?"

Callum is still for a moment, then he relaxes. "Aye. I've heard you barrel it in caves blessed by *Ghealach*."

"My clan will tell you that because of this, it brings the wolf to the surface more than any other whisky in the Northlands." Lochlan grins at me, and lowers his voice conspiratorially. "Really it's just the exceedingly high alcohol content." He winks. "Want to try it?"

I blink, surprised to have been asked. "Please."

He walks away and Blake falls into step beside him. "I'll join you. There's another matter I wish to discuss."

Lochlan inclines his head. "I had one my of men bring you a cart of moonflower, by the way."

"Excellent. My supplies were low. . ."

Their voices fade as they walk toward the group gathering around a barrel in the center of the stone circle. Callum frowns.

"He's up to something," he says darkly.

"Lochlan or Blake?"

"Blake. Whenever he lays on the charm, there's reason to worry." His eyes darken. "I didn't even know they were friends."

I touch his arm. "At least he can probably talk Lochlan into supporting you."

Callum sighs, his breath a plume of mist before his troubled face. "Likely with promises of what Lochlan can expect when Blake has put himself on the throne."

I squeeze his muscles. "You'll just have to offer him something better, won't you?"

"Did I ever tell you you're rather nefarious, Princess?"

I shrug and give him a coy smile, but Callum frowns.

"Are you feeling alright?" His tone is soft, and he touches my cheek. "Is it the fever?"

"What are you talking about?"

"You're looking a wee bit sweaty. Perhaps we should get you sat down." Indignation floods my system, and I shove him. I may as well be trying to move a rock for all the good it does. He arches an eyebrow, the corner of his mouth tugging up. "What?"

"Don't tell a woman she looks sweaty!" I shove him again. He doesn't budge an inch. "I'm sweating because I've just hiked up a big bloody mountain!"

He laughs. Loudly. "You should have said something. I would have carried you."

"I don't need carrying! I'm not completely fragile, Callum!"

He looks like he's going to say something, probably obnoxious, judging by the glint in his eye, but his brow furrows. At the same time, that thread of Blake's life force coils around my soul. I stiffen as it implodes, and ice crackles through my veins.

Blake stands with Lochlan and Arran by the whisky barrel. The wind drags its fingers through his dark hair, and makes his black coat flutter. His expression is careful, casual, but I catch a hint of ice in his eyes.

On the other side of the circle, the blonde priestess in the white dress has her hand curled around the young boy, Alfie's, arm. She appears to be scolding him, and his bottom lip wobbles as his eyes, big as saucers, fill with tears. The wind carries her voice toward me, as Elsie—his mother—storms across the circle, knocking shoulders with an older gentleman in her haste to get to him.

". . . an abomination. Your mother should be ashamed bringing you here. You're as tainted by darkness as she is, and you have no business—"

The roar in my ears tunes out whatever she says next. I don't know why she is punishing the little boy, but I won't stand for it. I have little patience for religious zealots, having been whipped throughout my childhood for my "sins against the Sun Goddess". I want to be respectful of the Wolves' culture, but I can't stand by and watch a young child be made to feel small by someone who claims to know the will of her goddess.

I stride toward them. "Let go of the child," I say.

The Moon Priestess's blue eyes snap toward me, and strands of blonde hair whip her face. There must be something in my expression she doesn't like, because she releases her grip on his arm. "You're the Southlands princess, aren't you? You're ignorant of our customs. But—"

"Careful." Callum puts his hand on my shoulder, as if to let me know I have his support. His heat sears my back, but it does little to warm the ice in my veins. I'm unsure whether it's my anger or Blake's that makes my body shake.

The priestess points at Alfie. "His mother is tainted. Promised to the God of Night—"

"He is a young child. An innocent," I say. "You ought to be ashamed of yourself." I hold out my hand to him. "It's okay, Alfie."

He grasps my fingers with his tiny hand, his black hair in disarray and his cheeks flushed and wet. I pull him toward Callum and me as Elsie shudders to a halt beside us. The wolf blazes in her eyes as she prods her finger in the priestess's direction. "You stay away from my son."

"I cannot conduct a ceremony to honor our goddess when a supporter of the God of Night is in attendance—"

"Elsie is no more of an acolyte than any of us here." Blake's voice is like a blade as he approaches.

Arran is beside him, and the large man's arm brushes against me as he grabs Alfie's collar and tugs. Tears shimmer in the boy's eyes, until Arran scoops him up and sits him on his broad shoulders.

"Come on, trouble," he says. "Let's go count the stones in the circle." He strides away, and I wonder if he doesn't want the young boy to witness whatever Blake has planned next.

"Apologize," says Blake, his tone like silk.

The night has quietened around us, as if Blake's presence has alerted both clans that something is going on. Elsie's cheeks redden.

"It's fine, Blake," says Elsie. "Don't you dare cause a scene. Not tonight. You'll ruin everything. I'd rather be in bed with a book than listen to this bitch drone on all night, anyway."

Blake keeps his gaze on the priestess. "Apologize," he repeats.

The priestess glares up at him. "It is forbidden to spill blood on this night."

"Who said anything about spilling blood?" The corner of his lip curves, and Callum tenses behind me. "I have a hallucinogenic in my infirmary that makes Wolves think their skin is melting from their bones. I have a paralytic that makes one long for death. Do you know what sound a wolf makes when they are deprived of air, again and again and again? I do."

A chill skitters over my skin that has nothing to do with my anger, nor the iciness in the Northlands air.

"That's enough, Blake," says Callum softly. "She's still a priestess."

"He's right, though." My words come out quietly, as if I can't quite believe I'm saying them. Every bone in my body is locked, every muscle tight. "She should apologize."

The priestess looks between Blake and me. Her eyebrows almost imperceptibly lift—as if something has dawned upon her. She dips her head. "I apologize."

She turns on her heel and strides toward the center of the circle. Elsie huffs sharply through her nose. Her dark hair whips her face as she spins around to face Blake. "I told you not to interfere." She shakes her head. "I'm heading back."

Blake grabs her wrist. "You have every right to be here—"

Her eyes blaze. "Drop it. And she'd better be alive in the morning." When Blake doesn't reply, she smacks his arm. "Blake."

His mouth pinches in the corners. "Fine."

He puts his hands into his pockets as she stomps away from us all. She casts one last glance at Alfie on Arran's shoulder before she disappears between the stones to head back down the mountain.

"What was all that about?" There's a crease in Callum's brow. "Does she worship Night?"

"No," says Blake. "She's tainted by her father's choices, that's all."

Not for the first time, I wonder who she is to Blake. Before either of us can ask anything else, Lochlan strolls up to us, four drams of whisky in hand. Blake conceals his emotion as quickly as I do.

"Is everything okay?" asks Lochlan.

"Fine," says Blake. He's watching the priestess as she talks to a group of women wearing yellow tartan beneath their cloaks.

Lochlan passes us each a drink. "Well... here's to old friends, new alliances, and broken birds escaping their cages." He winks at me.

Despite the discomfort of what has just occurred, we clink our glasses and drink. I can't shake the dark feeling that has come over me as the smoky substance burns my throat.

"Tonight is going to be fun," says Lochlan.

Chapter Nine

It takes a while for the tension to dissipate after Elsie's departure. Yet as more of Lochlan's whisky is consumed, the chatter gets merrier, and the scent of alcohol fills the air. I even catch Blake laughing with members of his clan, who, strangely, seem to like him.

The ceremony is more serene than I expected, though much has surprised me about Wolves since I arrived in the Northlands. There is a brutal beauty in this kingdom—in its wild peaks, and howling winds, and powerful alphas who can be gentle as well as deadly.

Callum has me tucked against his side as we sit against the stones in the circle, holding unlit candles while the priestess tells us stories of the Elderwolf, when darkness claimed the Northlands and monsters roamed the earth. Her own candle is alight and flickers in front of her face.

"When *Ghealach* was sentenced by the Sun to the prison in Night's Sky, before she ripped out her heart and sent it to the Elderwolf, she was only condemned to be captive for a century. However, she travelled to the depths of his prison to make a deal with him," says the priestess. "And thus, we experienced the first Dark Night.

"On this night, she vowed she would stay with Night in his prison for all eternity, if, in exchange, he would lock all the monsters who possessed his dark power within his cells. Her soul was one he coveted more than any other, so he accepted her terms, knowing it was the only way he could keep her forever. The vow was sealed with her power, and the monsters disappeared from our world. What Night did not realize was that, in his haste, he was tricked. For he, too, was a monster with dark power—and thus was locked within his prison too.

"On this night, which occurs every two and a half years, when *Ghealach*'s light is gone from the sky, we know she finds herself in the furthest depths of his prison once more. On this night, we commemorate the sacrifice she made, and shine our light for her so she knows that we remember."

The priestess walks around the circle, and we lift our unlit candles for her to light. We stand and I breathe in sharply as a shadow passes over the moon, and the land becomes dark. The Wolves sing in a language I don't know—the words rough yet soft—and they raise their candles to the sky. While I don't recognize the song, my heart knows it, somehow.

I lift my candle. Callum's smile is big and easy, and his eyes brim with joy when they lock onto mine. It's like he is pleased to be sharing this sacred moment with me, and warmth swells inside me.

I smile, too, as our small lights fill the darkness—casting the shadows away.

***

AFTER THE ceremony, Jack rolls a barrel of whisky, hidden behind one of the stones, into the center of the circle. He tells us it's courtesy of Lowfell, and a cheer fills the air. The fifty or so Wolves gathered swarm around him. The bagpipe player resumes her tune and the cold air fills with music and laughter. Callum pulls me against his chest, nips my ear with his teeth, then tells me he's going to get us some drinks.

I pull my cloak close as Callum exchanges warm greetings with a few of the Wolves in yellow tartan kilts. They laugh at something he says as he clasps one of them on the shoulder. He has an easy way with people, and I think that will be just as useful in us winning against James as his brute strength.

I've often thought that much of Callum's power comes from showing his more gentle side. My father would see that as weakness, but I'm starting to see that my father's cruelty was nothing but a mask he used to hide his fear.

Callum is making his way back to me when he stills about halfway across the circle. His body becomes rigid, and the humor disappears from his face. His expression becomes unreadable, the way it does when he's under threat, and my insides clench. The chatter in the circle dims, as more people cast their gazes into the shadows surrounding the stones. Their wolf senses are picking up on something that I cannot. Something is wrong.

A loud crack shatters the night. My heart leaps from my body. A few Wolves throw themselves to the ground. A crack forms in one of the tall stones as a bullet hits it. I look wildly around as the music shrieks to a halt.

Men carrying muskets emerge from the shadows between the stones. Adrenaline surges through my body. James strides through them. This is the wolf who attacked me, who gave me back to Sebastian, who bit me and almost killed me.

As tall and muscular as Callum, James makes his way toward the center of circle. The wind stirs his wild brown hair, causing it to brush against his broad shoulders. He wears a simple crown made of twisted branches—a crown he didn't wear the last time I saw him. It's a message to those gathered here.

He is the Wolf King.

"Hello, Brother," he says as people part around him, giving the two Wolves space. His guards remain at the edge of the stone circle—keeping us prisoner within.

"James." Callum's hands curl into fists. "I hope you're not here to spill blood on this holy night." His tone is dark, and he sounds as if the opposite is true, as if he longs for James to give him an excuse to expel the violence inside him.

James smiles, though it doesn't meet his eyes. "As king, it's my duty to uphold wolf law, not break it." He rolls up his shirtsleeves, exposing corded forearms—one of them inked with tattoos. "Though, if *you* were in breach of *Ghealach*'s rules, Brother, then I would be forced to take action—regardless of what night it was." His gaze moves to me, and I force myself to hold it. "You have something that belongs to me. Give her to me, and no blood will be spilt."

Callum's answering growl rumbles around the circle. "Rory does not belong to you."

My breathing is fast. My mouth is dry. I can't belong to another man, yet I can't figure out how we are going to escape this situation. Perhaps I should have let Callum bite me, yet I have a feeling James would have found an excuse to take me anyway.

"I bit her and she survived," says James. "Wolf law dictates that she is mine. She bears my mark. Unless you can say the same, you have no claim. Give her to me, or blood will be spilt." His men raise their muskets. "Do the Wolves gathered here today really want to die for the sake of a cunt-struck alpha and the daughter of their enemy king?"

A few of Lochlan's clan exchange whispers. I stiffen when the Wolf King turns his attention to me.

"Do you want to cause another war, Aurora?" asks James. "Do you want countless Wolves to die? Is that why you came to the Northlands? To stir up trouble between my brother and me on behalf of your father?"

Another murmur fills the whisky-scented air. I wonder if we have underestimated James. He has come here to turn Lochlan's clan against Callum and me, to make them reconsider joining his ranks.

"You were the one who caused a war between us, *Brother*," snarls Callum, "when you brutally attacked the woman I love."

I breathe in sharply as the word *love* rattles around inside my chest. He has never said that to me before. I don't have time to process it. The small child, Alfie, trembles as he hides behind Arran's big bulk, and a decision builds inside me. We are outmatched. We have no weapons, and if Callum spills blood, his claim to the throne will be ruined due to the breach of wolf law. I don't want to go with James, but I won't let these people die for me.

Whatever happens, Callum will get me back.

"Oh, for the love of the Goddess." Blake's exasperated tone comes from behind me. He hooks an arm around my waist, and wrenches me against his chest. He brings his mouth to my ear as my breath catches in my throat. "I apologize for this, Aurora, darling."

He sinks his teeth into my shoulder. Time slows down. I breathe in sharply, and jerk against him as he bites through my cloak. I arch my back, and pain flares through me as his canines penetrate my skin. I gasp.

Callum spins around, and the shock in his eyes is followed quickly by his wolf.

Shadows flood my body. The sound of dripping water fills my ears, and the taste of pine and parchment fills my mouth. The hairs on the back of my neck stand on end as a scalpel screeches against metal. A deep aching hunger consumes me. Far away, someone screams.

Blake releases me, and my knees almost buckle.

He steps past me and wipes my blood off his lips with the back of his hand.

"On this sacred night, with a priestess of the moon as my witness, I, Blake, alpha of Lowfell, claim Aurora as one of my clan." His tone drips with sarcasm. "I seal the claim by marking her with my bite. From this night, until *Ghealach* herself sees fit, Aurora is part of Lowfell and I her alpha. To dispute this claim is to break wolf law."

Chapter Ten

I'm numb. An icy wave of adrenaline crashes through me. Everyone stares at me, and their faces blur. My shoulder is hot and wet, and it throbs in time with my elevated heartbeat. It takes a moment to process what just happened, what's still happening.

James stands in the center of the stone circle. His men point muskets at us.

Blake just claimed me as his. His lips are stained red with my blood.

The wolf blazes in Callum's eyes.

Violence radiates from every ridge of his body. The wind howls around him and makes his kilt flap against his thighs. His chest rises and falls deeply, but his expression is stony. It's as if he's battling the beast that rages inside him. Or perhaps he is deciding who to unleash it upon. He has turned his back on James. His full attention is consumed by Blake.

James smiles wickedly. "I suppose the matter of which alpha Aurora belongs to is settled then." James gestures that his men lower their weapons. "We'll respect wolf law and leave peacefully. No blood will be spilled tonight."

James's voice is amused. He doesn't seem concerned to be leaving without me, and I'm filled with dread as I wonder if he wanted this to happen. Callum and Blake make a powerful, but fragile, alliance. Even though Callum has told me he doesn't like the dominant, alpha side of himself, he's protective of me. Blake biting me, hurting me, and claiming me as part of his clan could be enough to ruin their alliance.

James walks away. His steps are slow and unworried, as if he knows he has nothing to fear from us. His arrogance stirs the storm inside me, and I realize I'm shaking from anger, not shock. Anger at James, anger at Blake, anger at two males who bit me without my permission and think they have some form of ownership over me because of it.

On the other side of the circle, Lochlan leans against one of the jagged rocks, arms folded across his chest, eyes glinting with intrigue. From his expression, the alpha of Glas-Cladach could be watching a theatrical performance. James inclines his head as he passes.

"I'm surprised to see you here, Lochlan," says James. "Your father would turn in his grave."

Lochlan smiles. "As I was the one who put him there, that does not mean much to me."

James releases a low chuckle. He nods at another male in yellow tartan with messy blond hair. "Ian, isn't it? Have you heard from your brother lately? He was captured as part of the attack on Fort Dubh-Clach, wasn't he?"

Ian's face hardens. "What do you know of it?"

James shrugs. "I've heard he's in the Borderlands dungeons, prisoner of their new lord. Did you know he's offered to return any wolf prisoners to us in exchange for Aurora?" My blood stills. Ian's face pales, and he brings his attention to me.

"I'm not the enemy," continues James. He joins his men at the edge of the circle before turning. "Kneel before me, Brother. Apologize. I'll pardon your treason and exile you to Highfell. Aurora will be used as I see fit in the real war against the south, but you have my word, I will not harm her." His gaze slides to Blake, who smirks beside me. "Blake will be executed, of course—something you cannot deny will give you satisfaction. Do this, and we can put all this behind us. Refuse, and you will learn what it's like to have me as your foe."

Callum stands preternaturally still. His shoulders are taut beneath his coat, and his fists are clenched at his sides. "I'll see you soon, Brother." His voice is almost a growl.

James swallows, then walks away. His men follow. Silence stretches across the summit, and it feels as if everyone is holding their breath until they disappear from view.

A long breath escapes me. The relief that he is gone is short-lived. I feel Blake's attention on me, and something wild in my chest rears its head.

I do not belong to anyone.

I am Princess Aurora of the Southlands.

Blake had no right.

I spin around. His exasperation pulses in my chest, flickers across his face. I slap him. His head snaps to the side, and the sound of the impact echoes off the stones. A murmur travels around the circle, as if his clan can't believe I hit him. Jack turns his chuckle into a cough by the whisky barrel, while Arran shakes his head.

Callum strides across the clearing. He bunches Blake's collar into his fist, and slams him into the nearest rock. He curls his hands around his neck and squeezes.

The air supply is cut off from my lungs. I stagger back, clawing at the invisible fingers around my neck.

"*Callum*," I croak. "*Callum. Stop.*"

Callum inhales sharply, as if he's only now remembering the connection. The pressure eases as he pulls back. He's breathing quickly. A muscle flickers in his temple. He clenches his jaw, then brings his mouth to Blake's ear. "When the time comes, I'll enjoy killing you."

Blake only drags his teeth over his bottom lip, my blood tainting it like burgundy wine. His expression is bored, even if his cheeks are flushed and his dark hair is messy.

Callum shoves, then releases, him. He strides toward me and scoops me into his arms. Without a backward glance, he crosses the circle and walks away from the gathered Wolves. Agitated conversation fills the darkness.

"I'm quite capable of walking by myself," I hiss, my cheeks flaming. I don't know what the Wolves must think of me, but getting bitten then carried away was not the first impression I hoped for.

"I cannot let you go right now. Please do not ask it of me."

Callum begins the decline toward Lowfell Castle, the angular stone building small from such a height.

"At least we've established that James definitely doesn't have the Heart of the Moon." Blake's smooth voice follows us, and he sounds completely unaffected by what happened.

"Indeed," says Lochlan. "Why bring muskets, if you can use your teeth?"

Their voices fade into the night. Callum doesn't speak again as he carries me down the mountain, through the torchlit courtyard, and into Lowfell Castle. He takes me straight to our chambers. The fire is almost out, and embers glow in the hearth. He sets me down in front of one of the armchairs. His hands are on me again instantly, running up and down my arms, before cupping my face. His eyes are wild when his gaze drops to my shoulder.

"Are you hurt?" His voice is as gruff as gravel.

I shake my head. "It's just a bite." It's not, though, and we both know it. It's an assault on my freedom, and an insult to a territorial alpha who considers me to be his.

A low sound escapes him. "He shouldn't have done that."

"No." My jaw clenches. "He shouldn't have."

He touches my throat. "Did *I* hurt you?"

"I'm alright."

"Can I see?" he asks.

I nod. He unties my cloak and drops it to the floor. I turn and move my hair aside so he can undo the fastenings of my dress. I flinch, knowing he can see the scars that brand my back, but when I face him, his eyes are on the bloodstained fabric on my shoulder.

Gently, he pushes my sleeves down my arms, until my dress bunches at my waist. Cold air brushes my bare skin. I feel exposed, but he's not looking at my breasts.

Blood is smeared across my shoulder, oozing from the teeth marks that puncture the skin. The wound glistens in the low light. The blood makes it look worse than it is. It should heal quickly, but Callum swallows. Hard. He squeezes his eyes shut as he presses his forehead against mine. "Fuck. I want to kill him."

"You can't. Not yet." I touch his chest, curling my fingers into his shirt. "I'm okay."

"He claimed you—"

"I don't care what anyone says." My tone sharpens. "I don't belong to anyone. Least of all Blake." His chest is rock hard beneath my knuckles, his muscles strained.

He stalks away, into our bathing chambers. It's as if he can't bear to look at me.

"Callum?"

The air is cold against my bare chest, and I cover myself with my arms. I feel vulnerable, even more so than when Blake bit me. My skin pebbles, and I'm starting to pull my dress back up when the floorboard creaks.

I release a breath, and my grip on the fabric. Callum holds a washcloth and a small bowl of water. He has not abandoned me like I feared. He takes my upper arms, and steers me into the armchair by the fire. He kneels before me and places the bowl between my legs.

Dampening the cloth, he brings it to my shoulder. Gently, he wipes away the blood. I feel the warmth of his palm through the cloth.

The look on his face... I feel as if I need to comfort him, reassure him, even though I'm the one who has been bitten. When the blood is gone, the circular mark is barely visible on my skin.

"It's not deep," I say. "It will heal soon."

Callum wrings out the cloth in the bowl, and my blood dances across the water. "There is power in an alpha's bite. If *Ghealach* accepts the claim, it will scar. This may well brand your skin forever."

My pulse kicks up. "What?" For the first time since we arrived here, the fever rises within me, again. Sweat beads on my skin, and my insides feel like they're burning. I try to pull it all back, to cage my emotions, but all I can think of is how much I want to sink my teeth into Blake and tear him apart, limb from limb. "He bit me, knowing I didn't want it, knowing it would scar me forever?"

"Aye."

Blake has seen the scars that mar my back, given to me by the priest to suppress the wolf inside me. He was there when James's teeth sank through my flesh and almost killed me, branding my waist and torso. He knew this, and decided to leave his mark on me, too.

Amid the anger, something primal stirs. My stomach clenches and my teeth ache. Callum's face is close to mine, and I let that strong face, those bright green eyes, push out any thoughts of Blake and what I would like to do to him.

Now the lunar eclipse is over, the half-moon shines through the window and casts light onto the side of his face. His palm grips the side of my neck, gentle but firm. He pushes his forehead against mine and his skin is burning. "Fuck. I can't... I can't handle this, Rory. I said I would wait until after the full moon. I told myself I'd wait. But I need you."

I need him too. I need him to be rough with me, strong with me. I need him to rattle my uneasy soul, and give me something to focus my rage onto. I need to release this storm that's building inside me before I march back up the mountain to find Blake, and throttle the despicable bastard. I need him to push away all thoughts of that snake's glinting devious eyes, and his mouth at my throat, and my blood on his teeth.

I put my palm on his cheek. "Take me, then."

A low groan sounds in his throat. He captures my mouth with his, and kisses me deeply, tenderly. I pull him closer to me, and wrap my legs around his waist. "My control is thin tonight. My wolf presses against my skin as if you are the moon, and it does not like that another male bit you. I fear I will lose myself and bite you, too."

"You won't do that."

"You don't know that." He swallows, hard. "We need to do things my way, tonight, or not at all. Can you agree to that, for me?"

"I can handle it. I can handle you."

"Rory, please." His voice is strained. I stroke his cheek and nod.

He slides his hands beneath my thighs, and picks me up. He stalks across the room, places me gently on the mattress, then removes his clothes. He crawls over me. His face looms above mine and his warm breath tickles my lips. "If you feel the fever, if you need me to stop—"

"I won't."

His gaze darkens. "You must tell me."

I nod, then bite my bottom lip. Heat flushes my face. "If you're worried about losing control, I could always... well... I could be in control."

The corner of his mouth lifts, and some of the darkness leaves his expression. "As much as I would like to have you ride my cock, Princess, I need to be in charge tonight." He blinks, almost apologetically. "A wolf thing."

There is a question in his eyes. I don't think I could deny him anything right now. I incline my head. He shifts down my body, planting a kiss between my breasts, then on the soft skin of my torso. I breathe in sharply as the flames that flicker inside me build. He kneels as he slides my bunched up dress down my legs, his knuckles scraping my thighs, then tosses the fabric onto the floor. His hands are shaking, slightly, as he unfastens my boots and throws them aside.

"Are you alright?" I ask.

"Trying to restrain myself." He offers me a sheepish grin. "I'll be okay, momentarily."

He slips my underwear off, exposing me to him, and releases a shuddery breath. He dips his head, and without warning, drags his tongue over me. I make an embarrassing noise and clench the sheets as his growl fills our bedchambers. "Fuck. You taste like you're ready for me, Princess."

"I...I am."

Crawling over me, he rests one forearm on the pillow by my head, and nudges my thighs further apart with his knee. Breathing deeply, expression strained and full lips wet, he guides himself to my entrance. He groans when he pushes inside. My back arches, and a soft cry escapes my lips at the delicious pressure, the pinch of pain. He pauses when he fills me completely, closes his eyes and presses his forehead against mine to give me a moment to adjust to his size. He thrusts. It is deep and slow, and a rough grunt scrapes against his throat.

Sweat beads across my face as his scent floods my nostrils. I dig my fingers into the hard muscles of his back and kiss his neck. I need him harder. Faster. I curl my ankles around his back, and rock my hips against him.

He scrapes his teeth against the column of my throat and brings his mouth to my ear. "My way, remember, Princess?"

He moves tortuously slowly, drawing soft moans from my lips with each thrust. He's trembling, and I know it's because he's holding himself back. I try to respect his wishes, I try to be gentle, but my hips move of their own accord, and my fingernails pierce his back. My teeth *ache* and there's something wild within me that wants to tear into his flesh.

Bite. Bite. Bite.

I fear myself. I'm worried that if he doesn't give me what I want, I'll give in to this strange primal urge that is taking over me. Sweat beads on my brow as I suppress it, and the fever rises within.

"*Please,*" I gasp. "*Please.*"

He groans, and it's like my plea snaps something within him. He thrusts harder, deeper, and reaches the place inside me that I need him to touch.

When his mouth falls to my shoulder, and his teeth press against my skin, and his shoulders shudder beneath my hands, I get the sense that the urge to bite has come over him too. He wrenches away and claims my mouth instead.

I'm lost to him. To the sound of the mattress creaking, and his shallow grunts, and the dominant, branding thrust of his tongue.

Tonight melts away. I'm no longer under threat from the king, or being bitten by Blake, or a pawn, once again, in a game between men. I'm free. I'm powerful. I'm here with Callum, taking pleasure from his powerful body, while he struggles to maintain control.

"Come for me, Princess," he growls.

My back arches up from the mattress as I come wholly, completely, undone. All the fear, the darkness, the pain from this night is expelled from me. His pace increases, becomes fevered, before his back muscles spasm beneath my fingertips as he too groans with release. His face dips to the crook of my neck.

"You're mine," he mumbles against my ear as his heart thunders against my chest. "You're mine."

Yet, as my orgasm ebbs away, and I stroke the back of his neck, I can't ignore the slight protest within my soul. A small voice whispers through my bliss.

It tells me I belong to no one.

Chapter Eleven

Darkness.
Tendrils of shadow wind up my legs and coil around my arms.

I cannot breathe. I cannot see. I cannot. . .

My eyes adjust. Cold stale air floods my lungs. A corridor stretches into the distance, lined with doors. I approach one of them, and touch the symbol carved into smooth stone above the lock. It's a key with two crescent moons in the bow. The hairs on the back of my neck stand on end. It's the same mark that I saw in the chapel.

Something moves behind the door, and I jump back.

Distant footsteps approach, and I turn my head. Someone whistles. The tune is familiar but off-key, and I cannot place it. Fear grips my heart. Every instinct in my body tells me to run.

I edge away from that sound.

I run.

I must be dreaming, but I cannot shake the feeling that if I'm caught, there will be consequences.

"Where are you going, little soul?" A male voice echoes around me, and my blood turns to ice. There is something cold and powerful in his tone, inhuman. "You have found me, when many cannot, and yet you run."

I turn to the nearest door, and try to push it open. It won't move. I shove my shoulder against it so hard I think I bruise the skin. I suppress my cry of frustration as laughter resounds all around me. I fight the cold panic that threatens to debilitate me. I hurl myself at the door again.

"*Please*," I whisper. "Please open."

The scent of dark pine crashes into me as someone else throws themself against the door at the same time as me. It crashes open.

An arm hooks around my waist as we hurtle into darkness.

I jolt into my body—only I'm made of stone. I cannot move. I'm a statue in the palace gardens. I've been here before. I'm dreaming. I try to scream, but my lungs are stone and my lips are hard and my mouth tastes like old cemeteries.

Courtiers wander around in the moonlight. They comment on the neatly trimmed hedges, and the smell of the roses. Some of them look up at me.

"She almost looks alive," says a woman, before she and her friend walk away.

Blake saunters into view with his hands in the pockets of his breeches.

"Fascinating," he says.

Get out! I want to scream. *Get out! Get out! Get out!*

I'm paralyzed, powerless, trapped in this stone cage.

His eyes glint in the moonlight.

"When are you going to fight?" he asks.

***

I WAKE in the middle of the night.

I feel a strange pull toward the corridor, as if something I need is outside our chambers. I untangle myself from Callum, slip on a robe, and pad through the shadows. I open the door a crack. I breathe in sharply. Blake stands by the wall, at one with the shadows. His hair is messy, and his shirt is only half buttoned up. His bootlaces are undone, too. He puts a finger on his lips.

He reaches into the pocket of his breeches and pulls out a small pot. "Apply this to your wound."

The word *Moonflower* is written in elegant calligraphy across the label.

"My wound? The bite you gave me, you mean?"

He shrugs. "With any luck, it will fade the scar."

Fade, I note. *Not get rid of entirely.*

I snatch it, then turn and close the door behind me.

***

CALLUM'S MOOD is lighter when we wake up early in the morning. He faces me on the bed, a marking from a pillow crease on one side of his face, and brushes his knuckles along my arm. The sky is still dark outside the window when he tells me he intends to ride to a nearby territory. His friend has just taken over a clan, and he thinks he can talk him into joining us.

"Should I come with you?" I ask.

He brushes his lips against my forehead. "No. Stay here. Get some more sleep, then read your books and see if you can find anything out about your connection with Blake. That would be a better use of time."

"Okay. There's a whole section in the library about. . ." I stiffen, then frown. There's something in Callum's tone, and the slight glint in his eye, that reminds me of the times he has given Ryan a task to do that makes the boy feel important, but ultimately serves to keep him out of the way. "You don't want me to come with you, do you?"

The corners of his eyes crinkle. "No. I don't. Not after James's visit last night. I don't want to spend all day worrying about you. I want you to stay at Lowfell, where you'll be safe."

I sigh. "It probably *is* a better use of my time, anyway. It's not long before the full moon. I want to figure out how to break this bond before we get to Madadh-allaidh, so Blake can't use it against you after we've defeated James."

Callum plants a kiss on my lips. "Good lass."

He stretches, then rolls out of bed. Naked, he heads over to the armchair to grab his kilt and shirt, and gets dressed. While he's tying his boots, I slide out from beneath the covers and pull on a dress from the armoire. I turn so he can do the fastenings on my back.

"I'm supposed to be a fearsome alpha, not your lady-in-waiting," he says.

"You poor thing. What will all the other alphas think?"

"They will mock me, and I won't care." I hear the grin in his voice. "Though, I must admit, I prefer taking your clothes off to putting them on."

He hooks an arm around my torso, and pulls me into his lap before nipping my ear with his teeth and making a playful growling sound. I stroke his cheek.

"You'll make a better king than James," I say.

"I hope so. We've been at war with the Southlands for so long, and James is obsessed with vengeance. I cannot forgive the southerners for what they have done to my people, yet I wonder if there could be peace someday. You're the Princess of the Southlands, and I would be King of the Northlands. I wonder if you and I could bring peace." His tone is earnest and sincere, yet cold panic flickers in my chest.

He's not saying it aloud, but I know he's suggesting a marriage alliance between us. It's the kind of match I would have never let myself dream of before coming to the Northlands. Not because it's with a wolf, although I certainly wouldn't have imagined that, but because it's with someone I care for. I always knew I would marry for politics rather than emotion—it's part of the reason why I locked up my feelings for so many years. The thought of having both would have made my heart soar, once.

I don't feel that way, now. For our kingdoms to be united, Callum would have to strike an agreement with my father—the man who had me beaten by the High Priest, and who killed my mother.

Callum must hear my quickening pulse, because the humor disappears from his face. "A fantasy, perhaps." Nudging me off him, he stands. He takes my face in both of his hands. "Listen to me, Princess, because it's important. Whether we like it or not, Blake is your alpha now—"

"Don't be silly. Of course he's not."

"It's not up to you, or me, to decide. It's *Ghealach*'s decision, and if she accepts Blake's claim. . ." He bites his bottom lip. "An alpha can put the power of their wolf into their command. Their dominance forces other Wolves in their clan to submit, and to obey their alpha's will."

My eyes widen. "That's abhorrent."

"Aye, it is. The command is called the Àithne. It's not a practice that is widely used. If an alpha uses it, and someone in their clan resists, it calls into question who the stronger wolf is, which can lead to a challenge. If Blake has been accepted as your alpha. . ."

My muscles tighten. "He could do that to me. How will I know for sure if Blake is my alpha?"

He runs his thumb over my shoulder, where Blake's bite mars my skin. It's still sore, even after I put some of Blake's ointment on it. "I'm almost certain he is. As Wolves, we heal quicker, and better, than humans. But if any kind of claim is accepted by our goddess, the bite doesn't heal. We'll know if the mark remains. Either that, or Blake will use the Àithne, and you'll be forced to submit to him. I don't think he'll stoop so low until we take Madadh-allaidh. He needs us on side for his plan to succeed, but I wouldn't put anything past him."

"I'll be careful."

"Good lass." Callum offers me a smile that doesn't quite meet his eyes. He brushes his lips against my forehead and heads out of our chambers—leaving me alone at Lowfell Castle.

While he's away, I'm determined to get some answers. I need to find out how to break this bond between Blake and me. Our lives are connected—he bit me and claims he's my alpha, and I'm even dreaming of him.

I must break all ties with Blake, before he consumes me completely.

Chapter Twelve

I make my way up the spiral staircase to the library in the tower.

It's cozy within, with a crackling hearth that casts a soft glow onto the shelves that line the walls. The room is smaller than I imagined it would be for an alpha who likes books—probably because there are tomes all over the castle. I've caught glimpses of them stacked in drawing rooms and bedchambers, and there are likely more in Blake's room, too. There are still hundreds of them in here, and I've flicked through a few already.

The floorboards creak beneath my feet as I wander around, stroking the spines. There are a lot of medical books, which is what I'd expect for a healer, but also history, religion, and even fiction. Absently, I chew my fingernails as I try to decide where to start. I hiss when I accidentally tear a bit of skin from my finger, then I select a few of the big, leather-bound books at random.

The cushioned window seat looks out onto the loch and the burnt-orange mountains outside, and I place my pile on it. Outside, the water is covered with early morning mist. Even after all the violence I have seen in the Northlands, I'm awash with the sense of peace.

I'm about to settle down when a giggle permeates the silence. I startle. A small mop of dark hair peeks out from behind the door and I smile. "Hello, Alfie."

He grins. "I'm going to pick a book," he announces. "About flowers, or boats, or monsters."

Elsie appears moments later, dressed in an elegant grey dress with long sleeves. Her dark hair is tied in a bun that emphasizes her cheekbones and bright eyes.

She taps Alfie on the shoulder. "Go on, then."

The boy squeals, tears into the library, and starts pulling books from shelves. I cannot imagine Blake is going to be pleased about the mess. The thick air is uncomfortable, and I try to share a reassuring smile with Elsie in the hope it will put her at ease, but she doesn't react. I wonder if I overstepped last night, when I pulled her child away from the priestess.

Tense, I sit down and pick up one of the books.

She sighs, then walks toward me. "Thank you for looking out for him last night," she says.

My shoulders soften. "It wasn't right, the way the priestess treated you both."

"No. It wasn't."

She scans the bookshelf by the window seat. I feel as if there is something else she wants to say.

"Why did the Moon Priestess treat you like that?" I ask. "If you don't mind me asking."

Turning to me, she pulls up her sleeve. She has a tattoo on her wrist. It's a key, with two crescent moons in the bow. My heart beats faster. It's the mark from the chapel that reappeared in my dream last night. "I've seen this before," I say.

She steps back and readjusts her sleeve. "It's the mark of Oidhche."

"The God of Night."

"Aye." Her expression is defiant. "It's the symbol for his prison."

My insides tighten as I remember what Callum said about Night's Acolytes. Blake said Elsie was not one of them at the ceremony last night. I can't help but ask. "Why do you have this?"

She folds her arms. "My father worshipped the God of Night if you must know." The line of her jaw is as sharp as a dagger, and I know I've offended her. "He meant to sacrifice me to him, hence the mark."

"Oh. I'm sorry." I bite my bottom lip. "My father doesn't care too much for me, either. He used to have me beaten in one of the houses of worship in the name of the Sun Goddess."

I instantly feel as if I've overshared, and I'm unsure why I want to connect with this wolf so badly.

"You must know exactly how I feel, then." Her tone is sarcastic, and I blush.

"Where is your father now?" I ask.

"The night before I was supposed to be sacrificed, I prayed to the gods. They sent me my brother." She smiles, and something in her expression makes me shudder.

"He killed him?"

"Aye." She looks me up and down. "He's not good at showing it, but he likes you, you know?"

I lean forward on the cushioned seat, and my eyebrows knit together. "Who?"

"My brother."

"Your brother is here?"

"Aye?" Her forehead creases, and she looks at me as if I've lost my mind. "Blake."

"Blake is your brother?"

I'm not sure why I'm surprised. I take in her dark hair, sharp jaw, sensual mouth, and slightly bad attitude. I can almost see it. It explains her lack of deference to him, too, as well as the slight yearning I've felt when they interacted. I wonder if they have a difficult relationship.

"Half-brother. We share a father." Her nose turns up with distaste. "Bruce. He was alpha of this place before Blake got rid of him. He didn't tell you?"

"No." I align this with what I know. Blake told me once that he killed his father, and Jack told us Blake took a particular dislike to the alpha of Lowfell. I shake my head, my thoughts snagging on something else Elsie said. "And Blake doesn't like me."

"He's going to war over you, isn't he?"

"He's going to war for himself."

She shrugs. "If you say so." She slides a book from the shelf. "The night he arrived at Lowfell and found me in the chapel, bound and beaten, Night's mark on my wrist... I've never seen anything like it. It was like witnessing the wrath of the dark god himself. My brother is dangerous, make no mistake, but sometimes it doesn't hurt to have someone like him on your side." She passes me the book she's holding, and I frown as I take it. "If you like stories, you should read this one." I think I catch a hint of mischief in her otherwise serious expression. "Read it. It's enlightening."

Skirts brushing over the dusty floorboards, she heads to the exit of the library. "Come on, Alfie. Time to go."

The little boy grabs a book, hurtles through the mess he has made, and pushes past her to the stairway. Elsie pauses, and looks me up and down. "Hmm," she says.

"What?"

"Blake is hosting a feast tomorrow night so he and Callum can persuade Lochlan to join their cause. What are you going to wear?"

"I. . . I don't know?"

She nods, solemn, as if she's deciding something. "If you like, you can meet me outside after breakfast. Alfie and I are heading to the village. You can pick something out there."

"I. . . okay." Her footsteps fade as she descends the staircase.

I release a half-laugh. Perhaps I can make a friend in Elsie, after all.

Curiosity swells inside me as I look down at the small book she gave me. It's well read, and the spine is broken. *The Alpha and the Kitchen Maid* is written across the front in black ink. A story, perhaps?

The scent of cooked fish drifts into the library, and my stomach grumbles. Blake's clan don't usually adhere to formal meal times, but with Lochlan's clan arriving, Blake must be putting on a breakfast. I place Elsie's book on top of my pile, scoop them up, and head to the staircase.

I've been aimlessly reading for days, and have got no further to an answer. I know Callum wants me to stay out of Blake's way, but I have a better idea.

Plus, Blake didn't inform either of us that he intended to entertain Lochlan this morning. One of us should be present to keep an eye on him.

Chapter Thirteen

There are male voices in the corridor ahead, and I duck into an alcove on the way to the Great Hall, holding the pile of books close to my chest. There are five in total, all of different sizes, and one of them almost slips from my grasp.

"Is it under control, though, Blake?" A low, smooth voice. Jack. "You look like shit."

I peer around the wall. Jack has his hand on Blake's arm, and the two stand near the oak doors that lead into the hall. Despite my dislike of the alpha, I would not go as far as to say he looks bad. Blake's hair is messier than usual, and his skin looks a little pale, but he's still handsome, in his obnoxious way.

"How kind of you to say." Blake rolls his eyes. "I didn't sleep well."

"I wonder why." Jack's tone is steeped in sarcasm. "Have you spoken to Arran?"

"On an almost daily basis, funnily enough."

"Don't be a prick. I meant about—"

"I know what you meant."

"He might be able to help you manage things."

Blake sighs, and I feel a pulse of his weariness—sadness, even. "Please. Arran is barely managing."

"Perhaps you're right." Jack exhales. "I'm worried about you. Last night, you shouldn't have—"

Blake stiffens. I flatten myself to the wall. I feel him, then, that shadow inside me spreading its fingers. I try to push it back, to cage my emotions so he can't feel me.

Blake whispers something I can't hear. There's the thud of footsteps, and they disappear through the doors of the Great Hall. I release a breath. I can't help but wonder what Jack was about to say. Was he about to chide Blake for biting me, or did it have something to do with him threatening the Moon Priestess?

I wait for a couple of minutes because I don't want to speak to either of them. Holding my books, I step out from the nook and make my way into the Great Hall.

There are three long tables within, set for breakfast, that create an open rectangle. Twenty or so Wolves wearing yellow tartan sit along one of them, eating and talking to one another. I walk toward the Lowfell table, where there is more space on the bench, and pick a spot at the end so I can keep an eye on Blake.

He's talking to Lochlan at the table at the back, the crackling fire in the hearth casting his face in orange light. Jack sits beside him, and it strikes me as interesting that he's allowed at a table I'd presumed was for alphas. Lochlan inclines his head at me, a gentle smile on his lips, and I return it.

I pile my plate with oily fish from one of the platters, and take a sip of water. On the other side of the hall, Ian—the blond male who James singled out last night—watches me, his fork paused halfway to his mouth.

My heart beats a little quicker. James said the Borderlands had taken Ian's brother. Ian clearly sees me as an enemy, and I'll need to be careful around him. I offer him a polite smile, then select one of the books from my pile.

Fighting every instinct I have to keep Blake out, I imagine the thread between us as a tangible thing, and I feel for him. If Blake sees me reading something that will bring me closer to the truth, surely he will react in some way.

I flick through an account of the battle of Glen Marb, the valley that Callum took me through when he took me from the Borderlands. I feel only boredom as Blake sinks his teeth into an apple. I set it aside.

The next book is titled *Experiments: Book Three*. It's another of the horrifying tomes that I think Blake wrote. I glance up from the gruesome account of a wolf's eyeball being melted from his skull. Goddess. Did Blake do this to someone?

Even though Blake is the image of ease, darkness prickles beneath my skin. He leans back in his seat, one arm slung over the chair, as he converses with Jack. I feel him though. Uneasy. He doesn't like me looking at this book. I'm not sure if it's because it reveals secrets about the bond, or something else.

I pull his darkness closer and try to decipher his emotion. The cold hollowness he emanates reminds me of how I felt after the High Priest beat me. It feels like shame. I think he feels guilty for torturing his fellow Wolves.

I put the book to one side so I can look into it in more depth later. I release a breath, and only then realize how Blake's tension has wound its way around my body, squeezing like a deadly serpent

I pick up the book Elsie gave me, next. I flick it open, and skim through the pages.

It's a love story, from the look of it, between a woman who works in the kitchens of a grand castle and the grumpy male who is the alpha there. I flush when I catch a rather intimate description of the two characters in bed with one another. Heat coils low in my stomach. Across the hall, Blake clears his throat. I glance up at him. He's still talking to Jack and Lochlan, but one of his hands grips the edge of the table.

I go back to the story, flicking back the pages so I can read it properly from the start. Perhaps Elsie was making fun of me when she said it was enlightening. I get to the part where the alpha comes to the kitchens to tell the maid she looks good enough to eat.

A shadow looms across the page.

"Is Callum not satisfying you, darling?"

Every muscle in my body tightens and locks. Blake leans forward and tugs the book out of my hands. He flicks through, and stops at a random page. I feel his pulse of amusement.

"The alpha slides his throbbing member into her wet folds... Aurora, darling, where did you find this? This is quite shocking."

My cheeks flame. I grit my teeth and bite back my retort. I know he's trying to get a reaction out of me, and I won't give him the satisfaction.

"He flips her over onto her stomach and thrusts his hips—"

I jump up, and knock the back of my knees against the bench. A few Wolves look in our direction. I collect my pile of books, slide along the table, and march toward the exit of the Great Hall. Blake pockets the love story and follows me.

"You're not still upset about last night, are you?" he asks, and for some reason, the audacity of him asking me that question—the casualness in his tone, as if I have no reason to be upset that he bit and claimed me—provokes me more than anything he has done so far.

Rage erupts in my chest, stronger than the Northlands winds outside. My teeth ache and long to sink into something, into *him*. My knuckles whiten as I squeeze the pile of books.

He wants a reaction from me. I won't give him one.

I swallow my emotion.

I storm out of the Great Hall.

I feel him watching me.

Chapter Fourteen

I decide to take Elsie up on her offer to visit the village, and after putting my books in our chambers, I head toward the castle exit. I wonder if there's anything she can tell me about Blake that might be useful to Callum and me.

More than anything, I'd like to get some fresh air, away from Lowfell. Elsie—despite her horrible brother—seems like she might be nicer than I first assumed.

When I open the door, she is already waiting for me in the courtyard outside. She leans against the wall while Alfie chases a bird across the cobblestones. "I wasn't sure you'd come," she says.

My smile falters. "I did wonder if it was wise, after last night. James seems intent on capturing me."

"You'll be fine." She opens her coat, and pats a dagger sheathed in the belt around her waist. "I can take care of anyone who tries anything. It's only a half-an-hour walk, and we're not leaving Blake's territory. Besides, it looks like that big oaf will be protecting us meek ladies, anyway."

She rolls her eyes, though her cheeks flush slightly. I look over my shoulder, half expecting to see Callum. It's Arran who strides through the castle doors wearing a black shirt and a kilt of black-and-grey tartan.

"I thought you didn't want to come," says Elsie as he approaches.

"Changed my mind." His voice is hoarse, as if he doesn't speak much, and his mouth pinches in the corners. He doesn't sound convincing.

"Had your mind changed, more like." Elsie arches an eyebrow. Alfie trips on a stone, and wails as he falls onto his knees. Elsie scoffs. "Oh, come here, you!"

She marches toward him, picks him up, and brushes down his little breeches.

I glance up at Arran. "Blake told you to keep an eye on me, didn't he?"

"Is that supposed to be a joke?" he says. I frown, and he points at his eye patch. "On account of me only having one?"

My cheeks flame. "Oh, goodness! I would never. . ." I shut my mouth.

Arran is grinning, and Elsie shakes her head as she marches Alfie over. She slaps the burly male's arm. "Don't be mean," she says.

"You're joking." I bite my cheek. "You have a sense of humor, then? I wondered."

Arran lets out a gravelly laugh, and not for the first time, familiarity jolts through me. "Aye, Blake told me to watch you. Something about protecting his assets."

I exhale and my breath mists in front of my face. "Of course he said that."

He ruffles Alfie's messy hair with a big hand. "Come on. Let's get this over with. I hate shopping."

With Alfie wittering on about getting a glass of apple juice from the "apply lady" when we arrive, the four of us head through the tunnel in the wall, then cross the grounds.

I must admit, having spent most of my time in castles, so far, I'm curious to visit a village here in the wolf kingdom.

I'm even more curious to know what the people who consider Blake alpha think of him.

Light rain falls as we leave Lowfell behind.

We walk past the mountain path we ascended last night, and soon reach an overgrown track that cuts through a valley. Alfie races ahead. When some sheep grazing on the slope of one of the mountains scatter—afraid of the little menace tearing toward them—Elsie shouts at him to pack it in, then hurries after him.

Arran doesn't speak to me as our boots squelch through the mud, yet the silence is not entirely uncomfortable. There is something quiet and assured about him. Callum thinks he will have to fight him at some point. I don't like the thought.

He's a similar build to Callum—tall, broad, and packed with muscle—but I think he may be a few years older. From the neatness of his dark hair and beard, and the thin scars I catch on his hands and thick neck when the sunlight peeks between the clouds, I have a feeling he may have served as a soldier.

He also seems strangely familiar.

When Arran offers me an inquisitive look, I fight my blush. "Have we met?" I ask.

"I worked for your father." I stiffen and the corner of his mouth tips up. "I don't anymore. Obviously. I was in his army."

"But you're a wolf."

"I'm a half-wolf. I'd not been bitten yet when I moved to King's City. It was easy enough to hide."

"Blake was in the King's Guard, wasn't he? Is that where you met him?"

He inclines his head. "Something like that."

"And you came with him, to the north?"

"I did."

"Why?"

Arran chuckles. "You're very direct, aren't you?" He shrugs a shoulder, but darkness passes over his face. "I owe Blake my life. I'd follow him anywhere."

Ahead, Elsie pretends to be a monster whose diet consists of naughty "wee pups" who upset the livestock, much to Alfie's delight. A smile ghosts Arran's lips before his throat bobs.

"I came to the city the summer your mother died," he says. "My uncle took me out for her funeral. I'd never seen so many people gathered in one place before. People lined the streets, throwing flowers, sending prayers to the Sun Goddess."

My throat tightens as I remember that day—the scorching sun, the scent of incense, following the coffin into the domed Church of Light and Sun. Everyone was watching, and all I wanted to do was scream, yet I held it inside as I walked behind my father toward the front row of pews.

My brother, Philip, turned up late. He stumbled down the aisle, stinking of alcohol. Yet Father turned his back on him and hissed at me to pull myself together when a tear slipped down my cheek.

"She must have been very loved," says Arran.

Her people didn't know her, not really. They didn't know she smelt like lavender and horses, or that her eyes crinkled in the corners when she smiled. They never heard her stories about brave princesses who fought monsters.

Though perhaps—if she was a wolf—I didn't know her either.

"She was," I say softly.

It's not yet midday when we reach the village, and the rain finally stops.

Stone houses scatter across the sloping landscape, many with smoke coming from their chimneys. The streets are packed with people heading in the same direction as us, toward a market by the edge of a loch. The women wear simple dresses beneath their cloaks, and most of the men wear the same black-and-grey tartan of Arran's kilt. Blake's colors.

"They don't all wear the Lowfell tartan," I observe, as an older man stalks past us, wearing a blue-and-green pattern on his kilt that I've not yet encountered.

"Some of the older generation still wear Bruce's tartan." Elsie's lips harden. "Blake changed it after he'd killed him, but it didn't catch on with everyone."

"Do they not all support Blake as alpha?" I ask.

She shrugs. "Most like him well enough. Our father caused a lot of disruption. He was constantly grappling for more power, invading villages and taking nearby territories.

It was the villages like this one that suffered for it when other alphas decided to fight back. Blake has given them some semblance of peace, and most respect him for that, even if he is an outsider."

"Most?"

"He killed a lot of the Wolves who were in Lowfell Castle the night we arrived," says Arran quietly. "Most of them had family in villages like this one."

Elsie points at a building isolated from the others, with black stone walls that look like they've been charred. "Plus, he banned the worship of Night, which didn't go down well with some of the older folks. He's managed to dowse any sparks of rebellion over the past few years, but some wear the old tartan to remind him that they supported his father, not him."

Elsie keeps Alfie closer, now, as we pass vendors selling eggs, fruit, and grain from carts. A few say hi to her, and others dip their heads in deference at Arran—clearly recognizing him as one of Blake's close confidants.

We pass a stone building by the water's edge, with a sign reading *The Star Inn* above its doors. The faint scent of ale comes from within, and adds to the scents of fish and woodsmoke that come from the market stalls. Elsie tenses.

"I'll take him to get his apple juice," says Arran, putting his hand on Alfie's shoulder. "I have no desire to go dress shopping."

Elsie grips Arran's bicep, her gaze flitting to the tavern once more. "Just the apple juice. Aye?"

He stiffens, and a muscle ticks in his jaw. I tense because he's an imposing man. He doesn't seem like he has a temper like my father, but it's hard to truly tell. He steers Alfie through the crowd. When he's reached a cart filled with apples opposite the tavern, Elsie sighs and continues walking.

I don't want to pry, but. . ."What was that all about?" My voice is barely audible over the sound of a woman shouting about the cheap price of her fresh mussels. The water ripples in the loch, behind her.

"I probably shouldn't say anything, but he has a bit of a problem with alcohol. Ever since. . . well, he had some dark years, before he came to Lowfell." She offers me a terse smile. "He's doing well now, but. . . there are temptations in places like this."

Alfie's squeal cuts through the crowd. Behind us, Arran has the small boy in a headlock while he talks to a couple of men by the cart. "He seems like a good father," I say.

A dark laugh escapes her lips as she pauses by a cheese stall. "I wish he was the father." She shakes her head. "Alfie's not mine, either. Not biologically, anyway. His mother was my dearest friend. Blake. . . he scared me, that night when he killed Father. I left Lowfell, fled to a village close to Madadh-allaidh. Alfie's mother took me in." She bites her bottom lip. "Her husband was an abusive shite. I watched it happen, how he slowly killed her. She wouldn't leave him—even though I implored her to. Eventually, it was too late. He murdered her, and damned near killed the wee lad, as well. I got him out of there, and brought him here."

"I'm so sorry," I say.

She shrugs as if she's pretending to be unaffected, but her jaw sets. "The bastard never paid for what he did." She pats her dagger again. "One day, I'm going to make him pay."

"Where is he?" I ask.

"Castle Madadh-allaidh. You might have met him when you were there. His name is Magnus."

Ice spreads inside me as I recall the sallow-faced wolf with greasy dark hair. He was a prisoner in the Borderlands Castle when I met Callum, and he threatened me that night, and has done so numerous times since. The last I heard of him, Blake had poisoned him and left him in his infirmary.

"I had the displeasure of meeting him," I say. "Does Blake know all of this?"

"Aye, he knows. I asked him not to kill him. I want to look into his eyes when he dies. Blake's been torturing the bastard for the past few years." She shakes her head. "Magnus knows Alfie is here. He thinks Blake is keeping him hostage. It's how Blake has him wrapped around his little finger."

"You disapprove," I say.

"I've no qualms with him tormenting the bastard, but I wish he wouldn't use the lad to do it."

Sensing I've touched on a sore subject, I ask, "Are you and Arran together?"

She laughs a little too loudly for it to be real. "Us two? Together?" She waves a hand dismissively. "No. Of course not." I must not hide my skepticism, because she exhales and can't quite meet my eye. "He's a good man. He's been good to us both. He's even tried it on with me a couple of times over the years, but... well..." She bites her lip, some of the spark dimming in her eyes. She shakes her head. "The goddess has other plans, unfortunately."

My eyebrows pinch together. "What do you mean?"

"Ah, nothing. Just... his soul belongs to another."

"He has feelings for someone else?"

"You could say that. She's back in King's City, I think." Elsie shrugs. "He pines for her, sometimes. He thinks I don't know, but I do." She bites her bottom lip. "I wish I could look past it. After everything I've been through... I want someone who belongs only to me—heart, body, and soul. I think I deserve that."

"You do."

She grins suddenly, and her face lights up. "Have you started that book I lent you?"

"Yes. But then your brother took it off me."

"Did he now? I'll find you another." She points toward a stall by the side of the loch, laden with different colored fabrics, and speeds up. "Come on, let's get you a dress for the feast. I get all of mine from here."

I can't deny I'm a little excited as I follow her to the vendor. After everything that has happened lately, it's nice to have some semblance of normalcy. My fingers itch to pick something that will make Callum as tongue-tied as he was the last time I wore a nice dress.

***

ON THE way back to Lowfell an hour or so later, I have three new dresses draped over my arm that Elsie was kind enough to purchase for me. Arran is in a dark mood. I wonder if he drank something, and Elsie's nostrils flare a couple of times as if she's trying to determine the same thing. Sensing they might need a moment, I stride ahead to join Alfie. He offers me an apple, and starts naming the nearby sheep.

"Is everything alright?" Elsie's lowered voice carries in the wind.

"I'm not sure," says Arran. "Apparently people have been seen entering the chapel by the water. I have a bad feeling Night's Acolytes might be rising once more. There are rumors that the Night Prince is getting ready to free his master. It could make things difficult."

"Aye," she replies softly. "It could."

Chapter Fifteen

Callum returns to Lowfell that evening. He joins me in our chambers as the sun is setting over the loch. Settling in one of the armchairs in front of the hearth, he tells me about his day. It's drizzling outside, and his shirt is damp and clings to his muscular shoulders and torso.

Despite the bad weather, he's in high spirits. Flynn, the alpha he went to visit, has promised to support him when he goes head-to-head with James.

"I knew he would have my back," says Callum. "I've known him for years. He was my first friend when I moved to the south."

I don't bother telling him Madadh-allaidh is hardly "the south". I know he thinks anywhere below Highfell is southern. I tell him about my day, too. He frowns when I tell him what I overheard about the chapel.

That night, Callum makes love to me softly and slowly before we fall asleep in each other's arms. The next morning, I wake up restless.

The sun has not yet risen, but I can't get back to sleep. My dreams were agitated. I found myself stalking long endless corridors, past barred cells shrouded in darkness, with the ominous feeling that something bad was following me.

I have tasted freedom here, in the Northlands. But my dreams make me wonder if I still feel trapped—caught in a game between alphas I have little control over. The fact that the new Borderlands lord seems to have resumed the search for me makes me feel even worse.

I wonder if, when I slid the blade across Sebastian's throat, some vengeful seed was planted in my soul. It longs to be watered, fed, to grow and spread its vicious thorns. I wish to coil my hateful vines around James and my father. I want Blake on his knees, defeated and gasping at my feet.

I glance at Callum. He's lying on his front, covers pulled down to his waist as if he got too hot in the night—despite the chilly air. He looks gentle now. His dark-sand colored hair is mussed, his lips plump and soft, his body rising and falling with each breath. When James had threatened me, though, those relaxed muscles had tensed and he had become a hard, angry force. When Blake bit me, I thought he was going to kill him.

I know he won't let me put myself at risk. He will do anything to protect me, even if I want to be able to protect myself.

There is a childish part of me that wishes to incur Callum's wrath, his full strength, in the way my enemies probably will. I want to see his sizeable biceps clench, and his jaw to harden, and that low growl to build in his chest because I have angered him. I want his eyes to flash with his wolf, enraged, and to meet him with my own wildness, which I always swallow. I want him to take his pleasure from me roughly, as if he's not afraid that I'll shatter or break.

If he did, I would know he thought me equal to him. Someone unafraid of the parts he keeps hidden. Someone capable of looking after herself. Without thinking, I bite the edge of my fingernail, and the tang of blood creeps into my mouth.

Lochlan said Callum enjoys damsels. I don't wish to be a damsel.

I noticed yesterday that Ian and some of the other members of Lochlan's clan seemed hostile. I want to make sure I can protect myself.

I slide out of bed. Callum stirs beside me, a soft growl scraping against his throat, but he doesn't wake. The floor is bitingly cold on my bare feet and my legs, and I hurry over to the armoire—quietly opening it to pull on breeches and a tunic. I put on my boots and pad out of the room.

Lowfell Castle is dark and quiet as I navigate the narrow corridors. There are a couple of servants stirring pots in the kitchens when I pass. They must have been brought here from the village to accommodate Lochlan's clan. I keep my head down, turn down a long corridor, then hurry down the stairs to the infirmary.

I listen to make sure Blake is not inside, then open the door.

The underground room is smaller than the infirmary at Castle Madadh-allaidh. There's only space for one cot in the center, and a workbench and chair in the corner. The walls feel close together, partially due to the amount of pots and vials that are set upon the shelves. The air is thick with a musty damp scent, and a hint of blood. My stomach turns when I remember that Blake killed Bruce, the former Lowfell alpha, in here.

The log in the stone hearth against the far wall has not yet been lit, and I rub my arms as the cold seeps through my sleeves.

I head to one of the shelves, scanning the labels on the glass jars—*Milk of the Poppy, Mint, Moonflower, Motherwort*. They're organized alphabetically. I stroll to the other side of the infirmary, and smile when I read *White Poppy, Willow Bark*, then *Wolfsbane*.

The bottle of poison is too high for me to reach. I have drag the wooden chair from the corner, and stand on it, so I can pull it from the shelf.

I step back onto the ground, almost knocking over a jar on the lower shelf, and inspect the bottle. It's not the herb itself within, but a clear liquid version of the poison. About half has been used already, and I wonder who Blake has been poisoning.

There are some empty vials on the workbench, and I grab one and uncork the bottle. The pungent herby scent stirs bad memories of my mother's bedchambers, and my throat tightens. My father poisoned her with this. He then poisoned me with it for years after, small doses every day to try and suppress the wolf he suspected lived inside me.

I tip some of the liquid into the empty vial, cork it, and put it in my pocket. I pick up the next vial and start filling it.

"That's not for me, is it?" Blake's drawl comes from behind me.

Wolfsbane sloshes onto my hand and I curse under my breath before spinning around. Blake is leaning against the opposite wall, arms folded across his chest and an amused look on his face. With his dark hair and clothing, he seems to seep into the infirmary shadows.

His gaze takes in my wet hand. I drop the second vial into my pocket. I won't dignify his question with a response.

A dimple punctures his cheek. "If you're looking to murder someone. . ."

I raise my chin and stalk past him. He grabs my wrist, his fingers like a vice around the bone. I spin around, and bring my face close to his.

"Get your hands off me," I snarl.

His scent floods me. "Don't you want to know why I did it?"

"I know why you claimed me. You did it to provoke Callum."

"I have no interest in provoking your master, little rabbit."

I narrow my eyes. "To provoke me, then."

"Not everything is about you."

I turn my expression to stone. "No. You've made that clear. I'm nothing but a pawn in your little game of kings, to be moved around as you see fit."

"You could have been a queen. I gave you that choice. You still could be."

"If I ever become a queen, it will be without your help." I yank my arm out of his grip. "*You bit me.*"

"I de-escalated a situation." He steps closer, and invades my space. "We are not ready to fight James yet; *Callum* is not ready to fight James yet. You were about to go with him. I felt you."

I'm forced to look up. "Don't you dare turn this on me. What else was I supposed to do?"

"You had limited choices, as did I. If you'd gone with him, Callum would have overreacted. I had to play the villain to stop you from playing the hero."

"Have you considered that you did exactly what James wanted you to do? That James might have come here specifically to cause trouble between you and Callum?"

"Of course I have," he hisses. "Why do you think I gave you the moonflower? I don't want that territorial oaf getting worked up about it and acting irrationally. I don't want other people to think you're mine, either."

"Good. Because I'm not yours."

"Do you think I *want* you as part of my clan? You're..." He looks me up and down and I feel the weight of his gaze on my body. "A liability."

My muscles tighten as I lock down my emotions. I can't believe he has the audacity to call me a liability when he's plotting against us. "And you're a manipulative, obnoxious snake."

His face is close to mine. "At least I'm not a brat."

My cheeks heat as my blood runs hotter. "*A brat?*"

"Yes. A brat." There's a gleam in his eye now, as if he was fishing for a reaction and is pleased he has got one.

"You're behaving quite the opposite of how you should when I've saved your skin yet again."

"How, pray tell, should I behave when you sink your teeth into me like a bloodthirsty brute? Should I fall to my knees and thank you?" His smile widens and I have to suppress my snarl. "Yes, you'd like that, wouldn't you? I should have expected no better from a sadist. Is that how you like your females, Blake? Weak-willed and pliant?"

He arches an eyebrow. "Is that how you like your men?" There's something pointed in his tone, as if he thinks this of Callum. My fingers curl into fists and my nails dig into my palms. His voice drops to a dark caress. "I bet he's so gentle with you, isn't he? So afraid you might break."

My blood is wildfire, and my skin burns. I feel another wave of the fever coming for me, and I can't push it back. "How dare you speak to me in that way."

My senses are heightened. The scents of the infirmary overpower me—herbs and blood and Blake. I can see each individual eyelash fanning against his cheek, each fleck of gold in his irises. His heat wraps around me, and through it all, I hear another heartbeat, competing with my own like a war drum in my ear.

A slow, dangerous smile spreads across Blake's face. He grabs my chin. "Oh, hello, little wolf," he says. A wave of panic rises through me as I wonder if my eyes have changed.

I grab his wrist, and though he doesn't release me, his breathing shallows. A hiss fills the air, and I remember the wolfsbane I spilt on my skin. It's burning him. Though my heart is beating fast, though there is something unsettled in my chest that longs to break free, I smile.

"And I'm the sadist?" he whispers.

I'm about to retort, when I realize that though his skin is burning, I don't feel it. My brow furrows, and he tilts his head to one side as if he's trying to read whatever emotion I'm feeling.

I kick him in the shin. Hard. I yowl as pain flares in the same spot, and my wrist feels as if it's on fire. Blake makes a low, startled sound in the back of his throat and releases me. Both of us stagger back a step. My senses return to normal. The backs of my eyes sting.

"What was that for?" he asks.

"Do I need a reason?" I fold my arms. "I hate you." I don't want him to know about my discovery. His whole plan relies on Callum not wanting to hurt him in case he hurts me, too. He must feel my flicker of triumph, though, because he laughs.

"Don't get ahead of yourself. You didn't feel my pain because I decided you wouldn't." My shin stops throbbing, and my wrist feels as if it has been dowsed in cold water. "See? But I can bring it back. So don't get any ideas."

"Why did you stop me from feeling it?"

He shrugs. "To see if I could."

"How?"

"I caged my pain." He stares at my hand and I feel a pulse of his curiosity. "The more pertinent question is why doesn't wolfsbane burn you? It gave me a rash even before I was bitten."

"I was dosed with it throughout my childhood. Perhaps I'm immune."

"I dose myself with it too, and yet I cannot counter the effects entirely." He shows me his wrist—the skin is red and bumpy, as though he's been stung by a nettle. "Perhaps if you'll allow me to run some experiments on you—"

He grabs my wrist, and I stagger back. "Absolutely not!" Even if I'd not seen his ghastly books, filled with the horrible things he did to Wolves to sate his curiosity, I would not do anything to appease him. "Stay away from me."

I try to pull away, but his fingers tighten. The amusement in his eyes disappears, and that dark thread pulses around my soul. I follow his gaze to my fingers. My cheeks flush. My fingernails are torn, and there are bloody tracts down the sides where I've ripped off skin with my teeth. It's a habit I didn't used to have, I've just been feeling anxious, lately.

"Let me go!" I jerk my hand from his grip.

His expression becomes nonchalant once more. I could almost believe I imagined his reaction. He cocks his head to one side. "Are you scared?"

I tilt my chin up. "Of you? No." I probably should be—considering who he is and all he has done.

His gaze dips to my pocket, where the vial of wolfsbane is cool against my thigh through the fabric. "I'd keep that on you at the feast tonight. I don't like the way some of Lochlan's clan are looking at you."

That's why I got it in the first place, you patronizing snake, I want to snap at him.

Heart thumping, I turn my back on him and head up the stairs.

Some of my tension unwinds when Callum rounds the corner at the other end of the corridor. "I was looking for you. . ." His eyes darken when Blake emerges. They haven't spoken since Blake bit me. Both men halt, Blake only a few feet behind me, his body heat warming my back. "Blake." Callum's voice is low and guttural, almost a growl.

Blake's expression is unreadable. "Callum."

Callum's features are like stone. "I know you've never had a father to teach you such things, but biting a woman without her consent is not how a real man behaves."

Blake goes completely still. His handle on his caged feelings flickers, and my vision temporarily darkens as his emotions flood me. He's upset. Callum's blow has landed. I remember what he told me once, about how his father forced himself onto his mother.

"No?" Blake says, his voice like shadow. "Speaking of biting, have you seen your little pet's fingernails, lately?"

It's Callum's turn to still. A muscle flexes in his jaw as his gaze snaps to my hand. Heat floods my face as I curl my fingers into a fist. Callum's throat bobs. I don't know why, but Blake's jab seems to have hit Callum just as hard.

Blake strides past me, then Callum. He turns. "If you want to keep a pet in my castle, Callum, look after it."

He disappears around the corner.

Callum takes a deep breath, then crosses the space between us. He takes my hand, gaze taking in the torn skin around my cuticles. I try to pull away, but he laces his fingers with mine and tugs me toward the end of the corridor.

"What was that all about?" I ask.

"Come on," he says softly. He leads me back to our bedchambers.

When he has shut the door, Callum runs a hand over his mouth, then sighs. "There are a few things I need to tell you about Wolves."

Chapter Sixteen

"Wolves have something of an oral fixation." Callum's voice is as rough as sand.

"They. . . what?"

The fire has just been tended to. It casts its glow onto the side of Callum's face and turns his skin bronze.

"It's bad when we're pups, worse when we're adolescents. When we're adults, it becomes more of a sex thing." My cheeks flame, and Callum brushes his knuckles against one of them. He brings his lips to my ear, and his warm breath caresses my skin. "Wolves like to bite."

The hotness in my face spreads and surges lower. I don't know why such a thought would cause this reaction within me. He takes my hands in his.

"When you had a fever, Blake told me that before the first few shifts, the changes that happen to a half-wolf are akin to what full Wolves go through during adolescence." His expression becomes somber. "Your fingernails. . .

You've been biting yourself... I should have taken care of you. I should have offered you a vice for that particular fixation. I'm sorry, Princess. I forgot what it was like."

My forehead furrows as I try to make sense of what he's saying. "I... Callum... I don't want to *bite* you!"

"No?" Outside, the wind rattles the window and its soft haunting song drifts through the mountains. "I think you do, Princess." He runs the pad of his thumb over my lips. Gently, he forces entry, and the taste of salt and heat floods my mouth as he pushes down on my tongue.

An ache bursts between my legs, and something coils so tightly inside me that I think I may erupt. A whimper escapes me, muffled, as something wild within me urges softly.

Bite.

The wolf shines in Callum's eyes as he watches me, and the strange reaction I'm having to him that I'm trying to suppress. He steps closer, and slides his thumb further back. I should push him away. I should pull back. I should *not* be fighting the urge to sink my teeth into him with every ounce of my willpower.

My breathing quickens. Sweat beads upon my brow. Heat pools between my thighs, and Callum's nostrils flare.

"No? Very well." He huffs a soft growl, and pulls his thumb away. "I have not been as attentive as I should have been." His voice is hoarse. "It's a primal act. I worry I'll lose control of myself. The fever..." He shakes his head. "It troubles me. But if you need me, come to me." He takes my chin between his thumb and finger. "No more biting yourself, okay?"

***

WHEN EVENING approaches, rain drums against the castle walls. The torches flicker, as Callum and I make our way to the feast. I'm wearing my new dress. It's long-sleeved and blue, and I catch Callum trying not to stare at the low neckline

Noise hits us as we reach the doors to the Great Hall—raucous voices, the clatter of crockery, and music. We pause beside a man who plays the bagpipes, and I'm almost deafened.

The space is packed. I can't even see the alpha table at the back. Blake must have invited people from the village, because many wear Lowfell's black and grey tartan. I think there are more people from Glas-Cladach, too, who must have traveled for the festivities. Their kilts and dresses are wet from the rain, and the air is hot and damp.

"Ready?" asks Callum, threading his fingers with mine.

I nod. My shoulders bump against people's arms, as we weave through the crowd. Callum greets Wolves, his voice loud and warm. A shriek makes us both stiffen, and we both laugh when we realize the source of the sound was the small boy, Alfie—a disgruntled-looking Arran confiscates a goblet of wine from him. Elsie, beside him, takes it off him quickly, then catches my eye and grins.

"Looking superb, tonight, Aurora," says Lochlan as we reach the alpha table. He leans back in his chair, and the collar of his shirt shifts. Candlelight flickers over the edge of a tattoo on his collarbone.

I return his smile. "Thank you."

Blake is on Lochlan's other side, talking to Jack, but his gaze flicks up. Callum's hand tightens around mine. We take our seats beside Lochlan.

The tension between Blake and Callum is palpable. Neither of them acknowledges the other, yet Callum's biceps bulge against his sleeves, and Blake's fingers flex by his butter knife.

Both relax as food is brought out—large platters filled with salmon that must have been caught from the loch, steamed potatoes, and green vegetables. Goblets are filled with rich red wine. Lochlan makes small talk about his clan. The air is alive with music, laughter, and the loud unruly conversation I've become accustomed to in the Northlands. Everyone is in high spirits.

"So, Lochlan." Callum puts down his fork. Blake turns his head in our direction, his goblet of wine halfway to his lips. "Are we finally going speak about the reason you came here? I'm presuming you want something in return for supporting me when I challenge James for the throne?"

A slow smile spreads across Lochlan's face. "I have three conditions for my support."

Callum leans back in his chair. "Okay."

"I want Fort Dubh-Clach, the territory Sebastian took when he was looking for Aurora. It was mine before Kai, my beta, rose against me and claimed it as his. I doubt he's alive now." His kohl-lined eyes glimmer in the candlelight, and he smiles. "If any of his clan survived, they will pledge themselves to me. They were mine, once. The transfer will be peaceful."

Callum inclines his head. "I have no problem with that, though we'll have to win it back when I'm king. The fort will be under the control of whoever has taken over the Borderlands." Callum glances at me. "Do you know who the new lord will be?"

I shake my head. "Sebastian had no family. One of the lords of the nearby castles may have—"

"His name is Alexander," says Blake.

Something inside me freezes at the name. The memory of a man packed with muscle, his breath sour with wine, his hand gripping my thigh, flashes behind my eyelids. "If you're talking about Sebastian's bastard brother, he... he died a while ago. It must be someone else."

Blake looks at me curiously. "I assure you, he's alive, and has laid claim to the Borderlands in his brother's absence. My spy told me."

I shake my head. He's wrong. He has to be. I lean forward so I can see him properly, beyond Callum's big bulk. "My father will never accept him as a lord."

"He might, given the right persuasion." Blake arches an eyebrow at me, and I take a sip of wine so I have something to do with my hands.

"So, that's why he wants you, Rory," says Callum. He runs a hand over his jaw. "Fine. Done. I'll personally hand you his head while I'm at it. What else do you want?"

"I want to know if Kai, or any of the other Wolves from that clan, are alive."

"Kai is dead." Blake's tone is even, but that thread of shadow tightens. He's lying. He runs a finger along his butter knife. "They're all dead. My spy told me that, too."

Lochlan's eyebrows pinch together. "That is not what James seemed to think. If Alexander has Kai, and the lovely Aurora is here with us..."

Callum straightens in his chair. His fist clenches around his fork. He suddenly looks every bit the fearsome king he wishes to become. "Be very careful about what you suggest next."

Lochlan chuckles. "I'm not suggesting we actually trade Aurora for the prisoners, Callum. But if there are men, women, and children from my clan who are still alive, she could be used to trick Alexander into thinking otherwise."

I swallow. "You think he's holding children captive?"

"I do." He leans against the table so he can meet my eye. "Will you help me get them back, Aurora?"

"No." Callum's tone is final. "Rory will not be dangled like bait before him. When I'm king, I will make his death my priority, and if there are any prisoners that can be saved, we will get them out. But we must get James out of the way first."

I can't suppress my frown. It's not as if I would suggest barraging recklessly into harm's way, but if children's lives are at risk and there is something I can do to help, it's worth a conversation. I touch his wrist. "Callum. There may be—"

"No." A muscle flexes in Callum's arm beneath my fingertips. "And that's the end of the matter."

I narrow my eyes at his tone, his posture. "I'm not a member of your clan, Callum," I say under my breath.

"No. But I'll look after you all the same," he fires back.

"I'll send word to my spy," says Blake, before I can retort. "Let's find out if Kai is alive first. There might be something that can be done before we take any drastic measures. Jack?"

"I'll ride out tonight," says Jack.

Blake nods. "In the meantime, you're welcome to stay in my castle, Lochlan. But Callum and I have grown fond of our little Southlands pet. We'll kill you together if you decide to negotiate yourself a trade behind our backs. Callum likes to take a more forceful approach, whereas I. . ." The corner of his lip lifts as he runs a finger along the blade of his butter knife. "I like to play."

Lochlan laughs. "It's so nice to see you two getting along at last. Particularly after the other night."

Callum makes a low sound in his throat. "I wouldn't say that. But he's not wrong."

Lochlan ignores the two territorial alphas. "You're safe around me, Aurora. I swear it."

There's something sincere in his expression, and I believe him. Yet I can't pretend I've not noticed hostile glances throughout the evening from others within his clan. "What was your third condition?" I ask.

"Ah, it's a simple one," says Lochlan. "I merely wish for an audience with you, Aurora. In private. Tomorrow. Just you and me. What I have to say is for your ears only."

Curiosity rises within me, while Callum frowns. "Whatever you have to say to her. . ." A woman walks through the doors to the Great Hall. A crease forms on his forehead and he snaps his gaze to Blake. "You didn't tell me you'd invited Claire." His voice is low.

Blake runs his finger around the rim of his wine glass. "I didn't." I feel his intrigue ripple through me.

I frown as the woman walks toward us. She has dark hair, half tied back and half loose down her shoulders. She wears breeches and a loose shirt beneath a blue-and-green tartan coat, and there's a sword strapped to her belt. Most of her skin is covered, her clothing hugging an hourglass figure, and she walks confidently—as if she knows many of the Wolves in the hall have stopped their conversations to look at her. Her eyes are bright, her expression unreadable.

I recognize her name from somewhere.

"Claire," I say softly. I recall the time that Blake told me James liked bold women. "Isn't that—"

"James's former lover." Callum's tone is dark as his posture straightens. "Aye."

Tension curls in my gut because she could be here on behalf of our enemy.

It doesn't ease when Lochlan leans back in his seat. "I heard you tried to bed her at one point, too, Callum."

Chapter Seventeen

"That's enough, Lochlan," Callum growls under his breath as he stands to greet Claire.

His sharp rebuttal is confirmation that the claim is true, as well as the smirk that passes between Lochlan and Blake, and the soft laugh that escapes Jack. I try to be reasonable, to fight the dark shadow of jealousy that spreads unbidden through my body.

I assumed Callum would have been with other women before me. He's strong, and kind, and attractive. What's more, he's an alpha, and a wolf. I know the rules that apply to nobility in the Southlands—about waiting until marriage before physically expressing intimacy—don't apply here. From the way my brother would often sneak out to taverns at the docks, I'm skeptical about whether those rules apply to noble males in the south, too.

The idea that Callum wanted to bed the woman who walks confidently toward us still cools my blood.

She's flawless, and there is something about her that screams dominance—the steel of her spine, perhaps. Callum told me once he wanted to be with a female who was his equal, and I can see her allure.

I push my negative thoughts aside. There are more pressing things to worry about. Such as why she's here when her allegiance probably stands with James. I feel a slight twinge of irritation, too. I can't help but wonder *when* Callum tried to bed her.

Was it while she was with James? If so, it could explain why James was easily persuaded to ask for my hand in marriage. I think Callum has more honor than that, yet I wonder whether some of the contempt the two brothers hold for one another could originate from the female who halts before the table. Am I the second woman the two have fought over?

"Claire." Callum's tone is gentle yet wary. "I wasn't expecting to see you here. I hear you made alpha. Congratulations."

My eyebrows raise. I didn't think there were any female alphas.

Claire inclines her head. "And I hear you're trying to become king."

Callum eyes her warily, like he hasn't figured out whether she's a threat. "Did James send you?"

"James has no authority to send me anywhere. He's not my king." She smiles, though it doesn't reach her eyes. "I was on my way to Madadh-allaidh to see if I could negotiate an alliance with him."

Callum's brow creases. "An alliance? Your clan has always stood alone. Why now?"

"There are... things happening up north." A shadow passes over her features. "I want to move my people south."

Callum frowns. "Yet you came here first?"

She shrugs, her smile coy. "I thought I'd listen to what you had to say."

"How do I know you're not here to report back to James?"

"I don't play games, Callum."

"No?" Callum releases a dark laugh. "I'm not sure that's true."

Her brown eyes glint in the candlelight. "That was a long time ago."

Claire looks guarded when her attention turns to the dark-haired alpha of Lowfell.

Dimples puncture Blake's cheeks, but his eyes are cold. "Welcome to Lowfell. Please, come and join us."

Her gaze falls on me. She looks like she's assessing me, measuring me up, and I do the same. Finally, a smile ghosts her lips.

"It's nice to see another woman up here. Even if you *are* a southerner." She turns to Callum. "We need to speak. Alone."

He inclines his head. "Aye. Later."

She sits down beside Jack, who grins and starts a conversation with her. Callum drops into his chair and the music resumes. He squeezes my thigh underneath the table, as if he can see the questions in my eyes.

"*Later*," he repeats softly.

When the food has been cleared, the bagpipe music becomes louder and more unruly, and Wolves dance raucously in the center of the hall. Their violent movements as they spin one another around mirrors the storm brewing in my chest when Callum and Claire leave the Great Hall to speak in private.

I want my blood to stop howling, and my mind to still. I wonder whether the wolf that must exist inside me is making me feel like this. I don't like that they're alone together. The human part of me is just as unsettled, unhappy to be pushed aside once more while important matters are being discussed.

I swallow my emotion. I need to pull myself together. Callum needs to find out what Claire is doing here.

"Would you like to dance?" A male Northlands voice makes me start.

Lochlan stands in front of the table, elegant hand outstretched. His eyes dance with amusement. I'm not entirely sure what to make of him. Partially because he seems to likes Blake more than Callum.

I rise from my chair. "Of course. Though you'll have to teach me the moves."

"Your people didn't teach you the dances of Wolves?" Lochlan says, and I feel the slight challenge coming from him, the assertion that I don't belong.

"There are many things my people don't know about Wolves," I admit carefully as I walk around the table to join him. "We're at war, after all. But I've learned much, since I arrived here."

"We're not at war with your people," says Lochlan, when I place my hand in his. I frown as he leads me to the dancefloor. "We were once, of course. Many centuries ago, when they invaded Glas-Cladach in their longboats and ravaged our villages. When peace was sought, many of them settled and live among us now." He grins wolfishly at my perplexity. "Oh, you think I'm speaking of the southerners. No. I'm referring to your *real* people—the Wolves of the Snowlands." My heart beats faster at the mention of my mother's homeland. "Many of my clan were sad to hear of your mother's death."

The Wolves around me blur as they create two lines that face one another, and get ready for the next dance. "They knew of her?"

"The youth forget the Snowlands blood that runs through their veins. The elders prayed for her safety when she married your father."

The chatter, the clink of glasses, the crackle in the hearth—it all fades. "She really was a wolf?"

"Not many knew her true identity, of course, even here in the Northlands. We at Glas-Cladach suspected. Many hoped she would overthrow your father someday, and bring about a new era for Wolves. Alas, that was not the case." He assesses me. "Although perhaps hope is not lost yet."

My mind is whirling with information, but the music starts. It's so loud I can barely hear myself think.

"What was it you wanted to speak to me about?" I raise my voice.

"Tomorrow morning, meet my by the loch. For now. . ." Lochlan steps closer to me and grins. "Let's dance."

I quickly pick up the dance as Lochlan guides me through it.

It's a lively one that entails lots of looping arms with the nearest wolf, and swinging them around the dancefloor. My inhibitions start to dissipate, and it's not long before laughter spills from my lips. In the Southlands, I always felt constrained when dancing at balls in the palace—like a puppet who had to perform every move correctly. There is something more unruly in this dance, as if the steps don't really matter as long as fun is had.

Every so often, I feel Blake's gaze, weighted on my skin. I try to ignore it.

Lochlan tells me things about his territory every time I link arms with him—it's by the sea, he has the second biggest army in the Northlands, and many Wolves take a pilgrimage to the cliffs. Apparently, *Ghealach* was once said to have visited, and now a vast crop of moonflower grows there to offer small morsels of her power to those who smell its sweet perfume.

When the song ends, and the bagpipe player by the doors asks for any requests, Lochlan offers me his hand. Blake steps beside him.

My pulse kicks up, and my body instinctively tenses. I pull my emotions back, cage them in a box in my chest, desperate to keep them away from him. His posture is straight beneath his dark coat, and his expression carefully blank. When his eyes meet mine, the corner of his lip quirks slightly.

"Mind if I cut in?" he asks.

Chapter Eighteen

Some instilled sense of duty, of ladylike politeness, stops me from rejecting Blake on the spot, from slapping him in the face like I did two nights ago. It's so deep-seated that it's like instinct. My body locks up, and my smile doesn't falter. By the time my mind has taken charge of my body, Lochlan is stepping aside.

He surveys Blake, and I think I catch a hint of heat in his eyes before he grins at me. "Who am I to stand in the way of an alpha and the newest member of his clan?"

Lochlan inclines his head, then walks through the Wolves crowded on the dancefloor to one of the tables. Blake steps closer. His scent of night-soaked pine curls around me, and adrenaline courses through me, making the faces around me blur.

"I'm not dancing with you," I say.

"At least you're talking to me now."

A feral sound starts to build inside me, and I swallow it. I turn away. He grabs my arm, and I spin around. His face is so close that his breath mingles with mine.

"What do you want from me?" I ask. "You betrayed me. You linked our lives. You bit me. You intend to kill Callum. Can't you just leave me alone?"

"No." He drags his teeth over his bottom lip. "I'm your alpha. It looks bad, if you turn me down."

"Good." I don't even bother arguing that he is not my alpha. I won't give him the satisfaction.

"Don't you want to know about the bond?"

I *know* he's trying to provoke me. I can feel that dark thread of his inside me, curling around my emotions, trying to get me to react.

Don't bite. Don't bite. Don't—

"What about it?"

"You want to break it, don't you?"

He smiles slowly, irritating dimples creasing his cheeks. He has me, and he knows it. He holds out his hand, his meaning clear: *Dance with me and find out.*

I narrow my eyes. He must feel my cold pulse of anger. I don't even know if it's aimed at him or myself, because I'm actually considering it. My fingers flex at my sides. I feel the moment he thinks he's won—a triumphant burst of power in my chest. I can't stand it. I ball my hand into a fist and walk toward the alpha table.

"I could make you dance with me, you know." His voice slices through the sound of people talking, and I halt. "Ah, Callum told you about the Àithne, then."

"That would only work if you were my alpha, and you're not." I force my body to soften, and face him. Around us,

Wolves are lining up on either side of the dancefloor for the next dance. "You would not use it on me, anyway."

"What makes you so sure?"

I shrug, though as I say it, I'm certain it's true. "You're perpetually bored, Blake. You toy with people to entertain yourself. You would gain no enjoyment from forcing someone to do something against their will."

"Should we put your theory to the test?"

A challenge dances in his eyes, which glint in the candlelight. I raise my chin. "Go on then. Use your command on me. Order me to dance with you. It's the only way I ever will."

He angles his head slightly. Perhaps I'm playing with fire. I'm curious to see how it works. He may use this against Callum and me at some point, and I may as well prepare myself for it.

A slow, dangerous smile spreads across his face. He holds out his hand. "Dance with me."

I wait to feel something, anything, at his command. I fight my eyeroll. I knew he would have no power over me, because he is *not* my alpha.

He chuckles. "So pleased with yourself, little rabbit. Look at me." His pupils dilate and his irises become threaded with amber. My breath catches. Blake doesn't let his wolf surface often, and as it peers out from his eyes, it transforms his face. It seems to sharpen his jaw and accentuate his cheekbones. I'm looking at something feral, and beautiful, and deadly. "*Give me your hand.*"

This time, I feel him everywhere. His essence floods me—his scent, his heat, a dark unyielding dominance that I had not noticed before. I've always known him to be dangerous, but this... this *power*... The wolf is in his eyes, bright and beautiful, and I'm ensnared in his gaze. My pulse pounds as I fight the sensation, but all I can think of is my fever dream and the image of a rabbit in the maw of a great wolf.

I'd think he was doing something to me through the bond, but it feels slightly different. As if his command is slipping beneath my skin like a shadow, whispering, promising, coaxing. And when it strokes that feral thing inside me, that feral thing rubs against it.

It would be so easy to agree. So easy to do as he says. I want to please him. I'd do anything for him. He's my alpha, and I want to—

I grab those shadowy fingers that coil around my soul and shove them away. The Great Hall comes back to me, the crackle of the fire in the stone hearth, and the scent of buttered salmon and red wine. The bagpipe music starts. That feeling dissipates on a breath, and my first instinct is to bare my teeth at him and snarl. My second is to gloat.

I make myself look dazed, and place my hand in his. I want him to think he has power over me, so later, I can use it against him.

Blake's fingers curl around mine.

Where he touches me, my skin hums. The thread that links us seems to vibrate. I try to hide how my breath catches in my throat, and the way my pulse kicks up. His reaction is almost invisible, but his chest rises then falls, deeper than usual. His expression is too careful, too blank. He's hiding, like me. He feels it too.

His eyes shift back to normal, though they glint like a cat who has found a mouse to play with. "Isn't *that* interesting," he says – and I'm not sure if he's talking about his ability to use the Àithne on me, or whether he's talking about how taut and uncomfortable our connection feels.

He holds up my hand, as if claiming his prize, then leads me to the line of Wolves on the dancefloor. We stand at the end, beside Ryan and Becky. Ryan's grin falters when he sees who I'm about to dance with.

The dance is much like the last, but slower. It requires changes in partners as the females move down the line, but every time I'm to take the hand of another wolf, Blake takes their place. Until, close to the end of the line, he stops the pretense that we're part of this charade, and pulls me toward him.

The laughter and the clinking of glasses dims as he places a hand on my lower back. I reflexively put my palm on his shoulder, and my fingertips brush hard muscle. He pulls our bodies flush, and my breath dies in my throat. One hand still laced with mine, he spins me around.

He's manipulating me, I remind myself. He's going to take everything from me, including Callum. I have to stop him. I have to break this bond.

His movements are strong and graceful as we travel around the dancefloor, and again, I find myself thinking he's a good dancer. He told me he was born in a village, a half-wolf who later became part of the King's Guard. There is no reason he would be trained to dance.

"Why are you so good at dancing?" I ask.

"I said I had information about the bond, and that is what you wish to ask me?"

"Yes."

He dips me, and my breath hitches as I curl my arm around his neck. "Why are you asking?" he asks.

"Because I'm the princess. While the men in the castle were trained to fight, I was trained to dance."

He pulls me upright, and his breath mingles with mine. "You say that as if it's a bad thing. Do you not like to dance?"

"That is not the point."

"Kingdoms are not won by men fighting." He twirls me under his arm, and my skirt flutters around my legs. "They are won by men dancing and manipulating others behind closed doors."

"I'm not a man."

"No. But I'm sure you could bring a kingdom to its knees."

"That is your desire, not mine."

He only smiles. I wonder if it's a lie, that perhaps something inside me *does* wish to destroy and claim. To take something away from my father. I've felt the embers of something glowing in the pits of my soul since I found out what my father did to my mother.

"You're avoiding the question," I say. "How did you learn to dance?"

"Is it so hard to believe that I, too, was trained?" He cocks his head to the side. "Why do you want to know?"

"I can feel your emotions, and I know that you're hiding something."

"What of your secrets, little rabbit? I can feel you, too. I've sensed something within you, long before our lives were entangled this way."

My breathing quickens, even though he's talking nonsense. "Tell me about the bond."

"Make me."

My pulse thunders as some wild beast stirs in my chest. He'd implied he'd give me information if I danced with him. I should have known it was a lie. "You claim to be my alpha. That gives me a right to challenge you, doesn't it? I could do it right here, in front of all these people."

"Oh, please do, little rabbit." His voice is as soft and dark as a shadow.

"Do you think I cannot win? You cannot harm me without hurting yourself. You would look like a fool."

He dips me again, as if to prove he's in control and I'm floundering off-balance. "I have endured much pain in my life. And I have caused much pain."

"Do you think I have not?"

His hand shifts on my lower back. His finger brushes the spot where one of my scars brands my skin. I stiffen, and he pulls me upright. "I'm sure you have. But my experience with torture outweighs yours, I'm sure."

My blood chills as I think of his handwritten medical tomes.

"Go on," he whispers, his tone urging. "Challenge me. Show me how sharp those claws are."

The wild thing in my chest rears her head. His eyes glint as if he senses it, welcomes it. I take a deep breath. I know how to win this, and it's not by giving him what he wants. He wishes to play with me. I won't indulge him.

I release my grip on his neck and I step back. I curtsey. "Thank you for the dance, Blake."

He sighs. "You can ask three questions about the bond," he says. "I'll answer truthfully. Yes or no."

I turn around, hiding my smile. I take his hand once more. His scent curls around me as he brings me toward him. We continue our dance around the hall, and I ask him the most important question first. "Do you know how to break it?"

Something unreadable flickers across his face. He looks as if he's trying to figure out how to answer. Finally, he says, "Yes."

I overheard him tell Callum he read about the bond in a book. I need to have the same information as him if I'm to find a solution. "The book in which you read about the bond. . . is it here at Lowfell?"

"No," he says.

Again, I think he's telling the truth. I've been wasting my time in the library. I keep my features blank. "You've been living at Madadh-allaidh for a while. That's where the book is."

He opens his mouth to answer my question, but I shush him. I want to find out precisely where the tome is, so that when we take the castle, I can find it immediately.

"Your entire plan relies on the bond, so you wouldn't have left it out in the open." I search his eyes, and try to read the secrets that glimmer there amid the gold flecks. There was a wall of books beside his bed. "Is the book in your chambers at Madadh-allaidh?"

"Yes."

The triumph that tickles my lips dies. I don't have a chance of retrieving it until Callum has overthrown James. What's more, Blake betrayed James. James could have destroyed Blake's possessions. Blake's smile shows me he's well aware. Despite finding out where I can find some answers, the victory of this game belongs to him.

I'm surprised by the force of the anger that erupts inside me. My throat tightens, and my teeth tingle. I'm fed up of males like Blake thinking they can manipulate me. He thinks he's the only one who can play a game. I've been playing games with obnoxious lords my entire life. I don't see why Blake should be any different from the rest of them.

"I have another question for you, Blake." I curl my hand tighter around the back of his neck. I know he can feel the challenge that is coming from me, just as I can feel his intrigue.

"Okay. I'll play," he says. "One more."

I let my guard down entirely. I allow his darkness to flood me as I search for something that can be used against him. He breathes in deeply as if he can sense what I'm doing.

I smell pine, and parchment, and stale air. I hear a dripping well and someone screaming. I catch a glimpse of a dark cell, and the glint of a metal scalpel. I feel his essence—amusement, and danger, and something feral that lurks beneath. He feels like a viper, tightly coiled, that one day will strike.

I catch a whisper of something else, too. It's hotter. Hungrier. More dangerous. My blood heats as it takes its hold. I remember when I was in chains in the dungeons. His eyes flickered to my lips, just for a moment, and he'd stumbled back in disgust afterward.

His gaze, right now, is fixed on my face.

"Do you think I'm beautiful, Blake?" I ask.

He swallows, and a surge of power rises within me. For the first time, I think I've caught him off guard.

But then he smiles. He steps closer, and his heat and the scent of pine crashes over me, dark and all-consuming. He dips his mouth to my ear.

"Tread carefully, little rabbit." His warm breath brushes my skin. "That is not a game you wish to play with me."

A shiver travels down my spine as the song comes to an end. Blake steps back, and air fills my lungs once more. He inclines his head, the gesture polite, his expression as nonchalant as usual. His eyes are lethal in the flickering torchlight.

Wolves head to the tables to top up their drinks, and Blake walks through them. He leaves the Great Hall as the bagpipe player starts a new tune.

Jack stands by the exit, and watches him go with an uncharacteristically serious look on his face. He seems concerned for his alpha. He follows him.

It takes a moment for my pulse to calm and my breathing to steady. I'm playing a game with the most dangerous wolf in the kingdom, and his words were laced with threat.

I don't know whether I'm winning or losing.

But I think I just rattled him.

I smile.

Chapter Nineteen

The Great Hall is too hot. The scents of food and wine and sweat are heavy in the air, and my dance with Blake has made my skin feel tight. When I can't find Callum, I decide to get some fresh air.

I navigate the shadowy corridors, walk through the entrance hall, and slip out of the castle into the small courtyard. My breath mists in front of my face, and I rub my arms over the long sleeves of my dress.

I stand here for a few minutes, before the big arched door swings open behind me. Claire steps outside. She's clasping a goblet of red wine, and her dark hair tickles her face in the wind.

"Aurora. I didn't know anyone was out here."

Her stare is assessing—as if she's sizing up whether or not I'm a threat. I don't know if it's because I'm the daughter of her enemy king, or whether it's because of my relationship with Callum. I hold her gaze, equally wary of her.

"Callum is looking for you," she says. "Although he just got cornered by Ryan, so it could be a while before he finds you." She leans against the wall by the door and sips her wine. "The lad thinks he's going to storm Madadh-allaidh by himself."

"Oh dear." An awkward silence hangs between us. "I like your coat."

"Thank you." She nods at my dark-blue dress. "Nice dress."

We continue to stare at one another.

"Are you on our side?" I ask.

"I could ask the same of you."

"I'm on Callum's side. I have no love for my father, if that's what you're asking."

She nods. "If you want to know whether I've picked between James and Callum, I have not."

"You were on your way to Madadh-allaidh before you came here."

"My clan is based in the north, close to Highfell, where the nights are getting darker. An old threat seems to be returning." Her expression darkens. "There is something coming. We can sense it, and I want to move my people as far south as possible before it arrives." She swills the wine in her cup. "I'll respect whoever wins the challenge. James or Callum, it makes no difference to me."

"I heard you had a. . . history with James."

Her jaw tightens. "That was a long time ago."

"What happened between you?"

She bites her cheek. "My uncle was alpha then, and James and Callum's father was king. As a way to form an alliance, we were invited to Madadh-allaidh, and they agreed for James and me to marry."

My eyebrows raise. "The match was arranged? Did you wed?"

She laughs. "No. It never came to that. When I found out I was being offered up like cattle, I was furious. I stormed into James's bedchambers, slammed him against the wall, and put a blade to his balls. Told him I'd cut them off unless he put a stop to it."

A faraway look appears in her eyes, as if she is enjoying the memory. "It turned out he knew nothing about it. He fought against it, but his father was a prick. We began fighting publicly with one another at every opportunity we had. We pretended to hate each other, so everyone could see how difficult an alliance would be with us at the heart." A coy smile plays on her lips. "Secretly, though, we'd begun courting one another." She shrugs. "The ultimate act of defiance, I suppose. Until we realized. . . it's complicated."

I suck in my bottom lip. I want to ask about Callum, but I know it'll come across as insecure. I don't want her to think I feel threatened by her. Her brow creases, as if she's trying to decipher my emotions.

"Go on," she says. "Out with it. What do you want to know?"

I exhale. "Lochlan said you had history with Callum, too."

"Lochlan's a shit-stirring arsehole." She shakes her head. "I suppose we do, in a way. It was about five years ago, but it's not what you think. Callum didn't know I was courting James—we hid it well. Like everyone else, he thought we despised one another, and that I had a miserable future ahead of me. He could see his father wouldn't relent." She shrugs a shoulder. "He offered to take James's place."

I feel as if I've been doused with cold water. I thought he'd tried to bed Claire, but this is much harder to stomach. "He offered to be your husband?"

Claire rolls her eyes. "It wasn't like that. Callum... he's an honorable male with a weakness for a damsel in distress."

Her words don't make me feel any better. They're an echo of what Lochlan said. Callum rescued me, once. Is that the main reason we're together?

She shakes her head, her expression solemn. "He thought he was saving me from misery. He didn't realize I was never rebelling against being with his brother, but having my future decided for me by others. He wanted to rescue me, not marry me."

I look at her, taking in her curves, her bright eyes, and her delicate features. "I'm sure he didn't."

"You were betrothed yourself, at one point, weren't you?"

"Sebastian was not as pretty as you."

She laughs, and her stare becomes curious. "There are rumors that James killed him at the battle. Callum said James is lying. He says *you* were the one who did it."

Adrenaline swirls like wind in my chest. I clench my fists to stop my hands from shaking as the memory of slitting my betrothed's throat flashes through my mind. "Yes."

She must hear my pounding pulse. "I've had to kill in order to become alpha. It's never easy, and always leaves a mark on one's soul. You shouldn't regret it, though."

"I don't."

"Good," she says. "I'm glad you killed that bastard. He committed many atrocities against my people. Although I hear they have a new lord now, who is just as bad."

Worse, I want to tell her.

She finishes her wine, places it on a nearby window ledge, then walks across the cobblestones to the gates. "It was good to speak with you in private. Perhaps soon, we'll be allies, if Callum wins his challenge."

"And if he doesn't?"

She gives me a terse smile.

"You're going to visit James, now, aren't you?" I ask.

"Like I said, I need to make an alliance. But I'll respect the winner of the challenge." She disappears into the tunnel.

I slump against the castle walls, and place my palms on the rough stone. Callum asked another woman to marry him. It's not the idea that he envisioned a future with Claire that bothers me, as such, but his reason for doing it. Does he merely see me as a damsel he needs to protect?

I take a couple of deep breaths, and taste woodsmoke on the night air. I straighten and smooth down my dress, before tucking a couple of errant strands of hair behind my ears. I need to get control over myself. It's been so long since I've let myself feel anything, I fear I'm letting my emotions get the better of me.

It could be the wolf that stirs inside me that makes me feels territorial about Callum. It could be the princess who has never courted anyone—never even had a proper friend—who is scared of losing the one person who has cared for her since she was a child.

Callum has never given me a reason to doubt him. I head inside so I can talk to him. The door on the opposite side of the entrance hall opens at the same time. Ian strolls through. His blond hair is messy, and his eyes a little bloodshot. There's a red wine stain on his yellow kilt.

He smiles when he sees me. "Good evening, Princess."

My body tenses as he approaches. I'm not sure if it's his forced smile that puts me on guard, or the scent of alcohol that radiates from him.

Perhaps it's because James told him that Alexander wanted me in exchange for his brother.

I subtly reach for the wolfsbane between my breasts. "Good evening."

He steps in front of me and I curl my fingers around the glass vial.

"Is everything okay, Ian?" Callum emerges from the corridor behind him.

Ian tenses, then smiles. Callum is a head taller than him, and must be twice his width. He folds his arms, emphasizing his biceps.

Ian swallows. "I just wanted to let the princess know we're lucky to have her here."

"We are." Callum doesn't smile. He looks the younger male up and down, and Ian averts his gaze. "Go on. Back to the feast."

Ian dips his head. Callum doesn't stand aside, so the smaller male has to squeeze past him before he disappears from view.

I let loose a breath. Callum turns his attention to me.

Even with the threat to me gone, he seems tense. His jaw is a strong line, and his expression is stony. My pulse slowed at his arrival, but it starts to speed up again. He seems like he's annoyed with me.

"Is something wrong?" I ask.

"Let's go somewhere private."

I fall into step beside him. He threads his fingers with mine, and leads me past the festivities in the Great Hall, and up one of the stairwells.

"I'll have a word with Lochlan about Ian," he says. "I don't like how he was looking at you."

He opens the door to our room, and we step inside. The fire burns low in the hearth, casting a soft glow onto the leather armchairs and the four-poster bed.

I walk past him, and sit on one of the armchairs—the one facing away from the window, so I don't have to look at the half-moon that shines over the loch. Callum shuts the door, then lingers by the foot of the bed. There's something. . . off about him.

"What did Claire have to say?" I ask.

"There have been some unexplained deaths in a few of the villages in her territory, and people were seen entering an old chapel dedicated to the God of Night not too far from Highfell. She thinks Night's Acolytes are rising once more. They've been talking about someone called the Night Prince. We have enough to be worrying about with Lochlan and James right now."

"Is there something else? Something wrong?"

He chews his cheek as he leans against one of the bedposts. "You tell me."

"What do you mean?"

"I. . ." He drags his hands over his face. "I don't know. Probably nothing."

The room is silent but for the odd crackle coming from the fire, and the faint sound of bagpipes coming from the Great Hall. "Do you think I'm a damsel, Callum?"

His brow furrows. "What?"

"A damsel in distress. A weak female who needs saving."

He folds his arms. "Because I'm going to have a word with Lochlan about a male from his clan who was up to no good?"

"No." I know I sound petulant, but... "Do you think I'm your equal?"

He frowns. "Aye? Why?"

"You said once that you wanted to be with a female who was equal to you."

"I do." He cocks his head to one side. "I am."

"Yet you feel the need to protect me all the time."

"You're very small." When I don't return his smile, he exhales. "You told me you did not want me to suppress myself, my wolf instincts, around you. I'm an alpha, and you are my lass, and aye, I want to protect you. What's wrong with that?"

"I could help Lochlan with Alexander, you know?"

"I won't risk you."

I turn toward the flickering flames in the fireplace. "Claire's an alpha. If you were together, you wouldn't have to protect her, would you?" I instantly regret saying it. I sound weak. Foolish.

Silence stretches between us, and I long for him to fill it. I need him to say something. Anything. There's the thud and creak of footsteps across the floorboards. Callum crouches in front of the chair and nudges my knees apart to accommodate him. I'm not sure what I expect when I turn back to him. Annoyance, perhaps, or even confusion. It's not the wide grin that is spread across his face. I hate that it makes the corners of my lips twitch.

"What are you smiling about?" I say.

"So that's what this is all about."

"What?"

He slides his hands up my legs, pushing up my skirt, and nips my inner thigh with his teeth. "Fuck, I like that you're jealous."

My breathing hitches. "I'm not jealous."

He kisses my leg, and his stubble scrapes against the sensitive skin. "Oh, I think that you are." His hands move up and down my calves, leaving a trail of heat in their wake. "Perhaps I'm not the only territorial wolf around here."

"You asked her to marry you."

He looks up at me. "It wasn't like that."

I take his face in my hands to stop him from distracting me. "What was it like?"

"I was eighteen. My mother had just gone missing. My father was grieving. My brother was distant and distracted. I was far from my home." He shakes his head. "I was looking for purpose, I suppose. Claire and James seemed unhappy with the match, and I offered to take James's place. I wanted to prove myself to my father, to my people. It wasn't romantic."

"Claire seemed to think you did it to save her from an unhappy fate."

"I suppose that played into my decision, aye. Does that make me a monster?"

"No." I huff. "It makes you a good man, a good wolf. Someone who would rescue any woman in distress, no matter who they were. Just like you rescued me."

He frowns. "You did not wish for me to rescue you?"

"Of course. I'm happy you brought me here."

"Ah, so you don't have an issue with me protecting *you*," he says. "You don't like the thought of me protecting others? That's what makes you jealous?"

"No. It's not that, either."

I sigh. He doesn't get it. How can he? Callum is like a mountain—solid and strong.

"What is it then?" His gaze is searching, like he's trying to solve a puzzle.

I bite my bottom lip. I'm not used to expressing my feelings. I'm not sure how to explain that somehow, sometimes, Callum makes me feel weak. Not in the way that my father made me feel weak—with his control, and his dismissiveness, and his scorn if I showed emotion. In the way that he is so careful with me.

I wonder, sometimes, if it's my weakness that attracts him to me in the first place, when I don't want to be weak any longer. I want to be equal to the Wolves in this kingdom. I want to be equal to him.

"You're very. . . careful with me," I say, finally.

"I don't understand." His brow creases. "You would rather I was rough? Or cruel?"

"No. Of course not." I brush my thumb across his cheek. "All of my life, I've been taught to suppress my emotions and my opinions. All of my life, I've felt as if there was a scream building in my chest that I could never let go of. I worry, sometimes, that you suppress yourself around me, because you don't think I'm strong enough to handle the real you."

He pulls back slightly, and I worry that I've offended him. "My father didn't suppress his emotions. He was rough, and cruel, and he treated my mother poorly. So I'll hold back sometimes, because I don't want to turn into him. And aye, I'm careful with you, because you're precious to me. Is that so wrong?"

"I suppose not. I don't know. This is all new to me."

"Me too."

"It is?"

"Believe it or not, I've never courted a bonny wee Southlands princess, with fire in her soul, who drives me to despair on a daily basis."

My eyes narrow. "But you have courted other females before?"

His smile is soft but not remorseful. "I have."

Jealously crashes through me. It has thorns that ravage my insides. My canines ache, and the urge to bite something, to bite Callum, overcomes me. When Callum growls softly, I know he senses it.

"Fuck," he groans, dipping his lips to my leg once more. "That jealousy of yours makes me want to do some very bad things to you."

My lip twitches, despite my dark mood. "Do them, then."

His warm breath brushes close to the place where I'd like his mouth. "My wolf is very close to the surface right now. You want me to stop holding back with you? Let us wait until after the full moon, once you've shifted for the first time."

My jealousy twists into annoyance, then fear. I don't want to think about my body breaking and changing and my mind not being my own any longer. I want to be distracted.

I bet he's so gentle with you. So afraid you will break.

I find myself thinking about what Blake would do to get what he wanted. "Perhaps you're right. Perhaps, even after the full moon, we should not. . . act on our impulses."

"What?" The word tickles my inner thigh.

I rest my elbow on the arm on the chair and put my hand over my mouth to suppress my smile. "You know, as a Southlands princess, I'm not supposed to bed anyone before marriage. I should probably honor that, going forward." I catch the flash of the wolf in his eyes. "Perhaps I should not bed anyone again, until after I'm wed."

"No sex before marriage? That's how you do things in the Southlands?" His brow crumples, and I almost laugh.

"Yes. What do you think?"

I bite my cheek, sure he's about to pounce on me, sure I've won my little game with him. His breath is warm against my skin, and his shoulders brush against my inner thighs when he raises himself up.

"Okay," he says. "Marry me, then."

Chapter Twenty

My mouth drops open. "Marry you? Callum, I was not... I was... I was just..." I fumble for the words. I was not joking, as such, but—

"I know what you were doing, Princess." The soft glow from the fire flickers across his strong jaw. "You were trying to manipulate me. You should have known it wouldn't work. If you wish to talk seriously about this, then let's." He brushes a kiss on the inside of my leg. "Marry me."

"You're not serious."

"I am."

"What game is this?"

He huffs a laugh. "I don't play games, Princess."

"You... you're proposing marriage?"

He slides a hand along the back of my calf. Mischief dances on his lips. "I'm on my knees, aren't I?"

"This isn't a joke, Callum."

"I know. I want to marry you."

"For sex?"

He grins. "That's one reason. Aye."

Darkness spreads in my veins. "Are you expecting a political alliance? With my father?"

"No." He nips my thigh with his teeth. "In fact, I think he'd be rather displeased to know what this savage wolf wishes to do to his daughter."

"Do you wish to send a message to the Southlands, by marrying their princess?"

"No." He smiles. "I want you to be my wife."

I cup his face in my hands. His skin is hot, and his stubble prickles my palms. He truly means this. A few months ago, the thought of marrying someone like Callum would have been beyond my wildest dreams. It still is. Yet something feels. . . off. I feel. . . hesitant.

"Your wife?" I say.

"Aye."

"You want me to be yours."

His expression darkens. "Aye."

My muscles tighten. It's about ownership. The flames burn in the fireplace, and the log crumbles to ash. I wonder if that's all love is when stripped bare—people striving to own one another.

He swallows, as if he knows the direction of my thoughts. He takes my chin. "I'm a wolf, an alpha, and there are certain things I'm struggling with at the moment. I don't want to feel this way. But my brother has marked you. Blake. . ." A muscle twitches in his jaw. "Blake has bound himself to you and claimed you as part of his clan. So, aye, I want you to be my wife. Mine."

"Callum—"

"There is more to it than that, though. I want to be yours, too. I want to be your husband. Your equal. I want you by my side, challenging me, supporting me. I want a family with you, and to provide for you." He takes my hand in his, and brushes his lips across my knuckles. "You don't have to agree. You can marry me tomorrow—we can ride to Dawn's Craig in the morning and ask the Priestess to do. Or we can marry in ten years. We don't have to marry at all, if you don't want it. I'll still be here, at your side, striving to impress you until my soul sleeps with *Ghealach* and the stars. Think on it, okay?"

My mouth is dry, and my eyes burn. I nod, and squeeze his hands. "I will think on it."

He smiles, wide and open. Then he drags his teeth over his bottom lip. He cocks his head to one side, as if coming to a decision, and mischief ignites within his eyes. I've seen this look on him before. It means trouble. The corner of my lip quirks.

"What's that look for?" I ask.

"Perhaps I could give you a taste of married life, to help you make your decision." In a sudden movement, he grabs my thighs and pulls my knees over his shoulders. "Just a taste. . ."

I gasp as I'm dragged forward in the armchair. "Callum!"

He pulls my underwear aside. "What?"

"I thought you couldn't be manipulated." My voice is breathy and doesn't sound like it belongs to me. "It seems you're doing exactly what I want."

Slowly, torturously, he drags his tongue along my entrance. My hands find his head and my fingers curl in his hair to pull him to me.

"Who says *I'm* not manipulating *you*?" His lips glisten in the firelight.

I tilt my head back as he feasts on me as if I'm his favorite meal. He sucks and strokes and laps as if he's a rabid beast, and provokes sounds from me that I've never made before. I clamp my thighs around his head, and ride his face, rocking my hips until I'm nothing but liquid heat and the wind that howls through the mountains.

Somewhere, within the wild valleys and hurtling brooks that pass beneath me, I see his point. I would do anything he asked of me right now. If belonging to him means more of this, then I could give him everything I am.

Then all thoughts evade me and I'm only this feeling, this pleasure, as release crashes through me and I sink into never-ending bliss. I barely hear the voice somewhere deep within me, dark and primal and slightly annoyed.

Feral eyes. Amber.

A low growl.

You belong to no one.

***

I BLINK. I'm in my father's palace, in the ballroom. I sit at one of the many tables that are dotted around the dancefloor, and I'm concealed behind one of the stone columns that support the domed ceiling. People dance in their finery on the checkered tiles, and the crescent moon shines through the sun-shaped window above my father's throne. My brother Philip is by one of the tall arched windows, surrounded by adoring men and women alike. He throws back his head and laughs. His wine sloshes out of his cup.

Unease winds around my bones like a serpent. The notes of the string quartet are slightly off. The movement of the crowd is disjointed. The scent of liquor and sweat hangs heavy in the air. It's suffocating.

A man sits beside me. He leans closer. Too close. He is packed with muscle, with black hair shaved close to his head. He's drunk. Too drunk. His sour breath assaults my cheek, and as he slurs on about the glory he intends to bring to the kingdom, he puts his hand on my thigh. I stiffen. I know his history. I know the last time he visited the palace, one of my ladies-in-waiting was seen crying the next morning.

Touching me, on another night, would warrant his execution. Either drink, or the fact we are shrouded in shadow, has made him bold. My father wants me to talk to him, appease him. So, even though my skin crawls, I relax my posture, lean in for the jug, and refill his goblet with wine.

"You're being too forward, Alexander." My words are bold, but I force a coy smile onto my lips.

"I think you like it, love," he slurs in his Borderlands accent. "You need someone forward. A bit wild. Not like these stiff southern bastards in their silk and finery."

I nod at his black coat, embroidered with anchors and flowers. "You say that, yet your coat is one of the finest I've seen."

"It would look even better on the floor of your bedchambers, with the rest of your clothes piled beside it."

"Only my husband is supposed to speak to me that way."

"Play your cards right, and that could be me."

"My father would never agree to that." I pretend to be sad about the fact. "He will make me marry a lord, or a prince. Someone to strengthen the kingdom."

He slurps his drink, and brings his lips to my ear. "Fuck your father." My heartbeat quickens. "Does that make you nervous, love? Fuck, you smell good."

I force myself not to recoil, though I inch away slightly. "You don't like my father?"

"Who does? The miserable cunt." He takes another sip, and spills a little wine on the table. "You should do what I say, not him. After I've taken the Borderlands from my twat of a brother, I'll turn the Borderlands army to the south, put your father's head on a spike, and take you for myself. How does that sound?"

Like you've just signed your death warrant, Alexander.

I force myself to smile. "An appealing plan indeed."

He leans closer, and something inside me rattles against its confines. My fingers hurt, and I fear claws will erupt so I can claw out his eyes. He opens his mouth and his eyes gleam with hunger. I breathe in sharply. A blade protrudes from his throat. It's pulled back, and he slumps forward onto the table. The jug of wine tips over and spills onto the floor.

Blake stands behind him, and the muscles in his forearm flex as he sheaths the dagger. The moonlight illuminates the gleam in his eye, and the dimple that presses into his cheek. His dark hair is mussed, and his black shirt is baggy. The buttons are only done up to halfway—like he's been lounging on his bed.

This can't be happening. This isn't happening. This *didn't* happen.

The music stops. The people dissolve into shadow. A cloud passes over the crescent moon that shines on the throne.

My fear and unease dissolve. This is not real. I'm not a fourteen-year-old-girl, being groomed by a man almost twice her age. This is a dream. A memory. Nothing more.

My lips tighten. It's not something Blake should be privy to.

I straighten in my seat.

"Hello, little rabbit." Blake's lips curve into a wicked smile. "Have you been keeping secrets?"

Chapter Twenty-One

"*I made friends with a man in the Southlands, once.*" Blake repeats the story I once told him. He pushes Alexander and his chair onto the floor. He turns and leans against the table beside me, his thigh close to my clasped hands. "*My father thought he was plotting against him and I was told to dance with him, sit with him, fill up his cup. He was a devious, cruel man...*" A slow smile spreads across Blake's face. "No wonder you were so alarmed at the news that Alexander wasn't dead."

I fold my arms. "Very good. You have discovered my secret."

Blake laughs. "Here I was, thinking he wanted to marry you and stake his claim on the Borderlands. It seems he may have a personal vendetta against you, as well."

"I don't feel bad for what I did. He should have been executed."

"I imagine he feels otherwise."

I exhale. "You can be facetious all you like, Blake. You linked our lives together. Whatever happens to me, happens to you."

He shrugs. "I won't let him hurt you."

"You can stop him?"

Blake looks down at the body on the floor, and arches an eyebrow.

I roll my eyes. "I'm not sure killing the real Alexander will be as simple as killing a figment of my imagination. He had a lot of support in the Borderlands before... well, whatever happened to him."

I think of the bellows I heard throughout the palace after I'd told my father his intentions. I thought he had been executed—my father never mentioned him again.

"Lowfell is more or less secure," says Blake.

"More or less?"

The table creaks as he shifts against it and parts his thighs slightly. "I don't like how some of Lochlan's clan are looking at you. I'm starting to wonder whether a mysterious illness should appear among the lower-ranking Wolves in his pack. Nothing deadly, of course. Just bad enough to keep them weak."

"Oh yes, lets march a half-dead army, weak with sickness, onto Madadh-allaidh. James will be terrified." I give him a hard look. "Don't do anything."

Blake grins—a real grin, almost charming—and his annoying dimples deeply puncture his cheeks. "Fine. Perhaps not, then. Are there any other 'friends' of yours I should know about?"

"No one of note."

"What a relief. Does Callum know about this?"

"No. It doesn't matter that Alexander may have a personal vendetta against me. The outcome is the same." When Blake raises his eyebrows, I sigh and look away. "It will worry him and he has enough to deal with. I don't want him fussing over me like a mother hen."

"Quite right. Come to Daddy about things like this." He winks.

I shake my head, but have to bite my cheek to stop myself from laughing. "You're repugnant."

"Perhaps refrain from making any new 'friends' until we've dealt with this one. Yes?"

The corner of my mouth twitches. "You're the only 'friend' I've made recently."

"I'm glad to hear it. Keep the wolfsbane I gave you close by when you meet with Lochlan in the morning."

"You didn't give it to me. I took it."

"Of course you did, darling." His voice fades as the hall disintegrates around us. Shadows swirl around me as the dream ebbs away. "Let me know if Lochlan says anything interesting, won't you?"

***

THE NEXT morning, I wrap my cloak tightly around me as I walk through the grass toward the brown-and-orange waters of the loch. Lochlan is already waiting for me. He leans against the bough of an ash tree, his red hair a sharp contrast to the grey of the bark. His yellow kilt ruffles in the wind.

He smiles in my direction as I approach, then he looks over my shoulder. I follow his gaze. Callum leans against the outer wall of Lowfell with his arms folded across his chest.

He raises a hand to wave at Lochlan, the gesture playful—but the meaning clear. He's watching.

"Sorry." I shrug. "I tried to get him to wait in the castle, but he's as stubborn as an ox when he wants to be."

Lochlan's smile grows. "Not a problem. It was the other one I was more concerned about."

"Blake? Why?"

"We'll get to that." He holds out his arm for me to take. "Walk with me."

I asses the wolf before me—strong, lithe, a warrior. I'm glad of the vial of wolfsbane in my pocket. I loop my arm with his, and he steers me toward the woodland.

"What is it you wanted to speak to me about?" I ask.

"Sebastian."

Something cold floods me at the mention of my former betrothed. A vision of me straddling his lap in the carriage flashes behind my eyelids. *How about you show me what else you learned while you were being a whore to that Highfell beast?* Sweat beads on my brow, and I push down the rise of the fever that threatens to take me.

I push down my disappointment, too. I had hoped he wanted to speak to me about my mother.

"What about him?" I ask.

"He came to Glas-Cladach with a group of soldiers about six months ago."

"What did he want?"

"He was looking for the Heart of the Moon."

My eyebrows lift. "He thought you had it?"

Dry twigs and leaves crunch beneath our boots as the trees around us get taller. They stretch toward the grey sky with gnarly fingers. A rustle, and the scent of the mountains carried on the wind, lets me know Callum is not far behind.

"He believed it had been in the Snowlands at one time, but was then transported into the Northlands. Glas-Cladach is the nearest port to the Snowlands, so he reasoned we might have been holding onto it."

"Were you?"

"No. But we keep a log of all the boats that enter our territory. When he discovered there was a storm on the day your mother left her kingdom to marry your father, and her ship was diverted to Glas-Cladach, he became very interested. Particularly on seeing the crop of moonflower that grows on our cliffs—a crop said to only grow after the earth is touched by *Ghealach*'s power."

Lochlan steadies me as I almost trip over a fallen branch. "What are you saying?"

"Did she ever give you an heirloom? Something with a precious stone in—a necklace, or a ring, perhaps?"

"You think my mother had the Heart of the Moon?" I let out a half-laugh, though there is no humor in it. "She left me all of her jewelry. Much of it is adorned with precious stones. Some of it is back at the Borderlands, some in my father's castle." I shake my head. "None of it held any particular importance to her. If she had such a precious relic in her possession, she would have kept it close, surely. She did not have it, Lochlan."

"Hm, perhaps. I thought it was worth asking."

"What would you have done, if I had it?"

He shrugs, though something violent gleams in his eyes. "It's a very precious thing."

"In that case, I'm glad Callum is following us."

Lochlan smirks. We stop by the crumbling chapel, and I let go of his arm. "You didn't want Blake to overhear this conversation. Why?"

"All alphas want to get their hands on the Heart of the Moon, not just me. Whoever has it in their possession becomes the most powerful wolf in the Northlands. They'd likely become king. I thought you and Callum may appreciate me not passing on this information to him."

"You don't want Blake to take the throne? It's a relief to know that, at least. But why? You seem to get along with him."

"I told you, he intrigues me." The corner of his mouth tips up, but I sense sadness in him. He runs a hand over the back of his neck, and I catch another glimpse of his tattoos as he brushes aside his shirt collar. "The problem is, I tend to become intrigued by the wrong sort of men."

"Kai?" I say softly.

He releases a sad laugh. "I loved him, killed my father for him. He betrayed me and took part of my clan." He shakes his head. "Regardless, it looks like I'm going to attempt to rescue him. Jack returned from the Borderlands early this morning. One of my men overheard him talking to Blake. Two days after the full moon, Alexander plans to move a group of prisoners—Kai included—between the Borderlands castle and his castle on the coast."

"The Grey Keep," I say. Alexander boasted about his sea-drenched castle during the ball when I discovered his treason. I read about it, in the days after. It's close to the border and set upon cliffs. The rocks below are too jagged and perilous for boats to approach.

Lochlan nods. "I'm sure that Blake will lie and tell me he's dead, but you can inform Callum that if he wants my army, we'll rescue Kai, first." He raises his voice above the rustle of the leaves because he knows Callum is listening. "There's a craig in between the two castles, perfect for an ambush. When Kai is safe, Callum can have my army and we'll pay his brother a visit."

I smile. "I'll let him know."

His eyes glint and he shrugs. "My point is, I tend to be attracted to those who harbor darkness. And there is darkness in Blake. More than in most." His gaze sweeps over the ruin of the chapel amid the trees. "I fear what would become of the Northlands under his command."

I don't disagree.

***

THE BOND is like a thread, and it gets tighter as the full moon gets closer. After I escaped Sebastian, I told myself I'd be more open with my feelings, but I entomb them, to keep Blake out.

As the days pass, and Callum works with Lochlan to prepare his ambush, there's a part of me that wonders if I'm using Blake as an excuse. I wonder if feeling nothing is still easier than feeling something. I don't want to be overcome by fear of the full moon. My father killed my mother, and sometimes I'm so angry I feel like I'll combust. Callum is still being so gentle with me, and sometimes it makes me want to scream. And my mother. . .my mother hid that I was a wolf. She let herself be poisoned. Why would she do that?

No. I don't want to feel any of it.

I spend my time poring over books, trying to find something to break the link between Blake and me—or perhaps I'm just trying to distract myself, trying to stop myself from staring out of the window each night, as the moon gets brighter.

One morning, as I'm scanning the shelves in the library, pacing, chewing my fingernails, Elsie taps me on the shoulder and hands me a small paperback. *The Alpha's Secret* is written across the front. When I flick through, my lips twitch. "Another love story," I say.

"The old cook here at Lowfell used to pen them." She shrugs. "I wasn't allowed out, with my father being the way he was. These helped pass the time. This one is particularly good. You should read it."

There's a slight glint in her eyes, and she looks alarmingly similar to her brother for a moment. I'm sure it's due to the intimate romantic details I'm sure to find within. I thank her, and pocket it so I can read it in private, later. I go back to my frantic search.

It's not until the day before the full moon, when I'm eating breakfast, that I make a discovery. I'm reading a scripture that says all Wolves power comes from the moon. I breathe in sharply as Blake's darkness floods me.

The hall is quieter this morning. Lochlan and his clan are planning a hike to Dawn's Craig later as part of a Glas-Cladach ritual, and he's taken them outside. Ryan and Becky seem to be arguing by the doors, Callum is crouched in the middle of the flagstones and is attempting some kind of magic trick for Alfie, and Elsie and Arran are talking quietly while they eat breakfast.

Blake sits straight in his chair, and his hand is curled into a fist on the table. Beside him, Jack looks at him in concern.

The full moon is tomorrow. I walked in on Blake last month, shirtless, his muscles clenched and dripping with sweat. He was trying not to shift. I know he doesn't like being a wolf. Perhaps I'm merely feeling his anxiety, which rivals my own.

An idea takes root. The moon *was* shining brightly the night that Blake forged our connection. If Blake drew on the power of the moon to create the bond, then perhaps I could draw on the same power to break it.

It takes me back to my conversation with Lochlan regarding my mother, and the moonflower at Glas-Cladach.

What if the Heart of the Moon could be used to break the bond?

Chapter Twenty-Two

The evening before the full moon, I stare out of the window.

There's a solitary figure outside. His coppery hair is being blown around by the wind as he throws stones into the loch with his head bowed. Ryan seems to be having as hard a time today as I am. Though I presume his dark mood is related to his argument with Becky.

All my life, I've swallowed my feelings and entombed them in stone. If it ever cracked, I'd be accused of hysteria. It always struck me as unfair. My father executed anyone who stood in his way, and my brother emerged from King's City taverns bloody and bruised most evenings. Yet I was deemed emotional.

Now, my emotions churn like the waters of the loch that surrounds Lowfell. They howl with the gusts of wind that travel through the mountains. I try to fix my mask and act as impenetrable as I'm expected to be.

I feel the weight of Callum's gaze against my back. I feel night's shadows closing in on me. It's suffocating. I suppress a whimper. I cannot do this.

There's a rustle of fabric, and the armchair by the fire groans. Callum's footsteps approach, slow and steady, before his mountain scent wraps around me. One of his big arms curves around my torso.

"Don't be afraid." His words are warm.

"I'm not afraid."

He slides his palm over the dress I wear, up to my chest, leaving a trail of heat, and stops just beneath my breast. He lightly taps my ribs with two fingers. The pace is fast, a frenzied bird, in time with my racing heartbeat.

"Liar." He trails his lips along my neck, and something hot blooms amid the cool darkness. "Turn around. Tell me, Princess, am I afraid?"

He turns me to face him. He doesn't need to take my hand, callused palms rough yet gentle, and press it against his chest for me to answer. Nor do I need to feel the steady thump of his heart. Why would he be afraid? What would scare such a male?

His shirt stretches across powerful shoulders, and the sleeves are rolled up to expose thick, corded forearms. His hair is shorn close to his head at the sides—a warrior's cut. He was built to lead armies, to lead *kingdoms*. Even Blake seems to have conceded that he needs Callum in order to dispose of James and get what he wants.

He puts his finger beneath my chin. "I'll be with you, at your side. You have nothing to fear, I swear it." He presses his forehead against mine. "What can I do, Princess? Tell me, and I shall do it." He sounds almost as helpless as I feel. "How can I make you feel better? Let me in."

I wish his solidity, the hardness of his chest, and the steadiness of his breathing was enough. "I'm fine."

"I will kill him for you." His tone is low, almost guttural, and his hot breath brushes my lips. I know he's talking about James. "I will claim this kingdom for you, and he will pay for what he did. In a couple of days, we'll have an army."

I offer him a weak smile. I know he's trying to make me feel better, but justice doesn't negate what has been done. I have to live with the consequences of James biting me for the rest of my life, and I can't help but fear it.

A soft tap at the door makes both of us start.

"Come in," says Callum.

Very slowly, the door opens. A messy mop of dark hair appears through the gap, followed by a small flushed face.

Callum's answering smile is big and easy, and it instantly transforms his face. Warmth radiates from him. It eases some of the anxiety that coils in my chest. I can tell Callum likes children. I think he would make a good father.

"Hello, Alfie," he says. "Can we help you?"

Alfie blushes, and shifts from one foot to the other. He is clearly nervous to be speaking to the big scary alpha of Highfell. "My mum requests the princess's help in the kitchens."

"Does she now?" Callum's green eyes twinkle in the evening light. "She has obviously not tasted the princess's cooking."

I slap his arm, and he chuckles. Loudly.

"It's not that bad!" I protest, though the cook at Madadh-allaidh, Mrs. McDonald, who I was tasked with helping when Callum brought me to the Northlands, might disagree. "I'll be right down, Alfie."

His face reddens even more, and he bows deeply to us both, which seems to further amuse Callum. Alfie turns and scampers down the corridor.

"He's a spirited wee thing, isn't he?" says Callum.

"He is." I glance at the bedside table, where the new love story Elsie lent me, *The Alpha's Secret,* now sits. I smile. "I wonder what Elsie needs."

"Wolves fast on the day of the full moon, so often we have a big meal the night before. I'd not expected Blake to organize anything. Perhaps Elsie has taken it upon herself. You should go. It'll help take your mind off things. I'll go and have a word with Ryan in the meantime." He nods to the figure outside as he hurls another rock into the water. "The lad seems like he's wallowing."

"Goodness, he does, doesn't he? I saw him arguing with Becky earlier. I think she's getting fed up of him talking about Fiona all the time."

"That's the problem with us Wolves. We're very territorial. And very fixated on getting what we want." He brushes his lips against my forehead.

I stand on my tiptoes and plant a kiss on his lips. The wolf flickers in his eyes and he grins, then taps me on my behind. "Go on. Before I get any other ideas on how to pass the time."

***

WHEN I arrive in the Lowfell kitchens, the last thing I expect to see is Elsie chasing a lobster across the flagstones of the small shadowy room, while Alfie races around shrieking.

Her face is bright red, and strands of her dark hair have escaped her braid and stick to her rosy cheeks. I jump to the side as she swoops down, wrestles with the creature, and shoves it into a huge wicker basket—just as another crustacean emerges from the other side of the room and clambers onto the work surface.

"Oh, bloody bollocks!" she cries.

"Bollocks!" roars Alfie. He leaps back, hits the table, and knocks over a bowl of potatoes.

"Quiet, you! Don't use bad words!"

She grabs the escaped lobster, shoves it into the basket, and commands Alfie to pick up all the potatoes he's spilled. I crouch down, pick one of them up, and toss it to him. He catches it with a squeal, and I stand up and rub my now-muddy hands against my brown skirt.

"What on earth have I walked into?" I ask.

"Thank *Ghealach* you're here." Elsie leans against the counter and blows a strand of hair out of her face. Despite the searing heat in here, coming from the fire in the stone hearth and the large pot of water heating up atop it, she wears a long-sleeved grey dress that covers the Night tattoo on her wrist. "Blake wanted to organize a nice meal for tonight. I don't know whose bloody brilliant idea it was to bring six live lobsters back from the market. Arran's, probably. His idea of a joke. Still, they'll taste nice when they're done." My smile falters, and Elsie's eyebrows pinch together. "What is it? Don't tell me you don't like lobster."

I bite my cheek, then walk over to the hearth to peer into the big pot. "I used to. . . I just. . . my brother told me how they were cooked, once."

I was ten years old, and sitting at the family dining room in the palace—my mother and father at either end of the long table. It was her birthday—one of the last ones she would have—and she had dark circles beneath her eyes, but was trying to muster up the energy to act happy. My father didn't bother to make conversation, and soon, the silence was broken only by the snap and crack as he tore off the claws of the creature on his plate and bashed its shell with the small hammer.

I found pleasure in pulling apart the lobster myself—using the nutcracker to tear off its legs and the small fork to pick out its sweet flesh, rather than having the kitchen staff prepare everything like usual. Until my brother, Philip, leaned close with the acidic scent of wine on his breath.

"He said they were put in a pot of cold water while they were alive, then heated up slowly. By the time they realized it was boiling, it was too late. They would clamber over one another, screaming, trying to get out. They could not escape, try as they might. He said it to upset me—he could never bear me having a moment of joy—but the story always stuck with me." My throat tightens. "I've thought about it a lot since I came to the Northlands. Those lobsters. Their ignorance as their lives were taken from them, so slowly they didn't even realize they were trapped. How they didn't fight until it was too late. How they let themselves be killed."

I turn, and Elsie is staring at me. My cheeks heat, and I instantly regret speaking. I turn my gaze to the narrow window and catch a glimpse of an overgrown walled garden outside.

"You got out, Aurora," she says softly. "You escaped."

"My mother didn't." I glance at Alfie. He sits at the table and plays with a couple of potatoes. "Your friend didn't. Sometimes I wonder if I'll ever truly escape." I think about James, and the bite, and the fact that one day, Blake will try to kill Callum in order to be king. "Other times I wonder if, when I clambered out of that pot, I ended up falling straight into the open flames."

Elsie exhales. Loudly. She clucks her tongue, then slams her hand down on the counter. "Oh, bollocks!"

"Bollocks!" mimics Alfie.

My eyes widen. "What's wrong?"

"We can't eat the things now, can we?" Elsie grabs the huge basket, nudging a set of claws that pokes over the edge, and stomps toward the door. "Come on."

"Where are you going?"

"To free the lobsters!"

"What!"

"We'll take them to the loch. Come on!"

A soft laugh escapes me as Alfie squeals with joy and hurries after her. "Free the lobsters!" he cries.

"We can't do that," I say.

"Course we can."

"What will we have for dinner?"

She pulls a face, then glances at the muddy potatoes scattered across the table. "Potatoes? I don't know. We'll figure something out. Come on. Hurry. Before the men find out!"

With Alfie at her heels, she bustles out of the door. Unable to hide my grin, I hurry after her.

Chapter Twenty-Three

"Elsie, darling, what happened to the lobster I paid for?" Blake sits at one head of the alpha table and studies the mushed potato gloop that coats his spoon. His dark shirt is unbuttoned at the collar, and the candles that flicker in the center of the table cast light onto his sharp jaw.

The fire roars in the curved stone hearth at the back of the room, but does little to dispel the shadows. Arran, Jack, and Ryan sit along one side of the table, while Elsie, Alfie, and I sit on the other. Lochlan's clan have their own way of celebrating the night before the full moon, and have traveled to Dawn's Craig to meet with the priestess.

Callum sits at the other head of the table, and smirks at his bowl.

Elsie raises her chin. "They escaped."

Blake cocks his head to one side, as if trying to make sense of this. "What do you mean, they escaped?"

"I don't know!" she says. "They're gone! They got free!"

"How? Where, exactly, did they go?" Blake says. "Are they still here? Am I to find lobsters wandering around my castle?"

Callum turns his laugh into a cough, and Elsie shoots him a dark look. Alfie giggles.

Blake turns to the young boy. "Do you know the whereabouts of the lobsters, Alfie?"

"Swimming!" he says.

"Swimming?" He arches an eyebrow at Elsie. "And so the plot thickens."

"They're in the loch, okay?" She raises her hands. "What do you want me to say?"

There's a creak as Jack leans back in his chair, while the corner of Arran's lip pulls up.

A dimple punctures Blake's cheek now. "Why, may I ask, are they in the loch?"

Elsie points at me, almost knocking over her goblet of wine. "It was her fault!" There's a glint of humor in her eyes.

I put my hand on my chest. "It was your idea!"

"Only because you told me that sad bloody story about the lobster," says Elsie. "About how it didn't even know the water was boiling until it was too late."

I feel the weight of Callum's gaze on my heating cheeks. His expression softens. Some of the humor disappears from Blake's eyes.

"Well, it looks lovely," says Callum as he dips his spoon into the bowl. "What is it?"

"Tattie soup." Elsie juts out her chin. "What else?"

Callum takes a mouthful. "Mm. Delicious." He can barely contain his stupid grin, and the corner of Blake's mouth lifts when he struggles to swallow. "You can really taste the earth."

It's Blake's turn to conceal his laugh by pretending he's clearing his throat, while I slap Callum's arm. "I didn't see any of you gentlemen offering to cook," I say.

"I'm serious," says Callum, looking anything but. "I like it. It's got the gritty crunch I always enjoy with my tatties."

"Oh, piss off!" snorts Elsie. "One of you can cook next time."

"I do a good barbecued lobster," says Jack, a faraway look in his eyes. "Smoky sweet meat, cooked on open flames. Delicious."

"But then we would have been robbed of this treat," says Callum, and Jack grins.

"Lobsters mate for life, you know?" Ryan mumbles suddenly, hunched over his bowl.

All the humor drains from the hall. Elsie stiffens, while Arran looks down at the table. Callum frowns. Jack clears his throat. Blake stills, and I feel that shred of him inside me hardening, as if to stop me from feeling his emotion.

"Like Wolves," chirps Alfie.

It takes me a moment to figure out the strange tension, but then I recall what Callum told me once, about Wolves having mates that were chosen by the Moon Goddess. He said it was a connection more powerful than love. Didn't Elsie say *Ghealach* had other plans for Arran, that he had feelings for another? Was she talking about him having a mate?

"Aye," says Arran softly. "That's right, lad."

The air is too awkward. I want to say something to put people at ease, but words evade me.

"You're a ray of sunshine tonight, Ryan," says Blake, and everyone seems to release a breath.

"Becky finished with him," says Callum.

"Oi! That's private!" snarls Ryan, cheeks reddening.

Callum arches an eyebrow. "Would it hurt you to offer me, your alpha, a bit of respect every once in a while?"

"I would if you wouldn't go around proclaiming my private business!"

I touch Callum's wrist and squeeze, hoping he won't torture the boy any further. He rolls his eyes at me—the boyish gesture at odds with his big physique.

"Ah, young love." Jack grins as he slings his arm over the back of his chair, provoking another snarl from Ryan. "Come out with me tomorrow. We'll do some training to keep your mind off things."

"I'm better than you, anyway," says Ryan.

"Fighting talk, indeed," says Jack. "I suppose we'll see about that. You *are* good with a sword, though." Ryan sits a little straighter, chest puffing out ever so slightly. "Callum teach you?"

"Aye," says Ryan.

Callum grins and shakes his head as he goes back to his soup. Jack was trying to get Callum to fight him a few weeks ago, to learn how Callum fought. I suppose his implication is that if he can beat Ryan, he can beat Callum. Callum doesn't seem threatened by the blatant challenge.

"Aren't lobsters saltwater creatures?" says Arran suddenly, spoon paused halfway to his mouth.

"What? No! No, they're not!" says Elsie, looking at me, alarmed. "Those were freshwater lobsters. They'll be fine."

"I'm sure they'll live long and happy lives." Blake takes a sip of wine. "And soon, Lowfell will be overrun with lobsters. There will be shellfish all over the island, and I'll be known as the oddball alpha who lives in a castle among his crustaceans."

Alfie squeals with delight, clapping his hands together, and Jack pretends he has lobster claws on the other side of the table. A smile spreads across my face as Callum laughs beside me. If I didn't know better, I'd think he was starting to enjoy his time at Lowfell, and the company within its walls.

Strangely, I am, too. I think about what Lochlan said, about Blake collecting broken birds. There's Elsie, abused by her father, and little Alfie, who barely escaped his. Arran sits with a beaker of water, when everyone else has wine. And Jack, whose history I don't know, but whom I catch with a dark look in his eyes every so often.

There's a peace here that I didn't find at Madadh-allaidh, and that I certainly never knew back home. Blake may be an alpha, but he doesn't seem to take the role particularly seriously when the other alphas are not watching.

Yet as laughter spreads around the table, and Elsie pinches Alfie's side with fake lobster claws, I can't help but feel like this is the calm before the storm. Tomorrow night is the full moon. After that, if we manage to knock James off his throne, we will all be enemies once more.

Blake catches my eye across the table, as if he knows what I'm thinking.

I avert my gaze, and have a mouthful of soup.

The corner of my mouth twitches. Callum is right.

It tastes horrible.

Chapter Twenty-Four

The next evening, as the sun descends behind the mountains, Callum and I walk away from the castle walls. My fingers are laced with his.

The energy in Lowfell has been charged all day. As the hours raced by, tension built within me. It's not just fear that makes my skin hum. I feel as if something is awakening within me. Something that longs for release.

To my dismay, Callum left for a few hours, so I was alone with my thoughts all afternoon. I was unable to concentrate, unable to do anything but pace up and down our chambers and prevent myself from searching Lowfell for someone to pick a fight with—preferably Blake. Or Callum, because I didn't want to be left alone.

Now, I keep my emotions and my restlessness close and my head raised as we pass other Wolves gathering by the bank of the loch. Someone is playing bagpipes, Ryan is sitting on the bank with Jack, and the two pass a flask between them. A few Wolves in yellow tartan build a bonfire—assisted by Arran. To them, this is a night of celebration.

I hope the cold wind masks the sound of my racing pulse, and the scent of my fear. I grip Callum's hand more tightly than necessary, and he runs his thumb along my knuckles as the rain-drenched grass squelches beneath our boots.

Lochlan beckons us over, but Callum merely waves in acknowledgement and tugs me into the woodland. We walk in silence for a while, and pass the crumbling chapel. He leads me to a clearing. I halt.

A soft laugh escapes my lips and mists in front of my face. Warmth spreads through me, and some of my tension dissipates. "This is what you were doing today."

He stands beside me and curls his arms around my waist, resting his chin on my head. "Do you like it?"

Candles of varying sizes flicker at the edges of the clearing, about fifty in total, sheltered from the wind by the tall trees. A small campfire crackles in the center, a pile of rugs and furs beside it. The air smells like evergreen and woodsmoke.

I smile. "I like it very much. Thank you."

I walk toward the middle of the clearing, and Callum follows. I glance upward. There is a gap in the evergreen canopy, and the darkening sky strains through. My heart beats faster, and I release a shaky breath. It won't be long.

"Took me a while to find and light the candles." Callum grins. "Ryan helped. He moaned about Becky the entire time, which made it take even longer."

Callum tugs me down onto the rugs with him. He maneuvers behind me, raises his knees on either side of my body, and pulls my back toward his chest—tucking me safely into his arms. I melt against him.

Finally, I draw the courage to ask. "Does it hurt?"

"It's a good feeling. A release. I swear it."

I bite my bottom lip. My entire body is going to break and change, so I can't believe that to be true. There is a part of me that wonders if I should have asked Blake, because I know he would not lie to protect my feelings.

Callum sweeps my hair over my shoulder, and dips his mouth to the back of my neck. Shivers tremble through me as he drags his teeth across the sensitive skin there. "Do you want me to show you?"

"How. . .?"

He brushes his knuckles over my inner thigh, and the restlessness that has been humming beneath my skin all day crescendos. Slowly, deliberately, he pulls up my skirt, and skims his hand up my bare skin.

He brings his lips to my ear. "Do you want me to show you?" His tone is darker, lower.

My breath hitches. "*Yes.*"

He skims his knuckles over my underwear, and I gasp. "Surely it doesn't feel like that."

"I've not finished yet," he whispers, amusement in his tone.

"Show me."

He slides his hand into my underwear, and slowly drags a finger between my thighs. I whimper and arch into him. A low growl vibrates against my back at the slickness he finds there. He coats my bud with it, rubbing a torturous tight circle over the sensitive bundle of nerves. "How does this feel?" he murmurs.

All sensible thought leaves me. All rational fear. I'm just need, and desire, and the heat that builds with each expert stroke of his fingers. "I. . . good. It feels good," I gasp.

I grip his wrist and move my hips. I want him to move faster. Harder. To fill me with his fingers and ease this desperate throbbing ache. He keeps his pace tortuously slow and gentle. A feral moan escapes my lips, and my teeth tingle like they want to sink into something.

His dark chuckle fills my ear. "How about now? How does it feel now, Princess?"

"Frustrating," I growl.

He brings his other hand to my breast over the fabric of my dress, and runs his thumb over my peaked nipple, causing another jolt of pleasure, of frustration, to surge through me. He dips his head, and sucks the sensitive spot behind my ear.

"And now?"

"Please," is all I can murmur.

"This is what it is to be a wolf." He slides his finger down my slickness, and gently circles my entrance. An embarrassing moan scrapes against my throat. "To have something building inside you." He slides his finger into me, and I groan as he fills me. "To feel wild. Feral. Animal." He slides back out, then in, and sweat beads on my skin. "To always be on the edge of something." I arch my back, whimpering. "Never able to release."

"Please," I whisper.

"Until the night of the full moon." He nips my earlobe with his teeth. "Spread your legs."

I allow my thighs to fall open. He slides one finger in, and then the other, stretching me and filling me with delicious pressure. My moan echoes around the clearing, and he makes a low, satisfied sound in his throat. Finally, he gives me what I want. He pumps his hand faster. My head lolls back against his shoulder, and I move my hips against him.

"Fuck, you're so beautiful." He moves his other hand to my throat, and tilts back my head so I'm forced to look at him. I barely notice the wolf in his eyes, or the flush of his cheeks, or the hardness that presses against my lower back through his kilt. "This is what it feels like to shift."

He curls his fingers against my inner wall, hitting that spot deep within me, and it pushes me over the edge. My release crashes through me, more forceful than it ever has before. I writhe against him as the feeling is finally freed. Until, finally, whimpering, moaning, sweating, I still in his arms.

I blink, and everything comes back into focus: the clearing, the crackling fire, the trees swaying in the darkening sky. Callum. His green eyes are bright in the darkness.

I huff a laugh. "I don't believe you. It can't feel like that."

His grin widens. "Perhaps not quite. But it's a release. A good feeling."

He slides his fingers out of me, and I shift against him, tilting my head back against his chest to look at his face. When he holds up his hand, his gaze is drawn to the way his fingers glisten in the firelight. His expression darkens, and heat floods my face. Without warning, he puts them into his mouth and sucks, his eyes shutting for a moment as relief seems to flood through him.

"Callum!"

He opens his eyes, pulls out his fingers, and grins. "What? A wolf thing. I told you, we have an oral fixation.

Fuck. I cannot wait until tomorrow morning. I am going to devour you."

He told me he was going to give me all of him, and let his wolf off its leash, after I shift. Now that my orgasm is ebbing away, the tension coils inside me once more. The sky darkens through the treetops. "How long until it happens?"

"Soon. Can you feel it?"

"Yes." My skin prickles. Hums. Something stirs in my chest. "Yes, I do. I feel—" I gasp and my brow furrows. I feel like something is tugging at my heart and my soul. Pain surges through my body. Panic floods me. Dots dance before my eyes, and darkness seeps into the corners of my vision. Beads of sweat break out onto my brow. "Oh, goddess."

"Princess?" I'm vaguely aware of his jaw tightening. He's far away. I can't hear him over the roar in my ears. "Fuck. I'm sorry. The fever. Not again. Not now."

It wasn't you, I want to tell him. I can't speak. Something rises inside me, and I furiously try to push it down. I can't let it surface. I can't let it consume me. Another heartbeat competes with my own. My soul is frayed and unraveling. He mumbles something about not wanting to do something.

He scoops me into his arms, and strides across the clearing.

"Hold on, Princess." He pulls me into his chest as he mutters to himself. "Where the fuck is Blake?"

Chapter Twenty-Five

The trees sway. Twigs crunch underfoot. Shadows flicker across Callum's jaw. A fire crackles by the loch, and there is laughter in the air. It blurs and fades.

We reach the castle walls and I'm soaked with sweat. I want to shed my clothes. I want to shed my skin. I writhe in Callum's arms.

"Be still," he commands, as he powers across the courtyard. I snarl, and he snarls back—as if he's struggling to control himself as much as I am.

Then we're inside Lowfell Castle. The narrow corridors flicker around us. Doors to drawing rooms and places filled with books become prison cells and torture chambers. He kicks open a door, storms inside the room, and sets me down on something silky and soft. It's cool against my burning skin. The scent of dark pine wraps around me. My vision blurs.

"I need your help." Callum's voice is frantic.

"Don't be so hard on yourself. You can't be *that* bad in bed," Blake drawls, his voice a little slurred.

"Not funny," Callum snarls. "Help her."

Blake is already on his feet, setting down his glass on the ornate black fireplace. He half strides, half stumbles toward us.

"Are you drunk?" growls Callum.

The air is sucked from my lungs as Blake gets closer. *Blake.* The male I loathe even more than James. The male who linked my life to his, and uses me as a pawn in his games. Callum is saying something, reprimanding Blake, I think, but all I hear is my heartbeat thundering in my ears.

Blake's pupils dilate. The shadows flicker around him.

Monster.

A low, warning snarl rumbles out of me. My canines *ache* and his gaze drops to my mouth. Our connection is no longer just a shadow pulsing in my chest. The bond is a thread, and it vibrates between us like a living, breathing thing. The veins in his neck pulse. His face changes, hardens.

"Take your pet out of here. I don't want her in my bed." His voice becomes as cold as ice.

"What do you—"

"*Now*, Callum."

"This isn't normal!"

"It is for a half-wolf. Get her out of—"

I launch off the bed and charge at him. We careen back, and the wooden chair by his desk breaks and splinters as we crash to the ground. His body is warm, hard. My thighs clench around his hips, and my face slams into the crook of his neck. The taste of salt and dark pine floods my mouth.

I'm going to tear his fucking throat out.

He fists my hair, grabbing my head and yanking it back. My scalp is on fire. I growl and he arches back his head, closes his eyes, and exposes his throat. "Callum, get her off me." There's a trace of panic in his tone. I feel it. I *taste* it. It's delicious.

I lurch toward him, but an arm hooks around my waist and drags me off him. My feet are raised from the floor for a moment as Callum pulls me into him. He wraps his arms around my body, trapping me, imprisoning me. I thrash against him.

"*Stop it*," he snarls in my ear. It's a tone he hasn't used on me before—commanding and dominant. His alpha voice. "What's wrong with her?" The thing that rages in my chest stills, but doesn't settle. A growl vibrates in my throat. Callum is breathing fast, deep. Every muscle in his body is tight. "What's wrong with *you*?"

Blake is on the floor. He's pushed himself against the wall beneath the window. One of his knees is raised and his palms are flat on the ground, making the muscles in his forearms more pronounced. His dark hair is messy, and his broad chest moves up and down quickly.

The wolf shines in his eyes.

And what a sight he is, on the floor, cowering at my feet, his skin slick with sweat, glowing bronze with the light from the fire. A couple of strands of dark hair cling to his forehead.

Blake angles his head to one side. He returns my smile. It's a dangerous, wicked thing that makes my heart pound even faster than the other two pulses that thunder in my ears.

"Blake." Callum's tone is stern, a warning—though his voice sounds strained. His arms are tense around my stomach and he's breathing fast, too.

"Do you think I'm afraid of *you*, little rabbit?" Blake's voice is a cool whisper of silk. "Is that what you think? The full moon is coming. I'm afraid of myself, of what I might do. We can both scent what you want in the air. Tell me, is it me you want to fuck? Or Callum? Or do you want us both at the same time?"

"Blake, that's enough," growls Callum.

I launch myself toward him, and Callum pulls me back. Blake's head snaps toward the alpha of Highfell. "Get her the fuck out of here, then."

"I can't."

"What do you mean, you can't?"

"It's the full moon, Blake!" A frustrated growl rips from his throat. "If I move, I'm going to rip your fucking head off."

Power rumbles between the two of them, pushing and pulling me in two directions. Pine and shadow collides with the mountains at dawn. Peace and war. Love and hate. A whimper escapes me as the feeling heightens. My senses erupt. I taste seawater and rum at the back of my throat, rose thorns pierce my skin, the steel of battle roars in my ears, and wild bracken cracks beneath my feet. I can't breathe. Voices, whispers, fill my ears. Fingers claw my body. They pull at me. Taunt me. Try to take from me like everyone always has.

A low sound scrapes against Blake's throat and his head arches back. Every muscle in his body locks. "Fuck. I can feel her."

Callum's arms tighten around me as Blake rises to his feet.

"Stay where you are," Callum warns.

Blake cracks his neck. His features become cold and hard, chiseled from ice. The wolf is feral in his eyes.

"Don't." Callum jerks me back toward the door. "Don't you fucking dare."

He sounds far away. Every nerve in my body is alight. My soul is shattering, a million jagged pieces that pierce my insides like glass. I barely notice Blake moving toward us, Callum throwing me behind him and shielding me with his body, the two males making impact. I erupt. A bloodcurdling scream pierces my ears, and I think it's coming from me. Someone grabs me. A loud crash. My knees buckle.

Bright, blinding light.

Black.

Chapter Twenty-Six

Moonlight floods the room.

A low growl. Primal. Animal.

Bared teeth. Eyes glowing.

A whisper of fur. Two beasts. One black, one tawny. Both huge. A crash. Books cascade to the floor. A desk breaks. They're fighting, I think.

Howls permeate the castle walls.

Amid it all, a thought.

I have not shifted.

***

I'M BEING torn apart.

My cheek is pressed against the floorboards. I whimper and push myself to my knees. A snarl makes my head rear up.

Callum and Blake have shifted. They're both huge, the size of bears, though Callum is slightly bigger. The moonlight shines off their glossy coats. The desk is shattered around them, and glass glints on the floor in front of the fireplace where one of Blake's bottles has smashed.

Callum has the scruff of Blake's neck in his maw and as he bites harder, pain flares in the same spot on my neck.

"Stop!" I croak.

Callum's head snaps toward me, and his growl dies when his green eyes lock onto mine. I feel him, sense him—his scent floods my lungs, and with it, a calmness settles over me. He's still in there. He's still Callum.

My eyes widen. Blake hurtles into Callum's side. The tawny wolf flies across the room and slams into the wall by the door. He releases a whimper as he crashes onto the floor. Books, piled by the wall, cascade on top of him.

"Callum!"

I turn toward him, but there's a thud, and Blake looms over me. His paws are huge, and his claws dig into the floorboards. I try to crawl away, but he sinks his teeth into the back of my dress and drags me across the floor. I land on my back by the foot of the bed.

"Blake, stop it!"

I try to get up. A great weight presses down on my stomach, squeezing the breath out of me. Blake's body is stiff, his ears pulled back. Callum is on his feet, and the two lock eyes. Both growl.

I can tell Callum is still himself, but Blake feels different. Feral. Dangerous. His shadows, which exist inside me, move and spread in all directions, and I can make no sense of them. I shove him, and my fingers sink into silky fur.

"*Blake.* Get off me."

My vision blurs as Callum paces back and forth. Every time Callum gets closer, Blake's growl vibrates through me, and Callum inches back.

Another surge of pain crashes over me. My soul feels frayed, like threads of it are being pulled apart. I stiffen, then whimper. Blake's great weight pushes down on my stomach, squeezing the breath out of me.

Sweet darkness pulls me under.

***

MY FACE is pressed against something hot and hard, and the scent of male and forests fills my lungs. My skin buzzes, but I no longer feel as if my soul is being shredded apart. A soft sigh escapes me. I peel open my eyelids. My heart stills.

My face is crushed against Blake's bare chest. Our bodies are flush, and one of my hands is slung over his waist, as if I clung to him in my sleep. Blake's fingers brush the back of my neck.

Adrenaline surges through my body. I suppress the snarl that builds inside me as my teeth tingle. Something whispers. *Bite. Bite. Bite.* There's something wrong with me. Panic swirls in my chest, and my breathing is fast. I'm going to. . . I can't stop myself from. . . I open my mouth.

Blake stirs. He dips his chin, and panic flares in his eyes.

He is wrenched away from me. There's the thud of bare feet, the dragging sound of Blake trying to find his footing, then a slam and a rattle.

I push myself to my knees. Callum presses Blake against the wall by the cold hearth. My eyes widen. Both are naked. Their clothes are torn in shred on the floorboards, among splintered wood and books and parchment. Weak sunlight strains through the window and highlights the shuddering muscles in Callum's back.

"What the fuck?" he growls.

Blake's hair is a mess, and though he manages his usual bored expression, his cheeks are flushed. His eyes lock onto mine.

"Don't look at her." Callum grips his chin. "Look at me."

"Your cock is touching my leg."

Callum makes a frustrated noise in his throat. He releases Blake, but doesn't step back. "What the fuck were you doing last night? You were guarding her. Why?"

"Why do you think?"

"You don't want to know what I think."

Blake exhales. "She has a part of my life force inside her. Of course I was going to guard her."

"Oh, that was why, was it?"

I tune out their bickering. I sit back against the side of the bed. The fur that hangs from the mattress is soft against my back. I tilt back my head, and feel the Northlands sun on my skin. Outside, the wind rustles the trees and stirs the loch. The tips of the mountains are shrouded with mist.

Some of the anxiety that has been knotting inside me for weeks unravels. I still have too many questions about last night, about what's happening to me.

But a slow smile spreads across my face.

I didn't shift.

"Please. I have no interest in your pet," says Blake. "You shouldn't have brought her here on the night of the full moon. What did you expect?"

"For you to exercise a little self-restraint—"

"Next time, I will strive to be the picture of composure that you were last night, Callum—"

As they continue to argue, I cast my gaze around Blake's chambers. I'd not taken it in properly, last night. It's smaller than ours and simply furnished, despite him being the alpha of this castle, and having the pick of any room he wants.

The bed I lean against is barely big enough to fit two people, and is pushed against the wall. The mess is the outcome of the fight between Blake and Callum last night. The clutter, though. . . that must have been here already. There are books scattered across the floor, among the remnants of the broken desk, but they're also piled against the stone walls and stacked in the corners.

While he's distracted by Callum, I pick one up, curious about Blake's reading choices. It's full of sketches of monsters—winged beasts, half dead humanoid figures, a water creature with entrails curling out of its body like tentacles. My eyes lock with those of a serpentine creature, that—from the smudges around its scaled body—seems to wear shadows like a second skin.

There's a mark on its tail. It's the same symbol that is inked on Elsie's wrist. When I turn the page, the mark has been drawn in greater detail on the end of a hot iron. These are Night's prisoners, now bound to his prison in the sky. I wonder if Blake is taking the rumors about Night's acolytes, and the Night Prince seriously. I put the book down.

Numerous bottles of liquor stand on his mantelpiece, and one rolls across the floor, near Callum's feet as he continues to berate Blake.

The scent of lavender hits me, as well as another floral smell I don't recognize. Dried purple and white flowers scatter the floor—among bits of parchment. The lavender provokes an ache, deep within me, and I pick up one of the sprigs and twist it between my fingers. My mother used to stitch it into pouches, and place them beneath my pillow before bed. She said they would help me sleep, and keep the nightmares away. I wonder if Blake uses it for a similar purpose.

I drop it, and it lands on a sketch of a labyrinth with a hexagonal center.

"Can you two put some clothes on, please?" I say.

Blake and Callum both shut their mouths. Callum looks over his shoulder sharply. His expression softens. He releases Blake, crosses the room, and crouches down before me.

Still unclothed.

I should be used to it by now, but heat stains my cheeks.

"Are you alright?" He cups my face in his big hand.

I keep my eyes resolutely on his as Blake walks to his armoire. When he opens it and pulls out breeches and a shirt, my resolve wavers and I look. Raised white ridges crisscross the muscles in his back. I overheard him tell Callum he was whipped for being a half-wolf.

"I didn't shift," I say.

A slow grin spreads across Callum's face. "No. You didn't. You're not a wolf after all."

I feel Blake's emotion. That thread between us shudders, as if he is holding something back.

"You sound almost as relieved as I am," I say. "Did you not want me to be a wolf?"

He brushes his thumb against my cheek. "I know it's not what you wanted, that's all." I frown, because I'm not sure he's being entirely truthful. "Come here." He scoops me into his arms, and I reflexively hook my hands around his neck. Without a backward glance at Blake, he carries me out of the room.

"I hope you're going to put some clothes on," I say, as Callum carries me down the corridor.

"Don't need them." He kicks open the door to our chambers and grins. "Not for what I have planned."

He drops me onto the bed, and I squeal. "Callum!"

"What?" he asks as he crawls over me, then drags his teeth along my throat. "You know, it would be nice if, for once, I could spend the morning after the full moon with you *not* smelling like my worst enemy." He shifts down and plants kisses on my collarbone, then my torso, and then between my legs through the fabric of my dress. I breathe in sharply. "Last time, there was not much I could do about it. This time, I plan to rectify the situation."

"Is that so?"

He kneels on the mattress. His eyes glint when they meet mine—full of mischief. "I promise it will be very pleasurable for you."

Who am I to deny him?

***

CALLUM MAKES good on his promise.

We spend the morning in bed, with him drawing moans from my lips until I'm liquid in his arms. And then he starts all over again. He remains careful with me, though. Gentle. His promise to unleash himself upon me after the full moon is nullified. I didn't shift.

At noon, after getting some food brought up from the kitchens, he goes to meet with Lochlan and Jack to plan tomorrow's ambush. I spend the rest of the afternoon reading in the armchair by the fire, my legs curled beneath me.

As the sky darkens, so do my emotions. I was scared to shift, but being a wolf gave me an explanation for my mother's death, and a connection to her. It connected me to Callum, as well. I'm sure his high spirits this morning were linked to my inability to shift. I think he's glad I'm still human. *Still weak*, that wild part of me whispers.

I drop the book I'm reading onto the chair. I walk to the window. The bloated sky is dark grey, and shadows shroud the peaks of the mountains. The water ripples in the wind.

It doesn't make sense. There's something inside me, pressing against my skin. I've felt it since James bit me. I keep falling into fever. Lochlan believes my mother was a wolf, and my father must have thought I was like her, because he had me whipped so I would suppress it. I wanted to bite Blake last night. I wanted to bite him this morning. I almost did.

I can't accept that the human part of me would ever do such a thing.

Movement draws my gaze. A dark figure walks to the water's edge, hands in the pockets of his long coat. He looks out onto the loch, and the wind stirs his black hair.

I felt something from Blake, this morning. He knows something about me. Something he is concealing.

"Stay where you are," I whisper, even though I know he can't hear me.

I stride to the armoire, and pull on a warm coat and boots.

I'm going to find out what Blake knows.

Chapter Twenty-Seven

There's a light drizzle in the air.

It washes over me as soon as I walk through the tunnel leading to the courtyard and out onto the grounds surrounding Lowfell. It's dark, and the windows of the castle behind me flicker with soft orange light. Despite the rain, the air is crisp and smells like mud and woodsmoke. I pull my coat tighter, and, boots sinking into the earth, approach the figure who looks out onto the loch.

If he's embarrassed about what happened last night, or how we woke up this morning, he gives no indication of it.

"You feel different today." My voice is almost swallowed by the sound of the branches swaying overhead, and the rain hitting the loch.

Blake's shirt clings to his chest and torso beneath his open coat. A few errant strands of his hair stick to his forehead. "I always feel better after it's happened. Lighter."

"Is it the act of shifting you don't like? Or being a wolf?"

"Both. I cannot control it. I like to be in control."

"I noticed," I say. I catch a hint of one of his dimples. "Callum doesn't think I'm a wolf."

"What do you think?"

He's the last person I want to come to for help. Yet. . . "Am I a wolf?"

He drags his teeth over his bottom lip as he looks out on the mountains. "Yes."

"Why didn't you say anything? You let Callum—and me—believe otherwise."

He shrugs. "Callum wasn't too pleased with me this morning. As for you, I'm letting you know now, aren't I?"

I sigh, and my breath mists in front of my face. "How do you know for sure I'm a wolf?"

"I wouldn't have been able to share my life force with you if you were human." He turns to face me. Rain runs down his cheeks and moistens his lips. "I saw you, the night when I shared my life force with you. I caught glimpses of your dreams, your memories, your thoughts. Was it not the same for you?"

I think of the fevered images and sounds that filled my being—screams, and scalpels, and darkness. "Yes."

A pensive look crosses his face. "I found you. I saw your wolf form. She's the color of moonlight."

Something tightens inside me. I feel stripped bare, as if Blake has seen things of me that no one else has. It's not right. A part of me wants to get away from him, to run back to the castle and find Callum. My legs won't move. Even when he slips his hands into his coat pockets and turns back to the loch.

I think of all the experiments Blake has done on other Wolves. "Have you ever known a wolf to not shift on the night of the full moon?"

"No. Never."

"Why didn't I shift?"

His curiosity pulses inside me. "That's the question, isn't it, little rabbit?"

We both look out onto the mountains. The shadows hide their peaks.

"We have another problem," he says.

"What?"

"My source from Madadh-allaidh has delivered some bad news."

My pulse quickens. "Is Fiona alright?"

"As far as I know. It's Claire. Apparently she got herself captured by Alexander's men on her way to Madadh-allaidh." His jaw tightens. "Claire is James's... Claire is important to James. He'll want to get you quickly, so he can trade you for her."

I nod. "We should be ready by tomorrow, shouldn't we? After the ambush?"

"We'll have an army, if all goes well. Still, the thought that James might be panicking makes me uneasy. I think he'd do anything to get Claire back. He might make his own move against us." He runs a hand along his jaw. "It really is strange you didn't shift. Perhaps if you'll let me run some tests—"

I step back, and almost slip in the mud. I'm not as adverse to the idea as the last time he suggested it, but I can't forget that he's plotting against us.

A dimple punctures his cheek. "Do you think I'm going to hurt you, little rabbit?"

"I don't know. Are you?"

He shrugs, and turns his gaze back to the mountains to indicate the end of our conversation. "Let me know if you change your mind."

***

MORNING MIST shrouds the loch when Callum rides south with a small party of men, the next morning, to ambush Alexander and his men. I wanted to come along, but Callum was as alarmed about Claire being kidnapped as Blake. The two alphas think James might be waiting for me to leave Lowfell.

I watch them from the arched window in the stairwell outside the library, a cloak wrapped tightly around me to ward off the chill. The horses' hooves thunder against the wild terrain, and I can just about make out the yellow of Lochlan's kilt, and Jack's dark clothing, before they disappear into the mountains. I rub my hands together to bring some heat into them, then retreat into the library.

As the morning passes, the weather changes. The sky becomes heavy with grey clouds, and the air feels thick and muggy. Static energy prickles against my skin, and a ball of restlessness coils inside me, mingling with a twinge of anxiety. I think a storm is coming.

Sitting in the window seat, I pore through various texts, my vision blurring, my concentration waning.

I know Callum can look after himself, but I'm worried. Alexander is a fearsome foe, and I know now what my people do to Wolves. I recall the fur coat that hung in my wardrobe in the Borderlands, made from a wolf on the night of a full moon.

"Read anything interesting lately, little rabbit?" Blake leans against the doorframe.

I flick the page, and go back to the account I'm reading of an alpha in the Snowlands named the Shadow Wolf. It seems he was devoted to Night, and he was looking for the Heart of the Moon to free him from his prison. "Do you know, I think there may be a storm coming, Blake?"

He wanders over, and his boots thud against the floorboards. His shadow looms over me as he leans against the stone wall near the window seat by my feet. His scent of ink and night-soaked forests washes over me.

"I think you may be right," he says.

"Do the Wolves in your clan know you're a big baby who is afraid of thunder?"

"Obviously not."

I flick another page. "Let us hope they do not find out."

A dimple punctures his cheek. "Indeed."

There's a rustle as Blake picks up the book atop the pile by my feet. "This one is no good." He places it on the shelf beside him, and rifles through the rest. "Nor this one. This one is dull. And *this* one—if you wish for a more comprehensive guide to the Battle of Shadow and Snow, Erikson's is better." I grit my teeth as his pile of discarded books grows. "Ah, but *this* one. . . this one is interesting."

I make the mistake of glancing up. He's opening the book that Elsie gave me. *The Alpha's Secret*. An embarrassing sound scrapes against my throat as I lurch forward and snatch it from his hands. "Give me that!" I adjust myself on the window seat's cushion.

"I can have a word with Callum, if you like, little rabbit. Give him some tips, if he is not performing to your satisfaction."

I fight the flush in my cheeks. "Have you nothing better to do than attempt to vex me?"

"Attempt? I don't *attempt* anything. I always achieve my goals."

"Fine. Well done. You have succeeded at being the singularly most irritating male I've ever encountered. Go and congratulate yourself elsewhere."

"It's my castle. You're welcome to leave, if my presence bothers you so much."

I roll my eyes, and go back to my book about the Snowlands. "I have a theory about the bond, by the way."

"You do? I'm all ears, little rabbit."

I smile, because I sense him putting his guard up. He's caging his emotions so I won't feel them. I slide my feet from the cushion on the window seat, and turn so I'm facing him. I study his features—his light-brown eyes, framed by dark lashes, his chiseled jaw, his hand resting on the bookshelf. I want to be able to detect any change in his demeanor.

He leans forward, placing his hands on either side of my thighs, his fingers sinking into the cushion. His face is close to mine, and his eyes gleam, like he knows what I'm trying to do and he's showing me how unconcerned he is. Arrogant bastard.

I inch closer, so our breath mingles. "I think the Heart of the Moon can break it," I say.

His lips part, and he gasps softly. Triumph swells inside me, until I realize he's making fun of me. A frustrated noise scrapes my throat, and I jerk up my knee so I can hit him in the crotch.

He grabs my calf, his fingers curling around the muscle. My skirt has ridden up, and the heat of his hand sears my bare skin. He stiffens slightly. My breath hitches.

"You treacherous serpent!" I pull away, and he releases me.

He grins—one of his stupid real grins—and stands straighter. The bookshelf creaks as he leans against it. "Interesting theory. Although the Heart of the Moon has been lost for centuries."

"I have a theory about that, too, actually." I bring my legs back up onto the window seat.

"Ah, so that's why you're reading about the Snowlands. You've been speaking to Lochlan. About your mother's journey from the Snowlands, and the moonflower at Glas-Cladach, I presume?"

My head snaps toward him. "How did you know about that?"

His brow creases as his amusement pulses through me. "I was the one who told the Wolves to look for the Heart of the Moon in the Borderlands, remember?"

"You knew Sebastian had been there."

"Of course I did, little rabbit. I have eyes everywhere."

I pick my book up. "Fine. You're so clever. Why don't you go and bother someone else?"

"I'd rather bother you."

I nod at the dark grey clouds that roll over the mountains outside the window—dulling the orange and the greens in the wild landscape. "Shouldn't you start poisoning yourself in preparation for the storm? Like you did last time."

He sighs. "Perhaps. I think I've finally got the ratio right for a sleeping tonic that works on Wolves."

"Good for you. I hope you don't accidentally slip and give yourself too much wolfsbane."

A soft chuckle escapes his lips. "You'd better hope that's true. If I die, you die too, little rabbit." He pushes off from the shelf and strolls to the doorway. "If the tonic fails, perhaps I'll distract myself by discovering what the alpha's secret might be." He raises the book Elsie gave me, which I didn't realize he'd picked back up. His eyes glint. "If the other book you were reading is anything to go by, I'm guessing it has something to do with his abnormally large cock."

A soft growl scrapes, unprovoked, against my throat. "Oh, go away!"

He laughs softly to himself as he heads down the spiral staircase, and I'm finally left in peace.

***

BY NIGHTFALL, Callum has still not returned.

The shadows in the library are long and ominous and thunder rumbles through the castle. It's like a bad omen of things to come. Worry tightens my chest. I need to know that Callum is alright. I feel helpless, because there's nothing I can do.

I'm not usually afraid of the dark, but I shiver when I put my books away, grab my candle, and hurry down the stairs. The torches in the corridors burn low as I make my way back to our chambers. I want to be in bed, safe, under the covers.

I quicken my step. I hum the tune my mother used to sing to me as a child. One of the vials of wolfsbane I took from the infirmary is in the pocket of my dress, and I let its weight comfort me.

I sigh when I reach the corridor leading to our bedchambers.

There's a footstep behind me, and thunder echoes through the castle. I spin around. Ian, the blond wolf from Lochlan's clan, stands in front of me. I gasp and reach for the wolfsbane. He slams me into the wall. There's a sickening crack when my head hits the stone, and Ian's freckles blur while the corridor swims around me.

With all my strength, I knee him in the crotch. He doubles over and I scramble away. "Blake!"

He hooks an arm around my waist and throws me back. I land on the ground, the wind knocked out of me. I try to get up, but he lands on top of me and straddles my chest. Two more men appear from the shadows, and look down at me with merciless eyes.

"James was right," says Ian. "You're the enemy, not him."

"You're a fool," I gasp. "This won't work out the way you expect. Callum and Blake will kill—"

He pulls a cloth from his pocket and clamps it over my face. The acrid scent of chemicals floods my nostrils. I writhe beneath Ian, but I can't free myself. Panic crashes through me.

Ian grins. "It's time to meet the king."

His face fades, and darkness pulls me under.

Chapter Twenty-Eight

The darkness is suffocating. It takes a moment for my eyes to adjust. I'm in a long corridor, lined with cells. My heart jolts when I see the symbol etched into one of the cell doors. It's Night's mark. I'm in his prison.

A figure walks away from me. His breeches and shirt are stained grey by the darkness. His footsteps are hurried, and I wonder if this is his dream or mine. Is he as disturbed to be here as I am?

I can't quite remember what happened before I came here, but it feels urgent I reach him.

"Blake?" I whisper. Something hisses from beyond the door of the cell behind me, and my heart jolts. I hurry away from it. "Blake!"

He doesn't turn. I don't think he can hear me. I run after him. Even though my footsteps punctuate the darkness, he doesn't acknowledge me. I feel his warmth. I note the bunched-up muscles of his back. I reach for him.

"Blake! I need your help!"

The ground dissolves before I can touch him.

I fall through endless darkness.

I'm in the Church of Light and Sun, only the wilderness has taken it. Moss coats the stone altar, thick like green velvet. Vines burst through the ground and curl around my ankles. They snap from the walls and twist around my wrists to hold my arms outstretched.

But I didn't sin. A version of my voice whispers through the foliage that lines the domed roof.

All women sin, child. The shadows respond and they sound like the High Priest. *Your mother was a sinner. And you are a sinner too. Do you want the Sun Goddess to be angered?*

Vines crack down on my back and jerk me forward. Hot tears swell in my eyes. I don't want to plead. I don't want to beg. I try to remind myself that this is a dream, but my back is being torn open and blood pools on the floor tiles. A copper scent hangs in the air.

I'm screaming when a figure emerges from the crypt. His footsteps echo as he walks toward me.

His eyes glow, feral and amber.

"*Fight*," he says.

***

I BREATHE in sharply. I'm sprawled across the floor and my head is thumping. The air tastes like stagnant water, and my dress is damp. There's a barred wall in front of me. I've been here before.

I scramble to my knees. A cot is pushed against one wall, and there's a bucket in the corner. Shackles hang from the ceiling on rusty chains, and fear prickles down my spine. This is the cell in the manor house, a stopping point that Blake brought me to before I was given back to Sebastian. Blake taunted me here, then tried to get me to marry James.

It's close to the Borderlands. James must have organized a trade with Alexander, and he could be on his way now.

I shiver. I slide my hand into my pocket and grasp the small vial of wolfsbane. It's not much—James's army could be waiting for me outside these dungeons—but I can't go back to the south. I can't be the property of another Borderlands lord—especially not Alexander. I think he'll use me so my father will pardon him. I'm sure he'll hurt me, too. The ghost of his shouts in the throne room after I told my father he was planning to commit treason haunt the cell.

My head fuzzy, I start to form a plan.

I pray to any goddess that will listen for the strength to survive.

I pray that Callum is okay, and Blake knows I'm gone.

I'm sure that both of them will try to find me. I only hope they get here before it's too late.

***

WHERE IS he?

The torchlight flickers. The hours bleed together. I shiver on the cot with my knees pulled up to my chest. Everything in the cell is damp—the walls, the sheets, my dress. I ache with the cold.

I have felt like a prisoner for most of my life, but my gilded cage was very different to this one. I want to feel the sun, and the tickle of pine-scented wind on my face. The hike to Dawn's Craig, where the earth muddied my hands and the air was so crisp I could taste it, feels like a lifetime ago. I'm not sure how much time passes by, only every drip seems to count down to the inevitable. I'm going to be sent to the Borderlands—a fate that may be worse than death. Or perhaps James merely means to execute me to antagonize Callum.

At one point, a man in a blue kilt, his fair hair tied into a knot atop his head, passes me a hard bread roll through the bars. I recognize him from Madadh-allaidh. Duncan, I think his name is. I ask him what's happening, where James is, what James plans to do with me. He answers each question with a grim smile before turning his back and heading up the stairs.

I wait, my jaw clenched, for James to appear and seal my fate. I wait for Callum. I wait for Blake. Insecurities gnaw at my insides like the rats that scurry through the dungeons, their little feet tapping against the stone floor. Hunger hollows my stomach. My head thumps and I don't know whether it's dehydration or the onset of the short bursts of fever that keep washing over me.

Why hasn't Callum come?

I see faces in the shadows—midnight hair and feral eyes and taunting smiles. Blake haunts me. The darkness shifts, and I think it's him. Screams echo through the dungeons, even though I'm alone, and I hear the scrape of metal scalpels and Blake's laughter. I wake, tangled in the sheets, whimpering. Darkness rages inside me, cold and endless, and it tastes like pine and poison.

I vow to myself, to the Goddesses of the Sun and the Moon, that I'll survive this. Callum will end James and take his throne. I'll break the bond with Blake, and never return home to the south. We will both be free.

Yet Callum is not here. I'm alone.

I don't know whether it's day or night when footsteps approach. For a moment, I let myself imagine it's Callum and he has come for me.

There you are, Princess. You didn't think I'd leave you alone, did you? I imagine his thick Northlands voice, warm and comforting. I imagine his arms around me, and the solid safety of his body.

Duncan shatters the illusion. He is flanked by two men in green kilts, who enter my cell, grab me under my arms, and drag me into the corridor. My legs barely support me as they escort me up a narrow stairway. I'm cold and sweating as something wild inside me tries to surface.

"Where are you taking me?" I gasp.

"Quiet."

Noise hits me as soon as we reach the ground floor. Shouts infiltrate it from outside. I'm pulled past a window, and catch a glimpse of men guarding the building, their swords glinting in the moonlight. My heart beats faster.

I'm dragged around a corner, through some double doors, into what could have been a ballroom once. My heart almost stops. The room is vast and moonlit, and the wall is half torn down on one side. Cold wind blows through it and rocks the dusty chandelier. Six men sit around a long table.

James sits at one end. He leans back in his chair with his legs slightly parted in a display of dominance. His shirtsleeves are rolled to his elbows to display the floral tattoo on one of his arms.

Robert sits beside him—the alpha of the clan who wear green tartan. He's a huge male with a shaved head who took on the role of the Wolf King when James was absent. He leans toward James and whispers something as I'm pulled closer to them. James grins.

The other men who are facing me—no, the other *alphas*—are familiar, too, though I can't put names to their faces. Dread roils in my stomach. These are the alphas from Madadh-allaidh who support James's claim to the throne.

I fight every instinct I have to struggle, and keep myself limp. Pliant. Unassuming.

I'm thrown to the floor at James's feet, and I let myself crumple onto the chipped tiles, my dress pooling around me.

"I thought you wouldn't kneel before a false king, Princess." James's gruff voice echoes around the space. The alphas jeer. One of them growls. "How things have changed."

Adrenaline crashes through me. This is the male who bit me, who attacked me, who tried to force me to marry him. He's going to send me to a man who will hurt me. Loathing mixes with my fear. I don't think I can get away from all of these men, but I want him to know what it is to be afraid.

I take a couple of deep breaths to steel myself.

I launch myself at him like a rabid animal. I expect to knock him off his chair, but his feet are planted firmly on the ground. The chair merely rocks before he grabs my waist. A surprised sound escapes his lips.

"I didn't know you felt that way about me, Princess," says James, and Robert laughs. "But—"

I grab his face. The amusement drains from his eyes. A hissing sound fills the ballroom as his skin burns beneath my fingers, which I'd dowsed with my vial of wolfsbane. He grabs my wrists, and hurls me across the room. His roar reverberates off the high ceiling. I land, hard, on the cold tiles, the wind knocked out of me. My elbow bangs hard against the floor, and I suppress my whimper.

There's a loud bang, like the door slamming open, then uproar. Men shout. Chairs are scraped back as the alphas jump to their feet. "Tie her up," snarls James. Through the chair legs, I see one man get thrown to the ground. Boots thud. A growl fills the space. I don't know what's happening, instincts take over. I need to escape.

I scramble to my knees.

James's eyes shift as they lock onto mine. "*Get back down.*" He puts the force of his wolf behind his words. It's like being knocked back by an avalanche. He is using the Àithne—the alpha's command—on me. I grit my teeth and withstand it, before shoving it off. I get up and run.

Duncan grabs me under my arms and drags me to a column that supports the ceiling. He wrenches my arms around it and binds my wrists with rope. A male roar fills the air, but that wildness inside me wants release and I can't focus on it. A scream builds inside me, hollow and endless.

A smooth laugh cuts through the chaos like a blade. I breathe in sharply.

Blake strolls toward the end of the table. His black shirt is stiff and buttoned up to the collar, though his dark hair is as unruly as usual. He drops into one of the seats, and throws his arm over the back. He winks at me.

My heart squeezes. Callum is behind him, and I realize what caused the uproar. They must have just arrived. He is carved out of rage and thunder. He has a foot on the neck of one of the alphas, who must have risen to greet him, while a blond man in a light-green tartan kilt holds a dagger to his throat. Callum barely seems to notice.

It strikes me how unpoised he looks in comparison to Blake. His cheeks are flushed, and his dark-blond hair windswept, like he rode fast to get here. There's a tear on his shirt, and a streak of blood that I hope is not his. The wolf flares in his eyes as he stares at his brother.

"Touch her again, I dare you," he growls.

I can practically sense his wolf pushing against his skin—wanting to claim, to protect, to kill.

"Callum," I whisper.

"It's going to be okay, Rory." His voice is rough. "No one is going to hurt you."

"We'll see about that," growls James.

A dimple punctures Blake's face. "We're here to negotiate the terms of your release, little rabbit."

Chapter Twenty-Nine

We're here to negotiate the terms of your release, little rabbit.

Blake's voice echoes around the derelict ballroom. I'm breathing hard, and the bindings pinch my wrists. I don't want to negotiate. I want Callum to challenge James, and make him pay.

The alphas on their feet around the table look at me like I'm prey. Wolf eyes glint in the darkness. The man on his back, beneath Callum's foot, gasps for breath and Callum pushes his boot down harder.

Only Blake seems calm, though I know him well enough to guess it's an act. He sits back in his chair and straightens his collar. Beside him, Callum's chest rises and falls deeply, and veins throb in his neck.

"Let her go," he growls.

"No," says James. There are three blistered lines down both of his cheeks where I attacked him. They look like claw marks. "Not until I'm finished with her."

"If you touch her—"

"You'll what? Defy me? Betray me? Attempt to lead an uprising against the throne?" James's voice increases in volume. "It seems you're already doing those things, brother. We are at *war*. Our people are dying. And you see fit to set wolf against wolf, when our real enemies lie south of the border." The alphas murmur in agreement. The man holding the dagger to Callum's throat tightens his grip on the hilt, and his knuckles whiten. Callum doesn't seem to notice. "When our real enemy is *here*. You align yourself with the daughter of the conqueror who invades our lands, the prize of the lord who holds Claire in his kennels, the lass who was betrothed to the man who flayed our mother!"

The color drains from Callum's face. He clenches his fists, as if he can hide his shock and pain. Regret swims through me.

I'd broken the news of her death to Callum, but I didn't disclose my suspicions about how she was murdered, gleaned when James told me about the fur coat that had arrived addressed to his father. I'd wanted to spare him that pain.

I hate James for using this against him, as much as I hate him for what he has done to me.

Callum blinks a couple of times. "Rory is not our enemy."

"Sit down, Brother." The wolf disappears from James's eyes. "You and I have a lot to discuss." He nods at the man who holds a blade to Callum's throat. "Put that away, Hamish. You can all sit back down, too."

Hamish pulls back and sheaths his dagger. He sits, and the others do, too. Callum removes his foot from the alpha's neck. The male, who seems younger than the others, pushes himself to his feet. He narrows his eyes at Callum.

"Cunt," he mutters.

"Don't test me, Kenneth," snarls Callum.

Kenneth sits down and folds his arms as if he's unbothered, but his face is as red as his hair.

"There's nothing to discuss, James," says Callum. "You took my lass, and you will die for it. First, I shall be taking her back."

He strides toward me. Duncan points a blade at my throat. I gasp and raise my chin to stop my skin from puncturing. Callum halts.

"I'd advise you to reassess, Brother," says James.

Flexing his hand at his side, Callum walks back to the table. He seats himself at its head, opposite his brother. He points at Duncan. "You and I will be having words when this is through." Duncan pales as Callum turns his attention to the head of the table. "Talk."

"Your father would turn in his grave to see his two lads fighting over a southerner." The male beside James leans forward. He's older than the others, with grey hair. He has an angular face, and there's an absence of laughter lines around his eyes.

"Our father thought you a coward, Malcolm, after you ran to the High Peaks with your tail between your legs rather than coming to our grandfather's aid when he needed you," growls Callum.

Malcolm's eyes flash.

"He's right," says James. "Our father despised you. This is between my brother and me."

"I presume Alexander is on his way?" Blake interjects.

"He is," says James, and my stomach feels watery.

Blake drums his fingers on the table. "Shall we get on with it, then?"

"You're looking very smug for a dead man, Blake," says James.

"You're looking very smug for a wolf who expects to rule a kingdom after negotiating, yet again, with southerners," says Blake.

James's lip curls up. "As opposed to my brother, who surrounds himself with them."

Blake laughs, the sound cold. "Please. Aurora is no threat. As for me, I was on *your* council once, too, James."

James clenches his fist on the table. "And look how that worked out, you untrustworthy bastard." He shakes his head. "You're both a threat to this kingdom, and my brother needs to see it."

"Rory is not a threat," growls Callum.

"He's right," says Blake. "She's not. James, you're getting paranoid, just like your father did before his end. He said some interesting thing about you, you know?" A muscle feathers in James's jaw, and Malcolm narrows his eyes. "If you'd let Callum keep his pet, we'd not be in this mess, now, would we?"

James laughs, the sound gruff and humorless. "She's Callum's pet, is she?"

"Whose else would she be?" says Blake.

I try to contain my indignation for the sake of self-preservation, but I can't. "I'm no one's pet," I blurt. "I'm the princess of the bloody Southlands!"

Duncan presses his blade into my skin, and I tense. "Probably not the best idea to remind everyone of that right now."

A few men jeer, and Callum growls to silence them. "What do you want, James? You're my brother. We grew up together. We hunted in the forests round Highfell, and picked flowers for our mother. When I broke my leg, you carried me up Glen Ghealach on your back. You taught me to wield a sword, and I have supported you, loyally, always. I could have challenged you a thousand times, but I pledged myself to you." His expression hardens. "You have insulted me. You have harmed the lass I care about above all others. You hold her now, against her will. You knew how I felt about her, and you asked for her hand in marriage anyway. You have dishonored yourself, and brought shame to our family, to our mother. What's more, you're keeping Fi, one of mine, hostage. My honor will not let you walk away from this unscathed. You know that."

"Aye." James rests his arms on the table. "I know, at the moment, you feel that way. I only wish to show you something before you make any choices that cannot be reversed. Alexander's men will be here within the hour. If you allow me one small demonstration—a demonstration that will cause the lass no harm—I'll let her go and you can decide whether you want a head start, and take her away before Alexander gets here. Or whether you'll leave her with me so I can get Claire—one of our own—back from the Borderlands."

Callum releases a humorless laugh. "What is it you wish to show me, Brother?"

James runs a hand across his jaw. "I want to make a request of Blake. A simple task. If he completes it, you can go. I want you to pay very close attention to his reaction when I ask him this."

Blake's eyes glint in the slither of moonlight that creeps through the arched windows, as if he's intrigued. My chest tightens, though, and I feel his pulse of wariness. Callum turns his head, and Blake shrugs, one arm over the back of his chair.

"Go on, then," says Callum.

James turns his attention to the alpha of Lowfell. "You thought you were so fucking clever, didn't you, Blake? You turned Callum, my own blood, against me. You talked me into asking for her hand in marriage. You thought if I knew Callum wanted her, I would want her more. Did you really think that taking something from my brother would please me?" He shakes his head. "No. I decided I wanted her in spite of that. Do you want to know what it was that actually pushed me into asking her to marry me?"

"I'm sure you're going to tell me," says Blake.

"It was you, Blake." He huffs a dark laugh. "I've never seen you take interest in anyone in the whole time I've known you. Then I hear that you gave a Southlands lass your collar while Callum was assisting me in battle. Probably one of his games, I thought. Until I saw you dance with her on the night of the feast. You couldn't take your eyes off her, could you? I thought, what is it about this lass that has captured the attention of the elusive Blake? And she has caught your attention, hasn't she?"

I try to wrench my wrists apart, and the rope chafes. I've had enough of this. It needs to stop.

A dimple creases Blake's cheek. "She's the daughter of the Southlands king."

"Fuck off, Blake. That's not why. I had your chambers searched when you left. I found a very interesting book hidden away in there." I still. Does James know that our lives are linked? "It was full of torture, removal of organs, experimentation on Wolves. It was all pretty grim, though I'd expect nothing less from you. There was something else within those pages that caught my attention, though. You know what I'm talking about, don't you?"

The smile remains on Blake's face, but his shoulders tighten. "What is it you want me to do, James?"

James leans back in his chair. "Are you watching, Brother?"

Callum's brow creases. "Aye."

"Blake, I will let the princess go if you kiss her."

Chapter Thirty

Blake's laugh chills me as much as James's request.

Blake, I will let the princess go if you kiss her.

"Is that what gets you off nowadays, James?" asks Blake, and a few of the alphas around the table snicker.

My blood roars in my ears. I can't understand why he's asking Blake to do this. Logically, it's a small ask in exchange for my freedom. That is, if we can trust that James will keep his word. Yet my entire soul protests. I can't quite understand the force of my protest.

Blake kissed me before, once, when Callum was dosed with wolfsbane and he was trying to provoke Callum's wolf. It bothered me, then, but it didn't make my soul feel as if it were aflame. Perhaps it's because I know, this time, how much it will provoke Callum. I know Blake holds an inkling of attraction toward me, even if he pretends he does not.

James must be trying to cause a rift between the two alphas, using me to do so, because they make a powerful alliance.

Or perhaps my feelings have nothing to do with Blake, and everything to do with James taking away my autonomy. He already forced me to be a wolf, and now he has me tied to a stone column, and expects me to kiss a man against my will.

"I'm not kissing anyone." I try to pull apart the rope that binds my wrists, and it pinches my skin. Duncan presses the point of his dagger into my chin. I sill.

"Settle down," he says.

Everyone stares at me. Eight men, six of whom will probably revel in my humiliation. Callum looks like a statue carved of mountain stone. He's pulled back his emotions, the way he does when he's under threat. I can't tell what he's thinking.

"Well?" says James.

"No." Blake smiles, but his eyes are hard. "I'm not kissing Callum's pet."

James leans forward. "Why not?"

"You're not a strategist, James. If you mean to create a rift between Callum and me, it won't work."

"You won't kiss the lass, but you were happy enough to mark her and claim her as yours on the night of Oidhche Fhada?"

"So it seems."

James addresses Callum. "His reluctance is interesting, isn't it, Brother? It's just a kiss. It's not like I'm asking him to fuck her. He knows as well as I do that you'd get over it—given the circumstance. Particularly as it will likely save her life. What is it that he does not want us to see, I wonder?"

James gets up and strolls toward me. The marks I gave him are healing already, and the three lines on both of his cheeks look like faint scratches. Duncan pulls away the dagger and steps back.

"Don't you think she's bonny?" James grabs my chin, and his scent of bracken and steel assaults me. He turns my face toward Blake.

Blake's jawline tightens.

I try to pull away, but James's grip becomes painful. Blake straightens, ever so slightly, in his seat. "He doesn't like that, does he, Brother?" He releases me, and I edge away until my hips bang against the stone column. Chuckling, James strides back to his seat and drops into it.

I turn to Callum, sure he's going to challenge James and put a stop to this. There's a crease between his eyebrows, and he stares at Blake.

"Do as he says." Callum's low growl is barely audible, but it near deafens me.

My insides hollow, and darkness fills me. I thought he would protect me. I thought he would save me from this humiliation.

Blake turns his head toward Callum. "Seriously?"

"Seriously."

"Careful, Callum. Some things cannot be undone."

Both seem to hold their breath. Callum jerks his head.

Blake sighs. His chair screeches across the tiles as he pushes it back and stands. He drags his teeth over his bottom lip, then taps the surface of the table with his fingertips. I think he's trying to communicate something to Callum, but Callum stares at his clasped hands.

Shaking his head, Blake strolls past the gathered Wolves and makes his way to me.

This can't be happening. Callum can't be allowing this to happen. Robert jeers, and another wolf whistles.

Callum does nothing.

Nothing.

I want to shed my skin, to disappear into the darkness where no one can see me. The noise muffles around me as I struggle against my bindings. For a second, I'm back in the Church of Light and Sun, held by the Sisters of the Sun while the High Priest prowls toward me. Helplessness crashes through me. Like then, no one intervenes.

Callum doesn't intervene.

Blake's body heat and scent wash over me, and he stands so I can no longer see the men who jeer and laugh. His expression is solemn. Even though he's holding back his emotion from me, I sense his reluctance.

I shake my head. "*Don't.*"

He touches my bicep. He runs his hand down my arm to my wrist, and slides his thumb between my skin and the rope. I hold my breath, because it seems like he's testing how tightly I'm bound. As always with him, I'm unsure if he's going to help me or make things worse. I know he doesn't want to kiss me.

He cups my face with both hands, and his touch is gentle yet firm. His mouth is a breath away from mine. "I'm sorry about this, Aurora, darling."

He brushes his lips against mine.

His mouth is hard and unrelenting for a second, then he softens. His darkness floods me. His pine scent coils around me like a deadly serpent and refuses to let go. His heartbeat thunders in my ears, loud and unsteady.

Feelings that are not my own, feelings I cannot decipher, tangle with my fear and my anger and I cannot breathe. A word rumbles in my head. Intangible. The wildness inside me raises its head. My blood howls. My canines ache. Everything aches. I'm nothing but this dark, endless, aching void that needs to be filled. I'm an infinite scream, growing, raging, entombed in stone. I cannot bear it.

I part my lips, and he slides his tongue against mine. His grip on my face tightens. I jerk back, and Blake stills. The wolf blazes in his eyes. His pupils are blown and his irises flecked with the same molten gold that courses through my veins.

Jeers fill the air. Blake takes a deep breath. Movement catches my eye beyond him. Callum's breathing is fast. His nostrils are flared. He wears his emotion for all to see, and the anguish in his eyes is disproportionate to what happened when he could have stopped it.

Blake looks over his shoulder. Something seems to pass between the two men, and Callum pulls back his pain. He inclines his head.

Callum kicks Kenneth's chair, and Blake grabs Duncan. A second later, Kenneth and Duncan are both on the floor, and Blake holds Duncan's dagger. Blake slices the blade through my bindings, while Callum throws a chair through the air toward James. James dodges aside with a roar.

I stagger back as the rope falls onto the ground. Blake hooks an arm around my waist, and pulls me flush against him. He moves us both to the other side of the column, to block the sword of one of the men in green kilts. The ring of steel against stone, echoes in my ears. Blake pushes me back, twists, and knees the male in the crotch then slides the blade across his throat.

Callum pushes aside another chair, punches Kenneth in the face, and strides toward James. "Brother, I challenge you for the Wolf Throne. Face me now, or—"

The arched stained-glass window on one side of the ballroom shatters. He and James both raise their elbows over their faces to protect themselves from the shards of glass. Blake spins away from another male, his dagger even bloodier as his victim crumples to the ground. A rock rolls into the middle of the space.

Seconds later, men pour into the room from outside. Their shouts fill the space. Glass crunches beneath their boots. They're wearing the star sigil of the Borderlands on their chests. The alphas draw their swords, turning to greet them in battle. Alexander has clearly sent them to attack, not to negotiate a trade. More of James's Wolves spill through the double doors to join the fight.

James's eyes find mine. "I need the lass! Someone get the lass!" He strides in my direction. Callum charges at him, grabs him around his waist, and tackles him. They hit the floor tiles with a thud that rattles the chandelier.

"GET HER OUT OF HERE!" he roars at Blake.

Blake grabs my wrist. "Time to go, little—"

He pulls me into his chest and turns us both around as a loud crack reverberates through the ballroom. White-hot pain bursts across my shoulder, and both Blake and I grunt. There's another crack, and I feel it again, slightly lower. My legs buckle.

"*Fuck*," Blake hisses into the crook of my neck. He holds me tightly. My pain dissipates, but Blake's breathing is ragged.

On the other side of the room, one of Alexander's men holds a musket. Adrenaline crashes through me. Blake has been shot. Twice. The man turns and aims his weapon at another one of the alphas.

I grip Blake's back under his arm, and try to keep him upright. "Blake! Are you—" My words catch in my throat.

A tall male, packed with muscle, strolls through the space where one of the walls once was. His hair is black and shaved close to his skull. Even though he's human, and the wind is cold, he wears only a thin black coat over his breeches, expensive and embroidered. It's at odds with the brutality of his appearance. The moonlight highlights a mad glint in his eye, and the scar that cuts through his eyebrow.

"Alexander," I breathe.

He is even more fearsome now than he was in the finery of the palace. There are no rules here, no etiquette, no one to stop him from taking what he wants. He grins and flashes perfect white teeth as he strides toward us.

"Hello, love." His voice carries over the chaos. "It's been a while. I've been looking for you."

Chapter Thirty-One

Alexander strides toward us.

"Blake, we need to go," I whisper. "*Now.*"

Blake's legs buckle, and we almost fall. He buries his face in my neck and groans. A familiar scent hits me—a scent that reminds me of my mother's bedchambers when I was a child. Herbal and sickly. My skin turns to ice.

The bullets were dowsed in wolfsbane.

Men and Wolves are fighting all around us. Callum's roar reverberates around the ballroom as James straddles him and slams a fist into his jaw. Blood sprays the faded mosaic on the ground. My heart clenches. The sound of clashing steel and male shouts fills the air.

A wolf in a blue kilt steps into Alexander's path, sword raised. Alexander blocks his blow, then guts the man with another blade. Blood and gore, black in the moonlight, spills out of him. *Goddess.*

"Blake, can you walk?" His skin is pale and clammy. Black curls stick to his forehead. "Goddess, never mind."

I hurl his arm over my shoulder, and wrap my other arm around his hips, careful not to touch his bare skin with my wolfsbane-dowsed hands. I drag him toward the doors. We make slow progress. He slumps into me, a dead weight. He smells like blood and poison

"Horse... outside..." he rasps.

"Okay. Come on."

He's heavy, and I'm once again reminded that he's packed with muscle beneath his clothes. He's cold, too cold for a wolf. His shirt is sopping wet and I try not to think about whether it's with sweat or blood. Behind us, Alexander pushes one of his own men aside. He blocks Kenneth's blow and shoves the red-haired alpha aside.

"Where are you going, love?" Alexander's gruff voice follows me. "Don't you want to play?"

We reach the doors, and I drag Blake down a dark corridor. Blood runs down his fingers and drips onto the tiles. It leaves a trail behind us.

"Left," he mumbles, when we reach the end.

Footsteps echo behind me, and I know Alexander is coming. Callum roars, in pain or in victory, I don't know. I have to keep going. We pass what looks like a parlor, then a kitchen. I push open the door at the end of the corridor, and the night enters the house on a gust of wind. The scent of wild grass and the mountains floods my nose, and light drizzle sprays my skin. We stumble onto an overgrown path.

"I promised I'd come back for you, love, didn't I?" Alexander shouts.

There are three horses ahead, tethered to the trees a short walk away. I grit my teeth. Every bone in my body aches; every muscle is tight. Blake groans and alleviates some of his weight as we head onward. The mountains are dark ahead.

When we reach the copse of trees, Blake lets go of me and staggers toward a black mare. "You first," he rasps.

I mount, and he hauls himself onto the saddle behind me—I help pull him up. He hisses when my bare hands touch his wrists, but makes no complaint as he pushes himself upright, clenches his thighs around mine, and hooks his good arm around my waist. I grip the reins.

Twigs and stones crunch beneath Alexander's steady footsteps. He's whistling, slightly off-key. The tune is familiar, and it instils fear within me, even stronger than my fear of him catching me.

"*Go!*" Blake's breath tickles my ear.

I hold onto the reins and dig in my heels. The horse takes off through the trees. Her earthy scent floods my nostrils, along with the smells of forests and rain and Blake's dark poison. The wind brushes my hair back out of my face, and exhilaration twists with my fear. It's been so long since I rode a horse, so long since my mother and I would gallop through the countryside, yet it comes back to me like an instinct.

Freedom, my heartbeat urges. *Freedom.*

Hooves thunder against the ground behind us, and a low, rough laugh fills my ears. "You can't escape me, love."

Panic rises inside me. The lights from the manor fade, and the darkness creeps in. I don't know where I'm going. Blake's breathing rattles against my neck. He won't last long without his wounds being tended to.

He murmurs instructions to me, and I navigate the moonlit terrain as best I can while his chest rises and falls unsteadily against my back. My thighs ache as I clench the saddle. Blake slips behind me, and he grabs my side, his fingers digging into me.

"There. Ahead." His chin scrapes against my shoulder as he nods. "He won't follow us there."

A chapel comes into view on the slope of a mountain. There's an iron fence around it, and weathered headstones jut out of the wet earth in front. I push us on through the open gates. The steel has been shaped into crescent moons and stars. I bring my horse to a halt among the graves. There's nowhere else to go.

A rough laugh fills the air. My heart pounding, I raise my chin and turn the horse.

"Hello, Alexander," I say.

Alexander pulls on the reins of his horse and halts on the other side of the gate. "I've imagined our reunion so many times. The reality is even better." He holds out a hand, and I catch a glimpse of ink on his wrist as his dark sleeve rides up. "Come with me, love. I'll take you home."

I shake my head. "This is my home now, and if you think you can use me to get my father to pardon you, you're mistaken."

Alexander tips back his head and laughs. "Your father? Do you think I want the favor of that old fool? No. My plans for you are much sweeter, love. Come to me. I will give you glory."

"Why don't you come and get her, Alex?" Blake's voice is smooth, but he grips my waist tightly beneath my cloak, like he's afraid he's going to fall.

Alexander's grin widens. "Well, if it isn't the king's favorite pup. I missed you, Blake. I missed the sound of your screams. I dream of them, sometimes. Do you dream of me?"

My eyebrows lift. They know one another?

"Sometimes," says Blake.

Alexander gestures his head at me. "We can share her, if you like."

Blake laughs.

"No?" Alexander runs his hand over his shaved dark hair, then shrugs. "Fine. Another time. Bring her to the Grey Keep, if you want to have some fun. I've got one of our old friends there that I'd like her to meet. Before she fulfils her purpose, of course." He turns his horse and looks over his shoulder at me. "I'll be seeing you again very soon, love. In the meantime, I'm sending someone to visit you at Madadh-allaidh. I've grown very close to him over the past weeks. Make him feel welcome, won't you?"

He rides away.

Blake slumps against me.

Chapter Thirty-Two

I've got one of our old friends there that I'd like her to meet. Before she fulfils her purpose, of course.

I shiver. The trees in the churchyard sway in the wind. The graves around us jut from the earth like crooked teeth. It feels as if we are miles from anywhere. Blake grunts behind me. My mind reels with questions about Alexander and his link to Blake. I have to help him first.

Do as he says. I push away the memories of Callum's command.

"Are you conscious?" I whisper.

"Mm," he mumbles.

His arm is like a block of ice against my torso. If I can't heal him, we're both going to die. I steady my racing heart. "I assume you have the antidote in your pack?"

He grunts, which I take for a yes.

"Okay." I lead the horse toward the chapel, and stop by the arched door. There are more stars and crescent moons carved into the stone around it. This is one of Night's chapels.

Blake's arm is heavy as I move it to his side. He slumps as I slide onto the path. My knees buckle, and I put my hand on the side of the horse to right myself. My shoulder brushes Blake's leg. I take a deep breath.

"Come on," I say.

I hold out my hand, but he manages to slide down without my assistance. Dry leaves crunch beneath his boots as he lands.

"Fuck. I feel like shit." He knocks into my shoulder as he stumbles. He puts a palm on the chapel wall and bends forward. Dark strands of hair cling to his forehead, and his skin is as pale as moonlight.

I hurry to the saddle, and root around in his pack. I pull out the black case I've seen him use to heal people. I turn back to him. He leans against the chapel wall with a hand clamped over his shoulder. His head is arched back against the stone, exposing his throat. Blood spills between his fingers and pools on the flagstones at his feet. I've never seen him so vulnerable before.

I approach him, and he slings his arm over my shoulder. My hand around his waist, I nudge open the door and lead him inside. It closes behind us.

Inside, a few rows of pews lead to a stone altar. Above it, a stained-glass window depicts a key with crescent moons in the bow. Silver moonlight shines through it and creates a puddle of faint light on the flagstones. The air is thick with must.

"Wash your hands." Blake nods at a stone font by the entrance. I wash my hands thoroughly in the cold water while he makes his way down the aisle. I shake off the water, then hurry after him and hook an arm around his waist as he starts to stumble.

"Here." I put my hands on his hips, and turn him so he's facing me. I nudge him back against the altar. My knuckles brush against his chest, then torso, as I unfasten his buttons. His chin dips, and I feel his gaze on my face.

"How did you know where I was?" I ask.

"I have a source in Madadh-allaidh."

"Magnus?" I can't stop my mouth from pinching in disapproval.

The corner of his lip lifts slightly. "You've been talking to Elsie."

I undo the last button, and his shirt hangs open. Pale lines mark his chest, and there's a long curved scar near the sharp V of his right hip. A line of dark hair leads down into his breeches.

"Whenever you're done admiring me. . ." mumbles Blake.

I fight my flush as I help him slide his good arm out of his sleeve. I peel the blood-soaked fabric off his injured shoulder, then drop it onto the altar. He peers down at the two holes in his upper arm, both pumping out hot blood.

"Exit wounds. The bullets aren't inside me, at least. There's a tourniquet and syringe with the antidote in it in my pack," he says, and I nod.

I shuffle past him, and unfasten his case. It folds out and there are a range of scalpels, small vials, and a syringe arranged on one side. A leather strap, a roll of gauze, and a needle and thread are stored in the other. I pull out the strap, the gauze, and the syringe. It's filled with transparent liquid.

"Good," he says. "Find a vein."

He offers me his good arm. I wrap the strip of fabric around his bicep, and try not to think about how hard it is as my fingers brush against the muscle. As I tighten the tourniquet, veins bulge down the length of his forearm. I grab the syringe and slide the needle into one of them. I push the plunger, and Blake makes a low noise and tips back his head as the antidote enters his system. I pull it out, and place it on the altar beside him.

"There," I say. "I'll bandage—"

A low, feral growl vibrates in his chest. It echoes around the darkness and stirs the shadows. His face transforms and becomes cold. The wolf blazes in his eyes.

My left arm drops, useless, to my side. White-hot phantom pain spreads from my shoulder, and I feel blood that is not there pumping out of invisible wounds. A soft breath escapes my lips. As he loses his grip on the bond, his senses flood me. His emotions no longer make sense; they're pure animal. A word vibrates along the thread between us like a growl.

Hunt.

I stagger back. It's the antidote that is working, provoking his wolf, but I hadn't expected him to react like this. Callum didn't when he took the antidote. I feel as if I'm facing a wounded animal, not a man.

"Blake, don't."

He clenches one of his fists, and his knuckles whiten. He closes his eyes. When he opens them again, the wolf is stronger than ever. A slow, feral grin spreads across his lips. "*Run.*"

Adrenaline surges through me. "No." I fight the tremble in my legs. I step closer and he straightens. "I'm not doing that with you again. Get a hold of yourself."

His breathing deepens. His essence floods me, dark and primal. That shadow of him wraps around my soul. It's all-consuming. Suffocating. Sweat beads on my brow. Dots dance across my vision. He growls. *Hunt.*

"Blake. *Stop it.*"

Every muscle in his body is taut. My skin is clammy. The feeling... It almost feels like when he used the Àithne on me, but stronger. It provokes the wildness inside me. *Hunt. Claim. Bite.* I push back the fever that rises. I stand on tiptoes and grab his face with both hands. He snarls, and his breath mingles with mine. *Hunt.*

"Get a hold of yourself!"

A scream builds inside me. A need to be free. I feel like the moment before a storm breaks.

I shove him through the bond. I can't explain how I do it, but I take that shadowy part of him and push it back. His eyes flicker. The shadow inside me loosens its grip. A crease forms between his eyebrows. I feel his emotions start to settle. A low, rough noise escapes him as he turns away from me. He bites his arm.

"Blake! What are you...?"

His relief crashes through me with such ferocity that I barely notice the sensation of teeth sinking into my flesh. He releases a soft moan that courses through me. *Wolves like to bite*, Callum had told me. He takes a couple of deep breaths. He raises his head. His own blood stains his lips. He blinks, and his eyes shift back to normal.

We're both breathing hard. He glances at the open case on the altar. He nods at the roll of gauze. "Would you mind?" His voice is rougher than usual.

Shaken, I head to the case and take the roll of gauze. I stand on my tiptoes, and brush the tops of his shoulders. "I. . .I won't be able to do it properly unless you kneel down. You're too tall."

Slowly, he lowers himself to his knees. Covered in blood, and breathing hard in front of the altar, he looks like a fallen god begging for repentance.

I touch one of his shoulders, and feel his muscle knotted beneath. I wind the fabric around his upper arm and shoulder. A heavy, smothering silence falls upon us. It's weighted. Uncomfortable. His breathing is still fast. Blood spreads across the gauze, though it's already slowing. It's as black as ink in the darkness.

Finally, I tuck in the end of the gauze. "Done."

"Thank you." He clears his throat, then stands.

The door bursts open. Blake's hand moves to his stolen dagger, and I spin around.

Duncan stands in the doorway, breathless. His cheeks are flushed, and his shirt is stained with blood. "I've come with a message from the king." Blake unsheathes his weapon, and walks toward him. Duncan raises his arms, eyes widening. "The *new* king."

I grab Blake's bicep, and he halts beside me. "Callum?" I breathe.

"Yes, Callum." He looks between Blake and me warily. "Callum is king. He's on his way to Madadh-allaidh to join Lochlan and his army. He says you're to come. Immediately."

Chapter Thirty-Three

Duncan stands in the doorway. The wind blows his blue kilt against his thighs, and the night spills onto the flagstones before him. His shirt is bloody, and some of his blond hair has escaped its knot. There's a bruise forming over his eye, and I wonder if Blake gave it to him, or one of Alexander's men.

Callum is king.

Relief bursts in my chest, but it's quickly stifled. Duncan was my prison warden when I was kept in a cell. He held a blade to my throat. He could be lying. It's hard to believe Callum would send Duncan to find me, rather than come and get me himself.

Do as he says. I push back Callum's voice, and the feelings those words provoke.

Beside me, Blake's hand is curled around the hilt of his dagger. His arm is pressed against mine. He's still shirtless, his skin is pale and clammy, and we're both covered in blood. Duncan looks between us warily.

"I'm not lying," he says. "Callum sent me."

"The Borderlands men?" asks Blake.

"They rode away after Alexander left."

Blake uncurls his fingers from his weapon. "We'll meet you outside."

Duncan nods, then heads out of the chapel. The door swings shut behind him. When I take a deep breath, the scent of blood fills my lungs and reminds me that Blake's not yet at full health.

"He might be lying," I say.

"He's not," says Blake. "Or at least, I don't think he is."

"Why didn't Callum come after me himself?"

He sighs heavily. "Because you're with me." My eyebrows knit together, because this seems to exasperate him. He runs his good hand over the back of his neck "Or perhaps this is a trap, little rabbit. Shall we find out?"

Blake grabs his bloody shirt. He struggles to slip it on, and I help him fasten up the buttons. We walk down the aisle, and head outside.

Duncan is already on his horse by the chapel gates. The mountains loom behind him. Blake walks to the horse we rode here on, and pats her on the side. I halt and stiffen. We'd rode here in such a panic, it hadn't really occurred to me that our bodies were pressed together for the journey.

Blake looks over his shoulder and pulls a face. "Unless you'd prefer to ride with Duncan?"

Duncan straightens in his saddle, and I catch a hint of panic in his eyes before he resolutely looks away. I wonder if he worries what Callum would think.

I huff as I join Blake by the horse. "I'm holding the reins."

His left arm hangs limp at his side, and he rolls his eyes. "Obviously."

When I'm seated in the saddle, Blake hauls himself up behind me. His chest presses against my back, and every muscle in my body tightens. He grabs the saddle, rather than curling his arms around my waist. It satisfies me that, no longer on the brink of death, he's uncomfortable with this, too.

Duncan rides through the gates. Still marginally concerned about where he might be leading us, I grip the reins and follow him.

The trees rustle around us as we trot down a dark mountain pass. The peaks are hidden by darkness. Blake's legs rub against mine as the terrain becomes more uneven, and he keeps shifting to try and put distance between us.

He kissed me, earlier.

The weight of his kiss is heavy on my lips. I'm sure it'll get heavier when we get back to the castle. I'm sure there'll be consequences for both of us. All the alphas saw it. Callum saw it.

Do as he says.

"You know Alexander," I say, quietly, after a while.

"Yes." Blake's breath tickles my ear.

"You failed to mention that."

"I didn't realize I had to inform you of all my acquaintances." The horse stumbles on a rock, and his chest bumps into my back. "I can provide you with a list, if you wish."

"Don't be obtuse. You knew Alexander was coming after me, and you knew our history. It was pertinent information you should have shared."

"Why? You seem to think we are enemies."

"And you told me we were friends. How do you know him?"

Blake's sigh is warm against my cheek. "I was imprisoned a while back. I met him during my time of captivity."

"Why were you imprisoned?"

"For being a wolf."

My retort for how it was good he got some form of comeuppance for his behavior dies in my throat. "Oh. Sorry." There's running water by our side, though it's too dark to determine if it's a brook or a river. The sound is peaceful. "How did you know Alexander wouldn't follow us into the chapel?"

"Did you see the mark on his wrist?"

I glimpsed a tattoo in the same spot as Elsie's, and I guessed at the symbol that might be inked there. "He worships Night, doesn't he? We were in one of Night's chapels. Why would he fear it?"

"It's said that places of worship bring us closer to the gods and goddesses. Alexander isn't a true supporter. He tried to trick the God of Night into giving him power, or so I heard. Now, he fears retribution. He wouldn't dare set foot in a place like that."

"What do you think he wants with me?"

He shakes his head. "Let us hope we don't find out."

Dawn approaches when we reach the hill overlooking Madadh-allaidh. Birdsong fills the sky as it lightens over the castle—an angular building made of dark stone. An army of about three hundred surrounds the outer walls, and their kilts and sashes add a burst of yellow to the shadow-painted landscape. Morning mist coats the loch behind them.

Lochlan's army.

I can't determine where the alpha is himself, but I'm surprised—and delighted—to see that there are women warriors on horseback among the men.

"Did Callum and Lochlan free Alexander's prisoner?" I ask.

"Yes," says Blake. "Although, based on what Alexander said to us, I'm starting to wonder if it's a trap. It seemed a little too easy."

"He said he was sending someone to us."

"Exactly."

He shifts back on the saddle. "They're not going to bite, Duncan. Let's go." Duncan throws Blake an unpleasant look, then digs his heels into the horse. "We should go too, little rabbit. I'm sure Callum is overreacting because you're not there yet."

Do as he says. I push Callum's voice out of my mind.

I lead the horse down the grassy hill.

We make our way back to Castle Madadh-allaidh.

***

THE CASTLE courtyard is full of noise when we ride through the gates.

Morning mist coats the cobblestones. There must be thirty or so Wolves congregated in small groups, and the conversation is agitated. Some carry dead game, or buckets filled with chicken feed. Others have halted with bundles of hay in their arms. I catch Mrs. McDonald, the formidable cook, gossiping with Kayleigh, the kitchen maid, by the water pump—both rosy-cheeked and wide-eyed. People look out of the narrow windows looking onto the yard. Three women wearing blue tartan dresses swarm Duncan's horse to ask him for news. Isla, the woman from Highfell who was hostile to me, and clearly had feelings for Callum, flicks her mousy brown hair over her shoulder. She whispers something behind her hand to her friend.

I catch snippets of their conversations. Among the chatter, a phrase is repeated. *Callum is king.*

Some Wolves sound curious. Others hostile. Yet relief floods me that this is not a trap. Callum is here, and he won.

As we head further into the courtyard, the Wolves around us quieten. I'm reminded of the morning I first arrived here in the Northlands with Callum. People had been wary of the human woman with wild red hair, dressed in nothing but a nightgown, who rode on a horse with the alpha of Highfell.

I was frightened then. I'm not now, even if it's even tenser. People stop what they're doing and straighten. A woman pulls a freckled boy behind her. A couple of the men put their hands on their swords. Wolves have always feared Blake, but their fear seems to extend to me, too.

I'm not sure what they're most wary about. My wild appearance, having been held prisoner by James, Blake's equal dishevelment and his bloodstained clothing, or our affiliation with their new king.

Perhaps it's because we're both southerners. Or perhaps they heard what happened at the manor house. James forced Blake to kiss me.

Do as he says.

Blake pays the onlookers no heed. When I bring the horse to a halt, he presses against me as he slides his leg over the horse, then dismounts.

He looks significantly better than he did when we set off a couple of hours ago. Some of the color has come back to his cheeks, and though his dark hair is messy, it no longer sticks to his skin. He could pass for his usual self.

"Are you coming?" His eyes glint in the grey light.

I slide off the horse, and land close enough to him that his body heat sears into me. Ahead, Duncan strolls through the oak doors of the castle.

Blake snaps his fingers. "Kayleigh, can you take Nell to the stables, please?"

Across the courtyard, Kayleigh's face pales. When I worked with her in the kitchens, she seemed terrified of Blake. She looks as if she's contemplating bolting, but Mrs. McDonald gives her a shove. The two approach, and, her hand trembling slightly, Kayleigh takes the reins of the horse and leads it away.

"Well, if it isn't Her Royal Highness, here to grace us with her presence once more. Should I curtsy?" Mrs. McDonald's greying hair is frizzy around her flushed face, and her apron is dirty. She was probably preparing breakfast when Lochlan's army arrived. "No wonder you were so terrible at cooking."

I offer her an appeasing smile. Despite her hostility, I always liked the way she spoke to me as if I was no different to anyone else. "It's nice to see you again, Mrs. McDonald." I nod at the archway that Kayleigh walked Blake's horse through. The stables are in that direction, and it was someone different who came to greet us when Callum and I arrived. "Is Fiona—"

"The lass is fine. I'm sure she's on the warpath, currently, but she's unharmed. I made sure she was fed. Callum freed her as soon as he arrived. He was in an awful mood. You might be able to settle him." She shakes her head. "Two brothers, fighting over what their father worked so hard to achieve... It's a shame, though matters of the heart are rarely simple."

She looks Blake up and down and clucks her tongue. "As for you, I see you've been getting yourself into trouble again." She licks her thumb, leans forward and wipes a smudge of blood from his cheek. He stiffens slightly, but makes no remark. "You're needed in the infirmary. Callum's waiting for you."

My heart plummets. "Is he hurt?"

"He's seen better days, but he's fine. It's the prisoner that needs attention."

Kai. The prisoner Lochlan and Callum freed. Who Blake thinks was sent to us as part of a trap by Alexander.

Blake's jaw locks, but he nods.

"Come find me when you've seen to him," she says. "I'll make you that soup you like."

She bustles through a group of Wolves in blue tartan, and heads after Kayleigh. Blake wipes his face on his sleeve, but he doesn't say anything about Mrs. McDonald touching him. I've never seen anyone be so familiar with him.

I fall into step beside him as he walks through a group of Wolves to the castle doors.

"That makes sense, I suppose," I say under my breath, horribly aware that the courtyard is unnaturally quiet. "The two most fearsome Wolves in Madadh-allaidh would be friends with one another."

"Mrs. McDonald, and Kayleigh are both from Lowfell," says Blake, as we head into the castle. "They have differing opinions on what I did to the majority of their clan." He smirks. "I think Mrs. McDonald was quite pleased to be rid of her husband."

Disgust swells inside me, as I'm reminded that he's a killer. "You're abhorrent."

"Thank you."

"It's not a compliment." We walk through the entrance hall—adorned with banners, and tapestries and a wolf head mounted on the balcony level above. The doors shut behind us, and loud and restless conversation breaks out.

When we reach the infirmary, the fire in the hearth lights up the workbenches and medical supplies. Shelves line the walls, stocked with vials and jars. There are three cots in here, and there are patients in all of them.

Two men stand over one. Lochlan grips the shoulders of the man who lies there. He mutters under his breath. Beside him, Callum stands in front of the fireplace. I forget how to breathe.

He looks as formidable, as impenetrable, as the night we met. His shirt strains against hard muscle, and is stained with blood. There's bruising around his strong jawline, and his nose is swollen.

His expression is unreadable. His attention momentarily flickers to Blake, then me. His jaw locks. He looks at his enemies like this.

Do as he says.

My heart begins to race in my chest. I lift my chin, and hold his steely gaze.

He's jealous. No matter that he was the one who told Blake to kiss me. No matter that he could have challenged his brother before it got to that point. No matter that *I* was the one who was kidnapped, and forced to do something I didn't want to do.

I should be running into his arms. I should be asking if he is okay. He must have killed his brother, and—no matter how much I may dislike James—Callum must feel *something* about that.

My feet are rooted to the spot.

Lochlan picks up on the tension. Silence shrouds the room, punctuated only by the crackle of the hearth and Kai's raspy breaths. It feels like miles stretch between Callum and me, like we're royalty from two enemy kingdoms, like the past weeks spent in each other's arms never happened.

"Callum?" I say.

Chapter Thirty-Four

The fire in the infirmary blazes behind Callum and casts his face in shadow. He opens his mouth as if to speak. Blake stiffens behind me.

I'm attacked. Long dark hair distorts my vision as arms wrap around me and a chest bumps against my side. The scent of horses floods my lungs. I'm squeezed until I can't breathe.

"You're still shite at giving hugs." Fiona pulls back and turns me to face her with a smile on her face. I'd expected her to appear drawn and tired. She looks surprisingly healthy. Her dark hair hangs loose and is a little wild, but her cheeks are rosy, and her brown eyes are bright.

A soft laugh escapes my lips. "Fiona! Are you alright?"

"I'm fine. No thanks to James. I've been cooped up in my chambers for weeks. He didn't have the balls to lock me up in the dungeons, the bastard." She assesses me, and her expression darkens. "I heard what he did to you." She shakes her head, then frowns. "Why is it so tense in here?"

Callum blinks. Once. Twice. His expression softens and he clears his throat. "Rory. Are you okay?"

I release some of the emotion that bubbles inside me on a shaky breath. "I'm not hurt. Are you?"

He smiles, somewhat sadly. "No."

Fiona's forehead creases. She looks like she's going to say something, but Blake walks past me and slaps Lochlan's hand away from the man's shoulder. He leans over the wounded wolf, and I follow him, Fiona close beside me.

"This is Kai?" I ask.

Lochlan nods. The man on the thin mattress is barely breathing. I can tell that, under different circumstances, he would be handsome. He has jet-black hair and high cheekbones. His breeches and shirt are torn and stained with blood.

I balk when I realize he's missing a couple of fingers, and his ankle is twisted at an unnatural angle.

"Can you help him?" Lochlan is trying to appear composed, but his shoulders are stiff.

Blake pulls aside the collar of Kai's bloody shirt. There's a mark on his chest. I lean closer, and stiffen when I recognize it. Someone has branded him with Night's mark. The skin around it is mottled and burned, as if it was done recently.

Blake turns his attention to Callum. "We encountered Alexander a couple of hours ago."

Callum's eyes widen, and I realize that with everything going on, he must not have realized the new Borderlands lord had arrived with his men at the manor. "What?"

"He told us he'd be sending someone to us. He also expressed how keen he was to get his hands on Aurora." He walks to the workbench behind me, where knives and scalpels are lined up by vials of herbs and medicine.

"The ambush was a trap," says Callum.

"I'd say so. If Alex has broken him, he cannot stay. Neither can the others." He gestures at the men lying in the two other cots. "You know what needs to be done."

Callum slams his fist down on the workbench by the fireplace. "Fuck!"

I flinch, and Fiona stiffens.

Lochlan moves his hand to his sword. "I won't allow you to kill him. You need Glas-Cladach—"

The temperature in the infirmary drops, and the fire flickers out. Kai opens his eyes, and they are completely black. "*I know your scent.*" His voice is low and raspy, and the hairs on the back of my neck stand on end. "*The light and the dark. She always liked a good joke.*"

Blake darts forward, pushes me aside, and grabs Kai's throat.

Kai laughs. "*He's looking for you.*"

Blake squeezes. "Who?"

Kai frowns. The fire flickers back to life, and the black drains form his eyes to reveal honey-colored irises. Blake releases his hold and glances at Callum.

The man visibly trembles on the thin mattress. His breathing is ragged. He tosses his head from side to side, as if he can't figure out where he is.

Fiona grasps my sleeve, and her eyes are wide. Callum is completely still, and his hand is on the hilt of his sword.

Lochlan crouches down beside the cot. His skin is pale. "What happened to him?"

Blake shakes his head. "I don't—"

"It was bad enough when we were kept in those *kennels*—barely fed, beaten, broken." Kai's tone is monotonous. "Alexander arrived, and it got worse. He moved us to the Grey Keep. He tortured me. Made me betray my goddess." His voice breaks as he touches the brand that marks his skin. "Then he gave me to *it*."

"To what?" Blake grabs Kai's shoulders.

A haunted look creeps across his face. "He kept... something... caged in the kennels with us. We heard it clanging its chains sometimes, dragging itself up and down its cell. Hissing. The nightmares came. We tried to stay awake at night, fearing what would come if we succumbed to sleep. John, one of the biggest bastards I ever knew, woke trembling with terror etched onto his face." He shakes his head. "One night, Alexander told me it was my turn to meet it. He threw me to it."

He shakes his head. "All I remember is darkness, so thick I lost all of my senses. I wondered if I was dead, if this was what the afterlife was for those who had turned away from the moonlight. There was movement above me, and I saw deep obsidian eyes coming toward me. Then nothing. It's the last thing I remember."

Blake leans closer. "Do you know what it was?"

"The other prisoners called it the Dark Beast. There were rumors it was one of Night's prisoners, escaped from his prison. Alexander said he was breaking it in for when his special guest arrived."

Callum's brow creases. "His special guest?"

"He sent me here with a message. The Wolf King is to prepare for a battle, the likes of which the north has never seen." Remorse flickers across his face. "Or he can send him a gift, and Alexander will call off the attack."

Nausea rolls inside me, because I think I already know the answer to my question. "What gift?"

Kai's honey-colored eyes meet mine. "You."

Chapter Thirty-Five

A thick silence fills the infirmary.
"This conversation doesn't leave this room," says Callum. "Blake?"

Blake nods. Lochlan's eyes widen, and he starts to rise, hand on the hilt of his weapon. Callum curls his arm around Lochlan's neck and pulls him back. I breathe in sharply as Blake grabs something from the workbench and plunges it into Kai's neck. Lochlan roars, face red, as he thrashes against Callum.

"Relax," says Blake. Kai's eyes shut, and his body softens. Blake pulls out the needle. "It's a sedative. I'll need to interrogate him later."

Callum releases Lochlan, then walks past Fiona and me as if he doesn't see the wolf that blazes in Lochlan's eyes. "A word, please, Princess?"

I exchange a worried smile with Fiona, then head after him, my heart beating fast. Callum's pace is brisk as he strides through the castle. I half run to keep up with him. We pass armed soldiers wearing Lochlan's colors stationed in the corridors. Raised voices come from the Great Hall. Tension crackles between us.

I presume Callum is leading us to his old bedchambers so we can talk in private, but he turns in the opposite direction. I walk with him down a long corridor with narrow windows that let in the morning light. He opens a door at the end, and we enter a vast room.

A bed with ornate carved posts, red velvet curtains, and a pile of furs on the quilt dominates the space. There are paintings and weapons mounted all over the walls, and the red tartan banner of Highfell hangs above the bed. It's cold because there's no fire in the hearth, and the scent of bracken and steel hangs in the air.

"James's bedchambers," I say softly.

Callum swallows. "Aye."

He scans the room, then strides toward the desk by one of three narrow windows, and swipes something off the surface. His back muscles clench beneath the fabric of his shirt, then he exhales.

"It's not the Heart of the Moon." He turns. There's a round, white stone in his fist—the stone Sebastian gave James in exchange for me. "I was sure it wouldn't be—he would have used it against me, if it was. Yet I held a small shred of hope."

"You're sure?"

"The Heart of the Moon is an ancient relic, torn from the chest of our sacred goddess. I'd feel *something* if I encountered it, if I touched it. It would awaken my wolf. I'd feel it press against my skin." He tosses it onto the bed. "I feel nothing from this."

I offer him a sad smile. "I told you he would not trade it for me."

"Aye. You did. Foolish man."

The silence stretches between us. Even across the room, I can smell him—blood and sweat mingles with his mountain scent. He straightens and clenches his jaw, and my mouth dries. The way he's looking at me...

I had almost forgotten how formidable this man, this alpha—no, this *king*—could look. Even my father would cower before him. He's obviously angry, upset by what happened with Blake, even though he was the one who let it happen. I'm angry, too. Yet I want his comfort, and I want to comfort him.

He just killed his brother, who—up until recently—he served as second in command. He must have complicated feelings about it.

I take a tentative step forward. "Callum?"

I'm not sure if it's the uncertainty in my tone, the weakness, but his darkness shatters.

He crosses the space between us, and falls to his knees before me with a heavy thud. He wraps his arms around my waist and presses his forehead against my stomach, and relief bursts through me. He's still my Callum. His grip is almost too tight, and I want him to hold me tighter. I curl my hands around the back of his head while he mumbles something against my dress in a language I don't know.

"*Ghealach*, Princess." There's a watery film over his eyes. The blood from his nose adds to Blake's blood already staining my dress. "I'm so sorry. I'm so fucking sorry. I should have been there. I should have gotten to you sooner."

Do as he says.

I blink. "I thought you were angry with me."

He drags his teeth over his swollen bottom lip. "I am angry. I'm furious. I'm jealous. I want to rip Blake's fucking throat out and if you were not... connected to him, as you are, I'd have done it already. And I'm relieved. I'm so relieved that I feel like I'm floating out of my body. I'm so fucking happy to see you, to touch you, to know you're alright."

Something hardens inside me, and I force myself to look past the unfairness of his wrath. I brush my fingertips along the back of his neck, and he trembles. "How are you feeling about James?" I think about my own brother. I despise him, yet I can't imagine how it must feel to take his life. "I know that your relationship with him was difficult, but you're allowed to grieve—"

"He's not dead."

I still. "What? I thought you won the challenge?"

His shoulders harden, as if I've hit a nerve. "He forfeited. I knocked him out, then took over the fight against the southerners. I planned to deal with him later. He must have gained consciousness and escaped."

My blood cools. The vision of James's teeth when he sank them into me flashes behind my eyelids. The roar when I dragged my wolfsbane-dowsed fingers down his cheeks echoes in my ears. "He will come back to challenge you, Callum."

He squeezes my hip, then pushes himself to his feet. "And I will beat him again. I sent Ryan after him."

"Ryan?" My tone is incredulous, and a muscle twitches in Callum's temple.

"Aye. Ryan. He's like a wee brother to James. I don't think James will harm him. When I know where he is, I'll end this for good." He shakes his head. "It seems like we have bigger problems to deal with right now."

"Alexander."

"Aye."

Another thick silence stretches between us. Awkward. Uncomfortable. Usually, his emotions are easy to read, but his face is blank. Unspoken words hang between us, and I know we need to voice them. Something I'm not used to doing. I clasp my hands together. "Callum—"

"There's much I need to deal with before the day is through." He clears his throat. "I've had someone prepare your old room. The one in the tower that you stayed in when you first came here." My eyebrows lift, because I'd presumed we would share bedchambers, like we did at Lowfell. "I won't be in my chambers at all today. I need to find space for Lochlan's men. Rob is already trying to undermine me, and I need to get him under control if Alexander plans to attack. I thought you'd be more comfortable in your own space."

Hurt ripples through me. "The thing that happened with Blake—"

He closes his eyes. "Please, don't. Not now."

"Callum, I know you're upset—"

He opens his eyes. "I'm not angry with you, Rory, if that's what you're thinking. My wolf... I'm not in control right now. I need a bit of time to get my head around something, that is all."

"Get your head around what?"

He pinches the bridge of his nose. "I don't know. All of it. Things you don't understand."

"What things?"

"Not now. Get some rest. You've had a rough night. We'll talk about it later. I promise."

His lips are hard when he brushes them against my forehead. He strides to the door, heads out of the room, and leaves me alone.

The backs of my eyes burn. I want to scream. I sink my teeth into my finger, and revel in the blood that spills into my mouth.

I knew Callum would be upset, but I'm upset too. I was kidnapped, and held against my will. I was made a fool of in front of a room full of men. I was helpless, and not only was he witness to it, he encouraged it. I was almost shot, and Alexander tried to take me away. None of it was my fault.

I understand that he's under a lot of stress right now, but I thought I mattered enough for a conversation.

My mind whirls over everything that happened tonight.

I breathe in sharply as something comes back to me. James said he read something interesting in a book he found in Blake's chambers. Was he talking about the book that has information about the bond in it?

The bond complicates everything. Now Callum has taken the throne, it won't be long before he uses it against us.

Everyone is distracted. Blake is in the infirmary. Even though I'm exhausted, I don't think I'll find a better time to take the book.

I want to find out exactly what this connection is between us, so I can break it.

Chapter Thirty-Six

I hurry past the stairwell on my way to Blake's bedchambers. Downstairs, people are shouting and hurling insults at one another, but it's quiet up here. I pass Callum's chambers, and make my way further along the corridor to Blake's room. This is my best chance at finding the book that should give me some answers.

I push open the door.

The room has been torn apart. Ripped black curtains hang in shreds off the posts of the bed, and the armchair by the window is turned on its side. The books have been swept off the shelves, and are scattered across the floor. Shards of glass glint on the surface of the desk, and the scent of whisky hangs in the air. It mingles with the smell of bracken and the mountains—James's scent, I think.

Blake faces the window, and is arranging the littered parchment on his desk. He's wearing a fresh white shirt and breeches. He must have come here to change. My pulse quickens.

"Can I help you, little rabbit?" His tone is like silk.

He turns. The fire in the hearth casts soft light onto his face. When he leans back against the desk and supports himself with both hands, I realize he must be mostly healed. He is no longer the wounded animal I helped in the chapel.

"I came to check that you were alright," I say.

My gaze snags on a book that sits on the desk. It's the only tome that is not on the floor, and the way Blake leans... it seems as if he's trying to block it from view.

I lock a cage around my emotions so he can't feel the anticipation that buzzes beneath my skin.

Blake smiles. "I'm well now, thank you." He cocks his head. "Are you? You feel... nervous."

I step into his room, and the door clicks shut behind me. "It has been a long night, that's all."

"It has."

"Are your wounds healing?"

"Well enough."

He steps closer to the tome on the desk, and brushes the smashed bottom of a bottle aside with the movement.

"Let me check." I step closer.

"So concerned for my wellbeing, little rabbit."

"Your wellbeing is my wellbeing."

A dimple punctures his cheek. "True."

He unfastens the top buttons of his shirt, and slides the material off his shoulder. I walk toward him. The book is so close, I could almost reach out and grab it. It's blue, and I have the strangest feeling I've seen it before.

"Turn around," I say.

His dark eyelashes fan against his cheeks. He turns. My heart is in my throat. The muscles in Blake's back tense. I lurch toward the book. Blake reaches for it at the same time, grabs it, and turns. He holds it before me. "Looking for something, little—"

I slam my right hand down on the broken bottle. I cry out as shards of glass sink into my skin, and blood pumps from the wound. Blake makes a soft sound as he feels it, and the book slips out of his grip. It thumps onto the floor, and I grab it.

I half stumble, half run to the door. Blake grabs my wrist and tugs me back. I wrench away from him and clutch the book to my chest. My entire body stiffens. A snarl vibrates in my chest.

Mine.

This is mine.

Blake laughs, and I want to bite him. I'm going to bite him. It's all I can think about. My teeth ache. Everything aches.

"Settle down, little wolf. I'm not going to take it from you."

He lets me feel him. The shadows that coil around my soul feel soft, nonthreatening. I taste moonlit forests, and hear ducks in a river. The wild thing inside me settles, and I breathe out slowly. My cheeks heat.

"Wolves guard things that are of high value to them." He inclines his head at the book. "Keep it. I don't need it anymore."

I sense no threat from him. Perhaps this is the wrong book. Perhaps this is another of his games. I relax slightly, and pain flares in my hand. I'm bleeding onto the cover of the book.

Blake pulls his shirt back over his shoulder. He drags out the wooden chair that's tucked beneath the desk and pats it. "Sit." When I stand there, breathing hard, my grip tight on the book, he arches his eyebrows. "You're hurt. Sit down."

"I'm fine."

"You're in enemy territory, surrounded by Wolves who will not hesitate to kill you or hand you over to Alexander, and I'm the best healer in the Northlands. Sit down." I eye him warily. "I'm not going to hurt you. I'm not going to take the book. Come on."

I let out a shaky breath. I put the book on his bed—far enough away from him that he can't snatch it from my grip. I sit down.

"Good girl," he says.

Chapter Thirty-Seven

I lift my hand. Hot blood pours down my wrist. There are shards of glass protruding from my palm. From the ease in which Blake gave the book to me, I'm starting to think my means of acquiring it were unnecessary.

Beside me, Blake pulls a leather pack from one of his drawers and unfolds it on the surface of the desk. Outside, the sky is grey over the mountains, and cold sunlight makes his line of scalpels glint. I eye them warily, having read some of the experiments in his books, but he slides out a pair of tweezers. He kneels on the floor between my legs, nudging them apart slightly, and his body heat washes over me.

He holds out his palm. I offer him my bloody hand. A strange feeling hums beneath my skin when he curls his fingers around my wrist.

His gaze flicks to mine. "This may sting a little."

He grips the largest shard with the tweezers, and pulls. I withhold my cry as he slides it from the wound. I bite my bottom lip. He drops it on the desk and more blood pumps from the wound and coats his fingers.

He starts work on digging out the smaller pieces. It hurts, but he is surprisingly gentle. "Who took you from Lowfell and brought you to James?" he asks.

"Why do you want to know?"

"You know why," he says. I purse my lips and shake my head. "I'm guessing it was someone from Lochlan's clan. No one from Lowfell would have done it. Ian, perhaps?" I can't stop the quickening of my pulse. Blake drops another piece of glass on the desk. "Ian, then."

"I don't want you to kill him."

"Why not?"

I shake my head. "Alexander has his brother. He thought taking me would enable James to get the prisoners back. It doesn't excuse what he did, but I'd feel bad if he died for it."

"Would you have put someone in harm's way for the sake of *your* brother?"

"My brother is awful. It's not the same." I swallow. "You would have done the same for Elsie, wouldn't you?"

His grips tightens around my wrist. I've touched a nerve. He shrugs, and plucks out another piece of glass. "Has it occurred to you that I must kill Ian *for* Elsie? For my clan? For little Alfie? For you? I cannot have other Wolves thinking they can stroll into Lowfell and take what is mine."

"I'm not yours."

"No. But you're part of my clan. To Wolves, that means something."

I bite my bottom lip. "I don't want another death on my hands."

His brow furrows. "Another? Who else?" My lips harden and I focus on the flames that flicker in the hearth. "Oh. I see. Sebastian. Do you feel bad for taking his life?"

"No." My feelings are more complicated than that. I push down the memory of being trapped in the carriage with the man I was supposed to marry. I turn the conversation on him. "There was a storm, the night I was taken."

"There was."

"Why do you fear them?"

The wind blows through the mountains outside, and the fire crackles. I don't think he's going to answer.

"Do you remember what I told you, about what my biological father did to my mother?" he says.

Blakes fingers curled around my wrist when I tried to rip off the collar he gave me. He told me his father forced himself on his mother. Darkness twists in my chest. I'm not sure if it's coming from him or me. "Yes," I say.

"My mother didn't love me. I reminded her of him, I think, and of the crime that was committed against her. She feared I would have a wolf inside me, like him. For ten years, I showed no signs of it. She tolerated my existence."

He slides out the last piece of glass from my wound and gets up. He pours water from a jug into a wooden basin, then kneels back down again. He takes a cloth from the bowl and rings it out.

"Just after my tenth birthday, there was a vicious storm." He presses my knuckles into his palm, and gently wipes my hand with the cloth. "In the evening, just before it broke, I could feel the wolf. Half-wolves can sense storms, too, sometimes. My eyes changed, and my mother saw, for the first time, what lurked inside me. She dragged me to the church in the village and 'confessed' to the priest what had happened to her, and what I was. It was the first time I'd ever heard her speak of my father."

He puts down the bowl, and picks up a small pot from the table. *Moonflower* is written on the label. He twists off the lid, and puts some ointment on his thumb. He slides it on my wounds.

"The priest tried to get me to 'repent', tried to force the wolf to submit. The more afraid I was, the more provoked my wolf became. Finally, he grew tired of the beatings and dragged me to the well in the center of the village. He threw me down there and told me I could come out when I could control the wolf.

"All the while, the storm raged. My wolf senses were activated for the first time—not as strong as a full wolf's, but stronger than a human's. Every flash of lightning was blinding. Every crash of thunder near deafened me. The wounds the priest gave me were raw on my back. The rain beat down hard and the water rose to my chest. I couldn't stop the panic, try as I might. I didn't know what was happening to me. I thought I was going to die. A part of me wanted to."

In one of my fevered dreams, I remember shivering in a confined space, with water up to my chest. Was I there with him?

Blake grabs a roll of gauze from the desk. "I know it's irrational, but every time I sense a storm coming, I'm back in that well. Powerless."

This story explains more than his fear of storms. He told me before that his wolf condemned him to darkness from the moment he was born, and I know he doesn't like shifting on the nights of the full moon.

"I can understand that," I say softly.

He wraps the gauze around my hand, his touch firm but gentle as he winds it between my finger and thumb. It strikes me how competent he is at this. I knew he was a healer, but I've never seen him do anything but torment people before.

"What happened that night, when you were in the carriage, with Sebastian?" His tone is uncharacteristically careful. "Your emotions around it. . . they feel. . ." His brow furrows. "They feel like I'm ten years old again, trapped in the storm."

I shake my head. "It doesn't matter."

He continues wrapping the bandage around my wound. "I wonder, sometimes, if I ever left that well. It feels as if I am constantly clawing at its sides, trying to lift myself out. Yet every time I get closer to the edge, I slip further into the darkness."

My heart almost stills at the rawness of his confession, the vulnerability it displays. I realize that is the point. It's transactional. An unspoken bargain. He is offering me a part of him, in exchange for a part of me.

His eyes flick to mine. Serious. Expectant. I don't owe him anything. Yet the words bubble inside me. They claw up my throat, desperate to be heard. Even by him. Maybe only by him. Somehow, I know he won't judge me, nor try to protect me from them.

"James gave me a dagger to kill Sebastian with," I say quietly. "He sheathed it to my thigh. When I was in the carriage with Sebastian, I didn't know how to get it out without drawing attention to it. I. . . I sat in his lap. I could feel him, beneath me. He was..." I swallow. "I got the dagger, but he grabbed my wrist and disarmed me. He told me to show him what I'd learned when I was a whore to the Highfell beast." My skin cools. "He told me to get on my knees." Blake's jaw tightens. The shadows in the room seem to darken around him. "I felt helpless. The dagger was out of reach. I thought he was going to... And then James knocked the carriage over. It saved me from... I was able to get the blade. I killed him."

"How do you feel about that?"

My eyes burn. The confession, shameful and abhorrent, that has taken root in my soul swells and spreads vines up my throat. It threatens to rip me apart if I don't get it out. "It was my choice."

He angles his head slightly. "What was?"

"Sebastian." I stare at the ceiling. "I chose him. It was my fault. I chose my fate. My father told me to marry him, and I could have said no. I wanted to please my father. Even when I met Sebastian, and I realized he was a monster, I didn't run. If Callum had not escaped... If I had married Sebastian, the things he tried to do to me in that carriage... I would have let him, wouldn't I? I would have pretended it was my choice, because he was my husband, and I would have let him."

Blake's expression is unreadable. "Coercion and consent are not the same thing. And you do not deserve to be treated cruelly, regardless of what choices you make."

I'm embarrassed when a watery film creeps over my eyes. I've not let anyone see me cry since my mother's funeral, and I was scolded for it. I blink it back.

"I was helpless," I say. "I hate myself for it."

Do as he says. I push away Callum's voice.

I don't know why, but my next shameful secret spills from my lips. "I've started to hate my mother too, because she was helpless, as well. How did she not know she was being poisoned? Why did she not try to escape?"

Blake tucks in the end of the gauze. "Wolves guard things that are high value to them."

"You think she was trying to protect me?"

"Perhaps."

I pull my wrist back, and study my bandaged palm. "It doesn't matter now. It's all in the past. I'm tired, I think. I'm not sure why I said all that." I force a smile. "Ignore me."

"No."

Amid the darkness, a spark flickers. "What do you mean?"

"I cannot ignore you. Those that taught you to act small were fools. You don't need to do that with me."

I let out a bitter laugh. "We are not friends, Blake. You made sure of that when you linked our lives and decided you would plot to kill Callum."

"No. We're enemies, aren't we?" His gold-flecked eyes glint in the firelight. "And one day, we will face one another as such. When the time comes, I want all of you. I want you to throw everything you have at me. I want a glorious defeat."

"A glorious defeat." I shake my head, because I know he's mocking me. "You're one to speak, Blake."

"What do you mean?"

"You say I act small, but what of you? You told me once that you were always pretending. You're hiding something."

"When the time comes, little rabbit, I will give you everything I have. I promise." He stands, and puts his things on the table. "Your wound should be healed by tomorrow morning. Come back to me if it isn't."

"What are you going to do about Ian?"

"If I find him, he will die. He didn't come back to Lowfell after you were kidnapped. I'm guessing he ran away. If he's smart, he will not cross my path again."

"Thank you."

I get up and cross the room. I pick the book up from the end of his bed, and my fingers brush over his silky sheets. I expect him to stop me from taking it, but he rights his armchair by the window and drops into it.

I reach the door, then face him. "Are we going to talk about what happened last night?"

"What do you mean?"

"You. . ." *You kissed me. Took a bullet for me. Callum is acting strangely because of it.* "You know what I mean."

He leans forward and clasps his hands between his thighs. "Do you *want* to talk about it?"

"I. . ." *Do I?*

Blake is a snake. A pest. A monster. He plots against Callum, and uses me to do so. He has hurt people, killed people, *tortured* people. He talks of consent and coercion, yet he linked our lives together against my will. He is a liar. A manipulator. A cheat. Yet it occurs to me that he can be all of these things and still hold a shred of compassion toward me. He can be all of these things and. . . want me.

James certainly seemed to think so. Why else would he have put us through all of that? Why would Callum have been bothered by it?

I exhale. "Perhaps not."

Firelight and shadow flicker across his solemn expression. "Let me know when you do," he says.

Chapter Thirty-Eight

I sit cross-legged on the small bed with Blake's book on the white quilt in front of me. I'm in my old room, in the castle tower.

It looks the same way it did the last time I was here. It's simply furnished. Books cover almost every surface—the shelves, the writing desk by the small window, the bedside table. A candle burns low on the bedside table. Rain hammers against the window, and the sky is grey outside—a reflection of my mood.

Testing the Lore of Wolves is written in gold lettering across the front of the book. Golden stars dust the spine. The book is familiar to me, and it comes to me quickly. Blake slid this book from one of the shelves in this room, in front of me. He was secretive about it, and took it the morning when Callum rode out to help James.

As James said, it's one of Blake's books of experiments. The handwriting is neater than the scrawled notebooks I've read, and when I stumble on some experiments I've read before—the melting of an eyeball to see if it grows back, the testing of different metals on a wolf's skin, and the order in which bones break on the night of a full moon—I realize it's a write-up of the most interesting experiments. This book, I think, was meant for wider distribution.

I flick through, and hope that something will jump out at me. I'm alert for the word *connection* or *life force* or *bond* among the dusty pages. I'm tired, though, and the ink starts to blur.

When I jolt awake, the sky outside the window is dark. My dreams were restless. I found myself in dark corridors, passing barred cells, and being pursued by someone whistling in the shadows.

I'm dreaming of Night's prison, and I try to tell myself it's because of my encounter with Alexander, and the chapel in which I tended to Blake's shoulder, and all the talk of the dark god, of late. Yet my mother's stories have taken root in my mind and started to spread their vines. She told me Night would tempt desperate mortals, and offer them what they wanted the most in exchange for their souls.

I'm the daughter of one king, and the consort of another. Does Night covet my soul?

Someone taps on my door. I slide the book under my pillow, then pad across the room. I open it, and peer through the gap. Some of my tension dissipates.

"Fiona, what are you doing here?" I ask.

"They're throwing a feast for Callum downstairs. It's tradition when there's a new alpha or king. Put on a bonny dress and hurry!"

I frown. "Callum didn't tell me."

"He's been with the alphas all day. He told me to bring you down."

Her enthusiasm provokes a smile, even if I wish Callum had come for me himself. "Just a moment." I hurry over to the armoire, throw it open, and pick a dress.

I prepare myself for the feast.

***

THE SKIRT of my long-sleeved crimson dress brushes against the stone steps as I follow Fiona down the spiral staircase. I wish I'd had longer to prepare. Fiona burst into my room as I was doing my hair, and I only just had time to braid it and weave it into a messy crown. I haven't even bathed since I arrived here.

Fiona tells me how she spent the afternoon trying to help Callum keep the peace among the clans. "He's trying to prepare them for battle, given Alexander's threat, but it's proving difficult when some of the alphas keep trying to undermine him. Rob's the worst."

"He's the huge bald man who wears green?"

"Aye. His clan have always been trouble." She frowns at my bandaged hand as we spill into the corridor at the foot of the tower. "Are you hurt?"

"It's nothing."

Fiona and I part ways when we reach the entrance hall. She tells me she hasn't had chance to check her horses yet. I make the rest of the journey to the Great Hall alone. Brodie, the young freckled boy from Madadh-allaidh, is playing his bagpipes outside the double doors.

"You've improved greatly, Brodie," I say.

He plays a shrill note as I pass, and his cheeks flush as red as his hair. I recall how his chest had puffed up with pride when Callum complimented him the first time I came here. Like then, my amusement dies as soon as I step through the doors.

The Great Hall is loud, hot, and more packed than I've ever seen it. Fires roar in the hearths, and Lochlan's men stand guard in the shadows. The four long tables are packed with Wolves. They shout across the space to one another. A man in blue tartan pinches Kayleigh's behind as she hurries across the hall carrying a tray of meat, causing Mrs. McDonald to grab him by the ear, and shout at him until his face turns purple. When a brawl breaks out between two of the benches, and blood sprays across the flagstones, two of Lochlan's men stride over and break it up.

Callum sits on the wooden throne in the center of the alpha table. A tapestry of the Moon giving the Elderwolf her heart adorns the wall behind him. He looks like a king. His hair is brushed back from his face, emphasizing his strong jaw and his bright eyes. He wears a brown coat across his broad shoulders, with a red tartan sash across it. It must have belonged to James, because it has all the clan colors in it except for the yellow of Lochlan's clan. I imagine that will soon be weaved into the pattern.

Lochlan sits beside Callum, but his body is slightly turned away. I wonder if he's upset about earlier, with Kai, or whether they've been arguing about something else.

Callum's eyes lock onto mine, so intense that my mouth dries.

The noise in the hall dims, as if the Wolves can sense where their king's attention lies. Some of the faces that turn toward me are hostile. I'm clearly viewed as an enemy—not only because of my father, but for my role in this war between brothers.

Perhaps I should have stayed in my chambers.

No. I will not cower. I take a deep breath, smooth down my skirt, then walk between two of the long benches toward Callum. I catch whispered snippets of conversations.

". . . she caused all of this. . ."

". . . southern whore. . ."

". . . did you hear. . .?"

I feel the press of attention on my skin. Blake leans against the wall. A group of men wearing green kilts surround him. There's a strange look in Blake's eyes as he takes in my dress and the braided crown of hair on my head.

A tall, wiry blond wolf leans closer to him and I hear them speak as I pass. "Is it true you took a bullet for the lass?"

"Yes." The corner of his mouth tips up. "I'd hoped she would thank me for it."

The men laugh. "Did she?"

Blake's gaze doesn't move from mine. "Not yet."

The men gathered around him jeer. I felt like we had formed some sort of truce between us, but it shatters. He is blatantly trying to disrespect Callum in front of the Wolves in the clan who accept him the least. I turn my head away and keep walking. I block it all out.

Callum's expression is dark, but it softens as I approach. He gestures at the seat next to him, and I walk around the table, passing the alphas who witnessed my humiliation in the manor house.

Do as he says.

"You look bonny, Princess," says Callum quietly.

"Thank you."

He frowns. "You've hurt your hand,"

"It's nothing."

Lochlan offers me a smile as I sit down, but it doesn't quite reach his eyes.

The roast venison and potatoes that laden the table should make my mouth water, but Callum feels as if he's far away. We've still not talked, not properly, and we can't have a conversation in front of the Wolves.

We make uncomfortable small talk about the food and Brodie's progressing music skills. I ask about the wellbeing of Kai, and whether anything else has been discovered about what happened to him when he was a prisoner.

"He's alive," Lochlan interjects. "Which is more than I can say for some other members of my clan who seem to have mysteriously gone missing." He throws a dark look at Callum, who growls.

"For the last time, I have not killed Ian or any of the others. Make no mistake, if I ever see them again, they are dead. They were responsible for Rory—"

A murmur fills the hall, and there's a clatter as people put down their crockery.

Fiona has a man in a headlock, and hauls him between the tables toward us. She throws him onto the floor in front of our table, and he lands on his hands and knees, laughing. He's wearing a high-collared, tailored blue coat that looks expensive, breeches, and black leather gloves. His coppery red hair shines in the candlelight.

My heart hammers in my chest.

"If you wanted me on my knees, sweetheart, all you needed to do was ask."

The Great Hall falls silent. His accent is my accent—the accent of the Southlands. What's more, it has the musical lilt of nobility.

Fiona backhands him, and he groans and says, "If you keep treating me this way, I'm going to fall in love with you."

Callum's hand curls around his knife. "Who is this buffoon?"

"I found him lurking by the stables," says Fiona.

The man raises his head. His blue-green eyes meet mine, and I clench my jaw so hard it hurts. I take in his handsome face, spattered with freckles, his chiseled jaw, and the clef in his chin. Blood dribbles from his nose.

"My apologies," he says. "I must have forgotten my manners in all the violence. My name is—"

"Philip." I stand abruptly.

Dimples crease his cheeks.

"Hello, little sister," he says.

Chapter Thirty-Nine

Silence.

Then, whispers. They slither through the crowd like snakes. "It's the Southlands prince."

The air erupts. Wolves jump to their feet. One of the benches turns over. Shouts fill the air. They're hysterical. A woman's shriek for vengeance is so hoarse I expect to see blood pouring from her mouth. Lochlan's men push back those who run toward us.

I'm engulfed in the anger, and I know it's aimed at me, as well. My hands ball into fists. My breathing is ragged, like I'm trying to contain a storm in my lungs. Fire blazes through my veins.

"What are you doing here, Philip?" My tone is icy.

His smile widens and shows off his perfect white teeth. He doesn't seem even mildly concerned by the mob that bays for his blood.

He made my life miserable. He taunted me, mocked me, belittled me. He spent my entire childhood waltzing around the palace he was set to inherit as if he already owned it, and I was nothing but one of the objects within. He did as he pleased, drank as he pleased, bedded women as he pleased, and constantly made an exhibition of himself. He never received more than a slapped wrist for his behavior. All the while, I would be punished if so much as a crack showed in my perfect façade. Now he's *here*. He must have got back from the war he was fighting on behalf of my father and come straight to the Northlands to bring me home.

"I might ask you the same thing, Sister." He clucks his tongue over the noise. "Someone's been a naughty girl. Daddy will be displeased."

A low growl vibrates in Callum's chest, a sound that a wiser man would cower from. My brother has always been a goddess-damned idiot. Does he not comprehend that he's in enemy territory, surrounded by Wolves? Does he not sense the violence in the air? The thirst for blood—his *and* mine?

Lochlan leans forward slightly, and his brow furrows. Philip's grin falters, almost as if he recognizes the Glas-Cladach alpha.

Callum nods at Blake, who sits at the other end of the table.

Blake gets up and strolls toward Philip. In a sudden movement, he plunges a syringe into my brother's neck, and Philip crumples to the floor.

"I'll spend some time with him in the infirmary," says Blake.

Callum stands up beside me. His arm brushes against mine. "No one else touches him until I've decided what to do with him." He gestures at a couple of men, and they lift my brother and drag him through the mob toward the exit.

"He wouldn't have travelled alone," I say. "He can barely dress himself without his entourage, let alone travel across the entire kingdom."

"Lochlan?"

"I'll send out a search party," says Lochlan. His earlier darkness seems to be replaced by intrigue.

Callum whispers something to Fiona, then he and I follow Blake out of the Great Hall.

***

WHEN WE arrive at the infirmary, Philip is tied to a chair near the cot where Kai sleeps. His head lolls against his chest, and his hair is the color of tarnished copper in the soft light of the flames. His wrists are tied to the arms of the chair, and his long legs are spread slightly, his ankles bound to the feet.

I halt close to him, by the fireplace. Callum stands beside me. Blake dismisses the two men who brought Philip here.

Philip was supposed to be fighting in one of my father's wars in the kingdom of Rema, but if this has hardened him in any way, he wears no evidence of it. His long, high-collared coat is well tailored, he's as well-groomed as always, and his face—the only bit of his skin that is showing—is flushed with the flames, but not tanned by the warmer weather overseas. I can imagine him sitting in one of his big elaborate tents, drinking and eating and ordering others to do his—and my father's—dirty work.

Blake uncorks a vial and puts it beneath Philip's nose. My brother stirs, then groans. Blake walks to the workbench behind him and pulls a leather pack from one of the drawers.

He flicks it open to reveal metal blades and scalpels. My insides tighten. I loathe my brother. Still, after reading about some of Blake's experiments, I don't think I've the stomach for whatever Blake is planning.

I expect Callum to put a stop to this. Blake pulls out a small blade, and Callum's face is expressionless. Callum has always been so gentle with me that I forget that first impression I had of him. I'd thought him a bloodthirsty monster—as wild and untamed as the mountains he came from.

He's not a monster. He *is* a fierce warrior, an alpha, and now, a king. Philip being here is a threat to both me and his kingdom.

Philip tries to move his arms. There's a squeak as he grips the arms of the chair with his leather-gloved hands. I'm convinced now he will start to panic. My brother has not endured a single hardship in all of his life.

I'm not going to let Blake hurt him, but I can still enjoy his fear.

Philip peers up at Blake. "Bondage? You're not my usual type, but you're pretty enough, I suppose."

Blake leans against the workbench, and the small knife in his hand gleams. He flashes Philip a smile that most would cower from. My brother smiles back.

"Is your brother an eejit?" Callum's tone is a mixture of irritation and genuine curiosity.

"He's not a wise man," I say.

Philip stares down his nose at Callum, as if he's sitting on a throne rather than bound to a chair. "Perhaps you and I should speak in private. One future king to another."

Anger erupts inside me. Isn't that just typical of Philip? He's arrived on a mission concerning me, yet it's the highest-ranking male in the room who he wishes to have an audience with. Goddess forbid I have a say in my own future.

I grit my teeth. "He's not the future king. He *is* the king."

"Not for long, if the talk in the taverns is anything to go by."

"What are you doing here, Philip?" I ask.

"I had every intention of telling you, little sister. I've been so ill-treated that now I shan't." He shakes his head. "I had heard the Northlands Wolves were inhospitable, but I'd not expected such a cold welcome."

I step closer to him. He smells like ale. "This is not a game. Father is not here to save you, your title will not protect you, and you cannot pay your way out of this. You're in the kingdom of Wolves, and you're the prince of their enemy. You would be wise to show a little understanding of the seriousness of your situation."

His eyes glint. "You've changed, Sister."

"And you have not changed in the slightest, *Brother*."

"You might be surprised."

Blake drags a chair from the workbench and places it at an angle to Philip's. He drops into it, and puts an arm over the back. From the ease of his movements, his bullet wound must be healed already.

"You're looking better than the last time I saw you, Blake," says Philip.

A cold smile graces Blake's lips. "As are you."

I shouldn't be surprised they know one another. Blake was part of the King's Guard, so it's probable they would have encountered one another.

"Where have you been?" asks Blake.

"I don't see why I should tell you."

Blake rests his ankle on his thigh. He absently twirls the small blade in his hand. "Do you think Aurora will save you?"

"I think that you answer to her, don't you?"

Blake's smile becomes feral. "If that were true, I'd be very worried about your current situation."

Philip meets my eye. "She does this, you know. Bats her eyelids and wraps powerful men around her fingers. Plays the innocent princess to get them to give her whatever she wants."

Outrage blooms inside me.

"Is that so?" Blake says.

When did I *ever* get what I wanted? I want to tell him every bad thought I've ever had about him. I want to slap him across the face. The thought of snatching the blade from Blake and plunging it into his thigh is a strong one. My soul threatens to erupt.

I pull it all back. I cage my feelings, as if by having him here—a reminder of the palace—I'm regressing to an earlier version of myself. I hate that he makes me feel like a helpless, voiceless child once more.

Callum shifts closer. I step aside. I don't want the warm comfort he has denied me all day. I'm too far beyond thawing.

"You're dressed rather warmly, Philip," says Blake. "Keeping up appearances, or something else?"

It's a strange comment to make when the climate in the Northlands is considerably colder than that in the south. Philip's smile fades for a moment, as if Blake has touched on something. He stiffens when Blake leans forward and gently takes Philip's hand. My muscles tighten.

"Blake. . ." I say.

Blake peels off Philip's leather glove. The tip of his little finger is missing.

"Torture?" Blake drops the glove on the workbench to his side. "Or frostbite?"

My eyebrows lift. I can't imagine that my brother would have been exposed to either.

"You've been keeping track of me," says Philip.

"Naturally."

The door swings open. Isla swans into the room, and irritation sparks within me. I didn't see her at the feast. She wears a dress made out of the Highfell red tartan. The top part of her light-brown hair is braided into a crown, like mine, while the rest hangs loose and wild down her shoulders.

"Is there something you need, Isla?" Callum sounds weary, and I realize today is taking a toll on him.

"I was looking for you—" She halts. Philip angles his head to one side, and her nostrils flare. "There are two of them. Are we to be constantly inundated with southerners? When I traveled here from Highfell, I didn't expect to be so consistently surrounded by these people."

"What type of people did you expect to be surrounded by when you traveled south?" Blake says.

Isla's face blanches, as if she'd not realized Blake was here. She raises her chin. "I expected to be among my own people, *Wolves*. We're still in the Northlands."

"If you're looking for oil of evening primrose, I believe it's over there." Philip arches back his head, and indicates one of the shelves.

My eyebrows raise at his audacity, while Callum looks confused. Evening primrose oil was the remedy the palace healer would give me for easing the symptoms of my monthly bleed. Isla's eyes become icy.

She stalks toward Philip. She grips the back of the chair on either side of him, and brings her face close to his. "Brave words, princeling, but you forget you're among Wolves now. Your heartbeat is racing, and your scent... you smell of fear behind your rich perfumes and your pretty clothes. You're nothing but a spoiled little boy, acting as if you're not afraid, wishing you were back home among your silk and jewels." She bares her teeth. "You're a long way from home now."

Philip leans forward against his restraints, their faces even closer. "And what of you, *Isla*?" His voice is low, almost a whisper. "Your perfume—rose petals, lemon, and a hint of rosemary. I met a woman at a market once who swore those were the ingredients for a love potion. Your dress, tightly fitting, and the red tartan of your clan... It's the color of Highfell, a territory far from here, isn't it? You're a long way from home too, despite your apparent disdain for your surroundings. Then there's the striking features of your face, made more feminine with powder and rouge, as if you wish to seem more demure and delicate than you are—perhaps to appeal to a figure of authority. An alpha. A king, perhaps. Yet he has eyes only for my sister, doesn't he? Don't worry, Isla, *I* see you."

Her knuckles are white as her grip tightens.

"Now whose heart is beating fast?" His nostrils flare. "And is that another scent I detect? Have I caught your interest, little wolf?" Dimples crease his cheeks as he lowers his voice. "If ever you'd like to play with someone who can bite as hard as you can, let me know."

His eyes shift. His pupils dilate, and threads of silver glint among the blue-green of his irises. I inhale sharply. Isla's breath hitches.

My brother doesn't have the eyes of a man.

He has the eyes of a wolf.

Chapter Forty

Philip, the prince of the Southlands and heir to the throne, is a wolf.

Callum steps closer to me, as if—for the first time—he perceives my brother as a threat. His mountain scent curls protectively around me as his muscles harden.

I'm foolish to be shocked, but with everything going on, I'd not given much thought to my brother. If our mother was a wolf of course Philip would be a half-wolf like me. Though his eyes changed at will. His nostrils flared as he told Isla about her scent, and he claimed to hear her heartbeat. I told him he had not changed a bit.

You might be surprised, he had responded.

He has made the change. He was bitten, and was strong enough to survive. He is more of a wolf than I am. It's typical of him to succeed where I've failed.

Panic flares inside me. Philip's eyes confirm that I'm a wolf.

Why didn't I shift?

Isla steps back. Her cheeks are flushed, and I can tell she's caught off guard. She huffs. "It doesn't matter if you have some wolf in your blood. You'll never be one of us, princeling." She nods at Blake's small blade. "Besides, I don't play with broken toys."

She flick her hair over her shoulder, throws me a dirty look, then swans out of the room.

Philip sighs dramatically. "I think I'm in love."

"You'll be dead soon if you don't start minding your manners." Callum's knuckles crack as he clenches his fist. "Did you know he was a wolf?"

I open my mouth to respond. He's staring at Blake.

"It was hardly a stretch of logic, with your pet being the way she is," Blake says. "Plus, I know the wolf who bit him."

My insides turn to ice. "What? You knew about this and you didn't say anything?"

Blake rolls his eyes. "Not all this time. I presumed the palace healer had stopped the wolf venom from killing him. When he supposedly left for the war, I wondered if the bite killed him and your father covered it up. It wasn't until I met you, little rabbit, that I started to suspect differently. I sent Jack, recently, to try and find him. The rumor was that no sooner had Philip arrived overseas, he abandoned the war camp, and slipped off to somewhere slightly colder, never to be heard from again. Tell me, Philip, how did you enjoy the Snowlands?"

My head snaps toward Philip, and for the first time, curiosity outweighs my ill feeling. "You went to the Snowlands?"

"Yes," says Philip. "And as for how I found it..." He wiggles his tipless finger. "It was rather cold. I got frostbite within days."

"I... what... why?" I splutter.

Philip rolls his eyes. "Why do you think, little sister?" *To find out more about our mother.* "Perhaps we should save the family catch-up for later." He nods at the bindings around his wrists and ankles. "After my needless torture."

"Tell us what you're doing here, and you won't be harmed," says Callum.

"Release me, and I shall," says Philip.

A look passes between Callum and Blake.

"We know why he's here," I say. "He's come to take me back to my father."

"Not everything is about you, darling sister. I didn't come for you. I only found out you were here a few days ago."

"Why *are* you here, then?" I ask.

He nods at Callum. "I came for *him*."

Callum laughs. Arms folded, he looks Philip up and down. "You came for me?"

"Not to kill you. Goodness, must it always amount to violence among your people? I was sent by Ingrid Erickson, alpha of the Iceborn tribe, queen of the Snowlands. She believes an agent of the God of Night wishes to release the dark god from his prison. An army will be needed to push him, and his followers, back. She has a message for the Wolf King."

Callum frowns. "What's the message?"

"She wants to make an alliance to unite the two wolf kingdoms," says Philip. "She wishes to ask for your hand in marriage."

Chapter Forty-one

"Marriage?" Callum's eyebrows raise.

Shock hardens my body.

Philip has come with a betrothal request for Callum from the queen of the Snowlands. Of all the reasons I could have theorized for his presence in the Northlands, I would never have imagined it would be this. I would rather he had come for me.

"I see I've touched a nerve, little sister. Sorry about that," says Philip.

"Explain yourself," says Callum—when I need him to just say no.

"Around thirty years ago, our mother was sent to the Southlands by our grandmother," says Philip. "The Snowlands was being ravaged by a pack who were deeply devoted to the God of Night."

"They were led by someone called the Shadow Wolf," I say. I read about it in one of Blake's books at Lowfell.

"Yes," says Philip. "I don't know the exact terms of the agreement, but our mother married Father because he agreed to help the Wolves fight this Shadow Wolf. They were defeated, but lately, there has been a resurgence in this pack. They're stronger than before. More determined. They seem to think they have a chance of actually freeing the God of Night this time. There are rumors that the key to his prison is in the Northlands, and a wolf they're calling The Night Prince is looking for it. Soon, you'll face the same threat we have been dealing with. We need to unite."

Callum runs a hand along his jaw, and I wonder if he's thinking about all the strange things that have been happening in the Northlands lately—Night's chapels springing back into use, Claire's desperation for an alliance because of strange murders happening in the north, and Kai's claim that he faced one of Night's prisoners.

Philip nods at me. "My father will never agree to a match between the two of you, so you have no chance of an alliance with the Southlands. What I'm presenting... it's a sensible match. You've not seen the things I have seen." Callum opens his mouth, and Philip raises his fingers to stop him from speaking. "You don't need to answer now. Think on it. I will stay for a while."

Callum's expression is stony. "When I marry, it will be for love, not for politics."

"Then perhaps you're not ready to become king," says Philip.

"That's rich, coming from you," I say.

He shrugs. "It's different. I'm heir to the throne. One day, the Southlands will be mine, whether I'm ready to be king or not."

Obnoxious, arrogant fool. I bet he would let our kingdom fall into ruins rather than perform his duty as king.

"I was drinking in a tavern close to here," continues Philip. "Word is, not all support your claim to the throne. They think you're a southern sympathizer. It won't be long before you're challenged, and then what? Constant war among your people, when a bigger war is coming. An alliance with another wolf kingdom would be wise." He shrugs. "It would be for appearances only. You can still carry on with whatever *this* is." He waves his gloved hand between us, and his wrist strains against his constraints.

Callum's low growl rumbles through the infirmary. "Do not question my honor. My answer is no. When I marry a lass, she will have all of me—heart, body, and soul. I will expect the same from her. I will settle for no less."

"Why not offer yourself to Ingrid as a marriage prospect?" Blake asks Philip. I feel a thrum of curiosity that doesn't belong to me.

"The last time my kingdom made an alliance with the Snowlands, it didn't end well for them." A shadow dulls Philip's eyes. With the seriousness of his freckled face, and his hard lips, he looks like the prince he's supposed to be, rather than the waste of space I know that he is. "Ingrid won't marry me."

Questions bubble inside me. There's so much I want to know. I wonder what he found out in the Snowlands, and whether he knows Mother was a wolf. "We will talk about this later, Philip," I say.

"You were always insufferably bossy, little sister."

I narrow my eyes. "And you were always insufferable."

The door to the infirmary swings open. Lochlan and Jack enter.

Philip falls quiet as Jack strolls toward him. "Is this the heir to the Southlands throne?" For the first time, Philip seems uncomfortable. Jack grabs his hand, the one with the finger missing, and clucks his tongue. "Oh dear, what happened here?"

"I'm more interested in this." Lochlan approaches, grabs the high collar of my brother's coat, and tugs it to one side. Ink curls up Philip's collarbone and creeps down his shoulder. The tattoo must be new; he didn't have it when we lived in the Southlands. "I've heard that deadly warriors in the Snowlands bear these kinds of marks."

Philip shifts in the chair to cover it back up, and my scoff dies in my throat.

His face is hard. There's an iciness in his eyes that I've not seen before. His face... the way he's looking at Lochlan... For the first time in his life, he looks dangerous.

Until he blinks, and a grin broadens across his face. "The outcome of a night of debauchery and too much ale at the King's City docks."

Callum exhales. "If Alexander is planning an attack, I don't have time to look after a spoiled prince. Blake, find out what you can, then get rid of him." He tracks Lochlan's movements as the alpha pulls a chair toward Kai's cot and drops into it. "Has anything changed?"

"No," says Blake.

Philip straightens. "I'm not leaving. Not until you've agreed to speak with Ingrid."

Callum shrugs. "I've given you your answer. I won't force you to leave, but my people will tear you apart if you stay. I won't protect you." He walks toward the infirmary doors. "Princess, let me escort you to your chambers."

The desire to know more about what Philip has been doing, and my need to have a conversation with Callum, war inside me. My aching heart wins, and I follow Callum into the corridor.

I feel both Blake and my brother's eyes on me as I walk away.

Chapter Forty-Two

We make the journey through the castle in silence. Callum follows me up the spiral staircase, then leans over me to push the door open. His chest momentarily presses against my back.

Do as he says.

Inside, the candles are unlit, and the darkness lies heavily atop the many books and trinkets within the room. The door clicks shut, and the room feels too small to breathe. Callum strolls toward the window and looks out onto the shadow-drenched mountains.

"You—"

"Why—"

We both speak at the same time. I shut my mouth and allow him to continue.

"Can we trust your brother?" He clasps his hands together, and I get the impression that wasn't what he was going to say.

"No. He's rotten. But everything he said about the God of Night. . . Kai has Night's mark on his chest, and it seems like Alexander worships the God of Night. I think something is going on. What if Alexander is the Night Prince?"

Callum's jaw hardens. "It doesn't matter who he worships. If he means to attack my kingdom, if he means to take you, he'll face my wrath.

He runs a hand over his mouth. When he sets his eyes on me, there's such pain in them that I almost stagger back. I sigh. "Talk to me, Callum."

He walks to the edge of my bed and sits down. The small frame creaks beneath his weight. "I cannot get it out of my head," he says. "Even with everything going on, it gnaws through my skull. There's no respite. I close my eyes, and I see him with you."

My pulse quickens at the rawness of his confession. I want to be relieved that he's finally opening up to me, but it feels unfair. "I cannot get it out of my mind, either."

He makes a low sound in his throat.

"Not in the way you're thinking," I say. "I can't get it out of my head because of *you*."

"Why?"

"Why! Callum, you told him to do it." Callum opens his mouth, but I'm not finished yet. "Your brother took me prisoner. He bound me, and humiliated me in front of a room full of men who would gladly kill me. You could have done something to help me. You sat there, and you watched, and you *told* Blake to do it."

His jaw hardens. "I told Blake to do it because it was the only way one of us could get to you, to free you." There is something defiant in his tone, and he glances at the armoire in the corner of the room, as if he can't quite meet my eye.

I think back to the moment in the manor house. Blake tapped the table before he approached me, signaling something to Callum. He slid his fingers into my bindings, as if to test their strength.

Callum though. . . it seemed like he was listening to what James was saying. The way he looked at Blake, with suspicion, when Blake was visibly annoyed that James touched me.

Do as he says.

"I don't believe you," I say. "I think, perhaps, Blake went through with it because he was trying to free me, but it seemed like you had another reason."

Callum releases a bitter laugh. "You think *that's* why he kissed you?"

"Enough! Enough with this jealousy! You act as if you suffer, yet it's suffering of your own devising. You could have challenged James the moment I was brought into that room, but you didn't. You chose to do nothing. You chose to let it happen. Why? Tell me the truth!"

"I had to know."

"Know what?"

He puts his head in his hands. "I started to suspect, long before that night, that I had been cursed to want something that could never truly be mine."

"What are you talking about?"

He drags his fingers down his face. "Do you have feelings for him?"

"What? No!"

"Now who is not being honest? You expect me to tell you the truth when you're concealing it from me."

"I'm not lying to you—"

"I'm a wolf, Rory! Your heartbeat, your movements around him, your scent... Can you look me in the eye and tell me you felt nothing when he pressed his lips to yours?" I open my mouth and he shakes his head. "If you cannot be honest about this, I don't think I can get past it."

"You know James did this to get under your skin, don't you?"

"Of course I know!" He slams his hand against his chest. "Yet I wonder if in his own way, he was trying to help me."

"This is the wolf who attacked me, bit me, damned near killed me!"

"Answer the question."

"You're being ridiculous."

"Perhaps I am." He leans forward, and rests his forearms on his thighs. The mattress creaks beneath him. His shoulders are hunched, the muscles in his neck tense. He's such a sorry sight that if I weren't so frustrated with him, I would comfort him. "My wolf is so close to the surface when you're near, I cannot make sense of my emotions. I've never felt so out of control. I don't know if I'm overreacting, or underreacting. I don't know what's real. My blood is roaring and my teeth ache and I feel as if I could shed my skin and shift at any moment." His eyes shine in the darkness. "And that was always my father's excuse. He would lose his temper, and act jealous, and hurt the people around him, and he would say he did it because of the wolf. I don't want to turn into him. So I suppress it, and I tell myself I'm not right to feel the way I do, but I have to know, Rory. I need you to tell me. When he kissed you, what did you feel?"

I take a shuddery breath. I turn to the window, and place my hands on the desk, littered with books. I catch the slither of the moon that peeks from behind the clouds. The wind ripples the loch, and stirs the branches of the evergreen trees on its bank. "I don't know. I felt angry with you."

"And?"

I think of the moment he brushed his lips against mine. I felt like I was falling, and darkness was flooding me. I felt an intense ache, like nothing I had felt before. I felt heat in my blood.

"I felt his emotions," I say.

"And?"

I shake my head, and turn back to him. "That's all."

He makes a frustrated sound and stands. "I don't know if you're lying to me or yourself."

His footsteps thud as loudly as my heartbeat as he walks to the door and grabs the handle.

"I felt something!" The words tumble out of me, traitorous and painful, and he halts. The muscles in his back bunch beneath his shirt. "Is that what you want me to say? I felt a glimmer of something, perhaps. A fleeting moment. It was because I was angry with *you*. My feelings were mixed with his, and it was intense, and I was afraid."

He turns, and the wolf blazes in his eyes. He swallows. Hard. Then nods. "Thank you. Thank you for being honest."

He takes a deep breath, steeling himself. "I need. . . I need to calm down."

I walk to him and grip his hand. I'm angry and frustrated, yet I feel it needs to be said.

"I've met men like your father, Callum. You are not like him." I put his hand on my chest, over my heart. "And you say you don't know what's real? This is real. We are real. I took your hand, and I chose you that night in the Borderlands. I choose you now. But I cannot, will not, be the princess you keep locked in your tower while you spiral over things that neither of us can control. I did not want to kiss him. You know that. So go for a walk, swim in the loch, take the time you need to get past this. But get past it, because if you cannot. . ."

I can't bring myself to say it. He nods, and presses his forehead to mine. His skin is hot. He feels almost feverish. "You don't know how much I want you to be mine, Rory."

"Then stop being such a territorial beast. And stop pushing me away."

He releases a half-laugh, but there is no humor in it. He turns to the door again.

"Callum, wait." He looks over his shoulder. *I need you*, I want to say. *Stay.* But I feel as if I need some distance, too, after everything he has said. I think we both need to sort through our emotions. "You said you would not protect Philip, if he stays."

"Do you want me to?"

My insides twist. "I. . . I don't know. I hate him, but he's my blood."

I wonder if he—with his relationship with James—understands more than most how complicated siblings can be. "I shall tell my people Philip is our hostage," he says, "and we mean to use him to get to your father. Perhaps, once we beat Alexander, we will do so."

"Thank you."

"I'll have someone stand guard outside your chambers to make sure you're safe."

I can't help but think that one time, he would have guarded my chambers himself, all night if he needed to.

He opens the door and strides down the staircase, leaving me alone.

Chapter Forty-Three

Darkness trickles over my skin.

I try to make sense of my surroundings. I think I'm in Night's prison. The hairs on my arms stand on end. The air feels colder, and it seems to move around me when in other dreams it felt stagnant.

I extend my arms and expect to touch the walls. There is nothing on either side of me. I gasp, and it echoes, as if I'm in a cavernous space. Fear prickles down my spine. I inch forward, searching for a wall to edge along so I can find the door.

There's a scrape behind me, and my heart stops.

"Hello, little rabbit." A whisper like silk, calm and smooth.

I turn. I release a breath as my eyes adjust. Blake strolls along the length of a wall I couldn't see before. He seems to be inspecting something.

I swallow. "We're in Night's prison, aren't we?" Even though I keep my voice soft, it echoes around us.

"Yes."

I walk toward him. "What are you doing?"

"Look," he whispers. He pats the wall, and as I get closer, I see what he's looking at. There's a hole in the black stone, big enough that either of us could walk through it. A current of cold air trickles through. "Something has escaped. It shouldn't be possible. Only *Ghealach*'s power could have caused this."

"Does someone have the Heart of the Moon?" I ask. My blood turns colder.

"Doubtful. This doesn't look like it was done intentionally. The moon shone brightly on the night you killed Sebastian. I'd warrant it happened then."

"One of Night's prisoners is on earth."

"It seems so."

My pulse quickens as I recall Kai's account of the Dark Beast. "Do you think that the prisoner that has escaped is at the Grey Keep, with Alexander?"

Blake runs a hand along his jaw. "That seems likely."

I think of my mother's stories about dark monsters, soul-suckers, winged beasts. "Who do you think got out?"

Blake crouches and picks something up. Its thin, and black, and covered in scales. It looks like a piece of skin, shed by a serpent, and one of the images I saw in one of the books I found at Lowfell comes back to me. As he rubs it between his finger and thumb, it dissolves into a wisp of shadow.

Blake's expression darkens. "Something I really wish was still here."

The cell disintegrates around me and I fall through darkness.

I jolt onto my feet. I'm somewhere else. Pain screams through my body. My skin pulls taut on my arms, and there are hundreds of hooks piercing my skin and holding me upright. They're in my legs, my feet, my shoulders. There are translucent strings attached to them that extend into a cloud of darkness above me.

My lips are sewn shut, so my scream cannot escape. Tears well in my eyes.

I've been here before. It's my nightmare. I'm a marionette, controlled by an invisible hand in the palace's moonlit throne room. Around me, courtiers dance. They don't notice my anguish. They don't notice my silent scream.

My father's gold-adorned throne sits on the dais ahead. It's embellished with suns that glint in the moonlight. Its shadow swallows me.

Music and merriment floods the space. My invisible puppeteer moves the control handle, and I start to spin. I try to free myself, but I'm trapped.

I'm jerked to a halt.

The music stops. The courtiers are frozen in time. My heart clenches, because this is new and I don't know what happens next.

Loud footsteps click against the flagstones. The air stirs as Blake walks past me, up the steps to the dais, and he drops onto the throne as if it were made for him. He leans back and props an elbow on the arm.

"Isn't this horrifying?" he says. Moonlight illuminates one side of his face. The other is cast in darkness.

I try to speak, and I taste my own blood.

"I wouldn't do that, if I were you." His gaze travels up the strings to the control bar, which is cloaked in shadow. "Who controls you? Who would I find, if I climbed to the top, I wonder? Your father? Brother? Callum? Me? Perhaps your mother, or something more abstract—like duty, or honor. Has it ever occurred to you that *you* are the one pulling the strings? That you are binding yourself? That you could break free, if you wished it?" He drums his fingers along the arm of the throne. "Probably not."

I try to pull against the hooks, and warm blood dribbles down my arms.

"You looked like a queen tonight," he muses. "You could be one, if you wished it. Philip sleeps in my infirmary. You could creep down there while the castle sleeps. There's a beaker of water on the table beside him. A few drops of wolfsbane would do the trick. I would do it for you, if you asked me. Your father is old. He will die, eventually, and when he does, the throne would be yours."

He stands and straightens his coat. He strolls down the dais and stops in front of me.

"It pains me to see you like this, darling." I'm not sure if he's telling the truth. "Think about what I said."

He slips his hands into his pockets and walks away. His footsteps fade. The floor opens up.

I'm falling through endless darkness once more.

***

I JOLT upright in my bed. My skin is clammy, and the sheets stick to me. I can't control my wild pulse. The night is still dark, but I can't go back to sleep. I was dreaming of Night's prison. I was dreaming of Blake.

With shaky fingers, I light the candle beside the bed. I pull the book that has answers about our bond from beneath my pillow. I start to read.

The light of dawn is straining through my window when my eyes snag on a particular page in the book. Realization slams into me with brutal force. An emotion I can't understand threatens to tear me apart.

I dress hurriedly. I grab the tome and earmark it at the appropriate page. I hurry out of my room—almost tripping over the male who sleeps against the wall. He has a bushy red beard and a blue kilt. I recognize him from when Callum first took me from the Borderlands. Fergus, I think his name is.

He doesn't stir as I hurry down the stairs. So much for keeping guard.

I need to speak to Blake.

Chapter Forty-Four

The castle is awakening. I battle through the current of people who light the torches, carry food, and make their way outside with weapons.

That wildness in my chest I have felt since James bit me rears its head. My blood roars and my heartbeat howls. Dots dance before my eyes. My body is trying to shut down my emotions.

I pass the kitchens, and barely register Mrs. McDonald shouting at Kayleigh for burning the porridge. Blake strolls toward me from the direction of the infirmary. I grab him and shove him against the wall before he can speak. He makes a low sound in his throat. I grab his shirt and pull it out of his breeches.

He grabs my wrist. "If you're reaching for my cock, darling, that is off limits."

His voice is far away. There's a long scar that curves down his abdomen. My breathing is hard. Fast. My eyes flick to his, and the corridor swims around me. "Who did this to you?"

He nudges me back. "Does it matter?"

"Does it matter?!" I shove the book at his chest and he pulls a face. I open it at the page I earmarked. "*Do Wolves' internal organs grow back when removed? Incision was made on the right-hand side of the test subject's abdomen in order to remove the kidney.*"

I hit him with the book again, and he grunts. There is a diagram of a body, where there is a curved line on the abdomen to depict the incision point. It mirrors the worst of Blake's scars.

I recall that dark feeling that had twisted inside me when I read one of his books full of experiments in the Great Hall—so similar to the feeling I had every time the High Priest beat me. I thought it was shame, that perhaps he felt bad for harming other Wolves.

I had not considered there could be another reason: he might be ashamed that he let these things happen to him.

I shake my head, my hands trembling. "You led me to believe you wrote these books."

His expression is dark. "You came to that conclusion by yourself, little rabbit."

"All those experiments. . . all those terrible things. . . they were done to you."

"No." His tone is clipped. "I wasn't his only pet."

"Who?" I shove the book at him again. "Who did this?"

"Why?"

"I want to know."

He shrugs, as if it's inconsequential. "Who do you think? The Maester of Healing at the palace."

I feel as if I'm underwater. "Did. . . did my father know?"

"Did he know?" The corner of his lip tugs up, but there's no amusement in his eyes. "It was his program, little rabbit."

My pulse thunders in my ears, and I hear another one competing with it. I'd place Blake as three or four years older than me. That means he must have been somewhere in the King's City—perhaps even the palace itself—being torn apart, while I was attending dancing lessons, or preening in front of the mirror. My own naivety rises up in my throat on a wave of nausea. How could I have been so clueless as to what was happening?

Yet amid the shock and the anger that courses through me, something darker pervades. That wildness stills. My skin prickles, and the hairs on the back of my neck stand on end.

Any empathy is replaced by something cold and wary. I step away, and my back bumps into the wall on the other side of the corridor. All this time, I had thought I was a pawn in his game with Callum. He told me he hated the Wolves, and that he wanted to rule them.

It occurs to me now that he has just as much reason to hate humans. My father may be a far bigger foe to him than Callum, or James, or any of the Wolves. Perhaps taking the Wolf Throne is part of a bigger game, and my role in it won't be over if he defeats Callum. Perhaps he has something even bigger in store for me. Last night, in my dream, he tried to persuade me to kill Philip.

Perhaps he wants the whole world to burn.

"Are you going to hurt me?" I ask.

A tense silence stretches between us. My skin hums.

He drags his teeth over his bottom lip. "No."

I try to feel him through the bond, but everything feels dark. "Are you going to hurt my brother?"

"Only if you ask me to."

"What about Callum? Will you kill him? Do I get a choice in that?"

He runs a hand over the sharp edge of his jaw. "If he forfeits when I challenge him, I will let him go."

"And me? Will you let me go?"

"I haven't decided yet."

My skin prickles. He's lying. His choice seems to pulse in the air between us, dark and certain, and a word vibrates along the thread that links us. *No.*

I steady my breathing. "What happened to the Maester? Did you kill him?"

"That is not the right question, little rabbit."

"What is the right question?"

"If you ask it, I shall tell you." He tucks in his shirt. "But no, the Maester still lives." He walks away, in the direction of the Great Hall, and the tension is broken.

"Blake."

He halts. "Yes?"

"Last night, the dream. . . It was real, wasn't it?"

He inclines his head. Coldness fills me.

"Alexander truly has one of Night's prisoners," I say.

"It looks that way."

"What does he want with me?"

Blake shakes his head. "I hope we don't find out."

***

CALLUM SPENDS the day in meetings with Blake and the other alphas, talking strategy for the impending battle with

Alexander. Other than a few exchanged pleasantries over dinner that night, he doesn't speak to me.

The next morning, I get tired of waiting for him, and knock on the door of his bedchambers. He's already gone, so I spend the morning tailing Philip after he's released from the infirmary.

After being shown to his bedchambers on the first floor of the castle, he heads outside. He stops Kayleigh on her way inside from the kitchen gardens, and—after flirting with her—asks her if it's true that the Heart of the Moon is here.

He does the same thing to a couple more women, before he sits on the shore of the loch and looks out onto the mountains across the water. I watch him from a spot by the castle walls.

He's clearly looking for the Heart of the Moon. Is that the real reason he has come to the Northlands?

Philip gets up and wanders back to his bedchambers. When he doesn't emerge, I visit Fiona in the stables, share some bread and cheese with her on her break, then head back to the castle.

Back in my chambers, I pore over *Testing the Lore of Wolves*.

The experiments seem even more horrible now I know they may have been done to Blake. The sky darkens. The ink blurs. Frustration wells inside me, because I've scoured this book and can find no mention of a bond. I wonder if I'm wasting my time.

My heart jolts, and I slam my hand down onto the book.

There. The numbers change from page seventy-seven to eighty-three. I run my finger down the spine. There's a tear. Pages have been removed from the tome. I curse myself. I should have trusted my instincts. I knew he gave me it too easily.

If these pages weren't important, he wouldn't have removed them.

If I'm lucky, the alphas will still be in their meeting. *Blake* will still be in the meeting.

I slide out of bed. I head out of my room, and down the spiral staircase.

I make my way to Blake's bedchambers.

Chapter Forty-Five

Shouting and bagpipe music from the Great Hall filters up the stairwell as I pass it. When I reach his chambers, I press my ear to the door. There is no sound within.

Tentatively, I enter. I release a breath. It's empty.

There's a fire burning in the hearth. He has tidied since I last visited. The four-poster bed that dominates the space has been made, and the shredded curtains have been completely removed. The shelves beside it are creaking beneath the weight of his tomes.

His scent of dark forests lingers in the room, among the smell of woodsmoke and parchment.

I step into the room and close the door behind me.

It strikes me odd that Blake would leave his chambers unlocked, but I wonder if that is due to the arrogance of alpha Wolves. He believes no one would dare to break in. Most would not.

I take a deep breath. I must be quick. I don't know how long it will be until he returns.

I hurry over to the bookshelf, the floorboards creaking beneath my feet. I run my hands over the tops of the books, hoping I'll find a wedge of parchment stuffed away. Next, I rummage through the desk. There are two thin drawers in the dark wood, and I slide the first one open. There's a pile of letters within, crumpled like they've been removed and stuffed back in again. I flick through them.

Sebastian seeks the Heart of the Moon.

Sebastian plans to marry the Southlands princess. He will be distracted through the festivities.

They are all signed *M*. These letters depict Blake organizing the siege on the Borderlands castle with his spy. I put them away.

I find nothing of interest in the second drawer—a few maps of the Northlands, a list of poisonous flowers, and what looks like one of Elsie's romance novels titled *The Alpha's Fate*. I can't imagine him reading such tomes for pleasure, so I don't know why it would be here. I shove them all back inside and scan the surface of the desk.

My heartbeat quickens when I move a book about Night's Acolytes aside and find a piece of parchment, yellow with time. It's not one of the pages I want, but there's a handwritten note at the top.

I will not be able to write for a while. This may be of interest in terms of what you seek. I found it in Sebastian's office. M.

At first glance, it looks like a spiderweb of lines, but on closer inspection, it's a fading family tree that must stretch back forty generations or more. The name at the bottom of the diagram makes my heart still. *Freja Månsken*. It's the name of my great-grandmother.

I trace the lines of the diagram, passing the names of those who must be my ancestors. The two names at the top have been scrubbed out. Why would Blake be looking into my ancestry? Why would Sebastian? Does this have something to do with the Heart of the Moon, and Lochlan's theory that my mother had it?

I fold the parchment and put it into my pocket so I can study it more closely later. It's not what I'm looking for, but it feels important. Especially as I've started to suspect that Blake wants something more than just the Wolf Throne.

I check the armoire in the corner, sliding my hands through the fabric of his clothing and releasing his scent into the air. Then I check beneath the black sheepskin rug in front of the fireplace.

There are men talking outside the room. I throw myself behind the bed just as the door clicks open.

"Because I'm concerned about you." Jack's deep voice infiltrates the chambers. "You're not thinking clearly."

"I'm thinking perfectly clearly." There's an edge to Blake's silky tone.

"When was the last time you took someone to your bed?"

"What concern is that of yours?"

"I'm worried about your judgement. You're wound up. You're going to do something reckless. Again."

I barely dare to breathe. I keep close to the floor, and try to still my heartbeat. I wonder if I should announce my presence. I've burst into Blake's chambers before, and he has never seemed particularly bothered.

"Can you just do as I ask?" Blake sounds weary. "We need to know what this 'Dark Beast' is. For all we know, Kai is possessed. Aurora and I found ourselves in Night's prison recently. There was a hole in one of the cells. Something escaped."

Any thought of revealing myself slips away. I flatten myself to the floorboards and slide beneath his bed so I can hear the rest of their conversation. I stare up at the dark bedframe, not daring to turn my head to watch the two men speaking.

"Shit," says Jack. "You think Alex caught it."

"I wouldn't put it past him, would you?"

Jack sighs. "I'll see what I can find."

"Don't be long. I don't think Callum will keep me around for much longer."

"I'm surprised he's not thrown you in a cell already."

"Me too, if I'm honest." Blake sounds amused. Anger prickles beneath my skin. I don't like them mocking him.

Jack chuckles. "Just. . . hold it together while I'm gone. I don't like you being here alone. Arran, or Elsie, or *someone* should be here to keep an eye on you."

"I want them at Lowfell. Away from all of this. And when do I ever *not* hold it together?" There's a hint of sarcasm to his tone.

"I can call to memory a few times. . ." says Jack.

Blake laughs. He shuts the door and seals us both inside. The air is sucked out of the room.

Even though I get the sense I amuse Blake—that perhaps, even, he is attracted to me—I know that if he finds me, he will consider this a violation of his privacy.

I'm not sure how I can get away without alerting him. I lock the cage around my emotions. I try to still my pounding heart. Right now, he's not blocking me from feeling him. There is turbulence within him. He feels restless. Distracted.

There's a rustle of fabric as he takes off his shirt. He throws it aside, then walks to the bed. I put my hand over my mouth to stifle my breathing. He slips off his boots. He has a mark—a scar—on one of his ankles. He slides into bed, and the frame dips above me.

"What are you doing?" He sounds exasperated. I can't tell if he's speaking to me, or himself.

When he says nothing more, I relax a little. It takes a while before his breathing slows and he falls asleep. I wait a couple more minutes to be sure. I slide from under the bed and stand up.

I wince when the floorboards creak beneath me, but Blake's eyes remain shut. He twitches, like he's having a bad dream. One of his arms is flung over his head onto the pillow, and his other shoulder is bound with gauze. My gaze snags on the long scar that curves across his abdomen then disappears under the covers.

A low moan escapes his throat, and I freeze. There's a wad of parchment sticking out from beneath his pillow.

My pulse thunders in my ears. There's a slight shake in my hand as I reach for it. He turns his head on the pillow, and warm breath tickles my skin. His dark hair is inches from my knuckles. I start to ease it from beneath him.

Blake's eyes snap open. The wolf blazes behind them.

I snatch the parchment. He grabs me and rolls me over, so I'm on my back on his mattress with my arms pinned above my head. He straddles my hips. The shadows seem to darken around us.

The part of him coiled around me feels feral, like it did in the chapel A snarl builds in his throat.

"Blake!" I struggle beneath him. "Blake! Stop!"

Chapter Forty-Six

Blake blinks. The wolf disappears from his eyes.

"Oh, it's you. I thought you would have been sensible enough to leave while I was sleeping." His grip around my wrists loosens but he doesn't let me go. "Is there something I can help you with, little rabbit?"

His thighs press against either side of my hips. His scent is everywhere, dark pine and poison. It's stifling. Words evade me.

He arches an eyebrow. "I'm actually trying *not* to provoke your master right now, believe it or not. It's not the best time for you to visit me in my bed."

I roll my eyes. "Get off me. I was... It's none of your bloody business what I was doing!"

He laughs. "You're in my room." I try to clench my fist around the folded parchment without him realizing. I try to nudge him aside. He doesn't move. His gaze travels slowly from face to my hand. "Oh, I see."

I shake my head. I stretch my arm as he slides his fingers up it. His touch heats my skin. My knuckles hit the headboard. I try to twist away and knee him in the crotch, but I can't get out from beneath him. His chest is inches from my face when he looms over me, frees of one of my wrists, and plucks the parchment from my fingers.

He releases my other wrist, then kneels over me. He clucks his tongue. "Naughty little rabbit."

I get the familiar tingle in my teeth, the urge to bite him. Those pages are *mine*. Those answers are *mine*. He doesn't have the right to take them from me. I'm fed up of letting people take things from me.

Blake tenses. The ridges in his torso become more pronounced. He drops his voice to a whisper. "Whatever you're thinking of doing, I'd advise against it."

When we were in the chapel, and his wolf started to surface, I did something to him. I grabbed him through the bond, and I pushed the wolf back. I open the cage that binds my emotions and invite him in.

I feel him everywhere. That thread of him coils around me, and I grab it.

"Aurora. Don't."

Instead of pushing him away, I pull. His breath hitches, and it might be the most delicious sound I've heard. His eyes become amber and feral. Sweat breaks out on my skin. I feel his wolf, and it's agitated. It wrestles against my hold.

He falls down and clenches the pillow on either side of my head. He dips his mouth to my ear. "Why would the rabbit provoke the wolf?"

"Because I know you don't like it." My voice is strained. I'm losing my grip on him as he battles against me, and the room starts to swim.

His laugh is breathy. "Are you sure about that?"

He stops fighting. Lust surges down the bond, hot and restless. *Hunt.* The air thickens. He shifts his position on top of me, and nudges my knee with his thigh, spreading my legs. He's trying to distract me. He wants me to loosen my grip, to let him go, because he's afraid.

I cry out and I pull harder. His hand flexes by my head and a low groan escapes him. He presses his forehead against mine.

"Aurora. . ."

I touch something inside him. A hollow, endless ache fills me. It's like falling down a hole that has no bottom. I hold on. He mutters something under his breath. It sounds like he's counting. When I know I consume every inch of him, as he does me, I roll him off me. I snatch the pages from his loosening grip.

I let go of the bond, and I feel him retreating, fast. I can breathe again. The posts of the bed blur around me. I feel like the fever is coming for me as something wild floods my blood. I half stumble, half crawl, to the foot of his bed.

I unfold the parchment. I catch the words *Anam-Cridech*.

He is on top of me again. I try to fall down onto the pages to protect my prize, but he hooks an arm around my waist and pulls my back against his chest. "Don't," he whispers.

There's a tempest inside me. I have the answer I've been searching for in my hand, and he's going to take it from me. "I deserve the truth."

"You don't."

He snatches the parchment from my hand. His chest bumps against the top of my head as he leans over me and tosses it into the fire. It lands on the logs, and the flames take it.

A soundless scream tears from my lungs. Whatever thin line of peace that has existed between us lately snaps. Red clouds my vision. My blood howls. Wildness rises inside me, and I can't suppress it. I sink my teeth into his arm.

A low sound scrapes against his throat. His arm tightens against my torso.

"Fuck." His voice is strained. "Easy, little rabbit."

I snarl. Something takes over me and I bite harder. I don't think I could let go if I wanted to. I want him to hurt like I hurt. I want to make him bleed.

"Aurora—"

I try to stop, but there's something rabid inside me and it won't let go. His breathing is ragged. His heartbeat thunders unsteadily in my ears. His knuckles brush my torso as he clenches his fist. He groans.

"If you break the skin, you'll mark me. You don't want to do that."

I don't know what he's talking about, but panic floods me. This is not me. I'm not in control of myself. I can't stop. I moan against his arm.

"Okay. I've got you." He sends his emotions through the bond, a surge of them that I cannot decipher. They flood me. He's everywhere. His ice cools my fire. My vision blurs, and when darkness rises, I let it take me.

I slump onto the bed, and Blake crashes down on top of me.

***

FOR A moment, I'm falling through darkness.

I land in a dimly lit room. There are grates near the ceiling, and moonlight seeps through. A musty scent lingers in the air. I think I'm underground.

Someone mutters under their breath behind me. They're counting, I think. I turn. I stumble away and my back hits a workbench. Jars and scalpels rattle. Blake is strapped to a gurney in the middle of the room. He is shirtless, and covered in blood.

"Two... Four... Eight... Sixteen... Thirty-two... Sixty-four," he mutters under his breath. Something lurches inside me. I used to recite my mother's stories when the priest beat me. It took my mind off the pain, and stopped me from losing my mind. "Two-thousand and forty-eight... Four thousand and ninety—"

"Blake?"

His eyes jolt open. He frowns. "You shouldn't be here, little rabbit."

He wrenches his arms free. He pulls the strap from his neck, then his ankles. He slides off the gurney and prowls toward me.

"I've shown you mine, now you show me yours."

He grabs my arms and pushes.

The shadows rise and swallow us.

We hurtle through the darkness.

I land, and I'm somewhere else. My arms feel like they're jerked from their sockets. There's a rattle of chains. Metal bites into my wrists and my legs are wrapped around something. No. Someone.

Blake stands before me, and his hands grip my thighs. I'm shackled to the ceiling in the small cell in the manor house.

"If you kiss me, I will bite off your tongue." The words come from my mouth before I can stop them, as if I'm the puppet in my other nightmare. Panic floods me. This is a memory.

Blake smiles, only it's not Blake. He seems different, like he's a puppet, too. His eyes are black, and his skin is too smooth. "Depends where I kiss you, little rabbit." His voice sounds wrong in the darkness.

I jerk back as he drops to his knees. *No. No. No.*

The darkness stirs behind him, and the real Blake—covered in blood—slits his throat. The puppet melts into the shadows. Blake cocks his head to one side. My cheeks flame.

"This is your dream, not mine," I lie.

He shakes his head and a dimple punctures the corner of his mouth. He steps closer. His heat and scent ambush me as he wraps my legs around his waist. "I don't think so, little rabbit."

I stiffen. "What are you. . .?"

He brings his lips to my ear. "In my dream, I'm in chains, and you are on your knees."

My eyes widen. He grabs the chains and pulls. They dissolve like ink between his fingers. I fall, and my hands land around his neck as the floor disappears.

We hurtle through darkness once more.

We land in a pile on the floor. Grass tickles my cheek. The scent of summer floods my nose—flowers, and woodlands, and baked earth. I clamber from beneath Blake and raise my head. I breathe in sharply.

About one hundred meters ahead, a woman sits in front of a vast, moonlit lake. She has long wavy hair, and wears a baggy cream dress. A small girl is curled against her side, and the woman strokes her head. The full moon and infinite stars are reflected in the surface of the water.

My heart swells, then tightens. My throat is thick. I don't remember this exact moment, but I know my mother brought me here.

Turn around, I will her. *Turn around.*

She's talking, but the words sound muffled. I push myself up and walk toward her. Blake strides past me. I grab his arm, and my fingers curl around his bicep. This isn't his memory to intrude upon. I don't want him here.

He shrugs me off and keeps walking. There's something determined in his eyes. The voices get louder, but no less jumbled. I hurtle into his back, and this time, I take him to the ground with me. We hit the grass with a loud thud. My mother should be able to hear us. She doesn't turn.

Turn around, I will her. *Let me see your face.*

Blake pushes himself to his knees, and I pull him down. I crawl over him to get to her before he does. This is important. The weight of this moment hangs in the air. Blake feels it too. He grabs my ankle and drags me across the earth.

Mother! I have no voice. I elbow Blake in the side, and a soundless grunt escapes him. *Get off me!*

What is she saying to you? He looks like he's shouting, but no words come out. *What did she say?*

We're so close now we should be able to hear her. I can smell the water. I can see the kinks in her red hair, and the threads in her cream dress. The ground starts to shake and a crack appears between us. *No!*

I reach out, and my fingers almost touch her back.

She starts to turn.

The floor disintegrates, and Blake and I fall through it.

***

I'M TOO hot. Something hard and heavy pushes me down.

My eyes peel open. It takes a moment for my vision to adjust, for my mind to make sense of what is happening. Blake lies on top of me, and his arm is caught beneath my torso. His gentle breaths warm my ear.

We're at the foot of his bed. The fire flickers in front of me. The pages Blake stole are nothing but ash. The warmth I felt when I saw my mother cools. There is nothing soft inside me anymore. I slam my elbow into Blake's gut and he makes a low sound before rolling off me. I fall off the foot of the bed.

I land on the sheepskin rug "You snake! You treacherous snake!"

His legs hang off the end of the bed, and he plants his bare feet onto the floorboards. He stares up at the ceiling. His bare chest moves up and down deeply. I can't tell what he's thinking, but I feel a thread of his frustration wind around my own.

I stand up. I'm trembling. Shaking. There's a tornado in my chest and I can't contain it. I'm fed up of his games. I'm fed up of being used. I'm fed up of answers being concealed from me. He had no right.

"Break the bond," I snarl.

He pushes himself upright. "No."

"I will make you pay for this, Blake." I step closer to him. "I will haunt you. Every waking moment, I will make you feel me. Every dream, I will be there. Every moment of joy that you manage to feel in your sad little life, I will turn it into darkness. Break this bond, Blake, or I swear to every goddess, I will consume you until there is nothing left of you. I will ruin you. I will coil myself so tightly around you that you will beg me to release you, and still then, I will not let you go."

He rubs his face with both hands. "You already haunt me, Aurora."

"Then let me go!"

"I cannot!"

"Why?"

He leans forward and he clasps his hands together between his thighs. "I suppose I should tell you the truth."

Chapter Forty-Seven

The truth.

My breathing quickens and the scent of woodsmoke and pine fills my lungs.

The hearth is warm at my back, and the fire flicks dim light across Blake's chambers. It dances over the black silk sheets, crumpled from our fight, and the scars that mar his chest. For a moment, all I can hear is the crackle from the flames, and the wind that rattles the window.

Blake is promising me the truth. It's what I want, what I've been searching for, yet my muscles tighten. There is something in the way he clasps his hands between his thighs, his jawline sharp, that makes my stomach clench.

"Well? Go on then," I say.

He runs a hand over his mouth. "How could I have known?"

"Known what?"

His eyes snap to mine. "The events of that night, when James gave you to Sebastian. How could I have known what was going to happen?" He absently touches his bicep. There's an indent where I sank my teeth into him. "How could I have known James would bite you? When I tried to arrange the marriage between the two of you, I meant it when I said he would not hurt you. For all his faults, I did not think he would."

My brow creases. "I. . . I don't understand. Why are you telling me this? What has it got to do with anything?"

"If my entire plan rested on getting you to accept the bond between us, I would have needed to ensure you were in a life-threatening situation so I could save your life." He shakes his head. "How could I have planned the series of events that led to James attacking you? There were too many variables to control, too many things that could have gone wrong. Even I'm not that good."

"You said—"

"No. I didn't. You said that, not me."

I cast my mind back to the small bedchambers in Lowfell. I had accused him of planning it all, of creating the bond so Callum would forfeit the throne. And he had said. . .

My heart stutters. He didn't deny it, but he didn't confirm it, either.

"What are you saying?"

"I cannot break the bond, Aurora, because I did not create it. It's not in my power."

I step back. The fire is hot behind me, yet my blood runs cold. "You're lying."

"Do you think I want this?" His voice is uncharacteristically strained. "It complicates things for me."

My breathing is shallow. There is a sinking feeling in the pit of my stomach, a cold wind running through my chest. "I saw the words *Anam-Cridech* on the pages you burned. Is that the name of the bond?"

"Yes. That is one name for it."

"What is the other?"

His eyes bore into mine, dark and intense. "You already know."

I shake my head. "I do not."

"You do. A part of you knows. A part of you has always known. Just like, deep down, Callum knows. Just like I have always known."

My heartbeat thunders in my ears. "Tell me."

He twists his hands together. His lips part. "You'll have to figure it out for yourself, little rabbit. It looks like our time together is coming to an end."

I turn, just as the door opens. Lochlan enters the room, flanked by four of his men. A half-laugh escapes Blake's lips as he stands. "Really, Lochlan? You?"

"It's nothing personal, Blake." His kohl-lined eyes glint with violence, and belie his statement. I think he's worried about what Blake might do to Kai. "I have orders from the king. You are sentenced to imprisonment for plotting against the throne. Are you going to come peacefully?"

A dimple punctures Blake's cheek as he edges back a step. "I know Callum has told you I'm not to be harmed."

"He thought you might say that," says Lochlan. "He wants you to know that you've shown your hand. You've lost. We can hurt you, if we wish."

Blake laughs. It's a cold, contrived sound that makes the hairs on the back of my neck stand on end. A couple of the men share a look. He shrugs. "Very well. Let me grab my shirt."

Lochlan inclines his head. Blake grabs his shirt from the armchair and slips it on. I step away from him, and my back hits the wall by the fireplace. I tense as I wait for him to grab a sword and start fighting, or grab me to use me as leverage to get out of the situation. He fastens his buttons, then slips on his boots.

Lochlan gestures at him, and two of the men grab Blake's arms and pull them roughly behind his back. They slip shackles around his wrists, and the click resounds around his chambers. He doesn't resist.

They walk him toward the door, and he stops in front of Lochlan. "Will you give Callum a message from me?" Lochlan nods, and Blake's lips curve into a wicked smile. "He has not seen my hand yet. He doesn't even know what game we're playing. Come visit me when you've figured it out, little rabbit. I'll wait for you."

He's hauled out of the room.

Lochlan inclines his head. "Good evening, Princess."

He follows his men, and Blake, into the corridor.

I'm left dumbfounded, staring at the door.

Chapter Forty-Eight

Everything is still. Quiet.

It's the moment after a storm, when the world has been overturned, yet everything is expected to go back to normal.

I stand by the fireplace in Blake's chambers. If it weren't for the crumpled bedsheets, the few bits of mud on the floorboards that were stomped in by Lochlan's men, and the racing of my heart, I could be fooled that nothing out of the ordinary had occurred.

Callum finally made his move against Blake. He decided to lock him up—even though he knows our lives are linked. He didn't consider it an option before. We discussed it once, back at Lowfell, and decided Blake would starve himself, or hurt himself, to get to me.

Blake didn't even resist.

Callum is out of his depth. Blake is up to something.

Anam-Cridech. The word for the bond echoes in my mind.

I was so close to getting an answer, and yet a part of me is relieved that Blake was taken before he could reveal it. His words have taken root within me and I fear them.

A part of you knows. A part of you has always known. Just like, deep down, Callum knows. Just like I have always known.

I walk toward his desk and slide open the second drawer. *The Alpha's Fate* is tucked in the corner, nestled among the maps. I pick it up. Elsie gave me two of these books. She said they were enlightening. Blake took both of them off me. I thought nothing of it at the time, and yet...

A floorboard creaks behind me.

I shove the small flimsy tome into my pocket and turn. Callum stands in the doorway.

His eyes move from Blake's crumpled bedsheets to the spot where Blake was standing a moment ago. His nostrils flare and my pulse kicks up.

Does he think that something inappropriate happened between us? *Did* something inappropriate happen between us? I had been so caught up in getting the parchment, I had acted on instinct. I had not thought too hard about where I was, or who I was provoking. I bit him. My cheeks heat, and something cold moves beneath my skin.

It's certainly not proper for a lady to be in another man's bed, but I was angry. I was *fighting* him. I was trying to get answers for Callum, as well as myself. Still, shame spreads through me.

I get the sense that he's battling with his wolf. He breathes deeply, and his fists are clenched. His expression could be carved from stone, and I know he only pulls his emotions back when he feels threatened.

"Callum." I step toward him.

He staggers back as though I pushed him. Panic flickers across his face. He turns on his heel and walks out of Blake's bedchambers.

"Callum." I hurry after him.

He doesn't slow down, so I can't fall into step beside him.

"Callum!"

He halts outside the door of his bedchambers, clenches the top of the doorframe, and leans forward. His broad shoulders practically burst the seams of his shirt. He presses his forehead against the door. "His scent is all over you."

"It's not what you think."

He releases a bitter laugh, devoid of his usual warmth. "He touched you."

"I was trying to get answers—"

He spins around, and the wolf is in his eyes. "Were you in his bed?"

"Yes, but it's not—"

He makes a low sound, shuts his eyes, and bites down on his knuckles. A dribble of blood runs down his fist and drips onto the flagstones. It doesn't seem to offer him any relief, because his breathing is unsteady.

"Callum, please calm down." I reach for his wrist so I can stop him from hurting himself.

He lurches away from me and his back hits the wall. He drops his fist to his side, and blood drips onto the flagstones. When he opens his eyes, I almost stagger back with the force of his gaze.

"*Don't*," he snarls.

"I'm sorry. I just—"

"Do you want him?"

"No!"

"I'm a wolf, Princess!" He slams a hand on his chest and I flinch. He blinks back the watery film over his eyes, and shakes his head. "I saw you dance with him, you know? At the feast at Lowfell."

The memory of Blake twirling me around the dancefloor flashes through my mind. I shake my head. He cannot be serious. "I didn't conceal that from you. I was trying to get information from him." I hate the plea, the whine, the *desperation* in my voice.

A muscle feathers in Callum's jaw. "Is that what you were doing when you wound up in his bed?"

"*Yes.*"

He makes another low sound. My breathing is ragged. I've swallowed a storm, and it's taking all my strength to keep it contained.

"If you calm yourself, I shall explain what happened. Let us go inside and talk about it like rational human beings."

"I am *not* a human, Princess." Each word is rough and deliberate as he steps closer to me, his furious heat blazing my skin. "I'm a wolf."

"Right now, you're acting like a brute." My tone is harsh, yet some small part of me welcomes his fury as if I've been waiting for it. Let us tear into one another and shout and scream so that we can release it. Let him treat me to his wrath, for once, as though I can take it.

A frustrated noise rumbles in his chest. He shakes his head, turning his attention to one of the torches flickering on the wall. "I cannot speak to you when you smell like that."

He brushes past me and stalks down the corridor toward the stairwell.

"Do not walk away from me, Callum!"

"Have a bath," he snarls. "I shall deal with you later."

Indignation rises within me. "Deal with me?!"

"Aye! Deal with you!"

"What is the *Anam-Cridech*?" I say.

He halts. The muscles in his back shudder. His hand flexes at his side. My stomach lurches at his reaction. Blake was right. Callum knows what it is.

"Where did you hear that word?" he growls.

Coldness spreads through my bones. "What is it, Callum?"

He straightens. He doesn't turn. "Have a bath. I will talk to you later."

"No. You will talk to me now—"

"*Do not follow me.*"

His words power through me and I practically stagger back with the force of them. I feel him inside me—the taste of mountain air on the back of my tongue. His command grabs the wild thing in my chest and pushes it down.

He is using his alpha voice, his king voice, and trying to force me to submit to him—like when Blake used the Àithne. I'm not sure he knows he's doing it.

I grab it and push it off me, as easily as I did when Blake tried it. Yet as he storms away, I stand breathless and shaken.

I don't follow.

Chapter Forty-Nine

Somewhere beneath the castle, Blake is in the dungeons. I don't know what Callum is doing. Probably strategizing with the alphas because of Alexander's threat, or cooling down after our fight. I'm angry with them both. Blake burned the pages, and Callum walked away.

At least Blake was about to tell me something. I know I won't be able to get to him now.

My eyes are heavy as I stare at the paperback I took from Blake's room. I need to read it, but I fear it.

Blake's eyes were uncharacteristically sincere as he sat, hunched, on the edge of his bed—his hands clasped, the firelight dancing over his scars and muscles. Perhaps I don't want to know what he was about to say. Perhaps a thought has been planted in my soul—an explanation for the bond, for what James was trying to demonstrate and Callum's reaction to it. I want to cull it before its roots grow any deeper.

Callum told me about a wolf thing, once. When I first arrived here and he asked me to wear his collar. It sounded like a bond, of sorts, though he didn't exactly describe it as such. I glance at the battered paperback book, and wonder if I've been searching for answers in the wrong place. Blake has taken two of these books from me. This one was hidden in his drawer, as if to keep it out of my reach.

I nudge the book away. I drop back onto my pillows and pull my hands through my hair. I tug it, welcoming the sting on my scalp. The wind howls against the stone walls, and my mouth aches, and my skin is tight. I chew my finger. I break the skin and tear some off the side of my nail. I sit up. I pick up the book, my blood seeping into the parchment.

I open it, and begin to skim the neatly inked words. It's a story about a beastly alpha who lives in a castle, and who—in retaliation for a slight made by an alpha from a nearby clan—takes the alpha's daughter prisoner. Only, as they spend time together, they begin to fall in love.

It's not until near the end that I come across it. The two Wolves share a bond. It's named *Anam-Cridech*.

My heart pounds in my ears. The words on the page blur. I slam the book shut.

The shadows darken, and I'm underwater, thrashing for air. I kick for the surface, but something has hold of me and it's pulling me down. The thought that has taken root grows. I cut it back. I wish I could speak to Elsie, but she's back at Lowfell. I remember something she told me. *The old cook here at Lowfell used to pen them.*

Could it be...? I scramble off the bed, put on my slippers, and slide a robe over my nightdress. I grab the small book.

It's late, but if I'm in luck, the kitchens will not be empty. I tiptoe around Fergus, who is sleeping again, down the stairs, and make my way to the ground floor of the castle. There's a fire in one of the kitchen hearths when I arrive, and the woman I seek stands with her back to me, washing dishes in a soapy bucket.

"You should be in bed at this hour, lassie." Mrs. McDonald's voice is admonishing. She turns and folds her arms, her soapy hands wetting the sleeves of her brown dress. "And you certainly should not be parading around dressed like *that*." She clucks her tongue at how the robe, drawn in at the waist, clings to my curves.

I raise the tome. "Did you write this?"

Her eyes narrow on it. She turns back around. "Aye, I wrote it. A long time ago. I haven't the time for it now. What of it?"

Despite the questions that bubble dangerously close to the surface, the corner of my lip twitches. "Who would have thought you were such a romantic, Mrs. McDonald?" I say.

"Hm."

I walk toward her, and stand by the counter on the other side of the bucket she's washing dishes in. The window looks out onto the herb garden, and outside, the wind rustles the rosemary and bushes of thyme. I can't quite bring myself to ask her the question I want to know the answer to.

"You wrote about the *Anam-Cridech* in this book," I say.

"Aye. It's a rare thing, in reality, but I always put it in my books."

"The *Anam-Cridech*... if two Wolves shared it, would they be able to feel each other's emotions?"

"I like to write it that way. In truth, no one knows. It's rare for such a bond to exist, and even rarer for it to be accepted."

"It has to be accepted?"

"Oh, aye, of course. Why do you ask?"

"How does one accept it?"

She shrugs. "I don't know. The only wolf I know to have experienced the *Anam-Cridech* is James, and he was never forthcoming about the details."

My eyebrows lift. "*James?*"

"Aye. With that lassie he used to court. Claire. Or that's the rumor, anyway. People say she refused him, so the bond never solidified."

My pulse is hammering. "How can it be broken?"

She laughs. "Broken? Once accepted, it cannot be broken. Only the Moon Goddess would have the power." She goes back to her washing. "No. The *Anam-Cridech* is eternal. The bond is thought to surpass even death. Why do you want to know. . .?"

I'm already turning on my heel, walking on trembling legs out of the kitchens. I murmur my thanks, I think. My mind, my body, feel as if they're someplace else. The corridors blurring around me, I make my way to the stairwell.

An eternal bond, shared by two Wolves, created by the Moon Goddess, written about in love tomes—that would be upsetting to Callum. I grasp the banister, and suck in a breath.

You already know.

Nausea rises within. I remember what Callum told me when I first arrived at Madadh-allaidh.

It's a wolf thing. Rare, but powerful. Stronger, even, than love. Two souls chosen by the Moon Goddess...

I know what the bond is.

If I go in one direction, I could confront the alpha who lied and deceived me in the dungeons.

If I go in the other, I could face the alpha who hid the truth he must have suspected for weeks now.

The dangerous, horrible thought has grown vines so thick I can barely breathe. I fight it back with everything I have. I push it down, because I can't, *will not*, allow it to surface.

I'm not a rabbit. I'm not prey. I'm not a problem to be locked away in a tower. I'm not a helpless princess that needs protecting from the truth.

Someone has to pay for this.

Someone *will* pay for this.

Body trembling, heart thumping, chest heaving, I pick a direction.

Chapter Fifty

I burst into his chambers.

I barely notice the four-poster bed with the tartan throw, the fire in the hearth, the crescent moon that shines through the window.

Callum is in the copper bathtub. Even through my rage, my breath hitches at the sight of him. Powerful, muscular, yet completely at ease—the firelight dances across his wet skin and turns it bronze. His knees are raised, and his head is leaning against the edge, exposing his throat. His damp hair is the color of wet sand, and brushed back from his forehead in that way that makes him look younger.

He opens his eyes as the door swings shut behind me.

He grips the sides of the tub, and starts to sit. Water cascades down his chest, and I cannot deal with seeing any more of him right now.

"Stay where you are," I say. He stills as if he senses the growing storm in me. I know he doesn't fear me—could not fear me—yet wariness tightens his jaw.

"You need to calm down, Princess."

"You lied to me."

His expression darkens. "I did not."

My chest heaves, because that is not the truth and he knows it. There's a scream inside me, tearing me apart from the inside. My teeth ache, and I want to bite something. My skin hurts with the force of containing it all. My muscles vibrate; my bones shake. If I don't release it, I will combust.

"Rory. . ." Callum warns.

I storm toward him, grab the slippery soap that sits on the side of the copper tub by his hand, and hurl it at him. Then the washcloth. Water sloshes over the side of the tub as he raises his forearms. Both bounce off him and hit the floorboards.

"Are you done?" he growls.

"No. I'm not done!" I swipe the candlestick off the mantelpiece beside me.

"Don't you dare—"

I swing it at his head. He grabs the end and yanks it toward him. Instead of releasing it, I stumble, and have to grip the side of the tub to keep my balance.

"Am I going to let you do that?" he says.

My breathing is hard as that wildness in my chest struggles to escape. "No."

"No," he agrees. "Drop it."

"No."

"Drop it, or I shall make you." The wolf shines in his eyes.

"You won't hurt me." I'm as convinced of this now as I was when I first set eyes on him.

"Still, you cannot come into my chambers in the middle of the night and threaten me. I cannot allow it." His gaze darkens. "Drop it."

I try to wrench out of his grip so I can aim it at his face again. He lets go and I stumble. He hooks one arm around my waist and grabs my wrist with his other hand. There's a sloshing noise as I crash down on top of him, scuffing my knees against the sides of the tub.

Water spills everywhere. It careens over the sides of the bath, sloshes over the floorboards, and drenches the sheepskin rug. I release my hold on the candlestick, and it clatters to the floor and rolls beneath the bed. I gasp with shock as I'm drenched, and my core is pressed against his hard torso. He grabs my waist and holds me still. My legs are wedged between his thighs and the side of the bath.

"This is not the way we settle things," he says.

I suck in a deep breath, the room blurring around me. I taste mountains and soap and the familiar scent of woodsmoke. It's like ash in my mouth. "Do not tell me how I settle things, Callum McKennan." I grip his shoulders to push myself upward, and steady myself. My hair is draped against his chest. "You're a liar."

"I have not lied to you."

"You know the nature of the bond. Don't pretend otherwise!"

"Aye. I know."

A growl builds inside me. "You made a mockery of me."

"You believe *you* have been made a mockery of?"

He doesn't look like the Callum I know right now. There is nothing gentle or kind in his expression. Despite the intimacy of our position, he looks at me as if I'm a foe he's facing on the battlefield.

I can barely contain my rage. It rises up my throat and I want to scream. "You hid the truth."

"Because I did not want it to be true!"

"You had no right!" My body is tense against his, my chest heaving like I'm drowning. "How long have you known the nature of the bond?" His throat is bobbing. "*How long?*"

"I suspected on the night James bit you."

The fire inside me blazes and roars. "That long?"

His jawline hardens. "Aye, that long. And I denied it at first. But James told Blake to kiss you, and I couldn't hide from it any longer. I scented it, I saw the way he reacted to you, and I tried to tell myself I was mistaken. Until I read the pages in Blake's book the moment I returned to Madadhallaidh, and I knew it to be true." His accent gets thicker as he gets more agitated. "What am I supposed to do? Give you my blessing? You're his m—"

"Do not finish that sentence!" My nightdress and robe stick to my body. The water is warm, and splashes around my stomach. My curves press against his chest, and one of his hands is clamped on my waist—hot and firm as iron. "You're supposed to tell me so we can fix it!"

"You're not a full wolf. You don't understand." His hot breath mingles with mine. "There is no fixing it. There is no choice in it." A muscle throbs in his neck. "The bond is unbreakable, and I do not share. I want all of you, heart, body, and soul. I will take no less."

"What about what *I* want? Do you care about that?"

"You do not know what you want, Princess. You didn't know on the night I took you, and I don't think you're any closer to answering that question now!"

His heartbeat thunders in my ears with my own, furious, restless. "What's next, Callum? Are you going to keep me brushed aside, out of the way, kept in a room in your castle while Blake is locked away in—"

"Do not speak to me of *him*." His eyes blaze and his cheeks flush as he leans closer to me, pulling our bodies flush. "What would you have me do? You are the moon to me, Rory. Every time I set eyes on you, my soul is aflame. The wolf inside me presses against my skin, it howls in my blood, and roars in my ears—and you would not like the things it wants me to do. Every night, I have thought of you. I have imagined myself buried inside of you, sinking my teeth into you, claiming you as mine while cursing my goddess for not giving you to me. I have left my door unlocked, praying you would come while hoping you wouldn't."

Something coils, hot, inside me at his words. It aches. It burns. My teeth hurt, and my nails are claws. That wild thing in my ribs thrashes against its cage. A low growl builds, unbidden, in my chest.

Bite. Bite. Bite.

Callum's nostrils flare. He answers with a growl of his own and his hard wet chest vibrates against my peaked nipples. His fingers dig into my sides.

"Do not test me, Princess," he says. I know I should get a hold of myself. I know this is wrong and we need to talk. I know the nature of the bond changes things for him, and

I'm furious because of it. I can't stop. I tremble with the force of containing my emotion. He cups my face with his hands. "Princess, I advise you to get out of this tub and walk away. You don't want this."

"You don't get to tell me what I want. I'm fed up of people telling me what I want. *I* decide what I want!"

My chest heaves against his. I want him. Right now. I want him buried inside me while I take my pleasure from him. I want him moaning, gasping, beneath me. I want him to pay for all of this. I want him at my mercy.

His breathing deepens. Conflict flickers across his face as he presses his forehead to mine. "Rory, tell me what you want."

Chapter Fifty-One

Tell me what you want.

Callum's hands are firm yet gentle on my cheeks. My nightdress is sopping wet beneath my robe. My core presses against his hard torso. Both of us are breathing deeply.

I use his shoulders to push myself upright. The wet tips of my hair touch his shoulders, and his eyes darken on my chest where my nightdress has become translucent. His face is strained, like he's battling with himself. I take his hand and put it on my breast. He makes a low sound. He squeezes, then brushes his thumb over my peaked nipple. My back arches in response.

"You. I want you."

A low, guttural growl vibrates in his chest. In a sudden movement, he slides up, grips my thighs, and hoists me up as he stands. Water cascades off both of us as he steps out of the bath. He crouches down to lay me atop the sheepskin rug between the fire and the copper tub. He hovers over me, his knees between my thighs, and his hands on either side of my waist. My breaths are shaky as he crawls over me, and brings his mouth close to mine.

"I want... I want..." I can't express in words what I want, what I need. For once, I want him to stop holding back. "I want you to consume me," I breathe. "I want you to unleash. I want you to break me so I forget everything other than you. I want you to take me in the way that you want to."

He offers me a sad smile as he brushes a strand of wet hair from my cheek. "I will worship you." He brushes his lips against my throat. "Cherish you." He kisses me. "Honor you." He nips my earlobe with his teeth, and I squirm. "Tease you." His mouth hovers over mine. "But break you? No. You cannot ask that of me. If I'm to take you the way I want, I will have you gently, and deeply, and slowly." He brushes his lips against mine. "Can you accept that?"

And because I would rather have part of him than none at all, I nod.

"Good. Because there's no loch in the Northlands cold enough to dowse the fire in my blood right now."

He slides my underwear down my legs. Then he reaches between us, and guides himself to my entrance. My back arches as he pushes, slowly, inside me. We both groan. He fills me completely. Both of our pulses thunder in my ears. His scent overwhelms me.

He takes my face in his hands. "Your eyes," he whispers, and I know they must have changed.

Softly, he kisses me. He thrusts his hips in deep, languid movements, as though he's savoring every moment. It feels so good; *he* feels so good. I rock against him, and my fingers find his shoulder muscles and dig in. I curl my ankles around his back, and he shifts me so my hips are tilted up and he can hit deeper.

Something builds, hot and hungry, between us. I can practically sense his wolf, close to the surface, pressing at his skin. Mine answers, teeth bared, claws sharp. He groans and quickens his pace. My core slams against his abdomen, building sweet friction between us that makes me moan. His pulse thunders in my ears, frantic and unsteady, and I feel his control start to slip.

"It's okay," I mumble against his mouth. "Let go."

He takes two shuddering breaths. For once, he submits to my will, though he makes no question of who is in charge. He thrusts his hips, hard. I cry out. He grabs my wrists and pins them above my head, as he moves against me. His mouth moves to my neck. I rock against him, meeting his thrusts, desperate for more. He mumbles against me, words in a language I don't understand.

I writhe against him and dig my nails into his skin. He brings his lips to my throat. "*Fuck*," he murmurs against my ear. "*Fuck.*"

His expression is strained, his cheeks flushed. His whole body tenses, and a rough cry escapes from his lips as he lets go. It pushes me over the edge. For a moment, that wildness bursts from its confines, and I'm free. I'm weightless. The scream that has been building inside me comes out in a series of cries as he holds me together, and I melt in his arms.

He mumbles against my neck as I come back to myself. Finally, he brings his gaze to mine. He's as breathless as I am. He looks utterly undone—face flushed, eyes bright, lips swollen. I don't know what to say. I don't think he does, either. He seems familiar, yet strange at the same time.

He huffs a soft laugh, slightly sheepish. I return it.

He slides out of me, and rolls onto the rug. We face one another, and I stroke his hot cheek. He smiles, but there's sadness in it. "What do you want now, Princess?" The question is weighted, heavy, because he isn't asking about tonight, he's asking about the future. Our future.

I swallow. "You cannot make peace with it, can you?"

He places his hand on the small of my back and brings me close. "I tried to make peace with it. I tried to let you go. I tried to pretend it wasn't real, and that it was all in my head. I failed." He shakes his head. "The *Anam-Cridech*, it's sacred. If anyone found out what we have just done. . .if they knew what I had just done with another wolf's—" He clears his throat. "It's not done in our kingdom."

"You want to end things between us, don't you?" I should feel hurt, yet a strange calmness settles over me.

"It's the last thing in this world that I *want*. But you're bound to him, regardless of my desire." Tears glisten in his eyes as he strokes my cheek. "If things were different. . ."

I incline my head as my decision solidifies. "The moon's power can break the bond, Callum. I'm going to find the Heart of the Moon. I'll use it to break the bond, then I'll bring it back to you." A soft smile graces his lips, though there is a glimmer of disbelief in his eyes. "You don't believe me?"

"I don't believe the bond can be broken, Princess."

My jaw hardens. "I have to try."

He pushes his forehead against mine. "Fearsome creature."

"Wolf."

Chapter Fifty-Two

I wake sometime in the morning.

The fire has died, and there is only ash in the hearth. Darkness stains the floorboards, and the rain patters against the window. Still, I'm not cold.

Callum lies on his front. His heat sears me, and his scent is overpowering. I think I must be finally accepting that wolf part of myself, because I smell him all over me. Mountains and the dawn light, a hint of woodsmoke. His hand is inches from mine on the mattress, as if he reached for me in his sleep but fell short.

He seems so close, yet further away than ever. I understand now what plagues him. I understand how this bond—this unbreakable bond—with Blake tortures him, just like it tortures me. I understand that for him, it changes things. Things have changed, I suppose, for me, too, though

I like to think that if things were reversed, I would at least fight for him.

Perhaps it's because I'm not a wolf, or not a full wolf anyway. I've not grown up in the light of the Moon Goddess. Breaking a bond she has made doesn't seem like sacrilege to me.

In spite of everything, a strange peace settles over me. There's something growing in me that I don't understand. Something awoke within me long before I was bitten by James. The night I took Callum's hand, and came with him to the Northlands, it burst into existence, and it has been agitated since.

I've struggled to find my place here. I've always been defined by my relationships to other people. Even now, that is the case. The Wolves see me as either the daughter of their enemy, or the consort to their king, and—if the truth about the bond comes out—they will define me by my connection to Blake as well.

It's stifling. Constricting. I wish, for a short time at least, to be free of it all. To find out who I am outside of that cage. Blake was looking into my ancestry, Philip has made a strange allegiance with the Snowlands queen, and my mother... Lochlan thinks she had the Heart of the Moon at some point.

I want to do something for myself, for once. I want to learn about where I came from, and what happened to my mother. I want to break this damned bond.

I don't want the day to start. I want to stay like this, sore and sated, while he sleeps. I want to memorize his face, soft in a way most will never see. I want to trace the muscles in his back, revealed since the covers are bunched at his waist. I want to kiss the bullet scar in his shoulder and run my fingers through his hair—the color of wet sand.

He opens his eyes, as if he senses me watching him. "Morning, Princess."

"Good morning."

If he's embarrassed about last night, he doesn't show it. He smiles. It's the first sincere smile he has offered me since we arrived here, and it lights up his face. It makes him seem boyish. Mischievous. I can't help the twitch of my own lips.

"Last night was fun," he says, voice rough with sleep.

Visions of him pinning me to the rug as he thrust inside me flood my mind. "Yes, it was." We stare at one another. The light in his eyes dims, and I know he's remembering the conversation we had afterward. The warmth inside me ebbs. I sigh. "We need to talk about—"

"Aye." He exhales. "Aye. We do. There is something I must do first."

He rolls onto his back, then slides out of bed. Naked, he pads across the room, wraps his kilt around his waist, then slips on a shirt. A grim expression is etched onto his face when he throws open the chest at the foot of his bed and pulls out a couple of swords. I jolt upright.

"Callum, what are you. . .?"

He strides across his chambers and heads into the corridor. "I shall be right back, Princess."

I throw myself out of bed. I grab one of my simple dresses that hangs in his armoire and almost fall over as I pull it on. My messy hair gets caught in my mouth.

He can't kill Blake without me dying too. He knows this. "Callum! Wait!"

He's already rounding the end of the corridor when I stagger out of his bedchambers. I run after him, heartbeat pounding. I presume the dungeons are beneath the castle, but he strides past the stairwell and down another corridor, throwing open a door. I jerk to a halt beside him.

"Up. Now," Callum commands.

Philip groans, rolls over, and staggers out of the small bed by the window, arms outstretched. His copper hair is messy and it glints in the light of the low fire in the hearth. He wears a long-sleeved white cotton top, his tattoos covered. He blinks a couple of times as he turns to face us, as if confused. Yet when Callum tosses him a sword, he catches it with one hand.

Philip stares at him as if he is mad.

"You've overstayed your welcome," says Callum. "Outside. With me. Now."

Philip's eyebrows lift. Callum is already striding away. My heart beats quickly. I'm not sure what he's planning. I hurry after him. "I know he's despicable, but you cannot just kill the heir to the Southlands throne," I hiss.

Callum looks over his shoulder as he reaches the stairwell. "I suppose we'll see, won't we?"

Philip appears beside me a moment later, now wearing boots and a shirt over his undergarments. "Have fun last night, little sister?" His nostrils flare, and he pulls a face. "You smell like cock."

"Don't be disgusting." Goddess, I despise him. Yet. . .

I barge past him and hurry to stride beside Callum as he powers down the stairs. "Callum, what are you doing?"

"Testing a theory."

"Are you going to elaborate?"

"No." We make it to the entrance hall, and the torches are being lit by Kayleigh, who looks between us, wide-eyed, as we pass. Callum pushes open the double doors and steps into the Madadh-allaidh courtyard. "You'll see."

The courtyard is quiet. A few Wolves mill around—a servant carrying chicken feed, Fiona, who waves a hand before walking through the archway toward the stables, and Lochlan and a few of his men. I assume they have been training from the way their shirts cling to their chests, and the way they gather around the water pump. My breath mists in front of my face.

Callum turns to face Philip in the center of the courtyard. He draws his sword and drops the sheath onto the cobblestones.

Philip cocks his head to one side, his nose curling up. "Are you serious?"

Callum roars as he whips the blade through the air. In a lithe, graceful movement, Philip unsheathes his weapon and raises it to block Callum's blow. The sound of steel on steel reverberates through the courtyard. Birds nesting in the walls take flight, their wings flapping as they head toward the mountains. The Wolves around the water pump stop their conversation and turn to watch.

The force of Callum's blow should have shattered Philip's arm. Philip throws him off. The two males go at each other, and my lips part.

Callum is brutal, every blow deliberate and designed to overpower his opponent. His biceps ripple beneath his sleeves, and he grunts as he brings the sword down upon my brother. Philip blocks and dodges every blow. It's like watching fire battle water. A hammer clashing with steel. He is the opposite of Callum's brutality yet no less efficient—he moves as if he's dancing.

A muttering fills the courtyard as more people going about their morning chores stop to watch. I'm frozen, my mind not able to make sense of what I'm seeing. Callum is a battle-hardened alpha, while Philip is a spoiled drunken fool. And they are equally matched.

"Is that all you've got, princeling?" Callum kicks Philip in the torso, and sends him staggering back.

Philip glances up and smirks. He winks, and when I follow his gaze, I catch Isla scowling through the window above the oak doors. "Not quite."

Philip goes on the offensive, and I realize I was wrong. They're not a match. Philip is better. He slices his blade through the air and dances around Callum. His moves are ethereal yet deadly.

There must be twelve Wolves out in the yard now. They gather around the two with interest in their eyes. Callum's claim to the throne is already weak, and my brother is beating him. If he were to win, I dread to think of the violence that would befall both them and me.

Yet when Callum staggers back, a soft laugh escapes his lips. "Lochlan," he says.

He ducks back, into the circle of Wolves, and Lochlan darts forward to block Philip's next blow. He attacks Philip, and Philip adapts instantly. Lochlan's style is almost as brutal as Callum's, and his steps have some of Philip's grace, yet Philip outmatches him too. The two parry each other's blows, and Philip doesn't seem to tire.

This doesn't make sense. This is the male who would drunkenly bellow through the palace halls with a bloodied nose and the scent of perfume on his collar.

My eyes find Callum as he watches. A smile ghosts his lips. "A keg of ale to anyone who can knock this perfumed princeling on his spoiled southern arse."

The Wolves watching laugh. Two men dart forward and join the fray. Philip disarms one of them, and sends the other reeling back. Another raises his sword. Philip ducks, then swipes out his leg and sends him flying.

By the time Philip is holding his own against five Wolves, his blade a blur in the grey light, my fear ebbs away and all I can do is stare, dumbfounded.

"That's enough," says Callum, amused, when four of them are on the floor, and only Lochlan still stands against him—and even he is breathing hard.

Lochlan shrugs a shoulder at Callum. Philip glances up at Isla, whose mouth is parted. Slightly breathless, he bows elaborately, and her scowl reappears before she disappears from the window.

"You'll do," says Callum.

Philip turns on Callum, eyes widening. "Do for what?"

Callum strides toward Philip and clasps him on the shoulder. "Pack a bag. I've got a job for you."

He heads toward me, his expression softening. Something sad swells inside me when he towers before me.

"A word, please, Princess. I think it's time for us to have that conversation."

Chapter Fifty-Three

Callum takes me up a narrow stairway to the top of the castle's curtain wall.

He walks to the edge, and rests his forearms on the stone wall. I stand beside him, and his body heat stops me from feeling the early morning chill. Mist whispers across the loch far below, and thick clouds hide the peaks of the mountains. The evergreens to the left rustle in the breeze, their pine needles black in the low light. For a moment, we are silent—drinking in the peace. I wonder if, like me, he wonders how long it will last.

"My father took James and me up here on the first night we arrived at Madadh-allaidh," he says, his voice rough. "That way is the enemy, he told us." He gestures south, over the forest. "And that way is home." He inclines his head toward the mountains in the north.

"Highfell."

"Aye." He smiles softly. "I have thought a thousand times of what would have happened if I'd not stopped in that spot, by the loch, on our way there—if I'd not left you alone that morning. I should have held onto you tightly, ridden with you until you were safe in my castle, never let you go. It's the most foolish thing I have ever done, and yet, that night, with you, in the tent when you called me handsome—"

"I called you beautiful."

He grins, eyes shining. "It was the best night of my life."

My throat tightens. His face, full of emotion. . . it's like looking at the sun. I have to look away. "It was for me, too, Callum." I shake my head. "This bond, you speak of it as if there is no choice. . . as if I have no choice. There is always a choice."

"You still believe that?"

"You still do not?"

He shrugs a big shoulder. "You cannot choose if you are not free. You are tethered to him, whether we like it or not. The *Anam-Cridech* is unbreakable, created by *Ghealach* herself. I don't understand it, but for whatever reason, she has decided you and Blake are—"

"Don't," I say. "You're wrong. It's my choice. I'm going to break the bond. If the moon's power created it, then the moon's power can destroy it, too."

"I have prayed to her every night. I prayed for her to give you to me. She has not answered."

"My heart, my body, my soul—I'm the only one who gets to decide who to give them to."

Sadness flickers across his face as he turns toward the mountains. He makes a noncommittal sound, as if he doesn't believe me.

I exhale. "The Heart of the Moon might be able to break the bond."

"If we knew where it was. But it has been lost for many centuries, Princess."

"Lochlan thinks my mother had it at some point."

"I heard." He shrugs.

"You thought it was in the Borderlands on the night we met."

"Aye. I did. I came up here the night before I rode south. There was barely a cloud in the sky, and *Ghealach* shone brightly over the Borderlands. I thought it was a sign. Perhaps it was. Perhaps she led me to you." He runs a hand over his mouth. "You really want to look for it?"

"I do."

I half expect him to change his mind, to tell me I cannot go. "Okay."

"You're going to let me?"

"It's not safe for you here. Not anymore. Alexander wants you, and I don't yet have control of all the Wolves in my kingdom. I won't make the mistake of trusting too easily again. Alexander's men are getting ready to march upon Madadh-allaidh, and when the fighting begins, I cannot trust that no one will betray me." He drags his teeth over his bottom lip. "But I cannot let you travel alone. It's not safe."

A long breath plumes in front of my face. "You want me to go with Philip, don't you?"

"I had a conversation with him yesterday. He's annoying, but I could sense no ill feeling from him. He's your brother.

He will keep you safe when I cannot. I'm going to tell him to go back to his queen in the Snowlands, and to bring her back here." I snap my head toward him, gritting my teeth to stop the pain that shatters through me from escaping. He gives me a sad smile. "Not to marry her. To ask her to fight with us. I don't know what to believe when it comes to the God of Night. I feel we will need a bigger army soon enough. You said you wished to go to Glas-Cladach—their port is the closest to the Snowlands. He can accompany you there, and I recommend you go with him to your homeland."

"Okay."

His eyebrows raise, as if he had not expected me to agree. "I thought I would have a fight on my hands."

"I *am* fighting. Even if you are not."

"I always knew you had fire in your soul."

"I thought you were wrong when you said that about me. Perhaps... perhaps you were not." I peer up at him. "What are you going to do about Blake?"

Callum's big shoulders soften. "I'll let him go, eventually. He's no threat to me while you're away, and I cannot risk him getting harmed when your lives are linked. *Ghealach* knows, he has as many enemies here as I do. I just want to make sure you're out of the kingdom before he's free." He grips his hands together, knuckles whitening. "He'll come after you, you know."

"Yes," I breathe. "I know."

"Perhaps it would not be so bad, if he found you."

Hurt surges through me. "Why do you say that?"

He shrugs. "He won't harm you. Of that, I'm certain. There must be a reason for all of this. I had thought, at first, that *Ghealach* had created the bond because she wished him to be king, and wanted you both to bring the kingdoms together. But I cannot make peace with the idea that my goddess would want a southlander on the throne. There must be another reason." He shakes his head. "I despise the male, but I believe there is goodness in him, buried deep."

I believed that once. Now, I see shreds of it at times. But I had told Callum once that Blake may not be as bad as we thought and he had told me I was wrong. "What changed your mind?"

"The wee lad at Lowfell. Alfie. I realized why I recognized him."

I realize I never told him Alfie is Magnus's son.

"It's how we knew where James had taken you," says Callum. "Blake got a message to Madadh-allaidh, and Magnus replied. I'm sure Blake would have us believe he took the lad, and his mother, as hostages to control Magnus. But the wee lad was a menace—free to roam the castle, happy, healthy, undisciplined." He shakes his head. "No. I think he gave them refuge in his castle because he knows Magnus is an abusive piece of shit. I think Blake knows, as I do, that not all men are fit to be fathers."

"That doesn't make him a good man."

"No. But it gives me hope that he could be, under the right circumstance."

He sighs and his breath plumes in front of his face. The mist is clearing from the loch to expose the silver water beneath. I pick at a loose stone in the wall as I shake my head. "Things don't have to change."

"Things have changed, whether we wish it or not." His voice is rough. Quiet. The backs of my eyes burn because I know he's right. "I'll never forget the first time I set eyes on you at the dog fight. The way you held my gaze. Stubborn. Filled with fire. Beautiful."

I turn my gaze to the sky. "I will come back to you, Callum. This is not goodbye."

"And I will wait for you. Always." His voice is strained. He straightens and steps back, and I know everything is about to end. I'm not ready. How can I be ready?

"Will you hold me?" My voice is quiet. Unsure.

He takes a deep breath. There is an endless chasm between us, and I think he will walk away. His heat surrounds me as he steps behind me. He wraps his arms around me, pulling my back to his chest, and placing his chin on my head. "Aye."

I cocoon myself in his solidity, his safety. I try to suppress it, but a hot tear slips down my cheek. He sniffs behind me, his heartbeat thudding against my back.

Together, wrapped in each other's arms, we watch the sky over the mountains.

Chapter Fifty-Four

My heart is heavy as Philip and I ride away from Madadh-allaidh.

We must go west, to the small seaport at Glas-Cladach. First—on Callum's orders—we take a route through a valley to the north to avoid Alexander's army, who have been spotted riding in our direction.

I ride a small chestnut horse named Heather, prepared for me by Fiona, who hugged me tightly before I left and told me she hoped our paths would cross once more. Mrs. McDonald packed me a bag of bread, dried meats, and nuts—as well as another of her love stories, which she tucked within the other items with a wink. Callum brushed his lips against my forehead, eyes shining in the cold sun, and gave me the small silver letter opener I took from the Borderlands that I once tried to stab him with.

"Go for the throat," he reminded me, his voice strained.

"I'll find the Heart of the Moon, and I'll come back to you," I told him in response.

And then Philip and I were on our way.

I didn't say goodbye to Blake, though the bond tugs as the mountains rise up on either side of us. Darkness grows in my chest, and I'm not sure if it's linked to the sadness I feel, or whether I'm feeling his emotion. I think he knows I'm gone.

Philip rides ahead, his gait casual, only one gloved hand on the reins of his horse. He's dressed in his long blue coat with a high collar, and the sword Callum gave him is strapped to his back. I know he has daggers attached to his belt, too. Other than grumbling about his slumber being interrupted, and his despair that we left before he could have breakfast, he has had the good sense not to speak.

I'm not sure if it's compassion for my situation, or whether—like me—he feels awkward. We are both siblings and strangers. Back home, we played the parts of a prince and a princess who didn't much like each other. So much has happened to both of us since then, it's hard to know what roles we now fit into.

When clouds gather in the afternoon and the sky opens up, it does little to heighten my mood. I bring my horse beside Philip, irritated. "Are you sure you're going the right way?"

"Yes."

"How can you bear north when we cannot even see the sun? Callum said we should have reached a forest by now, at which point, we are to turn west." I taste the rain, and my cloak is starting to stick to my body.

"If you wish to take the lead, be my guest, little sister." His red hair is flat, and rain rolls over his mouth, but while I shiver, he seems at ease. "I didn't ask to become bodyguard to your spoiled arse."

"Must you be so constantly unpleasant?"

"Must you?"

I withhold my snarl, and turn my attention to the towering mountains, and the many shades of green and grey that surround us. Not for the first time since we set off, I wonder if I'm doing the right thing by traveling with him. I can barely stand his company.

By nightfall, I'm convinced we're lost, yet Philip seems triumphant when a woodland comes into view.

"There, see? The forest we were looking for. We'll make camp until dawn," he says, heading into the tall trees.

I follow, because it's better than roaming the mountains in the dark searching for the actual forest we were supposed to turn west at—I'm sure this is not it. The sound of the rain softens when I lead Heather beneath the evergreen canopy, and there is immediate relief from the cold wind.

Philip leads us to a clearing. We both dismount, and he orders me to light a fire while he waters the horses at a nearby stream, the sounds of which fill the pine-scented air.

I'm sitting on a log, warming my hands by the crackling flames, by the time he returns. He sits on a boulder opposite, and clasps his hands between his long legs. I pass him some food. We eat in silence. We finish. He sharpens his sword. I wring out my hair, and re-braid it.

A stubborn part of me wants to maintain the silence, to suppress all my questions because I don't want him to get the incorrect impression that I care about anything that happens to him. My curiosity outweighs it. His past is my past. I need to know.

"Are you going to tell me what happened to you?" I ask.

"That depends."

"On?"

"Whether or not you ask me nicely."

I glower at him over the crackling flames. "Oh *please* Philip, please tell me what happened to you. Because I *really* care."

"Sarcasm is quite unbecoming of you, little sister." He shrugs, then sheaths his sword. He props it against the boulder. "What do you want to know?"

"I don't know. Everything. Did you know mother was a wolf? When did you get bitten? Was it before you left the palace, or after?"

"Before."

Shock slams through me, and I try to pull back my reaction so he can't see my hurt. If it happened before he left, he must have known about Mother—about *me*—and never told me. I should expect no more from him, yet he's my family. His expression softens.

"I was not pleasant to you, growing up. I know that," he says. "In my defense, I didn't like you very much."

My hurt turns into irritation, and my fingernails dig into my palms. "Oh, well that's okay then." A thick silence extends between us and I can't stop the question that has plagued me for years from erupting. "Why?"

"I was jealous, I suppose."

"Jealous? Of what?"

He sighs dramatically. "I don't know. You spent your days swanning around the palace, dressing in fine clothes, preening, playing music, watching plays, embroidering. All the while, I had to train to go to war. I never wanted to learn to kill humans or Wolves. I certainly did not want to be up at dawn every morning, failing to impress our father, constantly being told what a disappointment I was." He shrugs. "Before she died, you were always Mother's favorite child, and I was Father's. When Father sent me to war, it was to 'toughen me up' because he believed I was too soft. I didn't see what was wrong with being soft. It always seemed to me that you got the better part of it all."

I had never thought of it this way, yet I release a bitter laugh. "I didn't, Philip. I was powerless. You have no idea what it was like to be a woman in that situation. I had no voice, whereas you always did. You got to escape it. Do you know what my escape was? I was supposed to marry Sebastian."

He looks up at the tree boughs overhead—as if he can't quite meet my gaze.

"I heard about that." He runs a hand over his mouth. "Since I met Ingrid in the Snowlands. . . I realize some of my perceptions may have been incorrect. I'm just saying, that's how I felt at the time. And, alongside my envy, there was a hunger growing within me that I couldn't understand. I tried to drown it out with drink, and fill it with women and men, and appease it by picking fights. . . yet I was never sated. You always seemed like you were at peace—it never occurred to me that you may be going through the same thing and were more adept at hiding it than me."

"You could sense you were a wolf?"

"I began to suspect it just before Mother died, yet I didn't ask her. I was afraid, I think. Of the discovery, of the answers, of her outing me to Father. When she passed, I started looking into Wolves. I read everything I could get my hands on in the library. If anyone saw me, I told them I was researching my enemy, so I'd know how to kill them better. One day, one of the guards saw me. He told me there were Wolves in the dungeons beneath the palace, if I wanted to see one up close."

Something coils, serpent-like, around my insides. Philip cocks his head to one side. "What?"

"Is that where you met Blake?" I ask. My voice is barely audible over the rain pattering on the evergreen canopy and the stream nearby.

"I'd seen him around, but that was the first time we spoke. One night, my curiosity got the better of me. I went to see what lay in the depths of our home. There he was."

You're looking better than the last time I saw you. Philip had said that to Blake when we were at Madadh-allaidh. "He'd been tortured."

"Yes. So you can imagine how my fear of discovery grew, on finding him and the other prisoners down there."

I shake my head, disgust writing within. "You did nothing."

"Would you have done differently, little sister?"

"I. . ." I shake my head. I like to think that I would have tried to help, but perhaps that is fanciful thinking. Perhaps I'm as much a coward as my brother. "I don't know, Philip."

"I tried to distance myself from what I'd seen. I tried not to think about it. It haunted me, though. It would be my fate if Father ever discovered what I was. Honestly, it had never occurred to me that you would share the same affliction, the same fate. I was too wrapped up in myself. The only saving grace was that I knew I was a half-wolf, and I had not yet been bitten."

"What changed?"

"The night of the full moon, I felt... restless. I snuck out to the docks, and drank so much I could barely stand. When I returned to the palace..." He shakes his head. "I was overtaken by a sick curiosity. I wanted to know what they looked like when they transformed."

"You went back to the dungeons."

A sorrowful look flickers across his face. "There were five of them in the cells. I was barely conscious, I was so drunk. I taunted a couple of them through the bars. I was bitten. I deserved it, I suppose."

"Blake said he knew the wolf who bit you."

"Yes. He's at Madadh-allaidh now."

My eyebrows raise. "Who?"

He snaps his gloved fingers, as if he's searching for the name. "The man with the dreadlocks and the southern accent."

"Jack?"

"Yes, that's right. Jack."

Shock blooms inside me. I had never asked how Blake met his right-hand man, but I didn't expect them to both have been prisoners within my father's palace. Darkness spreads inside me as something else occurs to me. "Jack is part of Blake's clan. That makes Blake your alpha."

The thought that Blake is playing a bigger game intensifies. It can't be a coincidence that he has managed to become alpha to both the prince and the princess of the kingdom that entrapped him. As much as I protest that Blake is not my alpha, his bite still marks my shoulder.

Philip shrugs. "He certainly thinks he is. He tried to use the Àithne on me when he had me in the infirmary."

"It didn't work?"

He shakes his head. "No. Although I let him think it did."

"I did the same thing."

A dimple creases his cheek. "After that, I realized I had to get out of the kingdom before the following full moon. Shifting in front of Father? Can you imagine?"

Despite my ill feeling toward my brother, the corner of my lip twitches.

Philip grins. "No, I decided I would spare myself that experience. I told Father I was ready to go to war. I took the guard who had told me about the Wolves in the dungeons with me, and—as soon as we had arrived at the war camp—we set off to the Snowlands in search of answers."

"Did you find them?"

"I found a divided kingdom. I found the fear of the God of Night." There's a distant look in his eyes. "And I found Ingrid."

"You love her," I say softly.

"It doesn't matter how I feel about her. It's unrequited, I assure you. I did little to warm her to me when we first met. She is. . ." He bites his bottom lip, his face uncharacteristically serious. He looks almost like the prince he should be. "She is quite extraordinary."

"Is that why you're looking for the Heart of the Moon?"

He laughs. "Nothing escapes you, Sister." He shrugs. "Yes, I'm looking for it. It wasn't my primary reason for coming here, but I spoke to a tribe in the Snowlands who said it was sent here, years ago. Although they have a different name for it there. It translates to Blood of the Moon. I thought Ingrid might forgive me of my sins, if I found it."

"The Blood of the Moon?"

"Yes."

I bite my bottom lip. "And you decided to try and arrange a marriage between this extraordinary woman and the man I am. . ." The words die in my throat, and I shift on the boulder. I'm going to return to Callum, and I'm going to fight for him, but he still wanted to end things between us. "The man I *was* courting. How brotherly of you."

A dimple punctures his cheek. "What does it matter, little sister? Blake is your—"

"Don't." I push down the rise of panic. "How did you know about. . . about the bond?"

He pulls a face. "Aside from the fact it's blatantly obvious?" He shrugs. "Every time you were both in the same room, he couldn't take his eyes off you. Be careful around him, though. He's changed since I met him. Back then, there was. . ." He shakes his head. "I don't know. There was something 'off' about him. He hides it now."

I agree that he's hiding something, yet I feel a little indignant on Blake's behalf. "Perhaps that's because you met him when he'd just been tortured, Philip."

"Perhaps." Philip lowers himself onto the ground by the boulder, and puts his pack down beneath him to use as a pillow before lying down. "Perhaps not." He closes his eyes. A smile spreads across his lips.

"What?" I say.

"Father would be so displeased to know what has become of us."

I lie down on the pine needles, and settle down for sleep. "Two half-wolves, each helping a different enemy kingdom. Yes, he would be, wouldn't he?"

Philip laughs. "Good night, little sister."

"Good night, Philip."

***

I OPEN my eyes. I'm no longer in the forest. The scent of pine is heady in the air. A fire crackles in a black iron fireplace adorned with books and a decanter of whisky. Blake's chambers. The mattress creaks behind me, followed by a muffled moan.

I turn and freeze.

I'm in Blake's dream. There is a version of me on my knees on his bed, framed by the bedposts and the dark silk curtains. I'm naked, and my skin glows like moonlight.

Blake kneels behind me. One of his hands is cupped between my parted thighs, the other roughly squeezes my breast. His teeth are at my throat, and he thrusts his fingers into me. The dream version of me moans and pushes back into him, and he groans.

My legs turn to liquid. I feel him. I feel him everywhere. He's not touching the real version of me, yet pressure builds between my legs, and my core aches.

I need to get out of here. But I'm transfixed. It's not just the fervent nature of Blake's movements, when he's usually so in control. It's the glow of my skin, almost goddess-like, as if that is how he sees me.

He pushes me down onto the mattress, and I snap to my senses. I stagger back. My back hits something solid and warm. I spin around.

Blake—the real Blake—stands before me. His gaze is fixed on the bed, and his lips are slightly parted. I grab his shirt, and push him against the wall by the fireplace. "Stop it."

His eyes flit to mine. Panicked. "I cannot."

A female groan—my groan—fills the air, and I can't breathe. The creaking gets louder, faster, drawing Blake's attention. The bond trembles, and I feel the word that builds like a growl. *Hunt.*

I glance over my shoulder, and my breathing almost stops. He has me face down on the mattress, one hand on the nape of my neck to hold me down, the other grips my hip as he thrusts into me. The look on his face... goddess... the look on his face.

My chest is too tight. My blood is molten gold. I swing back toward him. "Blake. You can't... you can't think of me like this..."

I feel the moment he changes. He feels like he did in the chapel. Feral. Animal. Not himself. His eyes shift, then glow. "No one would know."

"What?"

Almost delicately, he takes a strand of my hair and tucks it behind my ear. The gentleness is at odds with the look in his eye, and what is going on behind me. My breath catches.

"It's just a dream," he says. "We don't have to do it my way. I can be gentle, if you like."

My mouth dries. "Blake..."

He cups my face in both hands. "Let me have you. Just once. Please."

My insides combust. He is begging. Blake is begging. And I know he is manipulating me. I know he will do or say anything he needs to in order to get what he wants, because that is how his mind works. Yet my blood heats. I cannot move. I cannot think. He steps closer, and his body is flush to mine. His lips are inches away, and his breath brushes my mouth.

He smiles, a dark wicked smile, and tilts my head back. "It's just you and me. He doesn't have to know."

He.

Callum.

Ice crashes through me and dowses the traitorous flames. I block the moaning, and the slapping, and the deep grunts. I stagger back.

"You cannot think of me like this." I try to put a command in my tone, but my voice trembles. "This. . . this will never happen."

He has the audacity to look sad. I turn and crash through the door.

Chapter Fifty-Five

Something tugs inside my chest. There's a familiar press of attention on my skin, a whisper of air on my cheek. My pulse kicks up, as if my body senses a threat before my mind has caught it. I open my eyes.

The night is thick. I must have turned onto my side, because pine needles dig into my cheek. The fire burns low, and the orange embers glow in the darkness. The trees sway overhead. Philip snores gently, long legs stretched out, though one hand rests on the dagger at his belt. Everything seems normal, yet my blood thrums.

I blink a couple of times, then warily push myself upright. I breathe in sharply.

Blake watches me from the edge of the clearing. He sits against one of the tree trunks with his knees raised, his hands dangling between them. "Hello, little rabbit."

My stomach plummets. "What are you. . .?" My question dies in my throat as my eyes adjust.

He is not sitting in the forest a few feet away. He's on a cot, the mattress thin, and there's a dark stone wall behind him. There are books scattered on the bed around him, and his wrists are bound in shackles. His dark hair is messy, as if he's been dragging his fingers through it, and the top buttons of his shirt are undone.

Both the forest and the cell have a shimmer to them. It's like I'm seeing everything underwater. The sound of the stream nearby echoes in my ears, and everything feels far away. This is a dream, yet I've no doubt that the wolf before me is really Blake. Panic twinges inside me. It's not just because of the aftermath of our shared dream. I don't want him to know where I am. I believe Callum. Blake will come for me, when he gets free. I can't face him.

He tilts his head to one side. "Weren't you going to say goodbye?"

"I thought it best that I did not."

"I waited for you. I thought you would come."

I shake my head. "We're not friends, Blake."

"Perhaps not. Did you figure out the nature of the bond?"

"Yes."

"And?"

"It changes nothing. You may not have created it, but you manipulated me."

He tips his head back against the wall, exposing his throat. A laughs escapes him—cold and hollow. It echoes around his prison cell. "You still believe that?"

"It's true, is it not?" I sit straighter, twigs crunching beneath me. Stones dig into my palm. "Mrs. McDonald told me it needed to be accepted to come into effect. That's what happened that night, when James bit me, isn't it?" I think of the light I saw in the depths of my subconscious, and I remember Blake coaxing me to take it. "You tricked me into accepting it so you could use it against Callum, and my father, too, I imagine. Then you hid its true nature from me."

"Perhaps." He shrugs. "Or perhaps I merely used the bond to save your life, because I was the only one who could. Perhaps I've suffered the consequences of that decision every day since."

Anger stains my cheeks. "You ruined my life."

"Do you think you have not destroyed me?"

I shake my head. "You're playing a game, Blake. You said as much."

"Yes. But it's not the game that you think."

"And my part in it? Is it over?"

He clasps his hands together, and the chains binding him rattle. Regret flickers across his features. "No. I don't think so."

"It doesn't matter. You will not find me."

"Darling, I will always find you." His gaze flicks from me to my surroundings. "Your master let you go, then. Fool."

"He's not my master."

"Where are you?"

My laugh is as cold as Blake's. "I'm not going to tell you, am I?"

"Come back to me." A dimple punctures his cheek. "We can figure this out together."

"No."

"The trees don't grow that tall in the Southlands. Whatever your destination, he would have sent you north first, to avoid Alexander's army." Panic tightens my chest, yet I assure myself that Callum won't free him until a few days have passed, at least. "He shouldn't have done that. Alexander will come."

"We've taken precautions."

Blake shakes his head. "I know things about Alexander that you and Callum do not. He wants you more than anything, Aurora. He wishes to gain Night's favor, and he thinks your soul will help him do so."

"Why?"

"Does it matter? He's a zealot. A fanatic. He will come for you. He will track you down."

My heart beats faster as the trees rustle. "We're in the middle of nowhere. Alexander doesn't know these lands. He has an army of humans, and they're distracted by Callum. We'll be fine." I'm not sure if I'm trying to persuade Blake or myself.

His gaze moves to my brother. "You're with Philip. Did he tell you how we met?"

"Yes."

"Ask him who else was in that dungeon with me. Ask him what happened to Alexander when you told your father of his treason." His tone is pointed and my breath catches in my throat. I recall something Alexander said to Blake when he chased us to the chapel.

If it isn't the king's favorite pup. I missed you, Blake. I missed the sound of your screams. I dream of them, sometimes. Do you dream of me?

My mouth dries. "Alexander is a wolf."

Blake leans forward. "Listen to me, Aurora. Your life, and mine, may depend on it. I tried to use the Àithne on Philip. It did not—"

The wind changes, and my skin pebbles. I catch a scent, seawater and steel. I straighten, and look sharply over my shoulder.

Blake stiffens. "What is it?"

"I. . . I don't know. I thought I sensed something."

Blake looks over my shoulder, and his nostrils flare. He jumps to his feet, uncharacteristic panic etched upon his face. "Aurora, you need to wake up. Get away from—"

Male voices echo in the distance. I stumble to my feet. "Blake!"

He moves toward me, holds out his hands, bound in chains. I reach for him. My fingers slip through his and grasp only air. "*Run.*"

My eyes jolt open.

Philip is already on his feet, one hand on his sword, the other held out toward me. I grab it and let him pull me upright. The crunching of twigs surrounds us on all sides; the whispers of men twist with the rustling of leaves. Sweat and steel taint the forest-scented air.

"The horses are by the stream," Philip whispers, voice urgent. "Ride west. I'll kill—"

The air slices in two behind him. He shoves me back as his eyes widen. A thunk reverberates through the clearing as he staggers forward. He turns and flings one of his daggers between the trees. There's a cry, then a thud, as he hits his target.

My heart plummets. There's an arrow protruding from Philip's calf. He pulls it out. "Go. I'll follow."

"Together. Come on."

I grab his arm. He limps toward me just as something slices through the air once more. Philip takes me down with him as an arrow sinks into his side. His sword flies across the clearing. "*Fuck.*"

I try to drag him to his feet. Footsteps crunch toward us, and our gazes flick up.

A figure emerges from the shadow-drenched trees. Packed with muscle and dressed in a finely embroidered black coat with the Borderlands symbol—a star—etched upon its breast, Alexander smiles.

"Hello, love," he says. My heart stills. Philip starts to push himself up, hand curling around his other dagger. "*Down, pup.*" Alexander's eyes transform, blazing with the wolf he hides within.

Philip sinks to his knees and drops the dagger. A crease forms between his eyebrows, then his nostrils flare. "Aurora. *Run—*"

"Philip! What are you doing?" I demand.

"*Quiet*," says Alexander.

Philip shuts his mouth. Panic writhes inside me.

I shake my head. "Philip. . . what. . ."

"I'm sorry." His skin is pale. "I didn't know. I swear it. I didn't know. They had shifted. I thought it was Jack."

My throat is tight as more men emerge from between the trees. "Alexander is your alpha," I breathe in horror.

"You were pissed out of your mind, pup," says Alexander. "I'm surprised you even remember getting bitten. We both sank our teeth into you. It seems I won the claim.

Lucky me." He throws shackles onto the floor before us, and his eyes shift. "*Put these on your sister. We're going to the Grey Keep.*"

Chapter Fifty-Six

Silver cuffs bite into my wrists. My arm is wedged against the carriage door and one of Philip's knees is pressed against mine. He is in shackles too. The scent of his blood hangs in the air and he groans when we hurtle over a bump in the road through the mountains.

"Our father will see you hang for this." Philip's voice is hoarse.

Alexander sits opposite, thighs parted. "Your father's a cunt, and when I've achieved my goal, he'll be dead. As will you."

Waves of panic keep riding over me. I try to calm myself, but my breathing is fast, and my skin cold. This is too similar to what happened with Sebastian. I escaped that, yet I don't think I'll be so lucky this time.

How about you show me what else you learned while you were being a whore to that Highfell beast?

"What do you want with me?" I ask.

"Shh." Alexander leans forward and takes my chin between his finger and thumb. My soul recoils. "Save your strength for later, my love."

"Get your hands off me." I spit in his face and jerk back.

Philip stiffens. Alexander merely drops his hand and laughs—a low, gravelly sound that sends a shiver down my spine. He leans back, wipes the saliva off with his fingers, then sucks them. Fear tightens in my chest, and Philip shifts slightly, as if he can put himself between us.

Alexander's eyes shift. *"If she moves against me again, deal with her."*

Philip's jaw clenches. A vein throbs in his neck. I sense the wolf beneath his skin, as if it's fighting Alexander's command. If I'm going to do something, it needs to be now. I grab the letter opener Callum gave me from my pocket and hurl myself at Alexander. Philip's anguished roar fills the carriage as he grabs me by the middle and slams my head into the door.

Pain bursts into my skull.

Philip's eyes swim with tears. "I'm so sorry."

The last thing I see is Alexander's wide grin.

Black.

***

I GROAN. The scent of seaweed and sweat permeates the cool air. I peel open my eyelids and push myself onto my forearms. It takes my eyes a moment to adjust to the darkness. I'm in a cage. No. A cell. One of the walls is curved and barred. I touch my head—my hair is wet and sticky. Blood.

Panic tightens in my chest. Philip is not here. I'm alone. I'm going to die.

Someone is mumbling not far away.

"Stop your whining." The voice is rough and familiar, thick with the Northlands accent. My heart jumps. I turn toward the next cell. The wolf inside grins. "Hello, Princess."

He has the same powerful shoulders and almond-shaped eyes as Callum. For a moment, I let my heart tell me it's Callum who sits against the damp wall, that this man's kilt is the Highfell tartan, not the pattern that combines all the clans. Until I'm forced to confront the tangled brown hair that brushes his shoulders and the ink that covers his arms.

"*James?*"

"Shouldn't you be up there with that southern bastard?" He gestures with his chin at the ceiling.

"Where is my brother?"

"Your brother?"

"Alexander took him, too."

James tips back his head and a low, gravelly laugh fills the cell block. "They said Alexander was a mad dog, but he's kidnapped both of the heirs to the Southlands throne? Fuck me. We really are in trouble."

A low moan comes from the cell next to James's. "I should never have come here. I should never have fucking come here."

"Be quiet, lad," says James.

I straighten. "Ryan? Is that you?"

My eyes adjust. Beyond James's great bulk, Ryan sits with his back to the wall and his hands in his coppery hair. He looks up. "Hello, Princess." He tips his sharp chin toward James. "I found him."

"That you did, lad," says James. "And if we ever get out of here—which seems fairly unlikely given the circumstances—perhaps the next time my wee traitor of a brother sends you on a mad quest, you'll remember what happens when you follow his orders instead of mine."

I push down my rising anger at his insult to Callum. A growl, female and irritated, echoes off the damp walls before I can respond.

"Can everyone shut the fuck up for five fucking minutes?"

"Ah, allow me to introduce you to my delightful mate, Claire." James nods at the cell beside mine.

The woman who snarls at James through the bars on my other side is far from the pristine, well-put-together alpha I met at Lowfell. Her dark hair is wild and tangled around her face, her shirt is torn and baggy, and there is dirt on her cheeks.

She bares her teeth. "Call me that again and I'll rip your balls off and feed them to you."

"Don't mind her," says James. "She gets irritable when she hasn't eaten and starts acting like a—"

"Call me a bitch, I fucking dare you." Claire's eye flash in the darkness. James grins, and raises his big hands in faux surrender. Claire slumps against the wall. "That's what I thought. Arsehole."

"We've already met," I say.

"Of course." James rests his head back against the wall. "While you were planning your wee rebellion. How is that going for you, Princess? You're here, and my brother isn't, so I take it things didn't work out between the two of you. Shame."

I clench my teeth as my blood roars. "Your big plan was to rescue Claire, yet here you are, trapped in a cage alongside her. I take it your plans haven't gone particularly well, either."

Claire laughs.

To my surprise, James laughs, too. "No, they haven't."

I narrow my eyes. "You lack honor. You told me you'd let me stay in your kingdom if I killed Sebastian. I did as you asked, and you broke your promise."

"I'm not sorry for it. I'd do it again."

A snarl scrapes my throat, and the corner of James's smug mouth twitches. "Callum should have killed you," I say.

"He should have. My brother has always been too soft to do what needs to be done."

"Mercy is not weakness," I snap, aware that I'm somewhat contradicting myself.

"Then you must think highly of me for sparing my brother's life."

My spine is a rod. "Callum is stronger than you. He won the challenge and showed *you* mercy. Just as he would have won the challenge between the two of you years ago, if he had not let you win."

A muscle flexes in his jaw now, as if I've gotten beneath his skin, too. "No. I'm the dominant wolf. That's always been the case. But I love my brother. I didn't want to kill him for the sake of a southerner. Now, you have torn my kingdom apart."

My fingers curl into fists. "You did that. Not me. I never did anything to provoke such ill feeling from you. I was never your enemy. That morning we met, I offered to help you and your kingdom. If you had kept your word, if you hadn't sold me out to Sebastian, if you hadn't *attacked* me, none of this would have happened!"

James growls. "You are wrong, Princess. You are my enemy. Your blood is my enemy's blood. Your people are my enemy people. Since the time of the Elderwolf, you have ravaged our lands and taken from us. You have brought us war, and you tried to rule us, when all we ever wanted was peace. The moment I first laid eyes on you and smelt my brother all over you, I knew you were trouble. What did you expect me to do? Let you live? I knew it was only a matter of time before you left Callum and took our secrets to your people. You would have doomed us all."

"You doomed yourself, you pig-headed fool! I did not intend on spilling your secrets to my father. I did not intend on leaving Callum."

"Yet here you are, and where is he?" His raised voice echoes around the dungeons before he shakes his head. "It's not your father I worry about. I scented Blake on you, too, that morning, and I knew exactly what it meant. Two southerners—one a half-wolf from the Borderlands who became alpha of one of the most feared clans in the Northlands, schemed his way onto my father's council, and blatantly had designs on my throne, and the other the daughter of our enemy king. That, I thought, is not an alliance I want to contend with."

"I have no alliance with Blake."

"Of course you don't. . ." He runs a hand over his jaw. "I showed my brother mercy. I did not kill him, even though I could have. But I made sure he saw what I did. I made sure he'd read the book I found in Blake's chambers. Because I needed both of you out of Madadh-allaidh before you created any lasting damage, so that my brother could fight the war that your people started."

"I'm glad you got what you wanted," I spit.

"You think this is what I wanted?" He shakes his head. "I want to be drunk and warm with a lass in my bed. Thanks to you, I'm here. You were a threat to me then, Princess. You're a threat to me—"

The torches that line the wall flicker and dim, one by one, and James shuts his mouth. The shadows thicken and I feel them—cold and restless—writhing like snakes over my body. A low rasping hiss travels down the corridor, and the hairs on the back of my neck stand on end. I think about the bit of shed skin that Blake picked up when we found ourselves in Night's prison.

A hole is carved in my chest, and the darkness slithers up through my nostrils. That wild thing, deep within my soul, tries to break free.

I can't afford to lose consciousness. Not here. Not now. I clench my fists. I dig my nails into my palms, drawing blood. I barely notice James's grunt on one side of me and Claire's body stiffening on the other.

The sound stops. The torches flicker back to life. I let out the darkness on a long breath that mists before my face. I turn to Claire.

"What was that?" I breathe, but I think I already know.

"We call it the Dark Beast," says Claire.

"Night's prisoner," I whisper in horror.

James runs a hand along his jaw. "It's what we've been brought here to fight."

Chapter Fifty-Seven

The hours bleed together.

I bring my knees to my chin and clutch my legs in an attempt to keep warm. The torches flicker on and off. I've never been this cold before. My head throbs as blood trickles from the wound Philip gave me, then dries on my cheek. No one speaks. Despair hangs in the air, acrid and heavy. James mumbles something every so often. Ryan whimpers. I just want to sleep.

I fall between the nightmare I'm trapped within and the terrors that haunt my dreams. Both are dark and restless, filled with prison cells and darkness. They plague me until I can no longer differentiate between the two. All I can feel is the cold, oily terror that curls like a snake in my chest. It suffocates whatever wolf I have within me. It whispers that I will die. That no one will care. That my life will have amounted to nothing.

All of this has something to do with the God of Night.

Callum told me that his acolytes used to sacrifice Wolves to gain his favor. Does Alexander intend to sacrifice me? Will he kill my brother too?

Alexander must have guards. Perhaps I can persuade one of them that killing the heirs to the Southlands throne would be ill-advised. I don't want to use the name and title of my father—the man who killed my mother—to save myself, but I don't want to die, either. I need to save Ryan, too.

My mind frantically whirs through every possibility until dots dance before my eyes and I slump against the wall.

Hopelessness crashes over me.

I hear my mother's voice echo in the darkness.

Have courage, little one.

I don't know how much time passes before footsteps approach the door. Hooded guards enter the kennels and open all the doors except mine. Wolves are dragged into the corridor. They're too weak to fight and they're shackled, and collars are placed around their necks.

James grabs the bars of my cell before he's led away. "Does he know you're here?" he asks hurriedly.

"Callum?"

James looks at me pointedly as the guard shoves him forward. "No. Not Callum."

Darling, I will always find you.

Cold darkness spreads through my veins. "Yes."

He nods. "I'll try and buy you some time."

"What are we going to do?" Ryan asks behind him.

"You're going to do nothing, lad."

Chained together, they're led away.

***

A KEY turns in the lock, and I jerk my head upright as finally, someone comes for me.

I spring to my feet. "Listen, I don't know what Alexander has told you, but I'm the Southlands princess. My father would reward you greatly if—"

The man who walks into my cell looks like a phantom in dark robes with a hood that conceals his face. He grabs my arm, and his fingers tighten painfully around it. I catch a glimpse of a tattoo—a key with crescent moons in the bow—on his wrist. Night's symbol. My hope flickers out. Alexander's guards are zealots, like him.

"We don't answer to your father," he says.

He drags me into the curved corridor.

"Are you going to sacrifice me to your god?" My teeth chatter with the cold as he drags me up some stairs.

"We need to check you're the right one first."

"The right what?"

The man says nothing as I'm pulled through a door and down a corridor lit by flickering torches. The walls are damp and coated with a layer of lichen. The scent of salt and blood hangs in the air, and there is noise ahead—shouts and jeers, the rattle of metal and a roar of pain.

Ahead, two cloaked figures guard the exit of the corridor. I'm shoved past them into a dark amphitheater and the echoing roar is almost deafening. My heart stops. The Wolves are on their knees in a circle—beaten and bloody and chained—perhaps twenty in total. I search for Ryan, but my attention is stolen by the cloaked figures who watch them, watch *me*, from the tiered seating.

Alexander sits on what looks like a stone throne on the other side of the circle. My brother is on his knees, in chains, beside him. He's no longer wearing his coat, and his shirt is bloody. Torchlight flickers across his pale face. He lurches toward me, but Alexander hisses something—the wolf glinting in his eyes—and Philip slumps back down.

I turn to stone. I shake my head and edge backward.

There are two posts bolted to the stone floor in the center of the amphitheater. Shackles dangle from them. Beside them, a cloaked male stands with a silver-tipped whip in his hand.

No.

Alexander stands. "Our special guest has arrived." His grin widens. "Time to have some fun, love. If you survive, you can meet an old friend of mine." He nods at the man who brought me here. "Tie her up, and we can begin."

Chapter Fifty-Eight

The amphitheater dissolves around me. I grow roots. I can't move.

The cloaked figures jeering in the stands blend into the darkness, and the Wolves on their knees, clanging their chains, fade away. I'm in one of the holy rooms in the Church of Light and Sun, and the High Priest leans against the altar with a crop in his hand. *You have sinned, child.*

I stagger backward, shaking my head like a mindless beast, but I hit a hard chest. A clammy sweat breaks out over my skin.

No. No. No.

I cannot. Not again.

Hands curl around my upper arms, and it's not the cloaked male who brought me here, but the Sisters of the Church draped in their white robes dragging me forward. I jerk back and twist my ankle. I barely feel the pain. I'm thrust between the posts. I'm screaming, I think. Two men grab my hands and roughly raise them above my head. There's a click and a cold bite as the shackles close around my wrists and I'm trapped, chained between them. It's too late. All thoughts of dignity, of keeping my fear inside, slam from my mind.

I cannot do this. Don't make me do this.

I take deep, shuddering breaths. I'm ashamed that tears fall down my face. Men are jeering. They laugh at my distress. Alexander is saying something but I can't hear him over the roaring in my blood.

I take another deep breath. Then another.

I close my eyes and feel the sting of the cool air. I smell the lichen, and the woodsmoke from the torches. I focus on the bite of the shackles against my skin. I let the stone beneath my boots ground me.

I peel open my eyelids. Alexander stands in front of me, and I almost choke on my hatred. I can't stop this from happening, just like I couldn't when I was a child. I will not beg.

By the throne, Philip is trying to get up, but his wrists are tethered to a metal ring in the stone. Blood trickles from his nose. Someone must have hit him. I'm surprised he's trying to save me, as he didn't when I was a child.

"Why?" I ask.

Alexander brushes a tear from my cheek with his thumb. "Shh," he coaxes. "It's for your own good, my love. Your father did this to you because he wanted to repress your wolf, your power. They didn't take it far enough. I'm going to break you so you'll be free."

"You're insane," I breathe.

"Sometimes things need to be broken to be rebuilt, love. Your father broke me, in a cell beneath the palace, and I'm stronger for it. Now, it's your turn."

"Alexander, don't touch her," says Philip. "Whatever you want, my father will give it to—"

"*QUIET, DOG.*" Alexander's irises shift. He strokes my face and I try to scramble back, but the chains hold me in place. "It'll be over soon."

He steps back.

"Wait!" I blurt. "Tell me... tell me what it is that you want. It's something to do with the God of Night, isn't it? I've dreamed of him." I'm not embarrassed by the desperation in my tone. He is obviously mad. A zealot. If I can make him believe I can help him with his god, perhaps he will let me go.

There's a whisper around the amphitheater, and Alexander cocks his head to one side. "You have?"

A flower of hope grows among the darkness that fills me. "Yes! I find myself in his prison most nights. I could speak to him for you, if you like. Tell me what it is you want from him. I will ask him for you."

He scrapes a hand over his square jaw. "There's no need. I need to break you, if I want to repay my debt."

I shake my head. "You can give him my pain, my life, but he wants my soul," I say. "He... he told me. Only I can give him that. Set me free, and I will go to him. I will tell him whatever you like. I will offer him my soul, in exchange for whatever debt you owe him." I pray he thinks my heartbeat is racing because I'm afraid, not because I'm lying.

"He spoke to you?"

"Yes! He'll be angry, if you harm me."

I pray to both the goddesses of the sun and the moon that he will believe me. His forehead creases. His bright blue eyes glint in the torchlight. The cloaked man who brought me here whispers in his ear. The two step back to have a murmured conversation. The minutes stretch like empty chasms. Fear grips my heart, and the prickle of gazes on my body makes me want to disappear.

"Princess." A rough, familiar voice. My heart jerks.

James is on his knees, tethered to the floor by the entrance of one of four corridors that cut through the stands. His wrists are bound, and there's a metal collar around his neck.

"Your wolf." His eyes shine, the beast behind them. "The wolf part of you will protect you from the worst of it."

"I can't," I whisper.

"You can. You fought my Àithne, back in the manor. You're stronger than you look."

Alexander strolls back toward me. He smiles, almost lovingly, at me. "Nice try, love. I know you're afraid, but it must be this way."

I'm falling. My stomach plummets, and darkness claims me. Philip is shouting something. Alexander steps back, and the man with the whip stands near me. I'm losing feeling in my hands, but I manage to clench my fists. I grit my teeth.

I cannot do this. I cannot—

James roars. He elbows the wolf to his side in the face, and there's a crack as he breaks his nose. My eyes widen as I catch a flicker of blond hair, and a soiled yellow kilt. It's Ian, the male from Lochlan's clan. The two brawl, and the chained Wolves are knocked into one another. Shouting and snarling fills the air. Ryan tries to join in, and lands a hit on Ian, but quickly gets shoved back by James.

A female cry echoes around the amphitheater. The Wolves fall silent. James's gaze snaps across the circle. Alexander has his fist in Claire's hair. Her eyes are wild, furious, and a dagger is held to her throat.

She bares her teeth. "Get the fuck off me."

"I will, if your *king* behaves himself. Do I have your attention, Your Majesty?" Alexander mocks. A feral grin spreads across his face. "You will submit, or I will maim your mate, then throw her into the pit for my other special guest to play with."

James's steely gaze moves from Alexander to a trapdoor in the floor a few meters from where I'm bound. A hiss creeps through the cracks, and I suppress my whimper. *The Dark Beast.* We must be directly above its cell in the dungeons.

James releases Ian, and sinks back to his knees. Alexander throws Claire onto the floor. "Good boy." He nods at the trapdoor before dropping into his stone throne. "If you survive, Aurora, love, I'll open the door and you'll meet her. Let's begin."

Philip's eyes widen. A plea fills my lungs. Panic alights my soul. I jerk my head toward Alexander. "Wait—"

A crack fills the air and I'm jolted forward as a whip slices through my back. The burning pain comes a second later. Tears spring into my eyes. My fingers curl around the chains that bind me. The cuffs bite into my wrists. I take a deep, wheezing breath.

"Do it until she breaks," says Alexander.

My skin splits like butter. I'm burning. Dying. I cannot breathe. I cannot see. There is only pain and blood. I'm shrieking, I think. My knees are weak, and my shoulders jerk in their sockets. My fingers are numb as I clutch the chains. Tears stream down my face. I try to recite one of my mother's stories, but the pain is too great. I cannot focus on anything but my body being broken.

Something rises, angry, within. A scream builds in my chest that needs to break free. What good is screaming? What good is crying? Dots dance before my eyes, and I'm floating above my body—watching the broken girl, covered in blood, in the center of the amphitheater. My vision darkens, and I don't know if it's my life leaking away, or if that *thing* beneath the arena is making the torches flicker.

I can watch no more. I can bear no more. I retreat into myself. I hide with the emotions and the wildness I have contained since I was a girl. I coat myself in armor. I turn myself to stone. I let my soul flicker and blink out.

Alexander roars. The noise stops; the onslaught stops. I'm limp, my hair sticking to my tear-stained face, my arms pulling out of their sockets. My back is on fire. Alexander storms toward me, grabs my face, and jerks my gaze to his. His red face blurs in front of me.

"Why aren't you doing it, you stupid bitch?" He backhands me and my head snaps to one side. He grabs me again. "I know it's you. It has to be you. Show me your power. Show me your fucking power or I'll rip you apart—"

There's a gurgling noise behind him, and he turns. A blade protrudes from the neck of one of the men guarding the exit. His hood has fallen, and blood dribbles from his mouth. It spills down his chin and puddles between his boots. His eyes are wide. Shocked.

In a fluid movement, someone pulls the blade out, and he slumps to his knees before face-planting the floor.

Blake stands behind him.

His face... he is fury incarnate. His shirt is wet, plastered to his hard chest and torso, and a couple of dark curls stick to his forehead. His jaw is as sharp as the dagger in his fist. There's a sword strapped to his back, and two more blades holstered in his belt.

His essence overpowers me. It fills my hollow chest. It's dark and cold and inhuman, and puts out the fire that burns within. I thought I had felt his emotions before, but they were nothing compared to this. I cannot breathe. I cannot move. I can feel nothing but him. I'm reminded of that well that he told me about, and I wonder now if there is a bottom to the darkness.

The wolf blazes, amber, in his eyes as he holds Alexander in his steely glare. "Get your hands off my mate."

Chapter Fifty-Nine

My eyes meet Blake's.

Something erupts inside me. The wild and dangerous thought I've been trying to cull spreads through my body and sets my soul aflame. My breaths come out fast and shallow. *He came. He came. He came.* I feel the whisper of his attention brush over me, even when he moves his gaze back to Alexander.

Alexander releases his grip on my chin. My head is a ballast. I can't support it. It rolls onto my neck. My back is shredded. My shirt blood-drenched. It sticks to the welts that mar my skin, and every breath I take is excruciating.

A slow grin spreads across Alexander's face. "I wondered if you would try and take her from me. Too bad you're alone."

Blake's lips curve into a cold smile. "What makes you think I'm alone?"

"Hello, Alex." A low, smooth voice comes from the entrance corridor to my left. Jack leans against the stand and waves, a guard dead at his feet. His dark skin is wet from the rain, and it glints in the torchlight. He holds a bloody sword in one hand. "How have you been?"

"Long time no see." A gruff voice, thick with the Northlands accent. Arran blocks the exit to my right, big arms folded across his chest, his one good eye focused on Alexander. Two guards are sprawled before him, hoods askew and necks twisted at unnatural angles.

A murmur fills the tiered seating. The cloaked people rise to their feet all around me.

"How nice. A family reunion." Alexander turns on the spot, spreading his arms. "If we had Fenrir and Fara here, we'd have the whole pack back together."

Jack shrugs. "They were otherwise engaged."

"Get Fara's name out of your filthy mouth," growls Arran.

Alexander laughs. "Still pining for that bitch, I see. Too bad she rejected you."

Whatever Arran growls in response fades into the background as Blake bends down and plucks something from the pocket of the guard at his feet. It glints in the torchlight as he tosses it to James a few feet away from him—it's a key.

"No one you don't trust leaves here alive," says Blake quietly. "Wolf or man."

They're enemies, they despise one another, and I think James is going to say something unsavory to Blake. He nods. "Except for you, presumably," he says under his breath.

Blake smiles coolly. "Except for me."

James raises his shackled wrists and sticks the key into the lock of his collar as Alexander turns back to Blake. "You want her, Brother? Come and get—"

There's a flicker of steel, a swish of blades, and something slices the darkness.

One of Blake's daggers plunges into Alexander's torso, the other in his inner thigh. He staggers back. He grips one of the knives and pulls it out, then slumps to his knees. Blood pumps quickly out of his wound and mixes with mine on the floor. He clamps the gash with one hand, while moving his other to the second dagger's hilt and sliding it out with a feral groan.

He laughs. "You're a fool, Brother. You can't kill me." His voice is hoarse as he glares at the stands. "Kill them all. Except the Princess. She is. . . mine."

Chaos erupts in the amphitheater. The cloaked humans flood down the stands. James has passed the key around, and the Wolves are already freeing themselves and tossing their shackles aside. James is on his feet, roaring, as he strangles a blond man with his chain. He charges toward Claire.

Jack blocks the blade of one of the acolytes as it slices down toward one of the prisoners, before he pulls Ryan to his feet and sticks another sword in his hand.

The ground trembles, and I'm not sure if it's because of the thunder of feet, or the beast that lurks beneath us.

Blake moves through the tide of blood and destruction toward me. He barely blinks as he unsheathes his sword and decapitates a man who gets in his way. He stabs a man who is helping Alexander in the face, and then smashes the Borderlands lord's head with the base of the hilt. Alexander crumples into his own blood. Blake steps over him.

"Blake!" Arran tosses another set of keys toward his alpha. The guard who shackled me to the post is dead at his feet. Blake snatches them from the air and his scent of dark pine and poison engulfs me.

"Keep an eye on Alex. He can't die or we're fucked," says Blake.

"Aye." Arran powers toward the unconscious lord, slicing down a human in his path.

Blake presses himself against me, warm and solid, as he reaches for one of the shackles. There's a click, and my hand falls loose. My legs buckle, and he hooks an arm around my lower hips, careful not to touch my back as he frees my other hand. Gently, he lowers us to our knees. My blood and Alexander's seeps into our breeches.

He searches my face. He brings his hands to my cheeks and brushes away the tears and blood with the pad of his thumb.

My throat tightens. "You came."

"Did you truly think I would not?"

The ground trembles, and Blake's jaw sharpens when a low hiss comes from beneath us.

"There's. . ." My throat burns, and every breath opens the wounds in my back. "Night's prisoner. . .."

"Yes. If it gets free, we're all dead. I'm going to get you out of here, but it's going to hurt."

I blink back the tears. "I know."

"Good girl." He brings his arm around my waist and rises into a crouch. "Okay, hands on my shoulders. That's it." I whimper as the movement provokes a deep, burning ache in my back. "Shh, I know."

A film of water fills my eyes. "Can you feel it?"

"You're suppressing your emotions, caging your pain. I feel only a little."

He lifts me to my feet, and when he puts my arm around his shoulders, a low, feral sound scrapes against my throat.

"I know," he soothes. "It will only last for a short while. I have a sleep tonic in my pocket. I'll give it to you as soon as we're clear of the Grey Keep. Come on."

We start to move. I grip the collar of his shirt tightly, and every time my side bumps into his, I whimper. Every step is torture. My knees are weak, and if his hand was not firm around my hip, I would fall. Men and Wolves blur around us, black cloaks and kilts and chains. Arran is by my brother, pulling him to his feet. Jack and Ryan fight back to back. Claire twists the head of a man who straddles James, and he falls dead at her feet.

There is blood... blood everywhere. Nausea rises inside me.

"Why?" My voice is dry and hoarse, barely audible over the roars and the swishes of steel. I'm not even sure what I'm asking. Why did Alexander torture me? Why am I here? Why did Blake come?

"You know why." His mouth is close to my ear, and I'm not sure what he means. "Shh. It's okay. We're almost there."

The corridor I was brought through looms ahead. I let myself dare to hope, to water that small flower that raises its head in the darkness. We're going to escape. We're going to be free.

I grit my teeth. I grip Blake tighter and straighten my spine. He quickens his step.

The muscles in his shoulders tense beneath my fingers. The torches around the circle flicker, then die, and the amphitheater plunges into darkness. We turn our heads toward the trapdoor. Alexander has crawled to it, his black shirt slick with blood. He pulls a key out of the lock, and meets Blake's eyes, as Arran—blood spilling from his nose—charges toward him.

"You fool, Alex," Blake hisses.

Alexander grins and flings open the door. Dots dance before my eyes, and I squeeze them shut. I can't afford to lose consciousness. Not here. Not now.

I dig my fingers into Blake's shoulders and make myself look.

An unnatural quiet fills the amphitheater. Chains groan, then scrape along the floor, making the hairs on the back of my neck stand on end. A low hiss vibrates over the walls, and even the men in cloaks shrink from it. A sour scent, like decaying meat, floods my nostrils as a slithering sound fills the gloom.

"Moonlight and darkness. Freedom and chains. Power and destruction." An unnatural rasp seems to come from everywhere at once, and it reminds me of the voice that came from Kai when he first awoke. *"Does he know, do you think?"*

Blake hurls me back, and I withhold my scream as a tide of shadow spills out of the trapdoor and rears up, contained only by the ceiling. It winds around the circle, blocking the exits. The darkness moves like mist around a serpentine face and body. It blinks down at us with eyes of onyx.

"You've been so naughty."

Something rattles in the cage inside me and floods my body with ice. Sweat beads on my skin, and my vision begins to fade.

"Oh, I am so hungry. So very hungry."

The darkness crashes down into the amphitheater like a stormy obsidian wave. Shouts fill the air as men and Wolves scatter, and two males are plucked up as if they're weightless. A horrible crunch is followed by a squelch as they disappear, screaming, into the maw of the beast. Black blood spatters the ground.

My pulse is racing so quickly, I think I'm going to pass out. The fever is coming for me, and I can't keep it at bay. I fight it with everything I have, even though darkness would be a relief. I can't give up. I can't expect someone else to save me.

There's a flicker of darkness to my side, and Blake pulls me out of the way of the *thing's* tail. We land hard on the ground, Blake's arms curling around me, and I bite down hard to stop myself from screaming as the welts in my back are exposed to the air. It strikes again, scooping up cloaked men and Wolves, dead and alive, and swallowing them whole.

"Pick up your weapons!" James roars. "Next time it strikes, go for its eyes and mouth! Kill any southerners that get in your way."

I try to push myself up, and Blake helps me to my knees. He kneels before me and clasps my face in his hands. "Aurora, listen to me. You need to stop suppressing your power. You're the only one who can save us. If you don't, we will all die."

I shake my head. "I'm not a wolf."

Out of the corner of my eye, Alexander staggers forward, eyes set on me as the shadows writhe around him. Ryan is on the floor, bleeding. Philip is standing by James, the two of them barking frantic orders and getting the Wolves into formation, only for another three men to be plucked into the maw of the beast. Claire plunges a sword into a hooded male that lurches for her before turning to face the shadows—her eyes bright and feral, even though the blade trembles in her hand. Ian lies dead on the floor.

"Not your wolf, Aurora." Blood and gore splatter the ground beside us. Warm droplets drip down my cheek and onto his hand. "Your power. There's a reason why you didn't shift on the night of the full moon. A reason why *Ghealach* shone for you on the night of the battle with Sebastian. A reason why the Àithne doesn't work on you, why Callum has struggled with his wolf—gods, why I have—since you have been around." He grips me tighter, sliding his hands into my hair. "I think you've started to suspect it too. You feel it. It's not your wolf that you keep suppressing when the fever comes for you. It's a different power. The Wolves thought it was literal. A heart turned to rock, fossilized by time. What if it was not?"

What he's saying, it can't be true. I shake my head. "Even if you're right, it's deep within me, and I've been holding onto it for so long that I cannot let it go."

"Darling, people like you and me, we do not let go." He bumps his forehead against mine, and the wolf blazes in his eyes. "We unleash."

He breaks away from me and draws his sword. He meets Alexander's blade. There's a ring of steel as he throws the

Borderlands lord back before advancing upon him. A growl reverberates in his chest.

The serpentine beast rears up above us all, and I stagger back onto my palms as it turns its obsidian eyes on me. I no longer feel pain, nor my blood, nor heat. I'm numb. It's like looking into an endless abyss. Its scent ambushes me, ancient and primordial, and my clothes stick to my skin. It laughs, a raspy sound that vibrates through me and makes the hairs on the back of my neck stand on end.

"He will be so angry with me, when he finds out what I have done to you," it hisses. *"It will be our little secret."*

The darkness crashes down upon me, and something in my body rises up to meet it. A scream builds in my chest. My skin is clammy and everything is far away. The fever, it's coming for me, as deadly as the serpentine creature that hurtles ever near, its mouth opening, its fangs dripping with blood. Every instinct in my body braces itself.

Blake is right. I have started to suspect something. I have read through his books filled with experiments on Wolves, and not one of them could stop the shift, nor fight the effects of silver and wolfsbane. I have wondered why I've found myself in Night's prison and what it is he wants from me. I cast my thoughts back to the family tree I found in Blake's bedchambers, and who the two scrubbed names at the top may belong to. Lochlan thought my mother brought the Heart of the Moon to the Northlands. Blake and Callum thought Sebastian had it.

I have thought of my mother, of the reason she might have withheld the truth from me. She loved me more than anything. I was her heart, she told me, her love.

When the fever hurtles through my body, I don't fight it. I don't suppress it.

I close my eyes.

I release a breath.

For once, I let go.

Chapter Sixty

I'm falling, hurtling, crashing through darkness.

It rises to meet me.

I jolt into my body. My skin is stone. The taste of crypts and mildew is thick on my tongue. I cannot move. I cannot breathe. I'm a statue in the palace gardens and moss coats my skin like wet velvet. A scream builds in my chest, but my mouth is sealed shut.

The moon hides behind the clouds, and candles light the way through the hedge maze. Courtiers wander, long silk skirts trailing over the cobblestones. Some pause.

"Perfect stonework," says one.

"She almost looks alive," says another.

And I have had enough. I'm not a statue—with no thoughts, no feelings, no desires of my own. I'm not made of stone. I don't exist as decoration, for people to look upon, comment upon, as if I cannot hear them.

My smile crumbles. The ground quakes. The stone that encases me cracks and I shed it. It turns to dust, coating my naked skin, as I stand on a podium. I raise my chin, and a glimmer of moonlight touches my face. The courtiers around me start to scream.

Enough.

Then I'm falling once more.

My feet slam onto cold checkered tiles, and they crack beneath my feet. I'm in the Church of Light and Sun, only the wilderness has taken it. The stone altar ahead is coated with lichen, and a crescent moon shines through the domed roof. It's pale light puddles on the mosaic of the sun.

Vines burst though the ground and curl around my ankles. They snap from the walls and hold my arms outstretched. More of them snap down on my back, and I'm jolted forward. I bite down my scream and taste the copper tang of blood in my mouth.

But I didn't sin. A version of my voice whispers through the foliage, stirring the leaves.

Your mother was a sinner. The High Priest's voice echoes around the church. *And you are a sinner too. Do you want the Sun Goddess to be angered?*

What of my anger?

For so many years, I had thought I deserved it. I thought I was a sinner. I thought it was my fault that I was beaten. It was not my fault. Men wielded their power over me because it made them feel big, when I was so small. That was their choice, not mine.

The whip cracks down, and dark laughter fills the air.

I raise my chin, defiant.

I yank my arms toward me, and the vines fall to my feet. They uncurl from my ankles, and wither and decay until they're pools of thick darkness. I clench my fist, and sap runs between my fingers. The tiles crack and crumble around me. I raise my head to the glass dome.

Enough.

I'm falling once more.

I land. My skin pulls taut on my arms, and there are hundreds of hooks piercing me and holding me upright. I try to scream, but my mouth is sewn shut. I've been here before, in the palace's throne room. Once again, I'm a marionette, controlled by a hand I can't see. My father's golden throne looms over me on the dais ahead.

The invisible puppeteer is using the control handle as usual, and I begin to spin.

But I'm not a puppet. I'm not a pawn in the games of kings. I'm not someone to be controlled by others, to marry cruel lords for my father's gain. I can pull strings, too. I see them now, threads of power that glow like moonlight. They reach outward from my chest.

I pull my arms free, and the hooks tear through my skin and turn my white dress crimson. I pull the strings from my legs and my feet. The music grinds to a halt. Blood drips down my body. When it hits the floor, the puddle grows and creeps through the room.

I rip my sewn-up lips apart.

The wooden cross-brace hurtles from the ceiling, and the courtiers scream and scatter as it crashes onto the tiles before me. The floor shakes, then crumbles.

"*Enough.*"

I fall.

I land in a heap on the grass. The moon is full in the cloudless sky. It paints the lake by the nearby cabin silver. There are two figures sitting at the bank. A woman and a small child, around three years old, nestled into her side. Both have long red hair that brushes the ground behind them. My heart clenches. I push myself up and walk toward them. Unable to stop myself, I run. The grass tickles my bare feet and dandelions whisper between my toes.

"Mother?" I say.

"The moon is beautiful, isn't she, little one?" she says, and something erupts in my chest. It aches, yet it's warm. Tears spring into my eyes. I had forgotten what her voice sounded like, the musical cadence, the lilt of the Snowlands.

"Yes," I say, at the same time as the small child beside her.

My heart cracks, because it's not the adult version of me she speaks to. I don't think she can hear me. I try to walk around her. I try to see her face, but the scenery turns, and I end up facing her back once more.

My mother sighs. "There is so much I need to tell you. So much you'll need to know when you grow up. Yet I'm running out of time." She leans back on her hands, and her hair tickles the grass. The small version of me snuggles into her side. "I hope you remember these times, and you remember me fondly."

The small girl yawns. My mother hums the same haunting melody I hummed to Blake when he was in need of comfort, and the young version of me begins to gently snore.

"The Snowlands were at war when I was promised to your father. An alpha known as the Shadow Wolf had gained a loyal following. He devoted his life to the God of Night, and he was looking for the key to Night's prison to free his master. My grandmother—the alpha of our pack—could not risk him finding me."

"Why?" I breathe.

She looks down at the small sleeping babe at her side, almost as if she spoke. "It's in our blood, little one. Passed from generation to generation down the female line, getting stronger as each branch of our family tree grows.

"My grandmother believed that the next generation would be powerful enough to either release the God of Night or to defeat him. She feared the alpha would force a child upon me, and then sacrifice her to free his master." She shakes her head as darkness spreads its roots through my veins. "So my grandmother struck a deal with your father. Your father would support us in our fight against the Shadow Wolf, my grandmother would provide Wolves to help him fight his war in the kingdom of Rema, and I would be his wife to secure the alliance. Your father seemed kind, when she met him to discuss the terms. She thought I would be safe. I thought I would be safe."

"You were not."

Her breath is a whisper on the summer-scented breeze. "I was not. Your father... I loved him, at first. I was young, only eighteen years old. He showered me with affection. He bought me gifts. He made me his queen. He was handsome when we met, and I thought myself the luckiest wolf in the Snowlands to have escaped the war, and to have met such a man." I hear the sad smile in her voice as the moonlit water ripples before her, and I wish that she would look at me.

"I took the wolfsbane willingly at first. Just a small dose every day. He told me it was for my own good, to keep my wolf at bay. No one would love a queen with my affliction, he told me. His council would murder me, our people would turn on me, and he could not be with me... I had to keep that side of myself hidden at all times. He said the wolf was an illness, and the wolfsbane was the medicine. It would make me better. I took it for him. I tried to be 'better' for him. It was, of course, unnecessary. I don't have to shift on the nights of the full moon, because of the blood that runs in my veins."

She tips her head back to the moon, which is full in the clear night sky.

"I needed him to think that it was the 'medicine' that kept it at bay, not the power in my bloodline, though it pained me to take it. Because I knew that if I had a daughter, and the secret came out, she would be killed by your father's council because of what she represented to the Wolves."

She exhales. "He changed after Philip was born, now he had his heir. Or perhaps he was a monster all along, and I had chosen not to see it. Perhaps forcing me to hide a part of myself, perhaps making me feel shame for who I was, perhaps showing disgust if I ever slipped... perhaps that was abuse all along.

"When you were born, he started making me take larger doses of my 'medicine'. He told me he would take you and Philip from me if I did not. I can withstand it better than most, but I'm not impervious to its effects.

"I tried to escape with you and Philip, once. He caught me, and I was punished for it. This... this is the second and last time I will try to get you out of the kingdom."

The temperature cools, and a shadow passes over the moon. The water of the lake becomes agitated, and my mother's voice becomes harder.

"The next day at dawn, I tried to send you away with my lady-in-waiting. I instructed her to take you to the port at the White Cliff, and get passage on a ship to the Snowlands. There, I thought you would be safe. But your father's men came in the night, and took us back."

My heart stops. She is not talking to the sleeping child. She is talking to me.

"He locked me in my chambers, and made me take more and more of my medicine as punishment. He told me he would kill you, if I did not."

My breath mists in front of my face, and the soft grass hardens beneath my feet. A crack fills the air as the lake freezes, and snow falls from the sky. I knew he had killed her, had taken her from me, but the knowledge of how long his abuse lasted, and that my mother knew she was being poisoned. . . I cannot bear it.

"So I took it. I got weaker, day by day. I let him kill me, because I was afraid. Afraid of him, afraid he would harm you. And because I was afraid he would find out the truth."

Tears slide down my cheeks, hot in the winter air. My throat is tight. "What truth?" I whisper.

"*Ghealach* did not rip out her heart so the Elderwolf could be close to her power. She sent him her daughter, so that he would protect her. The power the Wolves seek. . . it was never a rock, or a relic, or a tool to be used. It was a person, and then a bloodline. We are descended from *Ghealach* and the Elderwolf, little one. You are the Heart of the Moon."

My heart shatters into a thousand jagged pieces. My fists clench, and my fingernails bite into my palms. The ice thaws, and the snow stops falling. The shadows shift, and the moon lights the lake once more. The summer breeze makes the green trees rustle. She kisses the small version of me on the head, then lays her down in the grass.

My mother stands up and looks out onto the water.

"What do I do now?" I ask her.

"Whatever you want to do."

Slowly, she turns. My heart almost bursts when I look upon her face. I had forgotten how blue her eyes were, and the way she wore kohl to underline them. I had lost count of the freckles that covered her nose, and I misremembered the warmth of her smile. I forgot how she smelt like lavender and snow and horses. And how that scent made me feel warm and safe and like no one could harm me.

Facing her as an adult, there are things I don't think I even recognized as a child. Like the grit in her stance and the steel in her gaze. My mother, I realize, was a warrior. She did not fight her battles in the field with swords and shields, but she was a warrior nonetheless. She fought every day to protect my brother and me, to keep us safe from the man who would harm us.

"First," she says, "you must fight."

"I miss you so much."

She touches my cheek. Her hands are delicate yet calloused. Warm. I had forgotten. "I'm so proud of the woman you have become."

A tear slides down my cheek. Her face starts to fade. The warmth of her touch disappears. The sounds of the summer become distant. Panic swells within me.

"Don't go," I plead. "I'm not ready. Don't go."

"They will make you feel as if you have no choice. There is always a choice." She smiles, and her voice sounds like it comes from a whole universe away. "Have courage, little one."

I'm hurtling upward. The wind tears at my face and my clothes. I squeeze my eyes shut. I cannot breathe. I cannot feel.

My knees slam onto hard earth. I open my eyes. Pain sears my back, and the sounds of battle fill my ears. I'm in the amphitheater and a wave of shadow crashes toward me.

I let myself feel the rage of losing my mother, the emotion I was beaten into suppressing, the wildness I was taught to prune. It fills my lungs, and makes my entire body vibrate with the force of it. It hurtles inside me. It presses against my skin. I push myself to my feet.

Enough.

I meet the obsidian gaze of the darkness.

And the scream that has been building in my chest all of my life. . .

I let it go.

No.

I unleash.

Chapter Sixty-One

A scream erupts from my lungs.

The jagged pieces of my heart tear like glass, and the wild thing inside me extends its claws. Power flares up from my soul. I taste it. Night, and untouched mountains, and moonlit forests, long before the first men came to this world. My back knits itself together, and the pain melts from my bones. My skin glows, and a bright blinding light flashes before my eyes.

As the tide of darkness crashes down, a wave of my moonlight rises to meet it. The serpentine creature rears back, and releases a bloodcurdling shriek of its own. Its eyes bleed like ink as it looks upon me, as if it's used to only darkness, and still, I scream. The shadows that shield its body dissolve and expose scales the color of obsidian. When my light touches its skin, the sizzle of burning flesh fills the air.

The creature flails. Its tail cracks the stands. Debris rains down upon me but still, I scream. Threads of light burst from my body, and they link me to the Wolves. I'm pulled in what feels like a thousand different directions. It's like the night of the full moon. My soul is being pulled apart, and I don't stop.

My senses erupt. I taste seawater and rum. Jack. There's a flicker of black fur beside me, and when he leaps past me and crashes into Night's prisoner, he is a snarling wolf with claws like knives. I catch the scent of heather and as a man swipes his sword at Claire, he finds himself pinned by a grey wolf. The smell of the battle and bracken crashes through me, and James shifts at my side and rips off the head of one of the acolytes.

I can't breathe. Whispers fill my ears. Fingers claw my body. They pull at me. Try to take my soul from me. I scream. I catch the scent of the mountains at dawn, there's coolness against my skin, then pine and shadow fills my lungs until they're all I can breathe. Blake is there, fighting. The thread that connects me to him is stronger than the others.

I tip back my head, and my light brightens. The serpent hisses and whimpers. It tries to retreat back into the pit from whence it came. I won't let it. It burns. Its head bashes against the ceiling as its flesh melts from its bones. It lets out a heart-curdling shriek that turns into a rasping laugh.

"She thought it would save you. He is coming."

Burning scales float like snowfall from above. They scatter and cover the blood and destruction with ash. They hiss as they touch my skin, then dissolve into shadow. My scream dies with the beast.

Silence.

It shrouds the amphitheater. My glowing skin is the only light in the darkness. Dark shapes cover the floor, and the blood is black and glistening. The coppery scent of death is overpowering.

It should be sickening, but everything seems far away. It's like I'm floating, and there's a primal song in my ears. The Wolves have shifted back into humanoid forms—covered in gore and shredded clothing. There are hardly any left.

James stands directly ahead of me, in front of the trapdoor. His bare chest rises and falls deeply. Blood paints his face and dribbles down his chin. My light dances off the tattoos that mark his biceps. My enemy. The wolf who bit me, who ruined the small shred of freedom I managed to find.

His lips are parted, and his eyes fill with awe. He drops to his knees. "*Cridche na Ghealach*," he breathes.

The remaining Wolves follow his lead.

Blake stands near the throne. His powerful shoulders move up and down deeply. Blood glistens across his scarred chest, and his dark hair sticks to his forehead. His lips curve into a slow smile, dimples springing into his cheeks. He opens his mouth.

Alexander appears behind him and slides his blade across Blake's throat.

Time stops. Blake's eyes widen as they hold mine. For a moment, I think he's fine. Then blood spills from the thin line across his neck.

Adrenaline erupts within me. The ringing in my ears gets louder. I don't hear Arran's roar as he charges at Alexander, knocks him off Blake, and decapitates him. I barely register

Jack lurching forward and catching Blake and dropping to his knees, or more of the acolytes charging toward the remaining Wolves.

The bond between Blake and me pulls taut. I feel as if my soul is being ripped from me. I see it between us, and it shudders. I follow it. I land hard on my knees beside Jack, who clutches Blake's wound with both hands.

"You'll be alright," he is saying, though he clearly does not believe it. "You'll be alright. We've been through worse than this."

Blood dribbles out of Blake's mouth. His skin is deathly pale. He tries to speak.

His pain sears my throat, and my breathing shallows. I shake my head. I lean forward and touch his cheek. He is cold. So cold. His eyelids flicker.

I wanted this, once. I wanted to defeat him. I searched for weeks for the answer to ending our connection. I wanted to break the bond. The power to do it crackles in my veins. I feel it. I could take it in my hands and snap it. If I don't do it now, he will take me with him.

He tries to reach for me, but his hand flops onto the floor by his side. His body twitches.

Emotion surges through me, raw and primal. It has been so long since I have let myself feel the things I thought I shouldn't—and this is the most forbidden feeling of all. It chokes me as the scent of his blood hangs in the air.

I need to let him go.

I cannot let him go.

He saved me once. I don't know how he did it, what words he whispered into the darkness, but I feel for the bond. The life is draining out of me, and my limbs shake. My breathing is as raspy as his. I shut my eyes.

"*Please. . .*" he gurgles.

And I feel it. He wants me to break the bond.

I push my forehead against his.

Darkness.

***

WE HURTLE down toward a pit of shadow. The sound of scraping scalpels and screams fills my ears. I wrap myself around Blake, and press my head against his chest, but his arms are limp and cold. I catch a glimpse of a dark room, a candlelit cell filled with books and the scent of citrus, a torture chamber with workbenches that creak beneath the weight of tools and jars. We fall through the ceiling of a small room lit by a fire in the hearth. A woman holds a rabbit while a small boy cries.

Water splashes as my body makes impact with the ground. I'm sinking into soft mud. Rain pelts my back, and the air tastes like lightning. I claw my fingers into the earth, and push myself onto my knees. Thunder rumbles across the sky. I'm alone.

I'm not far from the edge of a small village. Small stone houses stand on either side of a dirt road. Lights flicker in their windows. Blake is nowhere to be seen, but something tugs my chest, and I turn.

Lightning forks across the sky and illuminates a well in the distance. A thread of light links me to it, spluttering in the rain and the shadow.

I put my arm in front of my face to shield me from the rain that is coming down so fast it feels like it's cutting my skin. There's another rumble of thunder, and the ground shakes beneath my feet. The ground is like sludge, and it threatens to swallow me with every step I take.

I walk. The wind hurtles into me and blows my hair into my face. It tries to push me back, but I fight against it. I grip the edges of the well, and the moss-coated stone is slippery beneath my fingers. A small boy with ink-black hair cowers in the darkness, half submerged in water that is steadily rising. He is crying.

"Blake!" My voice echoes, then is swallowed by the darkness. The boy looks up.

He flickers, and changes into the man who tricked me, deceived me, manipulated me, saved me. His skin is white. He breathes in sharply. His chest and torso are bare. The wolf shines in his eyes, and his jaw clenches as lightening floods the well. "Aurora?"

The water drains, and the bottom drops beneath him. He gasps and grabs the sides, digging his fingers into the cracks in the stone. His biceps ripple and he grunts as he slides down. The bond between us jerks and pulls me forward. It flickers, a fraying rope between us.

"Break it," he shouts.

Thunder rumbles, and he flinches and slips down a few meters. I cry out as my torso slams against the edge of the well. I grab the bond between us with my numb fingers. It jerks and frays.

"Break it!" His voice echoes. "You have the power! You always have!"

"No."

"Don't be obtuse, Aurora!" Rain rolls down his face, his lips. "I'll pull you down with me."

I think of every dream he wandered into, smugness etched onto his face as he told me to fight. The hypocritical, condescending, obnoxious fool. "You are not even trying!" I shriek.

His throat bobs. The thread of the bond flickers in front of his face. Blake's gaze moves to it. I feel what he's about to do. Panic bursts within me. "Don't you dare." I grip the bond harder and grit my teeth. "People like you and me, we do not let go, Blake."

He's breathing as hard as I am. He's steeling himself for something, and I can't tell what. His emotions no longer run through me.

"You will regret this, little rabbit," he says.

"It's my mistake to make."

"Stubborn fool!"

"Obnoxious snake! Climb!"

He grunts as, inch by inch, he hauls himself higher. I bend over the side of the well, and stretch my arms as far as I can. He reaches for me. He starts to slip, and he roars as he swings and manages to grip onto my fingers. His hand is cold and wet. I cry out as I grab his wrist with my other hand. I pull with all my strength, but he is a dead weight. I reach for the frayed rope instead. I put all my anguish into it, and it mends, then strengthens beneath my fingers. He grabs my upper arm, and I hook my arms beneath his armpits. I scream as I hurl myself backward.

We fall from the well and collapse onto the ground. Blake's body pushes me into the mud. I can't catch my breath. The scenery dissolves.

We hurtle upward. I hook my arms around his back, and he presses his face into the crook of my neck. We break through the room with the woman and the rabbit, the torture chamber, the cell, and the darkness.

And we're back in the amphitheater.

I'm on top of Blake. People fight around us, but it all fades.

His eyes blink open. A tear slips down my cheek. He looks, for once, as if he's struggling to know what to say. He hooks his arm around my neck and pulls me into his chest.

"Thank you," he whispers.

Even though I shouldn't feel safe, he's warm and solid, and I melt into his embrace. He holds me tighter, and my nose presses against his shoulder. Everything that has happened crashes, full force, into me. My strength wanes; my bones turn to liquid. Everything fades away.

I don't know if a minute passes, or an hour, before I find myself scooped off the floor and held against a strong chest. The scent of pine fills my lungs as I'm carried away. I don't know where I'm going. I have no strength left to care.

He's alive.

James's rough voice sounds distant. "So, she's the Heart of the Moon."

"So it seems." Blake's breath brushes against my forehead.

"Why you?" says James. "Of all the Wolves in the kingdom, why would you be her mate?"

"I don't know."

But he does. Blake knows why. I feel this with a certainty that tightens my chest. I try to cling onto it, but everything fades away once more.

Chapter Sixty-Two

There is something soft beneath me. The scent of pine hangs in the air and mingles with woodsmoke. The wind roars, but I don't feel it on my skin. My body is like liquid, and my eyes feel as if they're welded shut. With great effort, I open them.

I'm in a bed in a small room. A fire crackles in the hearth, its light dancing over the dark stone walls and the thin rug in front of it. I wait for searing pain to flood my senses, but it doesn't come.

"Hello, little sister." Philip sits in a wooden chair by the bed, his long legs stretched in front of him. His coppery red hair sticks up in tufts, and his skin is pale, making his freckles stand out more than usual. The last time I saw him, he was bleeding, shouting orders at the Wolves as that serpentine creature reared before them. There was blood everywhere. And Blake. . .

I take a shaky breath, release it.

"Where is. . ." I swallow. It's strange that I feel disappointment that Blake is not here, that the first question I want to ask is his whereabouts. "Where is everyone?"

A grin crosses Philip's face. "He's dealing with the prisoners."

I push myself into a sitting position and frown. "Prisoners?" My throat is dry, and Philip nudges the glass of water that sits on the bedside table toward me. Candlelight flickers across its surface. I grab it and take a couple of deep glugs.

"Blake had the surviving Wolves rounded up. He's locked them in the Grey Keep dungeons."

"Why? Haven't they been through enough?"

The chair creaks as he leans back. Philip usually dresses in the height of fashion, so he looks strange wearing a dark shirt that's too big for him. It hangs off his lithe frame, and a couple of swirls of ink creep up above his unbuttoned collar.

"There weren't many left," says Philip. "He's given them a choice. They accept him as their alpha, so he can command them to stay quiet about you, or he'll kill them." He shakes his head. "The Blood of the Moon. Remind me never to get on your bad side again, little sister."

I sit up straighter. "What about Ryan?"

"He's fine. He tried to visit you earlier, but Blake has been a little bit. . . protective of you. You've been unconscious for twenty-four hours. He only just left your side."

"He's. . . he's okay?"

"Yes. Your mate"—I wince, and Philip's grin widens—"is okay."

I put the glass of water down, and my shirtsleeve swallows my hand. It's black and baggy, and smells like forests and fairytales. Blake's shirt. He must have changed me out of the bloody rags I was wearing when he carried me out of the amphitheater.

The crack of the whip and the wet sound of my skin splitting open reverberates through my mind, and I close my eyes and take a deep breath. Blake's scent curls around me, and I release a breath.

"Is it safe here?" I ask.

"For now, it seems. Alexander's army are otherwise occupied with Callum's army." Philip shifts in the chair. There's a leather satchel at his feet.

"Are you going somewhere?" I ask.

He glances at the door, then lowers his voice. "Yes. And I want you to come with me. We should stick to the original plan. Come to the Snowlands with me. I realize things might have changed between you and Blake, but there's something off about him. I still don't trust him. The Wolves will tear you apart when they find out what you are, and Goddess forbid Father ever discovers it. . ."

"I can't come with you. There's something I need to do."

He holds my gaze, his eyes searching, then inclines his head. "Okay."

"I saw her, Philip. I saw Mother."

His eyebrows lift before a pitying look crosses his face. "She's dead, little sister."

"I'm aware of that," I say. "I just. . . I don't know. Perhaps it was just a dream, or a suppressed memory, or my mind making sense of all the things I saw when I was young—but I know that what she told me was true. Father hurt her. He killed her, Philip."

He nods, and something like shame crosses his face. "I thought as much."

I bite my bottom lip. "Do you. . . do you want to help me?"

"I should. I wish I could. There's something I must do first, too. I've not been entirely honest with you, Sister. The reason why I was caught by surprise when Alexander could command me was because I was claimed by another alpha in the Snowlands."

"Ingrid?"

"No." He smiles sadly. "An alpha named Fenrir."

My eyebrows knit together as recognition jolts through me. "He is the wolf Alexander said was in the prison cell, with Blake and the others."

Philip nods.

"If both Alexander and Blake worship Night—" I say.

"Fenrir worshipped him, too. He made no claim to be doing otherwise. He was horrifying, and I committed many atrocities in his name. If I could go back and change things. . ." He shakes his head. "I thought he was dead. I didn't realize that my allegiance would fall back to Alexander after he'd gone." His expression darkens, and I get a rare glimpse of what my brother—the heir to the throne—would look like if he actually cared about ruling the kingdom. "The thing is, when Alexander died, something snapped then reformed. I felt him again. Fenrir. I think. . . I think he's back. And if he's back, Ingrid needs me."

"Because you love her," I say. Philip bites his cheek. When he doesn't reply, I smile weakly. "Go to her. I've a feeling we will need an alliance with her in the coming months."

Philip nods. An awkward silence hangs between us before Philip pulls me into an embrace. We have never hugged before, and I'm not sure what to do with my limbs. From the tension in his arms, I don't think he quite knows what to do, either.

"I'm not sure we should attempt this again." His words are muffled in my hair.

I pull back, the corners of my lips tugging upward, despite everything that has happened. "I'm not sure. Perhaps we'll get better at it."

He grins, then stands. "Be safe."

"And you."

He strolls to the door. "Good luck, little sister. Try not to get killed in my absence." He winks before disappearing into the corridor. I wonder if I'll ever see him again. The thought makes me strangely sad, considering out past.

And then I'm alone in the small room, with nothing to keep me company but the sound of the sea crashing onto the rocks somewhere below and the shadows that dance along the stone walls. Every time the window rattles, I flinch, and the memory of the whip, and Alexander, and the serpent made of darkness slams into me.

I don't want to be alone with my thoughts right now.

I can feel him. Blake. The thread that links us feels tighter, stronger, somehow. I think, if I follow it, it will lead me to him.

Get your hands off my mate.

I slide out of bed. My legs are a little shaky, and the skin on my back tingles, but I'm surprisingly well, considering what happened. When I slide my hand down the back of my shirt, I feel the ridge of one of my old scars between my shoulder blades, but no fresh wounds.

My legs are bare, but brown breeches are folded up at the end of the bed. Blake must have left them for me. I slip them on, alongside a pair of boots left by the wall. I creep through the door.

The torches along the walls aren't lit, and there are no windows. Darkness is thick on my skin, yet I can see the stairwell with sturdy black bannisters at the end of the corridor. I think it's my wolf sight. I think I may have finally broken the cage that was keeping my wildness locked within.

I head toward the stairwell, then down the stairs. The entrance hall looks like it might have been magnificent, once—it's large, with an arched iron door and a chandelier that creaks as it sways on the high ceiling. My footsteps echo as I stride across the hall.

On either side of me, streams of rainwater run down the walls and puddle on the black flagstones. The scent of seaweed is strong, and black algae almost entirely coats the anchor that has been attached to the wall above the door.

It's bitingly cold, but the temperature doesn't cause me the discomfort it usually would. I have a feeling that if I turn left, I'll find my way to Blake in the dungeons. Something compels me to walk in the opposite direction, toward the door.

It screeches as I push it open, then I slip out into the night. I find myself in a bleak courtyard within high fortified walls. It's raining heavily, and my clothes immediately stick to my body. Water rolls down my face, and I relish the feeling. It means I'm alive.

I head through tall iron gates, and I'm on the edge of a cliff with a path running down it. The waves crash against the rocks below. Ahead, there is nothing but perilous ocean.

It's not until I look down that I realize why I came out here and what I had to see. There's a circular stone building on an expanse of land that juts into the sea. One of the walls is crumbling. The amphitheater. The place where I thought I would die. The place where I finally let go and decided to fight.

A part of me wants to clamber down the path, cut through the rock, and make sure the serpent, the cloaked men, and Alexander are really gone. As I look, though, I notice thick smoke, darker than the night, pluming from its roof. A gust of wind brings the scent of fire and rancid burning meat.

"Oh, fuck off, James!" An irritated female voice is carried by the wind, along with the sound of boots thudding over wet stone. I turn to the path. "What do you want me to say? Am I supposed to thank you for coming to die with me?"

"Aye. That would be a start, you ungrateful—" The roar of the sea drowns out whatever insult James hurls at Claire. "I saved your life."

"That's what you were doing when you were chained and on your knees, was it? Aurora saved my life, you eejit. You did your usual fuck all."

"Aye? Well *you* saved my life, Claire. That acolyte was about to decapitate me. Remember that? Scared you were going to lose me?"

"Please. I was killing a southerner. It had nothing to do with you."

James laughs. "Keep telling yourself that, lass. You—"

He strides onto the clifftop twenty feet or so away from me, and his head abruptly snaps in my direction. He's wearing a drenched black shirt that clings to his muscles, and his kilt is stained with blood. He carries a torch and the flame struggles to stay lit as it fights the elements. Ash and grime coats his face, and my nose twitches at the odor of death that clings to him.

Claire clambers up beside him a moment later, slightly breathless. "Move, will you?" She barges into his shoulder. "Do you want to stop in a more inconvenient—"

Her mouth shuts as she follows James's gaze. Her hair clings to her cheeks, and she's just as grimy as James. There's a dying torch in one of her hands, too. She dips her head in my direction, then walks toward the tall iron gates behind me. "I'm done. I'm going to see if that southern bastard has any decent whisky in this shithole of a castle. Unlikely."

"Aye. I'll be with you in a minute," says James. He doesn't move his eyes away from me.

"That wasn't an invitation." Claire disappears into the courtyard, and James shakes his head as he strolls toward me.

I straighten. I can't tell whether or not he's a threat. He's my enemy, yet the memory of him falling to his knees before me flashes through my mind. He's not looking at me with deference now. There's more of a wry amusement in his eyes.

"Look who's awake. I'm surprised you're out here, alone," he says. He stands beside me, and nods at the amphitheater in the distance. "We burned it. Blake insisted. He's always struggled with his wolf, and whatever you did to him in there... well, he's been pretty intolerable since. Did my brother ever tell you about resource guarding?"

Wolves guard things of value to them. Blake told me that. "What do you want, James?"

He releases a dark chuckle, then swipes a hand over his stubble. "Simple things, I assure you. The same thing I wanted when I was in the kennels down there. To be drunk, warm, and well fucked. You've nothing to fear from me, lass. We may be enemies, but you've got the blood of my goddess in your veins. I won't hurt you. If my people discover who you are..." He shakes his head, and strands of brown hair stick to his cheeks. "My kingdom will tear itself apart to gain possession of you. I'll keep my mouth shut. You have my word."

Some of the tension inside me uncoils. James may not be as honorable as Callum, yet I believe him. He tried to help me in the amphitheater, even before he knew what I was. I have a feeling that there may be some good in him, buried deep.

James shrugs a big shoulder. "I know you found the idea of marriage to me abhorrent—"

"I find almost everything about you abhorrent."

"Almost? Are you warming to me, Princess?"

"No. You're not going to suggest we wed again, are you?"

He rolls his eyes. "That ship has long sailed away. Aye, you're bonny enough, but I only asked you before to piss off the Southlands, and because I knew Blake was up to something. You should be in the north, with the Wolves. With my brother. His honor won't let him marry another wolf's mate, but still, a marriage alliance with Callum would be sensible. I hate to say it, but with all this talk of Night lately, I think something worse may be coming. We may need to unite the kingdoms to defeat this threat."

"No," I say.

James arches an eyebrow. "Don't be stubborn. I know things are complicated between the two of you, but—"

"For our kingdoms to be united in marriage, my father would have to agree. He is ruler, not me." I shake my head. "Even if he was willing to work with the people he has oppressed and killed, even if Callum could be persuaded to join forces with a monster, I will not be presented to the Wolves as a political pawn."

My spine is like a rod as something wild and thorny jolts through me. I'm not sure why I'm telling James this, of all people, yet I feel like he'll understand.

"My father has ruled for long enough," I say over the roar of the waves. "He is not fit to be king. Philip has no designs on the throne, and with him in the Snowlands, there is only one heir left. With my father out of the way, the throne will fall to me. Maybe we need to bring the kingdoms together, but I won't come to Callum as the princess of nothing, with no power or influence, and ask for an alliance. I will come to him as his equal. I will come to him as the queen."

James's eyes glint in the darkness. "I was planning on heading back to Highfell to challenge whoever the new alpha is, but if you need some help killing southerners, I think I'm long overdue a visit to your father."

I assess him. Ruthless, with big powerful muscles and experience of ruling a kingdom. With me, he could shift at will, too. I don't like him, but maybe he could be useful. It's not as if I have many allies, so perhaps enemies with shared interests will have to do. "Hm. Perhaps."

He releases a dark chuckle. "You really are warming to me."

I open my mouth to refute his claim.

"Oi! Thanks for waiting!" Ryan shouts. He's climbing up the steep rocky path toward us, his copper-colored hair plastered to his skull. His face breaks into a grin when he sees me. "Princess! How are you—"

His face pales. At the same time, the velvety scent of the forest caresses my senses, and that thread that's coiled around my soul tightens. Ryan dips his head and scurries past James and me toward the Grey Keep. James shakes his head, amusement tickling his lips.

I turn around. Blake stands between us and the iron gates of the keep. The rain plasters his black shirt to his body, and the wind ruffles his hair. His eyes find mine, and that thread between us hums. At once, I'm falling and frozen.

Slipping his hands into his pocket, he walks toward us.

"Excellent plan, little rabbit," he says, and I realize he was listening in on our conversation. A dimple punctures his cheek. "Would you like my help?"

Chapter Sixty-Three

I forget how to speak.

As Blake stands before me on the cliff edge, the waves spraying the rocks below, I can partially understand Ryan's desire to dip his head and get away from him. Dominance I hadn't noticed before seems to roll off him. Perhaps I strengthened the bond between us, and now I'm more aware of him than before. Perhaps whatever links me to all Wolves senses the animal in him. He feels. . . dangerous.

It could just be how still he is as the elements rage around him, or the tension in his shoulders, despite the calculated dimple in his cheek. A streak of blood on his face mingles with the heavy rainfall, rolls down his cheek, and drips off his chin.

James grins. Widely. He grips Blake's shoulder and turns to me. "See this? Stiff shoulders, hard biceps, tight jaw." He points at Blake's face. "Classic guarding signs. If I touched you now, Princess, he'd probably try to kill me."

Blake flashes James a dangerous smile. "If you touch *me* again, I'll remove your hand and insert it up your areshole."

James laughs, and taps Blake lightly on the jaw. "Terrifying." He starts to walk away toward the iron gates of the keep. Blake turns and kicks him lightly on the back of his knee, causing him to stumble. "Prick!"

"Cunt." The corner of Blake's lip twitches as he turns back to me. The realization slams into me that even though Blake and James would happily kill one another, Blake was part of James's inner circle of alphas for two, maybe three, years. James knew Blake well enough to determine the true meaning of the bond before even Callum did. Perhaps they're friends, in a way.

As the gates screech shut, and James's footsteps are swallowed by the rain that hammers the ground and the sea, my stomach tightens. Blake and I are alone for the first time since I broke into his bedchambers and he was restrained by Lochlan's men. We're supposed to be enemies, working against one another, but he saved my life and I saved his.

He runs a hand over the back of his neck. He's caged his emotions from me, but I think he feels as awkward, as uneasy, as I do.

"How are you feeling?" he says, finally.

"I. . . I'm well. Thank you. And you?"

He releases a soft laugh and shakes his head. "I'm fine, little rabbit."

He sighs, and my muscles tighten. I'm sure—drenched and shivering as I am—he's going to tell me to go back inside, that I need to be resting. I don't want to go back to bed, not yet. I don't want to be alone with my thoughts. I don't want to risk the nightmares that I'm sure will come.

He strolls over to a boulder on the edge of the cliff and sits down so he's facing the ocean. I release a soft breath. I walk toward another rock a few feet away from him and sit down. My legs dangle over the side of the cliff.

In the distance, the amphitheater is almost completely consumed by black smoke. "James said you insisted it was burned," I say. "Why?"

"It was the bodies I wanted burned. The acolytes bore Night's mark, which means they've offered their souls to Night. I've heard stories that some of his prisoners are strong enough to possess the dead. It got me thinking about Kai, back at Madadh-allaidh, and the way his eyes changed."

"Do you think he was possessed?"

He shrugs. "I don't know. But they know the truth about you. I didn't want to risk it." He turns his head to look at me. "What you did in there... you were magnificent."

"Hm." My blood cools.

A crease forms between Blake's eyebrows. "What's wrong?"

"I felt... powerful for a moment. But then"—I shake my head—"I wanted to escape my fate. I wanted to feel like more than someone else's puppet. I didn't want to be an object anymore. Wars will be fought over me, won't they? People will try to kill me. Not because of who I am, but what I am and how people can use me. I'm a weapon."

"Darling, no." His voice, silk-soft, cuts through the roar of the wind. "You're not a weapon. You're a fucking tornado."

There is something so intense in his eyes I have to drag my gaze to the roiling waves.

"Alexander called you his brother," I say.

"We're not related, but we are brothers, in a way. Just as Jack and Arran are my brothers, too. Some bonds are forged by blood. Some by light and love and hope. Others. . . others are forged in the darkness."

"Where are Jack and Arran?"

"Arran went to check on Lowfell. Jack is making sure the Grey Keep is secure. They'll be back."

I suck in a deep breath of algae-scented air. "I'm ready to talk about it."

A long silence stretches between us. He clasps his hands between his thighs. "Okay. What do you want to know?"

"The truth. When. . . when did you know about. . . this?" I touch my chest, not wanting to say it aloud.

"I'm not sure. I thought I just wanted to play with you, at first. But the longer you were around. . . I told you before, I thought you seemed familiar when I first met you, even though we'd never met. Arran was kept prisoner with me, beneath the palace. So was his mate."

"Fara," I say softly.

He nods. "Our captor experimented on them and recorded it in the pages of the book you took from my chambers. I learned more about the mate bond than I ever wanted to know during those dark days. It's why I first took the book from my old room, not long after you arrived in the Northlands. I'd started to suspect something. I didn't know for sure, though. Not until I had you in the dungeons, with your legs wrapped around my waist."

I recall that moment—how he looked like he was going to kiss me, and seemed disgusted with himself for it.

He sighs. "So, later that night, when you were dying, I knew I could share my life force with you, because Arran and Fara had done it, time and time again." He shakes his head. "You think I tricked you. In truth, I did not. I did it because I didn't want you to die." The words sound raw against his throat, and I can find none to fill the heavy silence that stretches between us.

He shrugs. "I suppose the full truth of it is, I was arrogant enough to think I could pull away at the last minute—that I could grab you, like you did to me earlier, when I was in the well, and then let go without there being any consequence. But you gripped so tight. Honestly, Aurora, I did not mean for this to happen. Make no mistake, I had designs on the throne—I still do. Your part in my plan was over. I was going to blackmail Callum once we had taken Madadh-allaidh from James. I did not plan for. . . this. It complicates things for me."

"You hid it from me. You had no right to do that."

He releases a dark laugh. "What was I supposed to do? You were with Callum. I knew he wouldn't be able to handle it. The truth would have destroyed you both."

"And your plan, too, in the process."

"Yes. There's that, too." A smile plays on his lips. "You have the power. Break the bond now, if you must."

"I think I made it stronger, before. I feel. . . it feels. . . different."

"Yes. I think so too." The amusement dies from his eyes. "You may have missed your chance. You could have broken the bond when I was dying. Why didn't you?"

I drag my hands down my face. "Oh, I don't know, Blake. You're obnoxious, and devious, and manipulative. You have intentionally provoked me time and time again. You bit me. You plotted against me. You keep secrets and hide things and I don't trust you in the slightest. You are the most irritating person I have ever met in my life. And yet. . ." I sigh heavily. I feel exposed, naked, in front of him.

"And yet?"

I admit something that makes me feel more vulnerable than I have ever felt in my life. "You are my friend." My voice sounds small.

I expect him to mock me, taunt me. I await the sly curve of his lips and the antagonistic glint in his eyes. Instead, his expression is more serious than I have ever seen it. When he smiles, it's sad. I wonder if he has ever had a real friend before, or at least one that was not forged in the depths of a prison cell.

The truth is, though, that I have never had a real friend, either—no matter how much I have longed for one.

Overwhelming remorse floods me, before he pulls it back.

"Likewise, little rabbit."

The air feels awkward again. Suddenly, I'm exhausted. I shiver and rub my arms. I stand. "I'm going to go back inside. I'm tired."

He nods and pushes himself to his feet. "I'll come with you."

Together, we walk back into the Grey Keep.

***

DARKNESS.

It washes over me, so thick I can taste it.

THE NIGHT PRINCE

I breathe in sharply. I'm in a long, dark corridor and shadows whisper across the ground as if they have a mind of their own. They coil around my bare ankles. My pulse quickens when the scent of something old and ancient hits my nostrils. I creep forward, past locked doors. Something hisses behind one—the sound raspy and familiar.

I swallow the lump that forms in my throat and hurry past. I need to get out of here.

I walk through an archway into a hexagonal room. Something about the shape seems familiar, and I recall the drawing of the labyrinth I found in Blake's bedchambers.

"It's of no consequence to me." Blake's silky smooth voice comes from one of the archways to my left, where Night's mark is carved into the stone. "If you want an army, I can build you one."

My blood turns to ice. I follow his voice and I halt. I'm behind a large, obsidian throne. A male sits upon it, and fear grips me so tightly I can't move. He radiates a cold, ancient power that makes the hairs on my arms stand on end. I can't see his face, but I catch a glimpse of short hair as white as moonlight, and a tall jagged crown encrusted with diamonds. He drums his long fingers on the arm of his throne, and my soul knows who he is, even if I have never seen him depicted before.

"I do not trust you." The male speaks, his voice cold.

Blake kneels before the throne, his head bowed in deference. When he raises it, the corner of his lip lifts. "Is that not part of my appeal, Master?"

His face is younger, and his hair slightly longer and messier. Shock slams through me. This is a memory, like the others I infiltrated. A dream. Blake's dream. And we are in Night's prison.

Night laughs, a cold dark sound that makes me shiver. "You *are* one of my favorite toys. Hm. Very well. Take the Kingdom of Wolves in preparation for my return. It will pain *Ghealach* when I break her creatures. And find the key. Bring me the Heart of the Moon and you will be rewarded beyond your wildest imaginings. But fail me... fail me and your punishment will be severe."

"I will not fail you."

My heartbeat thunders. It's a cacophony in my ears. I inch back, and Blake's eyes lock onto mine. They widen slightly. A brief flicker of panic crosses his face before he schools it into nonchalance once more and brings his gaze back to his master.

"Is there something wrong?" The crowned male begins to turn, and clucks his tongue. "Is one of my souls misbehaving? Bring them to me."

I don't wait for the God of Night to see me. I don't wait for Blake to catch me. This may be a memory, but I have the terrible feeling there will be dire consequences if I'm caught. I run. I run faster than I have run in my life. My muscles scream; my feet slice on the tiles. My lungs feel as if they will burst as I crash back into the hexagonal room. Footsteps pursue me. *Blake* pursues me.

One of the archways glimmers with light. I turn to it, and pray it's the exit. I ram my entire being against the door within it. I catch the scent of pine and shadow.

It crashes open. Darkness engulfs me and I'm falling.

Bright blinding light.

Chapter Sixty-Four

My eyes jolt open.

I'm in the small room in the Grey Keep, and the embers in the hearth glow orange. Blake sleeps on the chair, with his head dipped onto his chest. I'm breathing too quickly, and I try to calm myself, terrified I will wake him.

A thousand emotions rattle around in my chest, but the one that slices through is a cold, icy fear. At some point in his lifetime, Blake called Night his master.

I need to get out of here.

Blake's eyes open. I'm restricted by the bedsheets. My pulse thrums beneath my skin. It's loud. So loud. I know he can hear it. I turn my body to stone, as if I can block out the sound, but it beats faster, faster. Faster.

His midnight hair is disheveled, and strands of it curl over his forehead. His shirt is unbuttoned at the collar. He looks relaxed, with the fire in the hearth flickering low behind him as he sits in the chair. He seems unthreatening.

Vulnerable. I wonder how carefully he practiced his act. Or perhaps lying just comes naturally to him.

He's working for Night. He has been all of this time. He's been looking for me.

I'm always pretending, he told me once. I should have listened more closely.

I know he's acting now. I can see it. His hands tighten on the arms of the chair. His back ever so slightly straightens. I feel that coil of wariness as it tightens around my soul. For so long, he has felt like a spring, wound tight. I think this is the moment when it finally snaps.

I know his secret.

My pulse becomes a cacophony in my ears.

Does he know that I know?

He stares at me, and there's the hint of a challenge in his eyes. *Say it,* he seems to dare me. *Bite.*

My breathing quickens. I need to get away. I need to warn Ryan. James, too, I suppose. I need to warn the whole bloody kingdom, and my people, too. I need to stop him from using me to release his master. My gaze darts to the door, but I know he'd catch me.

I force myself to relax. To release a breath. To smile. He hasn't hurt me yet, so he must be waiting for something before he makes his move. I have time. There has to be more time.

I can pretend, too.

"I had the strangest dream that I was being chased through a forest," I say. I settle back down on my pillows. I'll put him at ease, wait for him to go back to sleep, then I will run.

He blinks. Once. Twice. "That sounds frightening."

He shifts in his chair, and I try not to flinch. He puts his foot on the edge of my bed, and I think it's to barricade me in. But then the bottom of his breeches rides up. Too late, my eyes dart to the exposed flesh, and I realize his intent.

The mark I saw there, when I hid beneath his bed, is no ordinary scar. A key with two crescent moons in the bow has been burned into his ankle—the flesh around it is angry and mottled. Elsie and Alexander had Night's mark inked onto their wrists, but this... this is different. A fresh wave of horror crashes over me as I remember the book of drawings depicting Night's monsters. They were branded like this, too.

He's showing it to me. He wants me to confront him.

I look away hurriedly, and pretend I didn't see.

He sighs and slides his foot back to the ground. His boot hits the floor with a thud.

"Let's not play this game anymore." The way he says it—as if *I* am the tiring one, as if *I* have been caught doing something wrong—stokes a fire inside me that flushes away some of the coldness. "Let us be honest, for once."

"Honest?" The word tears from my lips. "You want to be honest?"

"Yes," he says as my gaze darts toward the door. "I know what you're thinking, so say it, and I can explain."

Power coursed through my veins earlier, but I feel anything but powerful now. Even if I understood how the power of the moon worked, what could I do with it? Turn him into a wolf, and make him an even bigger threat?

I clench the sheets. "You can't hurt me because of the bond," I remind him.

"That's not the reason I won't hurt you."

"You've been working for Night."

I wait for him to deny it. I *want* him to deny it. "Yes."

My breath catches. My soul splinters. My fear spikes. "The rumors that someone was trying to free Night and create him an army, they were about you. You're the Night Prince."

"Yes."

My pulse is beating so quickly now, it drowns out the sound of anything else. Adrenaline surges through me. *Run. Run. Run.*

"Aurora, we don't have time for this. Don't—"

I lurch across the bed toward the door, and the bedsheets tangle around my thighs. The glass of water on my bedside table spills. He grabs me around the waist, and throws me back onto the mattress. I open my mouth to scream, but he pins me down and clamps his hand over my mouth. He climbs on top of me, and his thighs clench against my hips. His scent floods my senses. I grab his wrist and curl my fingers into his bone. I taste the salt of his palm. *Bite, Bite. Bite.*

"*Don't.*" The wolf flashes in his eyes, feral and beautiful. "*Listen.*"

His essence floods me, dark and powerful and suffocating. It strokes and coaxes and is laden with such intense dominance that I almost whimper as I try to push it away. Something inside me wants to yield to it, to submit.

He is using the Àithne, like before, but fear cools my blood. He is more powerful than he was letting on the last time he did this. All this time, I thought it was Callum who was holding back with me. I see now it was Blake. Sweat beads on my brow. His words, spoken in his chambers at

Madadh-allaidh, come back to haunt me. *When the time comes, little rabbit, I will give you everything I have. I promise.*

Is this it? Is this his glorious defeat?

"Stop fighting, Aurora. Listen."

My own power rises to meet his. I reach deep inside of me and grab his shadowy fingers. His grip tightens, and I gasp as I'm held within his grip. Still, I think I could fight him off. As the telltale dots appear across my vision, and my breathing becomes rapid, I know that all I need do is let go.

I think he knows it, too. I think he's giving me a reason to acquiesce to him, a way for me to pretend that he forced me into submitting to him. Because he knows my truth, even if I can't stomach it.

I want to know what he has to say. I want to trust him. I want him to tell me this is a mistake, and that I wasn't wrong to save his life.

So, that traitorous part of me stills. Obeys. Submits.

I pretend I don't want to. I even let out a soft whimper against his palm. The corner of his lip twitches, as if he knows my game. I sink back into the sheets, and stop writhing beneath him. When I blink up at him, my body softens and becomes pliant.

His shoulders dip with relief.

"Are you going to scream?" he asks.

I shake my head, and he pulls away his palm.

"Good girl."

I'm breathing fast. So is he.

"I'm going to tell you the truth, Aurora, and I need you to listen carefully, because I fear we don't have much time. Are you listening?"

I nod. "Yes."

"Good. I'm not one of Night's Acolytes. I'm not some fool who dresses in a dark cloak with a symbol inked onto my skin. I'm much worse than that. I'm one of Night's prisoners, just like the serpent you killed, just like the monsters you have heard of. The prison I've pulled you to in my dreams, that was my home for a time. You've realized that, haven't you?"

"The brand on your ankle," I say.

"Yes. He brands all his prisoners with his mark. The acolytes copy it, as if they could ever know what it means."

He leans back so he's kneeling over me, and I can't settle my unsteady heart or the beast that has awoken in my chest. I'm still gripping his wrist, I realize. For some reason, I don't release him. His pulse thrums, agitated, beneath my fingertips.

"My soul belongs to the God of Night," he says. "So do the souls of the others who were trapped in the cell beneath the palace with me. You asked me once whether I'd killed the Maester of Healing. I told you that wasn't the right question. Do you know now, what the right question is?"

I inhale a shaky breath as I piece together everything I know, everything he has told me. Dread runs, thicker than blood, through my veins. I nod, the movement stifled by the pillow.

"Ask me," he says.

"How did you escape?" My words are quiet, barely audible as the wind picks up outside and the sea roars against the cliffs. It's as if the weather is reacting to the turbulence inside me.

A shadow flickers across his face, and that cold, endless ache that I felt from him when he kissed me, floods me. I feel as if I'm drowning.

"I didn't. In the cell beneath the palace, I died."

My heart stops. A powerful, unreadable emotion erupts from my soul and mingles with his darkness. "I... I don't understand."

He smiles, but there is nothing warm in his face. "That was Night's big trick. He covets desperate souls, and I was so very desperate. I made a bargain with him—I asked him to give me the power to escape from the Maester, and to set the others free. In exchange, I would give him my soul. He honored his promise, I suppose. He gave me my freedom in the form of death. Only, instead of my soul going to rest, he took it for himself."

Words bubble then die in my throat. I know, with certainty, that what he's telling me is true. I feel it with every nerve in my body. My skin is as cold as his eyes. I don't know what to say, how to react to such horror. That traitorous part of me wants to comfort him, just like I did when I found out what had been done to him in the palace. Like then, I realize the horrors he has undergone make him even more of a threat to me.

"I thought I knew torment. I did not. Not until I became Night's plaything. I would have done anything to gain my freedom. I was dead for months, but it felt like a lifetime that I was trapped. Over time, I realized Night was as desperate to get out as I was. I made him a new promise. If he let me go, I would give him what he desired. The dream you witnessed, the memory, it was the night when Elsie prayed to him because our father was going to kill her. I told him I could use Bruce to our advantage, and get a footing in the Wolf Kingdom. He agreed to let me go."

"How? Night doesn't have the key." *Night doesn't have me.*

"Night used *Ghealach* to do it. The walls of his prison are thinner on the night of the full moon. Not thin enough for him or any of the ancient prisoners to escape, but thin enough for me to slip through. He took me to her cell. I was so sure she'd find a way to stop me from leaving, but as I passed by her, she spoke to me." His eyes burn into mine. "She said, 'My heart is your salvation.'"

My fingers dig into his wrist.

"I thought the Heart of the Moon was just a rock. I thought I could use it to barter for my freedom, even if it meant unleashing horrors upon the world. Because the next time I die, I know what eternity will look like for me. I have no love for the Kingdom of Wolves, or the Kingdom of Men. One abandoned me, the other tortured me. What did it matter to me, if they both burned? But I didn't know, when I made that promise to Night. . . I didn't know that it would be you."

"When did you realize?"

"I started to suspect the more I got to know you. I was fairly sure on the night of the full moon when you didn't shift. When Alex took you, then I was certain."

I take a deep breath. "And now you know?"

"I cannot let you go." He says it as if it's so simple. And some deep, aching part of me wants to believe him. But giving me to Night is the only thing that will save him from eternal torment. Blake has lied to me, time and time again. He pretends, and manipulates, and deceives.

Earlier this evening, he coaxed me into breaking the bond, and it hits me that if everything he is saying is true, the bond could be the only thing stopping him from handing me over to his master. Anything that happens to me will happen to him, too.

His chest deflates as if he feels my hesitance. "I know I haven't given you much reason to trust me. But I believe that if Night, or any of his army, got their hands on you, you would be tortured and killed in order for you to release enough power to break the walls of his prison. So if you don't believe that I don't want to hurt you, then at least believe that my own self-interest will compel me to keep you away from the god I serve. But I need you to believe one of these options, and quickly. Because Alexander's soul belongs to Night, too, and now he's dead. He has told Night where you are. I saw it, just now, while I was dreaming."

My breathing quickens. My blood cools. A part of me knew more acolytes would come for me, yet I thought I would have more time to figure everything out. Slowly, he climbs off me, and stands at the side of the bed. I sit up.

"I know what you want, little rabbit. I heard you talking to James. You want an army, and a kingdom, and a crown. I can give you your vengeance. I will drop your father's head at your feet, if you ask it of me. You need to evade Night, and no one in this kingdom knows him better than I do. I can help you. I will help you. But we need to go." He glances at the window, which rattles in the wind. "Night's Acolytes, the beginnings of his army, any other prisoners that might have slipped through the hole in that prison wall. . . they are coming."

I swallow down my rising fear, and cling to some hope that we still have time. There has to be more time. "We need to tell Ryan and the others—"

"No. They are coming for *you*. If you want to keep them safe, we need to go, now. We'll draw them away. Just you and me." He holds out his hand for me to take.

"Callum—"

"Fuck Callum." There's an uncharacteristic sharpness in his tone.

I shake my head, because I'm so sure that his game is not yet over. "And what do you want in return for your help, Blake?"

He cocks his head slightly. "There is something I want above anything else. You know what that is, don't you?"

His eyes bore into me with such intensity that my breath hitches. The air in the room suddenly feels hot and thick. My skin prickles as the bond vibrates between us.

The dream I walked in on flashes through my mind—me on the bed, the flush of his cheeks, the way his face looked as he pushed me down onto the mattress. I blink the vision away because it's too dangerous to look at. "You want... you want your freedom."

"What you want, in exchange for what I want," he says, without confirming or denying my statement. "A simple bargain."

I look at his hand, still outstretched. Nothing is simple when it comes to Blake. I feel as if I'm making a deal with the God of Night himself. But Blake already has my soul. What more can he take from me?

Those dangerous dimples crease his cheeks. "Come on, little rabbit. We need to go. Now. They are coming."

Goddess help me, I put my hand in his.

Author Note

Thank you so much for continuing this journey with Aurora, Callum, and Blake. I can't wait for you to see what is in store for them in book 3, which will be the last book in 'The Wolf King' trilogy!

Make sure you're following me on Instagram (@LaurenPalphreyman), Facebook (@LEPalphreyman) or TikTok (@LEPalphreyman) for updates and teasers! You can also visit my website www.LaurenPalphreyman.com to find out more.

I hope to see you again for book 3!

Love,

Lauren

Acknowledgements

Thank you so much to everyone who read THE NIGHT PRINCE in its early stages.

In particular, thank you so much to my amazing team of alpha readers; Lauren F., Abigail Ballou, Caroline Reese, Ayu Chatterjee, Ida-Linn Möller, Yulia Shtanko, Keeley, Stephanie Basilius, Natalie Holmes, Maggie Drummond, Danielle Weston-Ford, Casey Hollingsworth, Lacey Spinks, Makenzie Staples, Kinsey Beyer, Jana Schuler, Charlotte Miller, Ashley E. Matters, Caitlin Connolly, Kristina Haira, Nikki Stier Justice, Lauren Rondou, Mariagiovanna Cacopardi, Danielle White, Valerie Cuellar, Rachel Graham, and **Daniella Draven**. Your feedback was invaluable, and really helped shape the story.

Thank you to Rachel Rowlands for all your hard work on the copy edits.

Thank you to Damonza.com for another amazing cover.

And lastly, thank you to you. Thank you for continuing this journey with Aurora, Callum, and Blake. I can't wait to see you again for the concluding instalment of The Wolf King trilogy!

You can also visit my website www.LaurenPalphreyman.com to find out more.

The Wolf King Audiobook

THE WOLF KING is now available as an audiobook, narrated by Zara Hampton-Brown and Shane East! THE NIGHT PRINCE will be released in audio later this year!

About the Author

Lauren Palphreyman is an Amazon bestselling romantasy author. She is best known for her The Wolf King trilogy. She writes books full of romance and fantasy. Her serial fiction has garnered over 70 million views online.

Connect with Lauren by following her on Instagram (@LaurenPalphreyman), TikTok (@LEPalphreyman), or Facebook (@LEPalphreyman). Or visit her website: www.LaurenPalphreyman.com.

Also by Lauren Palphreyman

Devils Inc.

The awkward moment when you exchange your soul for free Wi-Fi...

When Rachel accidentally signs away her soul to the Devil, she must join forces with a snarky Angel and a morally grey Bad Omen to stop the Apocalypse. Perfect for fans of Good Omens, Lucifer, and Supernatural.

Cupid's Match

He's mythologically hot, a little bit wicked, almost 100% immortal. And he'll hit you right in the heart...

Mythological mayhem ensues when Cupid comes to Lila's high school looking for his match. Perfect for fans of The Vampire Diaries